THE CLEANSING

Also by Mitchell S. Karnes

Water Grave
The Least of These

An Abbey Rhodes Mystery
Volume 3

THE CLEANSING

MITCHELL S. KARNES

WordCrafts Press

To **God** who is my everything,
Stephanie who refused to let me settle for less than my best,
Mike who encouraged me to dream, and
My audience for whom I write.
I couldn't have done this without you.

"For whoever keeps the whole law and yet stumbles in one point, he has become guilty of all."'

~*James 2:10*

Prologue

Friday, April 11, 6:45 PM—Ripley House

My phone chimed with a text message. I didn't recognize the number. It chimed repeatedly—all in all, six times. The person called me by name and spent five paragraphs congratulating me on a case that was well solved.

A final text chimed:

```
    My Dear Abbey, I see you're still
standing in the shadows of others. We
can't have that now, can we? Let me be
your Moriarty—your Lord Voldemort. You
may be great now, but I can make you a
legend.
```

I couldn't believe who signed the message.

Dallas leaned in over my shoulder. "Who's Skylar?"

Chapter One

Friday, April 11, 7:26 PM—Ripley House

"**I**t can't be Skylar." My voice a mix of doubt and terror. How did she get a phone? How did she get my number? What did she mean? *Focus!* "She's still in NCDC."

"Who is she, Abbey? What's NCDC?" Dallas asked. I could feel the heat of his breath on my neck.

Breathe! I took a deep breath as I stared at the text, waiting for the punchline—waiting for someone to say, "Just kidding." No one did. This was no cruel joke. This was my nightmare coming true. Dallas moved in front of me and asked again.

"NCDC is Nashville's Correctional Development Center for females. Skylar is a teenage inmate who thinks she and I have some sort of connection." I looked up from the phone and lost myself in Dallas's eyes, those rich brown eyes. They were a brief respite from the terrifying prospect of Skylar having access to technology. Then the gravity of his question pulled me back to reality. "She was involved in the deaths of two people. One was her own mother."

"Did you put her away?"

I nodded.

"Do you think she's out for revenge?"

I shrugged my shoulders. Was she? Did she still think we had some sort of attachment?

"Why is she texting you, Abbey?" He continued to press me for answers I didn't have. "Surely those facilities don't let the women have phones." He began pacing back and forth. I could tell his mind was racing too. He stopped, put his hands on my shoulders. "How in the world did she get your number?" It was a great question. I knew he wasn't criticizing me, but his tone and penetrating gaze put me on the defensive.

"I don't know." I'm sure he didn't mean to, but he was acting like it was my fault—like I invited her to text me anytime she wanted. I tried to explain that I never encouraged a relationship with the girl. But that wasn't exactly true. At first, I felt sorry for her plight and somehow projected my own abusive past onto her situation. Her rape tapped intense pain from my past. I did connect with her briefly, but we were very different people. What was she now, seventeen? Eighteen?

"Abbey, how did she get your number?" he asked again.

"I don't know!" I shouted at him. I didn't mean to, but it came out in one defensive burst. The blood drained from my face. My heart pounded. Would she come after me? After Susan?

Susan rushed out of the house. "What happened? You're white as a sheet."

"It's Skylar." It was all I could say. My knees went weak.

Susan stared into space. Her eyes vacant. I'm sure Skylar's name triggered Susan as much as it did me. Maybe more. "Skylar Watson? Is she dead?" Susan asked, her voice fading to a mere whisper.

Skylar was responsible for Susan's husband's death even though she never laid a finger on him. She used her body, looks, and persuasive nature to manipulate her youth minister into killing Pastor Mark Ripley. She used other persuasive means with her father, making him so angry and jealous of his wife that he killed her and stored her body in a deep freezer underneath his house. Skylar had a strange power over others, able to make them do things they knew were wrong. She got in their heads and twisted things around until they saw the situation through her eyes. Her methods almost worked on me. She somehow sensed a wound deep within me and exploited it. To think, I pushed to place her with the Ripleys as a foster family. Skylar was dangerous in so many ways.

"How do you know her?" Dallas asked Susan. His face betrayed his growing frustration—desperately needing an answer from one of us.

I answered so Susan didn't have to utter the words. "She was responsible for the death of Susan's husband, Mark."

Dallas's face filled with shame, wishing he hadn't pressed for an answer. I handed Susan my phone and let her read the texts. "Please, Abbey, tell me she's not out." Her voice trembled. Her hands shook. She rubbed the chill bumps from her arm. "That girl is mentally ill." We heard a noise, and Susan jumped. It was just the neighbor's cat that had captured a mouse and was playing with it before she settled in for the kill.

After a few awkward moments of silence, Dallas pushed us for more answers. "Who is she? Do you think she'll come looking for either of you?" Poor Dallas was trying to get information from us, but we were both terrified at the thought of Skylar's escape. We didn't know how much to tell him.

Susan kept her focus on me. "My goodness, Abbey. She set fire to her foster home, and she nearly shot Sam."

Dallas perked up. "She shot Sam?"

"She missed," I said, somewhat casually.

"Somebody, please tell me what happened?"

"Abbey shot her."

I stole a glance at Dallas but quickly turned back to Susan when I saw his eyes widening. I couldn't deal with his fears right now. I had to keep my focus on Skylar. Where was she, and how did she get the phone?

"If you shot her, how is she still alive?"

"I just winged her."

Susan got the number from the text and called it. She put the phone on speaker so we could all hear. "You've reached Doctor Emily Teague, Psychologist. I'm currently away from my phone, but if you leave a message, I will return your call as soon as possible." When the message ended, Susan hung up.

"Is that Skylar's doctor?" Susan asked. "Why would she let Skylar use her phone?"

I was sure she didn't *let* Skylar have the phone, which could only mean…

"Why is this girl contacting you?" Dallas asked, gently directing my glance to him. "What aren't you telling me, Abbey?" His eyes penetrated my soul.

As long as I stared into them, I couldn't resist him. I looked away, pretending to study my phone in Susan's hands. "Nothing, Dallas. You know as much as I do." It wasn't true. He already knew more than I wanted him to know about it. I grabbed my phone back from Susan and called Sam. "Sam, I need you to check on a psychologist named Emily Teague."

"Sure. Why?"

"Skylar Watson used her phone to text me."

"The crazy girl? That can't be good."

"I'm afraid she's escaped." My voice was surprisingly steady, despite my anxious thoughts.

"I'll call you back as soon as I have something," Sam said. "Until then, stay tight." He paused but didn't hang up. "Abbey?" His voice was shaky. I'm sure he was remembering the shot too. "Am I off speaker?"

I took the phone off speaker and put it to my cheek. "Yes."

"Watch your six. Are you alone?"

"No. I'm with Dallas and Susan." They were both staring at me.

"Good. Stay there and stay inside." As he often did, Sam slipped into the protective father role with me instead of equal partner.

"I will, Sam. Just get back with me as soon as you can." When I passed Sam's message on to Susan, she hurried us inside, locked the door, and called Hannah in from the backyard.

Once all the doors and windows were secured and the blinds shut, she asked, "Abbey, what did Skylar mean by, 'Let me be your Moriarty—your Lord Voldemort. You may be great now, but I can make you a legend'?"

She quoted the text word for word. I couldn't respond. Truth be told, I wasn't sure myself. I recognized the names, but their significance eluded me. My mind was in overdrive, listing possible steps I'd take if Sam confirmed my fears. I said nothing. My mind continued running multiple scenarios for Skylar's message. If we faced each other again, would I shoot her in the shoulder or the heart this time? *Don't go there, Abbey. Don't let her get to you.* I put my right hand under my leg to hide the quivering. Why would Skylar want to make me a legend? Was that a good thing? Weren't legends famous dead people? It wasn't until Dallas explained the significance of Skylar's choices of characters that I truly understood the gravity of my situation.

"Moriarty is Sherlock Holmes's nemesis," Dallas explained. "That, I get. But Voldemort is Harry Potter's enemy, hellbent on his destruction and death. Those are two entirely different scenarios."

Susan chimed in, saying, "Solving riddles and crimes fits Abbey. Skylar thinks she can make her great by doing something awful and challenging Abbey to catch her so everybody can see." They were talking as if I wasn't there. Susan put her hand on mine as we sat on the couch. She patted my leg like a mother trying to encourage her young daughter. "I never read the Harry Potter books, so I don't understand the second part."

Dallas sat on the other side of me and took my other hand. He leaned forward and looked around me at Susan. I felt like a little child sitting between her parents as they discussed adult stuff. "Voldemort made Harry stronger and more popular by trying to kill him *and* anyone who supported him." This time, he looked at me. "I think you need to start at the beginning and let me know exactly what happened between you and this Skylar."

I did. As hard as it was to say in front of Susan, I gave a thirty-minute summary of the Mark Ridley case and how it involved Skylar. I gave Dallas details of her pregnancy and the horrific death of her mother. I didn't, however, tell Dallas how Skylar and I connected. I kept my dark past in the past. After all, Dallas preached that's where the past should stay. "They diagnosed Skylar as a psychopath."

"I'd think so," Dallas said.

"I knew she was a sociopath, which is bad enough, but I studied the difference. According to my research, it's extremely rare for females to be psychopaths and incredibly dangerous to those around them," I explained. "She's extremely intelligent but has no empathy whatsoever."

"That's a horrible combination," Susan said.

My body felt as though it would sink through the couch. My face must have revealed my confusion and fear, because when I looked toward the hallway, I saw Susan's daughter, Hannah, sitting on the floor crying. I was her rock, her fortress, and she saw my panic. If I was visibly afraid, she knew it was bad. I felt a buzz in my back pocket. It was Sam. "What did you find out?"

"NCDC confirmed that Skylar was released for a home visit with Doctor Emily Teague, a world-renowned psychologist specializing in personality disorders. She's written all kinds of books on the topic."

"I guess that's what connected her to Skylar. Sam, we need to see what happened to Doctor Teague."

He was direct and to the point. "If Skylar has her phone, we can assume she's either dead or about to be."

It had been about forty-five minutes since I received the text. Maybe Skylar was torturing her and still on site. If so, we might have a chance to catch Skylar. "Did you find out where she works or lives?"

"She works out of her home. I'm sending the address to you now. Meet me there as soon as you can. Tell the others to lock the door behind you and wait."

The address wasn't on Harding Place like I expected; that ruled out an office at the NCDC. Why would Skylar be away from there for any reason? All mental health personnel came to see the patients, not vice versa. Specialist or not, she should have come through the security of the facility. I was growing more concerned by the minute.

Chapter Two

Friday, April 11, 9:16 PM—Home/Office of Dr Emily Teague

We met a group of officers from the West Precinct at Dr. Teague's home office. She lived in a southern traditional two-story brick home at the back of a gated community called Sylvan Park. Dr. Teague's home was symmetrical in nature with chimneys extending from each side. Other than a lone hall light in the entryway, the house was dark. We knocked several times with no response.

"We believe Dr. Teague is in mortal danger," Sam said.

"Okay, everyone, let's spread out and check for unlocked doors and windows," one of the officer's barked at his team. "Let me know if you see anyone inside."

"Be careful," Sam warned. "Her patient, an escaped psychopath, is already responsible for the deaths of two others."

It was true, but I didn't expect Skylar to still be on the premises. We'd taken too long to get here. Besides, she was too smart to hang around after she sent the message.

The team of officers spread out and checked the doors and windows. One officer remained at the front door, knocking and announcing, "Police! Open the door." The other officers flanked the home, which had a fenced-in back yard. Flashlights spread light in every direction on the darkened property. The singular streetlight stood three houses down the road and barely penetrated the dense canopy of the aging trees in the front yard. Darkness enveloped the rear of the lot.

Sam and I followed the team of officers moving around to the left. Every window was closed and secure. We followed a stone pathway to a gate accessing the back yard. It stood slightly ajar. I followed the first officer through the gate, searching with my light, which was limited in distance and lumens. The lead officer gave us a signal to wait while his officers checked the perimeter of the back lot. The officers secured the yard, making sure no one was hiding behind any of the shrubs that filled the lot. My mind raced with the possibilities of chaos Skylar could release on Nashville. A sharp whistle broke the silence, and we were motioned forward.

I made my own quick sweep of the backyard with my flashlight. My eyes drifted to a ten-by-ten aggregate pad located in the center of the yard just twenty feet away. The table and one of the four chairs were overturned. I knelt to examine the scene and noticed a patch of smashed flowers which spread out to the side of the fallen chair. As I leaned my head near the ground to look beneath the shrubbery surrounding three sides of the pad, something caught my attention. Donning my gloves and reaching beneath the bottom branch, I grabbed the handle of a large black rubber mallet. The scene was coming together in my mind.

Skylar and Dr. Teague sat on either side of the small table, discussing Skylar's lack of progress. While Dr. Teague made a few notes, summarizing their conversation, Skylar jumped to her feet and struck the unsuspecting woman with the mallet. She must have landed on the table and tipped it as her body fell. I flashed the light back to the flattened flower bed. This is where she fell in a limp heap. Yes, this patch of smushed flowers once held the body of Dr. Teague. My eyes traced the outline until I found the ruffled trail of mulch and torn grass. It led to the house.

"Sam, over here." He left the side of the yard and came to my side. "I think Skylar knocked Dr. Teague out. There's no sign of blood." I pointed to the trail where the body was dragged toward the house. "Dr. Teague might still be alive."

"Which means, Skylar may still be here." Sam whistled and

called the team to us. With all the lights focused on our location, we pointed out the trail leading toward the house.

Sam explained our theory, but was interrupted with a radio call announcing, "We got a body down inside."

The team checked the back doors and windows, and they too were locked. We joined the other team at the front of Dr. Teague's house. One officer pulled a battering ram from his trunk and breached the front door. The officers fanned out, flipped on the interior lights, and began to search both stories. Room by room, they called out, "Clear." The first-floor team continued until the lead officer made it back to the room where the body was spotted and called out, "Detectives, in here."

We followed the sound of her voice to a small office with books lining three of the four walls. She pointed to an area surrounded by four leather chairs. A white woman in her late forties lay in the middle of the room with what looked like a letter opener buried deep into her chest. It held a folded piece of paper with my name written on the top. I put my fingers on her carotid artery. No pulse. Glancing at the photos on the desk, I made a quick assumption that the victim was in fact Dr. Teague. I looked at Sam and shook my head.

I turned to one of the officers and said, "Get CSI here to process the site. We'll look around until they get here." I studied the books and photos on her bookshelves. "So, Skylar Watson has escaped," I said dryly. "How did she get out, Sam? Why would they let her come here?"

Before Sam could answer, a deep male voice boomed from an adjacent room, "I have another body."

We left Dr. Teague's office and moved down the hall to a sitting room just off the entryway. A young black woman lay on her back. A crimson circle surrounded her head like a red halo. Her throat was slit from ear to ear. I leaned over and read the ID tag that lay on her stomach like a tag on a present. "Alex Carson, technician. She worked for the Nashville Correctional Development Center."

"I think we just got our answer of how Skylar got here," Sam said. "Now, we need to know why she was here." He immediately dialed Spence and asked him to call the NCDC to inform them of the two deaths and ask why Skylar Watson was released for a visit to Dr. Teague's home. Sam called out to the officers, saying, "All right, everyone, let's go back over every inch of this place again to ensure Skylar Watson is not hiding in some crease or crevice. If she's still here, I want her." She was nowhere to be found.

CSI arrived and processed both bodies and the house. They took photos, diagramed each room and the back patio. Angelique, one of the members of the CSI team, introduced herself. She pulled the letter opener from Dr. Teague's chest and unfolded the note. "It's addressed to someone named Abbey."

"That's me," I said. She handed me the note. Fear gripped me, and I handed the note off to Sam. "You read it."

He took out his glasses and read the note as I bagged the weapon as evidence. "Abbey, a cleansing is coming, Skylar."

Skylar knew where Susan lived. Pulling me to the other side of Nashville would allow Skylar direct access to Susan. I called Susan and gave her a quick update, emphasizing they should stay away from the windows. I texted Dallas and asked him to stay with her until I was free from the crime scene and could relieve him.

"Sam, do you mind working the other body? I'd rather investigate Dr. Teague and her office. Skylar left me a personal note attached to her body. She wants me in here for some reason."

He got up to leave. "Watch yourself, Abbey. She could be playing you for a fool."

"Maybe, but I don't think so. She thinks she's superior and has nothing to fear from me."

"She's two years older now, Abbey. Be careful."

"I will, Sam." I paused and looked at the body. "Skylar manipulated her dad into killing his own wife and beating Skylar within an inch of her life so we'd focus on him. She also twisted Jonathan around her little finger, somehow convincing him to kill Pastor

Mark Ripley. Now, she's escalated to killing with her own hands. Dr. Teague's death looks clean, but Miss Carson's is violent and messy."

"You don't know what happened to her in that place. Sometimes, putting a young girl next to other mentally messed up women changes her for the worse." Sam let out a heavy sigh. "Anyway, I'll see what clues I can discover about Miss Carson; you take this room and see what you can find."

I should have let Sam make the decision since he was the senior detective, but Skylar's note bothered me, and I wanted to figure out what she wanted to tell me. In the back of my mind, I acknowledged it was a manipulation, but my curiosity got the best of me.

As Sam left to gather clues in the other room, I knelt beside Dr. Teague's body. Her eyes remained wide open with a look of fear and surprise. "What do we have so far?" I asked the technician named Angelique.

"There are no visible signs of a struggle. No defensive wounds. No tissue under her fingernails. As far as I can tell, nothing in the office is out of place."

"Did the mallet kill her?" I asked. "There's no blood anywhere around the letter opener."

The lead member of the CSI team cleared her throat. It was a subtle message to the young technician that she was sharing too much without authorization. Angelique didn't answer my question. Instead, she turned to the scribe and said, "The blade measures five inches."

"It was buried right up to the handle," I added.

I imagined Skylar watching with a mixture of fascination and delight as the woman lay unconscious or dead. She found the stationery, took time to jot the note, and decided to attach it to Dr. Teague's body by burying a letter opener in her chest. Skylar's mental disorder deepened at the center. There was no doubt.

"She was already dead."

I'd said it more to myself than the CSI crew, but the one in charge answered. "Yes, the wound was made post-mortem."

If she was willing to answer that inadvertent question, I thought I might see what else she would share. "How long would she have to be dead for the chest wound not to bleed?" I had so many questions. Obviously, Skylar took her dear, sweet time.

This time, the CSI lead answered. "You know the drill, Detective. Our office will notify you when the results of our study are in." She felt Dr. Teague's head: the front, the sides, and then she paused as she felt underneath. "There is a sizeable indention in the back of her skull." She pulled her hand out gently, easing Dr. Teague's head back to the floor. She carefully rolled the body over to visually examine the skull.

I knew from the scene outside that Dr. Teague was dead before Skylar went to all the trouble of dragging her body back in here. Why not leave the body outside? Why bring her to this room? What did she want me to see?

A technician kneeling near the door to the hall found a small black streak where the rubber from Dr. Teague's shoes rubbed off on the tile floor. I stood in the hall separating the two victims. The door was opened to the sitting room. "Sam, Skylar's not that feeble little girl anymore. She hit Dr. Teague hard enough to kill her."

The male member of the CSI team said, "That theory is consistent with my preliminary findings, but the ME's office will give you a more detailed and official pronouncement in the next few days." He called out, and someone rolled a gurney into the office for Dr. Teague's body. Sam and I moved to the site of the second murder.

"Nothing strange about this death. A fast, clean cut of her throat—execution style," Sam said, letting me know his observation. "After she was executed, her body was rolled over and the identification tag placed on her abdomen."

"It's like they're both presented as gifts."

"To you, unfortunately."

I felt through the evidence bag and pressed against the letter opener's edge. "She didn't do it with this. It's too dull."

"So, we have at least three different weapons," Sam said, stepping out into the hallway, "the mallet, a letter opener, and a knife." He motioned for me to join him in the sitting room. As I entered, he pointed to the blood splatter and stains on the floor. "Alex Carson was killed right here, but I haven't found any weapon." He called out to the officers from West and told them to look for any sign of the knife. It was the only one we were missing.

"Sam, look at the blood pattern. It's perfect—no obstructions. Somehow, Skylar knocked Dr. Teague out and managed to reenter the house to surprise Miss Carson." I stared at the blood. "Skylar's changed."

"Anyone who could live in a house where her mother's body was hidden in a deep freeze could easily do this." Sam called Skylar a dark soul. He rubbed the chill bumps from his arm as he looked back at the body at his feet.

"How could Skylar do such a thing? I always thought she manipulated the others to survive. She went out of her way to do this. My mind can't wrap around it, Sam."

"And yet here we are with two dead bodies and a note left by Skylar telling you a cleansing is coming. She texted you, Abbey, and she used her doctor's phone to do it."

"Okay, Sam, you've made your point." Skylar was sending me a message. I heard it loud and clear. Game on. "I still can't understand why she was here. Isn't that against NCDC policy for someone like Skylar to leave the premises?"

"We both know she can play the innocent as well as anyone, Abbey."

It was true. She played me during the Ripley case. As usual, we had more questions than answers at this point in a case. "Any word from Spence?"

As if on queue, Sam's phone rang. "Go ahead, Spence. You're on speaker."

"Finally got through to someone in administration. With HIPPA, it took a few minutes to get any pertinent information. You were right. Dr. Teague is a specialist in personality disorders. She was studying Skylar because she is considered a rare female psychopath. Something about researching for a book. Anyway, Skylar was taken there by a staff member at four-thirty."

"That's two hours before her text to me." I walked back to the office and leaned in. "We need a specific time of death."

"You'll have to wait on the official report." The CSI team was digging in its heels.

Sam was still talking with Spence. "Did no one notice she hadn't returned?" Sam removed his gloves and ran his fingers through his salt-and-pepper beard.

"They wouldn't comment."

"Spence, I want to know who had contact with Skylar Watson since she's been there? Did other inmates talk with her? Anyone visit her? Anyone call her? Write her? Dig, Spence. Find me something."

"I'm on it. Anything else?"

"I want to know her daily habits."

"The director said I'll have to complete a form and get a judge to sign off on it first."

"Why? The visitor logs should be public."

"I think they are trying to cover their bases and keep this out of the news." Spence gave more details about the facility manager. "I have a suspicion that Skylar's offsite visits were not approved. I don't know for sure, but I think favors or money may have passed hands. I'll look into their financials."

"You'll need a warrant for that, Spence. Lean into them. Get a warrant for both items."

"I'll take care of it and let you know," Spence said before ending the call.

"Why would Skylar do this?"

"She wanted out."

"Then why not do it and slip away? Why text me and announce the killings? Why make herself a target of the law?" I began walking through the sequence of the killings. "She manipulated Dr. Teague into going outside where they could be alone. She hit her. Left to go kill Miss Carson. Came back outside to drag the body to the office and left me a note. She waited long enough for Dr. Teague's blood to settle before attaching it with the letter opener. Sam, she wants me to find her and stop her."

Sam cautioned me about assuming. "Remember, let the facts lead you to your conclusion, not the other way around."

"I know, Sam. My mind gets ahead of me all the time." It was true. My mind constantly ran scenarios, especially in murder cases like this.

"Abbey, you know her better than most. What do you think she meant by *A Cleansing*? Those words ring a bell?"

"I don't know, Sam, but with Skylar, it certainly spells trouble. She left the note stuck to Dr. Teague in the office. There must be more there."

Sam and I returned to Dr. Teague's office. "What did she want me to see?" I scanned everything left out in plain sight. The bookshelves, the chairs, and the desktop. There was a brown folder peeking out from under a leather desk protector. I slipped it out and opened the folder. "Skylar's file."

There was a handwritten note on top dated for today. I read it aloud. "'I, Skylar Watson, give permission to Detective Abbey Rhodes to open and read my file.' She even signed it, Sam." I couldn't help but smile. She didn't want me to get into trouble. "This must have been what Skylar wanted me to find."

On the other side of the note, Skylar added, "Let me know your thoughts. I think she's a narcissistic quack, although she did have some good insights."

Dr. Teague's last note said, "Skylar's obsession with Detective Abbey Rhodes is of great interest. She feels a strong reciprocal relationship. I must speak with the detective to see how she responds.

Skylar claims Abbey is the Yang to her Yin, which suggests she understands she is the opposite of Detective Rhodes—a negative to her positive. It also shows Skylar's belief that they need each other for perfect balance. She mentioned two fictional antagonists: Moriarty and Voldemort. This also means Skylar assumes the relationship is not only ongoing but growing in intensity. This is a dangerous development. There's something strange about Skylar's eyes today. They are cold and…" A squiggly line trailed off from the letter "d" to the end of the page.

"Dr. Teague must have been writing the observation as Skylar struck her." Focusing on the note was possibly enough of a distraction for Skylar to gain the advantage. The doctor must have reached for the table to steady herself. I bagged the note separately for evidence. I would have to check with legal before reading any more of the file. Knowing Skylar, she probably left the permission note to build trust between us, all the while setting a trap. Skylar would know I needed properly completed forms to read the file's contents. Maybe she was anticipating a trial and would use my lack of patience to throw out the file. She was clever that way. Either way, I felt like I was being played.

Chapter Three

Saturday, April 12, 6:00 AM—Homicide

Bright and early the next morning, Sam and I both studied the evidence we'd gathered from Dr. Teague's home. Such was the life of a detective—late nights and early mornings. Even though MNPD assigned shifts to the homicides teams and there was one dedicated for the weekends, we worked on our case no matter the hour or day. Since Skylar was an escaped inmate with mental health issues and a person of interest in a double homicide, we put her information into the National Crime Information Center, otherwise known as NCIC. We also requested a teletype describing Skylar and the situation be sent to nearby agencies in all counties connected to Nashville's Davidson County, as well as neighboring Kentucky counties. Finally, we requested the local news channels run a feature with her picture and a brief description, asking the public to help us locate a person who might have information about a double homicide.

I was exhausted, both physically and mentally. After I left the crime scene late last night, I went by to check on Susan and assured her we would catch Skylar. Dallas and I ran a sweep of Susan's neighborhood, which turned up empty. I got in bed a little after two. My mind ran scenarios until the fatigue finally took over and I fell asleep. What seemed like minutes later, my alarm sounded, and off I went to the homicide offices.

"Abbey, are you deaf?" I turned. Sam had one hand on my shoulder, gently shaking me. "Where's your head today?"

"Sorry, Sam. I'm just tired. What were you saying?"

"You know her better than anyone; what do you think she's going to do next?"

I thought for a moment. "Still trying to piece it all together. She sent the cryptic text, saying she was going to make me great. Then the note saying a cleansing was coming—whatever that means." I stopped for a moment to see if I could wrap my mind around the clues. "She intentionally left the file where we could find it."

"According to Dr. Teague's note, this girl is really obsessed with you," Sam said. "Doesn't that bother you?"

"Of course it does, Sam. I get chill bumps just thinking about her." I hadn't told anyone, but I'd awakened several nights a month over the past year with the image of Skylar's mother's twisted body looking up at me from the freezer. A shudder ran down my spine. I had to focus my attention on this case. I opened the text. *Moriarty. Voldemort.* "Today, I need to do a little research on those names she used. Maybe that will help me figure out her next move."

"Okay. If we're lucky, we'll get a tip as to her whereabouts soon. In the meantime, I'm going to check on those orders and see if a judge signed them yet."

Sam left. I scooted up to my computer and typed in the name Moriarty. Just as Dallas said, Professor James Moriarty was a criminal mastermind and nemesis of Sherlock Holmes. I searched several sites for anything that may connect with Skylar and me. Two specific pieces of information stood out in multiple articles. Moriarty was not only a mastermind and brilliant criminal strategist, but he assisted other criminals with strategies.

The second piece, the more ominous part of the information, explained that Sir Arthur Conan Doyle, the author of Sherlock Holmes, created Moriarty as an equal but opposite force to Sherlock Holmes with the goal of using Moriarty to end his great detective. Is that what Skylar wanted to do? Was she going to be my equal but opposite power, making me great in the eyes of the public? Eventually bringing about my death to show she was always greater than I was? Another chill ran down my spine, and my body shook involuntarily. I glanced around to see if anyone had seen the spasm.

I made several notes about Moriarty before moving on to Voldemort. What a strange character. Voldemort was the evil villain set on destroying his nemesis, Harry Potter. Did Skylar know she was evil? Was I good? I could easily see how that sort of relationship connected us. It didn't bode well for me if that was the case. Voldemort killed Harry's parents and tried to kill Harry as a baby. Somehow, the attempt backfired, and the child was saved. I stopped as I read another note. Only Harry had the power to stop Voldemort, and according to the plot summary, Harry wins in the end. This was the opposite of the Moriarty analogy. Did Skylar know this? Maybe Skylar was saying we would be at odds with each other until one of us eventually died. Maybe she wasn't sure which way it would end. That gave me a little hope.

I filled my pad with notes about the two villains and my theories as to what their stories meant for Skylar and me. In either case, Skylar was going to keep at it until she was caught or killed. A cleansing? What was she going to clean?

I scanned back over our notes from the crime scene. Dr. Teague's car was still in her garage. Skylar escaped in Alex Carson's car. That car was found in Franklin, Tennessee, two towns south of Nashville. It had been wiped clean. There were no doorbell cameras in the neighborhood that could confirm which direction Skylar drove away. Where did she go from Franklin? Her first priorities would be to eat and find shelter. Surely, someone would see the news and recognize her.

Sam returned just before noon and brought me a salad. It was from a fast-food place and was mostly iceberg lettuce, but it was a wonderful gesture and a refreshing break. We took the time to sit out in the courtyard and eat our lunch. "That girl is beyond crazy," Sam said. "She wants to make you a legend."

"A legend isn't a bad thing." I was trying to put a positive spin on things, more for myself than the case.

"Maybe on the surface." Sam stroked his beard. "She plans on making you great by going on a killing spree."

"I'm not naive, Sam. Of course, I know she means a killing is coming. I just can't connect that to a cleansing. If she was killing criminals that would make sense. But she started with her psychologist and a worker at NCDC." After we bantered for a while, letting off some of the steam that had been building since Skylar's text, I filled Sam in on my findings. He knew about Moriarty but only had superficial knowledge of Voldemort. "Do you think she's going to clean the streets of other murderers, or is she going after people who hold them accountable?"

"Who knows. We've got to find this girl before she gets the chance to show us what she means."

We finished our lunch in silence. I don't even remember eating my salad, but the bowl was empty. Skylar's reappearance was doing a number on me.

Chapter Four

Sunday, April 13, 10:25 AM—Living Water Church

I went through the motions of listening during Bible study and worship. Susan and Dallas guided me to the sanctuary and our pew. I mindlessly followed. I couldn't even tell you what this morning's lesson was or the name of the song we just sang, but I perked up when Dr. Kelly, the new pastor, set his Bible on the plexiglass pulpit. He was a young man about the same age Mark Ripley had been. He had short blond hair and one of those beards that looked neatly groomed but was supposed to say, *I forgot to shave today*. He boasted a broad smile that could disarm his worst enemy.

"My name is BJ Kelly. Yes, I have a doctorate in theology, but that's the last time I'll mention that. The only thing that matters is that I love Jesus, and I want everyone else to love Him too." He got several hearty *Amens*. "You can call me Pastor Kelly or just BJ. I'll answer to either." He waited for the laughter to subside. "Today, we're going to seamlessly connect the Old and New Testaments as we discuss the need for ritual sacrifice."

Great. Old Testament lessons. These were always judgmental in nature. That's why my father loved them so much.

Pastor Kelly continued. "In many ways, these sacrifices served as spiritual cleansing. A sacrifice was presented that covered the sins of the people." A cleansing? That certainly grabbed my attention.

He began in the book of Leviticus and discussed God's command concerning sacrifice. He gave a quick summary of the various kinds of sacrifices. I had no idea there were different kinds. I thought a sacrifice was just a sacrifice. Either my father never discussed the differences, or I failed to pay attention when he did. Anyway, Pastor Kelly said there were burnt offerings, grain offerings, peace offerings, sin offerings, and guilt offerings. Each offering was specific to the need of the person offering sacrifice. Of course, the priest would present the sacrifice on the person's behalf.

"I could spend a month discussing these, but I hope you see the importance of sacrifice as a restoration of perfect fellowship between a Holy God and a sin-filled people. Unfortunately, the problem remained. These sacrifices only served to cover up their sins, which means they basically threw a blanket over them. The sins underneath remained."

I dog-eared the pages in the Bible that Dallas had given me so I could find the verses Pastor Kelly mentioned later. They may come in handy with the Skylar puzzle. The pastor mixed in personal stories and a spattering of Old Testament Scripture to support his claims. Then, he turned to the book of First Peter and read a passage I'd heard my father share on multiple occasions.

"The prophet Isaiah foretold of a sacrifice that would offer forgiveness of sins. I believe the New American Standard Version describes it best, when in Peter's first letter, the third chapter and the eighteenth verse, it says, 'For Christ also suffered for sins once for all time, the just for the unjust, so that He might bring us to God, having been put to death in the flesh, but made alive in the spirit.'"

He moved from there to the fifty-third chapter of Isaiah and showed how Jesus fulfilled every minute detail of the prophecy—how "His willing sacrifice of self on the cross paved the way for eternal life and the forgiveness of sin."

I knew about the crucifixion and resurrection from my days as a missionary's daughter, but I'd never made a connection between Jesus and the lambs, goats, and bulls mentioned in Leviticus.

My mind was shooting off in all directions, wondering what Skylar had up her sleeve. If these sacrifices connected to her cleansing, what kind of sacrifices was she going to offer? Then I wondered, did Skylar consider herself some kind of priestess? Even if she did, her sacrifices would be in vain, for—according to Pastor Kelly—Jesus already paid the ultimate price, and no further sacrifices were needed or accepted for that matter. I wanted to shout out my many questions. What about the Jews who didn't believe in Jesus? Did they still have to sacrifice? If not, where did confession come into play for them? *What did he just say about blood?* I couldn't keep up. I was flipping through my Bible, trying to find the next reference, only to get sidetracked again.

I felt someone tugging on my arm. I looked up and Susan was trying to pull me to my feet. The sermon was over, and the congregation was singing the invitation song. How much time had passed since he mentioned Isaiah? I stood between Susan and Dallas, but I didn't sing. My mind was fixed on Skylar. What was her plan?

"Coming over for lunch?" Susan asked.

"I can't today, sorry. Sam and I are meeting to work on the case while there's still a chance to find Skylar before she does anything else." I kissed Dallas on the cheek, pushed through the crowd, and walked swiftly to my car. This information was too interesting not to share with Sam, so I recorded my thoughts on my phone before I lost them.

Chapter Five

Monday, April 14, 9:47 AM—NCDC

With warrant in hand, Sam and I entered Nashville Correctional Development Center for women. Spence was back at Homicide digging into the facility's financials and the personal finances of the center's manager to see if any money had changed hands concerning Skyler's offsite access. We were there to see videos of Skylar's visitors. She had three. One was a regular.

The tech guy sat us in front of his screen and produced the videos we needed. A young man sat opposite Skylar. We listened as he told her how beautiful she was. Skylar smiled and threw in a word or two of encouragement. He promised to write to her. The visit amounted to nothing more than an admirer who was interested in nothing but Skylar's looks. It reminded me of our conversation where she told me men constantly showered her with compliments and offers. She said that's why she found it so easy to direct them where she wanted.

The second visitor was an older woman who offered to pray for Skylar while she was incarcerated. She tried to elicit a response from Skylar, but she rose and walked away. The visit was approximately two minutes.

"What about the regular visitor?" Sam asked. "How many times did she see Skylar?"

He checked his notes. "Five times. Do you want to see each one?"

"Yes, please," Sam said.

He typed on his keyboard, and the first video played. She was a short redheaded young woman with pale skin and orange freckles. She introduced herself as Penny Thatcher and said she was interested in the Old Testament temple. Skylar sat across from her. Nothing seemed to register on her face. Penny wasn't fazed by the lack of response. Instead, she sat there describing the Temple and its ornate aspects. She went into great detail of the materials used in its construction.

Something in what she said seemed to pique Skylar's interest. "Tell me more."

The young redhead grinned as she leaned forward and described the Temple's inner chamber called the Holy of Holies. "Can you believe the priest only visited it once a year? What did the people do the other days when they needed forgiveness?"

"Time. Let's wrap it up." The officer standing in the corner of the room motioned for the visitors to leave.

We watched the second video. It was much the same. "She brought Skylar Watson books on the Temple, along with a few commentaries," the tech said, looking at his notes. "They were checked and approved."

As we watched the other visits, it seemed the two women hit it off. Skylar began asking detailed questions based on her readings. Penny's excitement grew, and she promised to continue her visits. That was the final one. It was three weeks prior to the murder of Dr. Teague.

"Well, it's obvious where Skylar got her inspiration. "We need to get the address of this Penny Thatcher and check her out," I said.

Sam nodded.

Chapter Six

Tuesday, April 15, 11:02 AM—Home of Penny Thatcher

We knocked on the door of Penny Thatcher's home. No answer. We'd tried to call her, but the phone went straight to voicemail. Sam and I peered through the windows on either side of the front door. The home was dark.

"Let's look around while we're here," Sam said. "No harm in seeing what we can find."

We looked through the first window to our right. A kitchen with a small table. "There's a plate, Sam, and it looks like it has food on it. Maybe she's here and doesn't want to answer."

"Keep looking."

We went around back and looked through the window. "Sam, the place has been tossed."

He pressed his face to the glass and said, "Call it in. Someone's been here looking for something."

I called for backup. We climbed up the stairs of the back patio and tried the door handle. "It's unlocked." I pulled out my Sig and turned the handle. "Police. Is anyone here?"

I stepped inside. Sam followed. We made our way through the little house and found the den. Someone cleared the bookshelves. Books and nicknacks lined the floor. The furniture was strewn about, most of which still lay upside down. I pushed the chair aside. "Sam, I have blood." It was dry, several days old.

He was on the phone with dispatch, describing the scene and calling for CSI. While we waited for the others to arrive, Sam and

I searched the house for any sign of the attacker. The home was clear. The police arrived first. CSI was quick to follow. They found patches of blood in four separate places near the den. Streaks of blood indicated a body had been dragged to the front door. No sign of blood from there.

"Sam, it looks like a rug used to be here by the door. I think someone wrapped the body and carried it out."

"Probably. Let's comb this place from corner to corner."

This didn't make sense. "Why would Skylar kill Penny Thatcher? She seemed to have a connection with her."

"You can't assume it's Skylar Watson. Let the clues reveal the attacker. Besides, don't try to think logically when it comes to Skylar. She does whatever she wants and whatever accomplishes her goal."

I suppose Penny served her purpose. "I wish I knew what books are missing. That could give us clues as to who and why." If it was Skylar, this made three kills. How did these deaths make a cleansing? A psychologist, a technician from her detention center, and a young, enthusiastic visitor. What was their common denominator?

I examined every part of the house, doing my best to come up with a profile of Penny Thatcher. By the looks of things, she was deeply religious. The walls were lined with posters of Bible verses, mostly from the Old Testament. We found five different Bibles, all different translations. The poor girl didn't know what she was getting into when she decided to visit Skylar Watson. Where was her body? Why would the person who ransacked the house take it away? What was the point in that? I know I wasn't supposed to jump to conclusions, but it was pretty obvious the three deaths all connected to Skylar.

What was she going to do next? Sam and I gathered everything we could, made extensive notes, and headed back to Homicide to discuss the two cases. Were they connected, or was this just a random case of a burglar caught in the act? We checked Penny's workplace, The Frame Shop. She'd been missing since Thursday. That was the day before Skylar escaped.

"Sam, we may have a different killer."

Great! Just what we needed, another case to distract us from Skylar Watson.

Chapter Seven

Friday, May 2, 4:10 PM—Homicide

"**N**othing! It's like she vanished from the face the earth." Sam tossed the folder onto his desk. It slid against the back wall, spilling its contents onto the floor. "How can that girl go off the radar completely?"

"She's smart, Sam. The fact that we have no other killings remotely resembling a sacrifice or slit throat shows me she probably left the note to distract us while she made her escape. Besides, didn't you tell me Monday, 'Relax; it's only been a month'? Maybe Skylar realized how crazy her idea was. Speaking of crazy, I wonder how she's coping without her meds."

"That's another reason she should have been easy to spot," Sam said, bending over to pick up the papers and photos. "She's probably out there bouncing off the walls."

"Every lead we've gotten has turned up nothing." Finding nothing triggered old wounds about Sam's family whose murders were never solved. We both fought feelings of inadequacy and failure for different reasons. Lieutenant Stallings took the Penny Thatcher case from us and gave it to the other members of our homicide team. They were coming up empty-handed as well.

Sam sat and lowered his head in his hands. With his fingers, he rubbed tiny circles around his temples. After a few moments, he looked up and asked, "And Skylar hasn't reached out to you at all?"

"Come on, Sam. You know I'd tell you immediately if I heard anything." That reminded me of something. "Did you hear the public relations office had to upload her information again? Somehow, it keeps getting deleted."

My mind flitted off to Pastor Kelly's latest sermon. I became a student of the Old Testament sacrifices and could easily rattle off a list with descriptions of each. I even interviewed Pastor Kelly a couple of times to see if he had any idea what a modern cleansing without Jesus might look like. I coupled that information alongside my intensive interviews with Skylar's counselors at the NCDC, and I was able to create a detailed psychological and spiritual profile. Her story was sad and dark. It made me wonder if she went to Living Water Church for anything other than a physical relationship with her youth minister, Jonathan.

I found it difficult to believe Skylar spent most of her last two months at NCDC studying the Bible and conservative commentaries, filling her sketchbooks with drawings of altars, Old Testament priestly clothing, and sacrifices where fire came down from heaven to consume the animals offered. To say she was obsessed with the topic would be an understatement. Apparently, it was all she thought about, so it was highly unlikely that Skylar would give up on her mission of a cleansing. One counselor said she even made notes in Hebrew. We had them translated by a local scholar who said they were prayers, pleading God to use her in mighty ways. Some of the later entries made me think Skylar believed God was answering her prayer and promising her freedom. She wrote that two nights before the double homicide.

My body twitched as a shiver ran up my spine. "If Skylar ever chooses to fulfill her fantasies, we'll be in a mess of trouble."

Sam stopped what he was doing and turned around in his chair. "I know it's wrong, but I kind of wish she would do something. I hate waiting. Besides, if some sort of cleansing begins in Nashville, we'd have a fighting chance of catching her."

I didn't know how to feel about his wish. On the one hand, we could put an end to this case. On the other, it would mean she killed again. As it was, we were spinning our wheels—going nowhere fast. What was she doing? What was she waiting for? Was I on the right track with this *cleansing*? Maybe it had nothing to do with sacrifices at all.

"I'm calling it a day, Kid." Sam looked at his watch. "How's it going with the preacher boy?"

"Preacher boy? His name is Dallas Gatlin, and he's a professor of English and Biblical Studies at Belmont."

"So, he's out of your league then?" Sam punched my shoulder as he left.

I rubbed the spot. "Thanks for the encouragement, Sam." I was already convinced I had no long-term chance with Dallas. Why was he interested in me anyway? Then I remembered we were supposed to go bowling with Susan and the kids tonight. That would be safe enough. Maybe I wouldn't make a fool of myself.

Chapter Eight

Wednesday, September 10, 7:10 AM—Home of Jonathan Buxton

Four months passed since the murders of Dr. Emily Teague and Alex Carson and the disappearance of Penny Thatcher, and we'd found no sign of Skylar Watson. The trail had gone completely cold. Captain Harris had her image and bio resent to all Middle Tennessee counties. Skylar was eerily silent. No texts and no messages of any kind. Whatever plan she concocted never panned out. I was in the process of giving up on *The Cleansing* and moving on with my life. There were plenty of other homicides in Nashville to keep me busy. September tenth was no exception.

At six thirty-five, Wednesday morning, we were sent to the home of Jonathan Buxton. His wife, a nurse, came home after her graveyard shift and found him dead. She called the police, who, in turn, called Homicide. The officers made a point to prepare us for the oddity of his death and staging. It's never a good sign when the officers use the word *staging* to describe the victim. It always hints at a possible pattern, which meant more killings would follow.

Mr. Buxton lived in a middle-class neighborhood in Nashville, in a white two-level home with a small front porch. We made our way up the sidewalk, which was flanked on both sides by a variety of colorful Mums. I thought of the irony. Beauty and life on the outside, death on the inside. We stepped up to the yellow crime scene tape and held out our credentials for the recording officer.

"Detectives Tidwell and Rhodes," Sam said. We ducked under the yellow boundary and stepped into the house. I could smell fresh paint. I paused to examine the doorframe. No visible forced entry. I pulled the door to me and looked behind it. Nothing on the wall. I looked down and noticed a doorstop fastened to the floor. Kneeling, I examined the bottom of the door and felt a slight indention where it would have contacted the doorstop. Could be old—could be new.

"We can look at the door later, Abbey," Sam said, encouraging me to follow the officer. I got up and glanced around the foyer. Everything looked neat and tidy. No children's toys in sight. Just beyond the eight-by-eight tiled entryway, rich cherry hardwood steps rose to the second floor. We were directed to the right, past a baby grand piano and sitting room. It was immaculate and looked unused. Probably just for display purposes.

"The body's in here." In the other room, a young female officer directed our attention to the site. She was thin and had twisted her jet-black hair in a bun that pushed tightly against her hat. "I've never seen anything like it," she said as she held her left hand over her mouth. "You guys must get this kind of thing all the time, but it makes me nauseous."

I nodded and made my way to a hallway displaying family photos. I say *family*, even though there were no pictures of children, just a young couple in various locations. I looked down beneath the wall of photos. I suddenly understood the young officer's nausea. This was a horrifying site, and the stench of death was strong. A young man's body lay belly down, stretched out in the shape of the letter X. His hands and bare feet were bolted to the floor. His head rested on his chin, which made it obvious that someone slit his throat from ear to ear.

Just like Alex Carson. Could this be connected to Skylar Watson's case? Was she finally revealing her plan? Blood formed a small puddle beneath his neck. I noticed multiple bloody footprints leading down the hallway to his left. Initial assessment—three killers. I tried to imagine how his wife felt coming home this morning after a long shift. She must have been exhausted and ready to crawl into bed, only to find her husband like this. I imagined her scream—her outrage. I turned to the officer. "Any ID?"

"Yes." She handed me his wallet with her gloved hand, keeping her other hand over her nose. "Jonathan Buxton."

"Thanks." We assumed as much since his wife made the call, but it was proper procedure to verify the victim's identity whenever possible. I slid the driver's license out of its slot and matched the picture to the face of the man at my feet.

"His wife is upstairs in her bedroom lying down. We have an officer with her."

"She's still here?" I asked, somewhat surprised.

"She refused to leave."

"Thanks, we'll talk to her after we get a good look at our crime scene. How far do those go?" Sam asked, pointing to the prints.

"They lead to the back yard and disappear in the grass."

"We'll follow those a little later," I announced, "after we examine the body. Is CSI on the way?" She nodded.

"See if we can get a team of dogs up here," Sam told the officer. "It's a longshot, but maybe they can show us which direction the killers went."

The CSI team entered a few moments later, hauling their equipment through the front door and apologizing for the delay. At their arrival the officer asked, "Am I through here?" Sam nodded, allowing her to move away from the graphic scene.

Knowing the CSI team would move in on the body, I quickly examined it. Obviously, he was killed on that spot. I could tell from the blood spatter and pooling. Oddly though, there wasn't as much pooled blood as there should have been. A cut like that would have drained most of his body's blood. It only took a moment to discover why the puddle was so small. I followed the blood trail two feet to his left where it led to a floor vent, through which the remainder of his blood disappeared. By sharp contrast, there was no blood where the bolts or screws penetrated his hands and feet. They obviously were in no hurry after killing him. They took the time to display the body post-mortem. Large washers, almost as wide as his hand, kept the screws from ripping through the flesh. They meant for the body to stay right there in that specific place. Why? What did the staging tell us?

"What's your first impression, Abbey?" Sam asked. He was ever the mentor, challenging me to talk my way through the scene. Sam was trying to make me more of a team player, sharing my thoughts as I had them. He kept telling me he wouldn't be around forever, and the next guy might not be as patient.

"Why go to so much trouble fixing a dead body to the floor? If they meant to torture him for pleasure or information, they would have drilled him to the wood while he was alive." I thought for a moment before adding, "So, what was their point? His death was swift and decisive—almost merciful."

"Good. Go on." He knelt beside the body and studied it as the CSI team set up around us.

"Since we know he wasn't tortured and the staging was done after his death, whoever killed him wanted to make sure his body wasn't moved from this spot. It must be significant." I studied the body. Why prop the face forward on his chin, and why point him in this direction? "I don't know if his body was stretched out to make an X on purpose or just stretched out and fastened to the floor facing this direction." I looked up at the wall. What did the killer want us to see? "There's something about this wall—these photos. It's almost like the killer, or killers, wanted him to stare at the images in death—to remember something." I paused to reexamine the body. "But that doesn't make sense either. If he was supposed to face the photos in death, he should have been posed either kneeling in front of the photo or fixed in a standing position stuck to the opposite wall. So, why like this where he could only see the base of the wall?"

"Great question. Look at the family photos, but don't look at them," Sam said.

"His wife is the next of kin, and she discovered the body."

"Or did she?" Sam asked with one eyebrow raised. "Remember not to assume anything at this point."

I knew what he was suggesting. It was a fair question. We could easily check with the hospital to see what time she left. This staging would have taken time. Something about the way his body was secured was of equal importance. "I don't know, Sam. I think we need to dig into his occupation and his family. What he does for a living may be significant. We know family is an important clue, but I don't think it's everything. I don't know about you, but does everything in this house look brand new?"

"You may be onto something there. Let's see if we can dig up any skeletons," Sam said. "See who might have wanted him dead." He shook his head and sighed. "We never get ordinary homicides anymore. What ever happened to the classic drive-by?"

I turned my attention to the man's arms as the older CSI agent knelt to exam his neck. "Sam, look." There was something carved into his right hand, nearly hidden in the fleshy crook between his thumb and forefinger by the large washer. "It's the letter V."

"Maybe the V and the X are clues," Sam said. "Good catch. The killer may have written a message on the victim's body. See any more letters?"

Sam and I scoured for additional clues. "No." We studied the home. There was no forced entry, so he either let the killers in or left the door unlocked and they surprised him. I made a note to check with his wife about his security habits. "Any sign of struggle or resistance, Sam?" He shook his head. I studied the pictures on the wall. Most were Jonathan and his wife in various locations around the world. "He had enough money to travel. These all look recent."

"What makes you say that?"

"He hasn't aged from location to location."

Two pictures at the far-left end caught my eye. Jonathan and another man stood on either side of two large fish hanging by their tails. One was of a huge Marlin, the other a Great White Shark. I made a note to find the identity of the man. "A brother?

A friend?" I wasn't asking Sam. I was becoming painfully aware of my bad habit. I needed to keep my thoughts inside. I turned my attention back to the deceased, stood between his feet, and looked at the wall directly aligned with his head. There were two photos of Jonathan with an older man in the same place but taken several years apart by the older man's appearance. "Sam, look at these. Buxton and Son Bolt and Screw. It looks like a warehouse for parts." I looked down at the body. "Bolt and Screw. I bet they sell washers too." Somebody was sending a message.

"I bet you're right; we need to look closely at his workplace," Sam said. "See if they stock these materials and dig into his relationship with his father and their employees."

"I agree. This washer has a light scoring—possibly from a socket attached to a drill."

Sam knelt beside the body and examined the hand. "Makes sense. You'd have to use a power tool to drive it through flesh and bone. This would have taken a lot of time—long enough for the blood to drain. They weren't in a hurry, and they weren't concerned with noise."

"It suggests the killers knew the home and the wife's schedule. They knew what he was doing and came prepared for the staging. The familiarity suggests they've probably been here before and knew about the wall of photos."

"You keep saying *They,* Abbey. What makes you think it's a group? My first thought was Skylar Watson."

I thought of her first too. Skylar was petite. If she did this, she would have had to have help. "Look how the body is stretched out. Even with a dead body, somebody would have to hold the arm down flat to attach it like that. Plus, his body is taught in all directions. Call me sexist, but I don't believe little Skylar could overpower him, kill him, stretch him out, and drill through his hands and feet. She isn't strong enough."

"She knocked Dr. Teague out with one hit to the head. Don't underestimate her."

"Believe me, I don't, Sam. But there are also three distinct sets of footprints in the blood."

I made another entry in my little notebook. This was certainly an odd case. "If this is the cleansing, Skylar has recruited help."

"Maybe that's why she took so long to start," Sam said.

After taking detailed notes and my own pictures of the crime scene, Sam and I inspected the three separate sets of footprints in the blood spatter. I say footprints because that's exactly what they were—bare feet with no shoes. The big toe on the smallest set of prints had a scar running its length. That could be helpful. "Proof we have more than one killer," I said. "We have at least three, and they were all barefoot." Sam followed the prints, and I followed him. Just as the officer said, they led to the back door of the home and disappeared into the neatly manicured grass. Such a weird detail to add to a crime scene—footprints. "Who goes barefoot to a crime scene?"

Sam pulled off his gloves and ran his fingers through his curly hair. "Get closeups of each print and one of the three together for comparison of sizes. We can analyze them back at Homicide." I did, and we reexamined everything once more.

After Sam and I completed our search of the crime scene, we went upstairs and interviewed the victim's wife, Cheryl. According to her, they were happily married. Jonathan was doing well at work, and with the extra income, they were able to travel like they always dreamed they would. He was a great man, and everyone loved him. Isn't that what they always say about the dead? Cheryl Buxton said her husband never locked the doors. He never felt the need to since he always carried a gun, even around the house.

A gun? That was upsetting. We checked the body again; there was no hidden gun or holster. Now, the killers had a gun. "How did they subdue him if he always carried a pistol, Sam? I don't see a bullet hole anywhere. He must not have gotten a single shot off."

"Apparently, he didn't see the need."

"Another reason to look at family, friends, and employees."

We gave instructions for the officers to canvass the neighborhood and see what they could tell us about the Buxtons. We also told them to look for neighbors with doorbell cameras.

Chapter Nine

Wednesday, September 10, 2:42 PM—Homicide Headquarters

As soon as we returned to Homicide Headquarters, I dug into the background of Buxton and Son Bolt and Screw on Elm Hill Pike in Nashville. It was founded in 1981 by Vince Buxton. Vince? "Hey Sam, Jonathan's father's name is Vince—like with a V."

"That's curious, Abbey. You think his father killed him, branded him?" I shrugged my shoulders. Too early to tell. "Any history of bad blood between the father and the son?"

"I don't know, Sam, but I'll find out." I was determined to flesh out my growing theory, so I dug deeper into the company's history, looking for anything about the relationship between Vince and Jonathan Buxton. Jonathan's wife didn't mention his father at all, but that didn't surprise me. She was focused on her husband.

The articles I found praised Vince Buxton's ingenuity and hard work. He built the company into an industrial giant from a small, rented space and one-man shop. Buxton and Son was currently the number one supplier of bolts, screws, washers, and pretty much anything related to those items in Tennessee and Kentucky. Vince sounded like a great businessman with a reputation for community involvement and philanthropy. He donated the money to build a community playground in North Nashville. No mention of Jonathan.

I kept searching while Sam investigated Jonathan's finances. After about two hours of perusing articles on Vince Buxton, I finally found one introducing his son, Jonathan. The article, dated June twenty-third of this year, examined a leadership controversy over the company's direction. Jonathan Buxton took over as president of the company after having his father declared mentally incompetent. Vince was diagnosed with early stages of dementia and forced out of leadership. According to the article, Jonathan was deeply concerned about several mistakes his father made, costing the company nearly a hundred thousand dollars. With the help of his own primary physician, Jonathan moved Vince to a facility for around-the-clock care of dementia and Alzheimer's.

Around-the-clock care? That didn't sound like appropriate treatment for someone in the early stages. Maybe they were trying to cover up a more advanced cognitive issue so they wouldn't lose the confidence of their clients. If that were so, why would Jonathan consent to the article, which would make his father's condition public knowledge? Maybe he wanted to publicly assure his clients that he would personally keep things going smoothly. Maybe he seized the opportunity to justify his takeover.

If Vince was under constant watch at a memory care facility, I could scratch his name from the persons of interest. I read further. Jonathan was quoted numerous times rationalizing the "abrupt transition of leadership." According to the article's author, the "forced takeover" was an unpopular move with many of the Buxton employees. So much for unbiased journalism. So much for his wife's claim that everybody loved him.

"I have a list of people I'd like to get more information on, Sam." He stopped and looked over the top of his reading glasses. "Jonathan forced his dad to give up the business and had Vince committed to a memory care facility."

"When?"

"In early June."

Sam smiled. "Well, that explains the jump in his income. It nearly tripled from June ten on."

"That would certainly give somebody loyal to Vince a motive

to murder Jonathan. There were no signs of struggle and no forced entry, which would point to someone Jonathan knew and trusted—like an employee. It would also explain the killers fixing him to the floor with bolts and washers in a sign of submission. He'd be fixed *below* the picture of his father in front of the business. How symbolic is that? As for the means, I bet they have a warehouse full of washers and bolts, and you can pick up a sharp knife anywhere. Motive, means, and opportunity. What an idiotic move."

"Sounds like you've wrapped it up already, Abbey. Let's go home." I knew it was Sam's shot at my habit of making assumptions rather than letting the clues lead us to a logical conclusion. "I guess you no longer need me. Maybe I should go ahead and retire."

"Oh, shut up, Sam! You'll always be indispensable." He'd been floating the idea of retiring ever since we became partners. I wasn't ready for that. Neither was he.

"You and Spence did a fine job on the Swain case when I was in the hospital," he said rubbing the scars on his shoulder and chest.

"A case built on your hard work." He knew I was right. Had he not gone back over to the homeless camps and been shot, I probably never would have given the place another thought.

He looked at his watch. "It's getting late, and you have a date. Get it? Late and date?" Sam laughed. "I'm a poet and don't know it."

"When will you stop with these Dad jokes? Besides, it's not a date; we're meeting for Bible study night at church."

Bible Study. Those words sounded so foreign to my ears, yet they rolled naturally off my tongue.

"I still say it's a date. It's not like you to worry about church stuff." He shuffled papers into stacks and shifted them around his desktop. "My mind is shot for the day," he added.

"Just because Dallas will be there, doesn't make it a date." He was right, though—on both counts. I was excited because I would see Dallas. To be honest, I was also beginning to warm up to the church people and their ways. Living Water Church differed from the church I grew up with. There was no condemnation at Susan's church. No criticisms. No fear that I would make a mistake and be called out for it. Even grumpy old Duke Stearns had a positive disposition as of late. He welcomed me, and he was sharing the Gospel message with some of the new families. I guess an old dog can learn new tricks. The people at Living Water spoke of the Jesus I dreamed about as a little girl. Even with all of that, I was still hesitant to trust Christians, and I knew two shining examples. My past was hard to shake.

"Well, let's call it a day anyway. What do you want to pursue tomorrow?"

"I'd like to visit the warehouse and get reactions from the employees. I'll see if anyone matches the size of the footprints."

"A modern Cinderella," Sam joked.

I ignored his flippant comment and said, "I'd also like to match the screws and washers to their inventory. What about you?"

"I'd like to visit Vince Buxton and see how much he knows and remembers. You get a list of employees. Remind me to check the visitor log to see if his daughter-in-law or any employees have been there recently."

"Will do, Sam. We'll meet back here after." I grabbed my stuff and looked at the time on my phone. If I headed straight there, I could make it for supper. I smiled as I pictured Dallas waiting for me. Having someone like him was a dream come true. But the sad thing about dreams—you eventually wake up.

"Don't forget to come here first. You know Lieutenant Stallings will have his thing in the morning."

"Oh, yeah. I forgot. It's nine-eleven tomorrow. I'll be here." It was an annual event at Homicide. I grabbed my things and rushed out the door to fight the Nashville traffic.

Chapter Ten

Wednesday, September 10, 6:05 PM—Living Water Church

I arrived just in time for supper but missed the opening blessing, which was fine with me. I was still struggling with the concept of prayer, whether or not it made any difference. On a bright note, Dallas and Susan saved a seat for me at their table.

"You made it," Susan said with a smile. She looked so cute in her black sweater which made her red hair pop. Susan was always dressed trendy but modestly. Hannah and Danny jumped up from their seats and hugged me. I was getting used to their physical contact and no longer flinched or pulled away. It felt nice to have people I trusted and could let inside my defenses.

Dallas gave me a big hug, too. "I'm glad you came." He let go, but I didn't want the embrace to end. I loved the hint of cologne he wore. It was mild and reminded me of amber. He didn't overdo cologne like some men. "I didn't think you would make it."

"Yeah, Sam made sure we quit on time." I looked at Susan and said, "He still ribs me about coming here, though. He thinks it's creepy that I stayed around after the investigation." It was out of my mouth before I could stop it. That investigation solved the murder of Susan's husband. How could I bring that back up again?

She seemed to let it pass and focused on Sam. "Maybe we can team up on him, Abbey." Susan said it with one of those looks she gave when she sensed a challenge. Her blue eyes sparkled in the fluorescent light of the fellowship hall. "Church would be good for Sam." She nudged the kids and said, "We better get in line before it gets too long. I haven't seen this many people on a Wednesday night since Mark was pastor."

"I think everyone is excited about Pastor Kelly," Dallas said. "Sunday was crowded, and everyone was trying to corner him for a conversation."

The fellowship hall was packed, and additional tables were set up in the library and courtyard. "Are we starting the fall Bible studies tonight?" I asked. "There are so many people here."

Dallas answered immediately. "All the adults are meeting in the sanctuary with the pastor. He wants to kick off the fall by reiterating the new church vision. Next week, he said we'll start all the study groups."

We finally reached the front of the serving line and got our plates. My mouth watered. I loved Italian food and found it difficult to choose between lasagna, spaghetti, or fettuccini alfredo. Dallas put his hand on my lower back to gently nudge me forward. I savored the tingling feeling that rose from his hand to my head. It had taken several months for me to welcome his touch without tensing up or moving away, but I now treasured it. Dallas was so patient with me. That was one of the many things I enjoyed and admired about him. He seemed to understand my need for security and time. We dated for nearly a month before he kissed me on the lips. I was beginning to wonder if he ever would. "How was school today?" I asked.

"Four classes of American literature," he said. "I suffered from déjà vu all day. I couldn't remember whether I'd just shared that information in my current class or if I said it in an earlier one." He went on to describe the trouble of teaching the same lesson four times in a row.

I wasn't a fan of school; I only stayed in it for the sports and the diploma. School allowed me the opportunity to play soccer, and I was good. It amazed most Guatemalans to see a white girl excel above the locals. As for my professional education, most of my knowledge came from individual research and study. Mr.

Morales, the man who took me in after my parents kicked me out at the age of fourteen, gave me access to anything I needed and encouraged me to learn as much as I could on my own. But I had no patience for *group learning*. I did what I had to in the Army to qualify for MP, but I wouldn't choose to go to a formal school if I didn't have to. Thankfully, I was lucky and picked things up quickly by just reading the material for myself. Dallas continued to speak about American Literature. "Sorry, but it sounds boring," I said, guiding him away from the topic.

"Oh, no," Dallas said, turning me around. "I enjoy the subject, but I couldn't focus. My mind was on you. I couldn't wait to see you tonight."

I smiled. It felt nice to be wanted. "Well, here I am. Look all you want." I turned a circle.

"You know I meant to be with you, not just look—although that's nice too." He blushed when he said it.

"Aw. You're so sweet." I put my hand on his cheek and stared into his eyes. "I could look at you all day."

"What did I say about the two of you?" Susan asked, reminding us for the hundredth time that she put us together. "Am I a good matchmaker, or what?"

"Sorry. That probably sounded really sappy." I'd forgotten we were standing in a room packed with nearly a hundred people. For that moment, it felt like there were just the two of us.

"No, it was precious," Susan added. "But you might want to move forward. We're all getting a little hungry."

Where was my head tonight? I looked forward and realized no one was in front of us. I quickly made my salad, selected a dessert, and grabbed a glass of sweet tea to go with my fettucine. Given my past, I never thought I'd be this way with a man, but it felt so natural with Dallas. One thing still bothered me—his desire to teach and preach the Bible even after his interim duties ended. Even though the two were nothing alike, I couldn't shake the shadow of my father or his degrading words. They haunted me and affected my ability to relax and trust anyone fully. Dallas did nothing to make me doubt or question his intentions, yet the dark past forced negative and paranoid thoughts into my head. No matter how hard I tried, I couldn't silence those old, critical voices. Those tapes ran deep in my soul.

We sat at our table. "Are we still on for Friday night?" I asked, taking a bite of salad.

Dallas nodded and asked, "Aren't you going to hint at our destination?"

"No. But I will say dress comfortably and have a jacket." I insisted that I choose the activity this week, and I wanted to surprise him. It was part of my strategy to keep the relationship equal. I had this thing about not giving anyone the upper hand.

"So, it's probably outside. That's scary."

I hated surprises. I suppose it was rooted in my deep trust issues—at least, that's what my counselor said. But being on the other end of the surprise excited me. I could tell Dallas was easygoing, but he didn't like the unknown either.

After supper, we moved to the sanctuary. Some would hear the new pastor's vision and mission for the first time. "What I'm about to share with you isn't unique, but it is profound and will change how you look at God's Word and His church. I know it changed my paradigm completely." He had my attention. He was such a good speaker. "I've been saying this since I came in April, but you'll need to get used to hearing it, because I'm not going to stop. God's vision for Living Water Church is simple. Love God and love others. I didn't coin the phrase. I've seen pastors who have argued over its origin, and they're all sadly mistaken."

He took a few steps to the left of the pulpit. "Jesus said it in the Gospel of Mark, but it wasn't just a New Testament thing. Jesus was quoting Scripture from the books of Deuteronomy and Leviticus." He smiled and said, "I see some of the faces contorting. Yes, those are the Old Testament books of the Law." Dallas smiled and nodded. "In these books, Moses tells us to 'Love the

LORD your God with all your heart and with all your soul and with all your might.' God's message of love hasn't changed since the beginning of time. He also says, 'you shall love your neighbor as yourself.' Now, when he said that, he meant we should love our neighbors as much as we love ourselves."

I couldn't help but think of my neighbor Aaron. He hurt me and used me. He called me damaged goods. It would be hard to love him after all that. I didn't know any other neighbors. To be honest, I didn't want to. I still liked my privacy.

Pastor Kelly explained the simple but powerful vision God had for Living Water. It was a vision of love. "We first need to focus on loving God. Then He enables us to love our neighbors, especially those who are unlovable." It was almost as if he was reading my mind. Aaron was unlovable. But I had a deeper question at that moment. I was supposed to love my neighbor as much as I loved myself. Did I love myself? I was trying hard to see myself through Susan's and Dallas's eyes. They saw something of worth in me. Shouldn't I? It was one thing to trust my ability to solve a murder case. With Homicide, I had purpose and was experiencing moderate success. But that was more of what I did than who I was. I never felt worthy of someone else's love after I was cast away. What was *love* anyway?

"We must learn to see ourselves and others through the lens of God." The pastor stepped down from the stage and stood in the center aisle. "The Bible tells us God desires that all men be saved." Before I could form an objection, he added, "Yes, ladies, that includes you as well. The writer meant mankind as in humankind." Susan smiled and turned to me. She knew what I was thinking. He continued, "It also tells us He loved us so much He sent His only Son to pay the price to make that possible." He walked up the aisle and addressed those seated further back. "What should the church do with such knowledge?" He received several responses. He managed to affirm each tactfully. He was not much older than I was, but he carried an air of wisdom far beyond his years. He was one of those people you meet that makes you feel like you've known them forever.

"One of my favorite verses tells us, 'The love of Christ compels us.'" He gave us a disarming smile. He seemed to read the thoughts of those present and quickly dismissed their fears and doubts. "It's not that God forces His will upon you and makes you love Him. The message is for the saved—those of us who call ourselves by His name—Christians. It means the love of Jesus should drive every choice and action you make. That's our vision."

"He's so like Mark, it's scary," Susan said. I just nodded. I had other things on my mind.

The new pastor spun a good tale. I totally agreed with him in principle. The problem remained in the great chasm existing between what should be and what was. I'd heard men speak of love in Jesus's name and watched their actions say the opposite. I'd come to accept this hypocrisy in the church as a part of its natural order. However, I learned that there were exceptions to that rule, such as Susan and Dallas. But those were exceptions. I first discovered it in my investigation in the death and life of Mark Ripley. God still had a long way to go to convince me that the church people loved others as much as they loved themselves. I was not convinced, but for the first time in a decade, I wanted God to prove me wrong.

After the meeting, we walked to our cars. Dallas took my hand and pulled me close. I thought he would kiss me right there in front of everyone; instead, he whispered in my ear. "I know you don't believe it yet, but you will one day. I have faith enough for the two of us."

I bristled at the thought of his faith carrying me, but I forced down my walls. I knew he wasn't trying to control me or force me into it, but the comment resembled arguments of earlier days about church with my family. For a moment, I wondered what my parents were doing these days. It was a fleeting thought and quickly faded away. "It sounds nice, Dallas, but I've seen so much pain caused by people claiming to be the church and saying they loved others…" I didn't complete my thoughts. Right now, I was with Dallas, and he deserved my full attention.

"It takes time Abbey. Think how long it took to harden your heart to the church. It will take time to soften it." I started to object, but he put a finger on my lip. "Abbey, you'll always find people who are selfish and dishonest, but I promise—if you look hard enough—you'll also find people like Susan who live out the love of Christ every day."

I leaned in, put my head on his chest, and listened to the steady beat of his heart. I took a deep breath of his cologne. I felt safe and loved. I admired his optimism. I wished it would rub off on me. My past with the church as well as my experiences as a cop and a homicide detective robbed me of that luxury. If Dallas saw what I saw every day, he'd smile less. He saw eager college students at the beginning of a journey, people filled with hope and a dream. If I could help it, Dallas would never see the darkness and death Sam and I lived with daily. I'd rather Dallas stay in the light of hope.

"I'll pick you up Friday at seven. Remember, wear comfortable clothes and bring a jacket."

Chapter Eleven

Thursday, September 11, 7:30 AM—Homicide

Lieutenant Stallings still looked like a marine. His uniform fit snugly across his chest and around his muscular arms. He entered the homicide room and called for attention. His 9/11 speech had become a standard for our department, and even though I'd heard it each year, it still moved me. He described his experiences as a marine in great detail, facing gunfire and searching a myriad of caves in the hills of Afghanistan. He spoke with a sense of fond sadness.

"There were days I didn't think I would survive. On those days, I remembered my brother whose building crumbled to dust. He probably died the moment the first plane hit his floor of the first tower. Thankfully, I can rest in the fact that his death was immediate, but it still haunts me. He was a civilian, not a soldier. They brought the war to our house." He paused to survey the room of detectives. "That's why I joined the Marines. That's why I served. He's the reason I hunted for the enemy in Afghanistan." He paused again and gulped water from a bottle. It seemed he was still trying to quench that desert thirst as his eyes glazed over. I could only imagine he was revisiting the scene, mentally scouring the hills with their numerous hiding spots, avoiding enemy fire. He took another long drink.

Lieutenant Stallings spoke vividly of a day we will all remember. He called it our generation's Pearl Harbor. He described the moment he heard the news of the attack on the Trade Center

Towers—how he rushed to the nearest television and watched as they played the crash over and over. He spoke of the shock as a second plane crashed, and he, along with the rest of America, realized the first crash was no accident. His brother was dead. We were under attack.

"I want you to spend a few moments with your partner to share each other's story. Tell him where you were when the planes hit. Share your feelings the moment you learned it was a planned attack on America. Then, at seven forty-six, we will pause for seventeen minutes of silent reflection—the time between the two plane crashes. I know that will seem like an eternity. I know it will feel awkward. I want it to. As long as I'm here, we will never forget the seventeen-minute stretch of time that changed our world forever."

I looked at Sam and said, "You know my story."

"Yes, but it's important you share it again. This means a lot to Lieutenant Stallings—and to me."

Spence and I were much younger than the others in the homicide department. We were mere children when it happened. We certainly didn't understand the attack's significance or didn't take life-changing action like Lieutenant Stallings. I was embarrassed as I overheard conversations around our cubical. My story was insignificant. "Sam, I was only one-and-a-half years old. My family was living and serving in Honduras at the time. I don't remember what I was doing at the time. I know my family remained in Honduras for a while after that. Then we moved to Guatemala. I remember hearing references to it, but it didn't seem to change my father's ministry any. My sister spoke about hearing the news of the attack. She said she was afraid—being an American in a foreign country." I stopped. That was my pitiful story. "Your turn, Sam."

"I was married and had an eleven-year-old daughter, Molly. His face drooped. Even though he spent hours with his counselor, finally dealing with their deaths, Sam still felt the pain of his loss. "I was on the phone, telling my wife, Kathy, Metro was honoring me with the position of detective, and I would be stationed in the South Precinct, when I heard the commotion in the hallway. Just as I was listening to see what was happening, Kathy shouted, 'A plane just crashed into one of the twin towers.'" Sam paused. I'm sure he was remembering the sound of her voice. "Of course, I ran to the break room to see if it was true. We all sat around the television in shock, especially when the second tower was hit. When the tower crumbled and the people fleeing down the street were showered with dust and ash, I had to turn away. I returned to my desk and prepared for the worst. I thought we were seeing the beginning of World War Three." Sam continued with the details that followed that moment. It moved him to tears.

At precisely seven forty-six, Lieutenant Stallings said, "Okay, everyone. Let's stop and quietly reflect as the first plane strikes."

We sat quietly for seventeen minutes. The silence was deafening and awkward, especially for someone like me who was too young to remember the event. That didn't mean I was oblivious to its impact. I just had no personal reference or memory of the moment. I looked around the room. Even the toughest of men had watery eyes. Sergeant McNally let his tears fall unabashedly.

"Thank you all for participating in my annual reminder," Lieutenant Stallings said. "Now, let's get back to it and make Nashville a safer place." It was strange that these men were moved with emotion, only to turn the switch when the allotted time expired. I guess I'm not the only one who lives with emotional walls.

Chapter Twelve

Thursday, September 11, 1:05 PM—Buxton and Son Bolt and Screw

After I stuffed down my lunch, I headed to Buxton and Son Bolt and Screw. Something was telling me this case was much bigger than Jonathan Buxton. I pulled off Elm Hill Pike into the warehouse parking lot. I'd called ahead and said I wanted to talk with all the employees one at a time to see if anyone could help us with our investigation. Of course, I had a suspicion that the killer might be found among the employees, but I didn't have enough to call for an official investigation of any particular employee. Thankfully, the general manager was eager to assist me and worked out a schedule for each employee to speak with me, sixty-eight in all, representing each of the three shifts.

The company was much larger than I anticipated. It included an enormous warehouse holding the stock of materials waiting to be shipped to various locations. I didn't expect to see the small factory attached at the back. As of last year, Buxton and Son Bolt and Screw began manufacturing some of their products in-house. According to the manager, it was part of Vince's vision to expand the business.

During a quick tour of the place, I found the exact washer size used to hold Jonathan Buxton to the floor of his home. I pocketed one, with the permission of the manager, and then set out to interview workers. Metro Nashville's DA's office sent a memo earlier in the month highlighting the differences between Reasonable Suspicion and Probable Cause. We were under the microscope, so all detectives at homicide were operating strictly by the book. I had to keep my hunches in check and stop using the term *suspect* until we gathered enough evidence to charge someone.

The newest employee went first. A young, pimple-faced, greasy-haired girl with major hygiene issues entered the small office they gave me to conduct interviews. Thankfully, she didn't know the father or the son. She'd seen them and had even spoken to Vince once, but I could tell she had little to no investment in their lives or their controversy. I quickly moved on, dismissing her and shutting the door after she left. I took a small can of disinfectant spray from my pocket and showered the tiny room. It didn't remove all her body odor, but it helped. I opened the door and waved it back and forth before going down the hall to get the next employee.

The second and third employees said nothing nice about the son, but they also had little personal investment. Most of their opinions were formed by hearsay. When I reached a group of employees who'd worked for the company at least three years, it suddenly became apparent they shed no tears over the young Buxton's death. They described him as a self-serving, narcissistic bully.

"We're just numbers to him," one said.

Another said, "As long as things were good, he avoided the production line, but if a department was falling below expectations and quotas, Buxton's voice could be heard from one end of the building to the other, calling us all kinds of nasty names."

"Which Buxton?" I asked for clarification.

"The son," a hard-looking woman said. She had the appearance of a boxer who'd been hit too many times. She wiped sweat from her forehead with the back of her hand. "He'd blame us when sales weren't good. Like that's our job." She stretched her neck to the side until a loud pop sounded. "Vince would jump in the line occasionally to help. He wasn't too good to work with us." She had a great deal to say about Vince and his way of doing things.

"I think Jonathan's doctor drugged Vince and stuffed him

away in that facility so no one would be the wiser," an older man said in a later interview. He was the first to put a first name to the son. "It's shameful to treat anyone that way, let alone your own father." He shook his head and looked at the floor.

"What makes you think Jonathan's doctor would do such a thing?" I asked.

"I overheard him say he'd do anything for him." He scratched his chin. "I think they went to college together at Florida State."

"So, Jonathan and his doctor were friends?" This was an interesting twist.

"Oh, yeah. Jonathan would brag about their fishing trips and argue over who caught the biggest fish," said a chatty employee. He'd been with Vince since the beginning. He obviously had no love for the son. I put his name on my list even though he was old and frail. I doubt he could have managed the physical aspect of the kill. "They sure loved to fish and preferred the ocean to fresh water."

Fish? The picture of Jonathan and the other man popped into my head. Then I remembered the article which said he had Vince admitted to the memory care facility with the blessing of his personal physician. "Do you happen to remember the doctor's name?" The older man shook his head. I made a note to find out.

I spent another three hours speaking with the rest of the employees of Buxton and Son Bolt and Screw. Any employee who knew Vince and Jonathan well had an opinion. It was all positive of Vince and negative of Jonathan. According to the employees, the men were polar opposites in nature and management styles. By the time I was finished, I was secretly wishing I could let this case go unsolved. Jonathan Buxton was a selfish beast. He'd sold his father out to keep the money and control for himself. But the law was the law, and I was sworn to keep it. I couldn't wait to hear what Sam discovered from his visit with Vince.

Forty-two employees had the desire to see the man harmed or at least given "his just desserts." Forty-two employees had the means by which to do so. Now, I just needed to see who had the

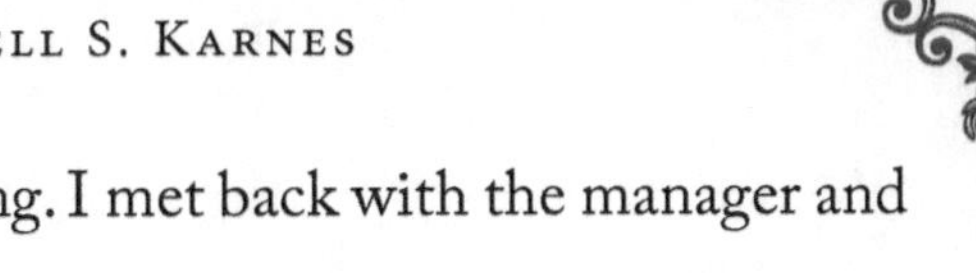

opportunity early that morning. I met back with the manager and asked, "Is this everyone?"

"Yes..." he stammered.

"Anyone else I should know about?"

He thought for a moment and added, "You might want to talk to those two new girls who quit last week."

"Two new girls?"

"Strange girls. They only worked three weeks. Both young and just about your size—maybe a little shorter."

"Do you remember what they looked like?"

He scratched his head. "Both short and kind of plain. One brown hair, the other blonde."

"By any chance do you have pictures of them?"

"We should. We take pictures of all employees for their ID badges. Let me check our system." He settled into an old leather office chair far too big for his desk and began typing. Maybe this could be the break I'd been waiting for. Was it possible I'd just stumbled across Skylar and an accomplice? What were the odds of two young girls working here for a short time and quitting days before the murder? Of course, neither would know the father and son well enough to act upon the injustice.

"Here you go. Meagan Harlin and Lisa Gatewood." He turned the screen where I could see their pictures. My heart sank with disappointment. It wasn't Skylar. Meagan Harlin, the brunette, boasted a big smile, the kind the passport people don't want you to make. The blonde had the opposite look, like she was already bored with the job.

"Could you print out their names and addresses so I can check their whereabouts on the night in question?" He nodded. "Any chance you could print one with names and pictures?" He nodded again and started the search. Before he hit print, I asked if he could flag all employees not working during the time of Jonathan's death. This time, he waited to see if I wanted anything else in the search. I shook my head, and he printed the pages. I planned to cross-check the employee list with those who visited Vince recently.

He pulled the paper from the printer and handed me the list. "It's a short list. We had a huge order to get out that day, so several employees pulled doubles that night."

"This helps us greatly." I thanked him for his time and cooperation and let myself out.

Sitting in my car, I glanced over his list. Only eighteen employees were off at the time in question. I checked the names against those from my interviews who fit the approximate shoe sizes to match any of the bloody footprints. My list was down to six. Oh, I planned to check all eighteen out, but I had particular interest in those six. I looked at my phone and realized it was already after five. I called Sam. "Do you want to meet and compare notes?"

"Let's meet back tomorrow. I promised my sister I'd come over for supper tonight, and she eats early."

"Alright. I'm going to the office and work a couple more hours to plan for tomorrow. Tell Maggie I said hi."

Chapter Thirteen

Friday, September 12, 7:27 AM—Homicide

I moved my running time an hour earlier and shortened my course so I could beat Sam to the office. I sorted through my notes from the Buxton and Son Bolt and Screw interviews. I knew all but eighteen of their employees were on the clock the night of Jonathan Buxton's death. Last night, I put the notes pertaining to those eighteen on my desktop. I'd set the rest in a small bin between our desks.

Matching the eighteen names to the list I made of the forty-two employees wishing Jonathan harm, I was still left with thirteen people. Everyone with the right sized foot was still in the mix. That brought me some satisfaction. The worst part of this process was the haunting knowledge that we were looking for multiple murderers. Why would they go to the trouble of staging a scene like that unless this was about Jonathan and Vince? I flipped back a few pages of notes. There were three sets of distinguishable footprints in Jonathan's blood. By the size and shape, we determined there were two women and one man. Sam had teased me about doing a Cinderella test, but the idea may actually be better than I originally thought.

I slid the photographs from Jonathan Buxton's file and set them next to mine. The bloody footprints led from the source, Jonathan's neck, to the grass of his back yard, dissipating each step of the way as the blood transferred to the floor. I pulled out my magnifying glass and analyzed the footprints, coming back to our initial theory of three individuals. I chose two photos that gave the best detail of the three separate prints. It was one of the female prints that showed a scar running the length of the right big toe. The scar would be a unique identifying factor. Maybe, I could get the employees in question to volunteer prints of their feet or ask the manager to *encourage* participation. Otherwise, I would have to persuade a judge to grant an order for them—hoping no lawyers got involved until we secured a match. Still, with the new DA's rigid guidelines for warrants, I'd better find another way to discover the killers or be certain whose prints I need. I'd bounce the idea off Sam and Spence before pursuing it further. If anyone could run it by the book, Spence could.

"What are you doing, Abbey?"

"Morning, Sam." I turned and handed him the two photos. "I think we can find our murderers by matching prints of their feet, much like we would do of a cast, especially this one with a scar."

"I take it you have just a few persons of interest?" He set his briefcase beside his desk. "Otherwise, we'll be searching for a needle in a haystack."

"I'm down to thirteen from the company. Five of those have shoe sizes like one of the three footprints. Only three of those are women." Sam glanced over my shoulder at my list and sat down. "How'd it go with Vince?"

Sam rolled his chair over to mine. "We have a dead end there." He scratched the top of his head. "He's heavily sedated."

"Why?" I put the photos on the desk and gave my full attention to Sam. "Why would they sedate him? I thought he was in the early stages of Alzheimer's. Was he hallucinating or behaving erratically?"

"I couldn't get a lot of answers thanks to HIPPA," Sam admitted. "The nearest living relative is Jonathan's wife, and there was no point bothering her with that now." Sam sighed heavily. He had a tired look in his eyes. "I sat with Vince and watched him for nearly an hour." He pulled out his notes and scanned through a few pages. "I did meet another resident who seemed clear-minded enough. He said Vince was talkative when he arrived and had a lot of energy." Sam flipped the page in his notebook. "Chester. Yeah, Chester Baker said the following day he stopped by Vince's room, and he was catatonic."

"That sounds awful, Sam, but keep the source in mind. You said he was a resident too."

Sam shrugged and said, "Then I got nothing."

"What about the visitor list?"

"They said I'd need a judge's order to get that."

"So, get one." It seemed easy enough to me.

"We don't have enough to even ask right now, and the new DA wants solid evidence first. I guess we're left with your footprint test, but you'd better be prepared to lobby your need for it."

"Yeah. It'll be a tough sell with her."

I filled Sam in about the two girls who quit recently and shared my disappointment that Skylar wasn't one of them. "I plan to track them down for an interview anyway. I doubt they're involved, but I need to make sure they can account for their whereabouts during the time in question." Then I filled Sam in on my interviews, highlighting the consensus that Jonathan was a controlling jerk with an abusive attitude towards his employees. "The atmosphere changed overnight. No one liked Jonathan. I didn't find a single person who cared that he was dead." I paused for a moment, wondering if I should admit it or not. "I know it's our job to find his killer, but I wish we didn't have to."

"Hey, Kid, I've been there before, but we do our best whether the dead deserve it or not."

I spun back to my desk. "We've got to get some prints." Suddenly, I couldn't hold back a laugh.

"What's so funny?"

"Just a dumb thought," I admitted, but it was an irony my mind couldn't ignore. "We didn't find a single fingerprint at the crime scene. Nothing was out of place."

"Yeah, so? They wore gloves."

"If you're going to that much trouble to hide your identity, why walk barefoot through blood? I read an article the other day about forensic podiatry, where they can identify a person by his footprint and his gait." Sam stifled a laugh. "I'm not kidding, Sam. Their research determined the ridge patterns on a person's toes are just as identifiable as his fingerprints."

Sam put his hands up in mock surrender. "Okay, professor, let's say we do your footprint test. We'll still need a search warrant for that."

"I know you're teasing me, but I'm serious." I was just a high school graduate. "It makes no sense, Sam. They were meticulous in every other sense. Why leave obvious footprints for us to find? They had to leave the footprints intentionally." Was it a mistake? Maybe just a red herring? A taunt? Or was it a message? If so, for who? I turned and Sam was reading something on his computer screen.

"Hey, Abbey, grab your coat. We're going to visit the Forensic Center. Mandy's finishing her autopsy and wants to see us."

"She wants to see you, Sam—not us." I often hinted at Mandy's flirtatious nature. He gave me a dirty look and grabbed his coat. We headed out the door, and I took the opportunity to tease Sam once more about his connection with Dr. Coleman, or *Mandy* as she wanted him to call her. She was the forensic pathologist for the Middle Tennessee Forensic Center. She always made a point to make personal comments with Sam beyond the case. Unfortunately, flirting with Sam was like throwing an egg at a wall and hoping to knock a brick loose. Mandy was a hopeless romantic. Sam was just hopeless.

Chapter Fourteen

Friday, September 12, 8:42 AM—Forensic Center

"Morning, Sam." Without taking her eyes off Sam, Dr. Coleman added, "Good morning, Detective Rhodes."

"Mandy." Sam's reply was as short and as dry as a dusty Guatemalan village road.

"Dr. Coleman."

"How's Maggie?" she asked.

"She's fine. She said to tell you hello if I ran into you."

"That's sweet."

"Now, Mandy, I know you didn't call us down here to socialize or ask questions about my sister," Sam said with a little break in his voice. "What do you have for us?" He reminded me of this old black and white show Mr. Morales used to watch where the dry and dusty detective would say, "Just the facts, ma'am." Sam was trying to keep to the case, but I noticed he couldn't look at her very long without suddenly turning his attention elsewhere. It was like a little boy looking at a girl but making sure he wasn't caught looking. It was cute. I knew Sam liked her, but he'd often said that dating anyone would feel like he was cheating on his wife. I don't know how long it would take for him to feel like he could move on without guilt. Maybe never. He was that kind of man.

"Okay, Detective Tidwell," Dr. Coleman said in business-like tone. "Your victim is over here." We knew the routine by now and put on our protective lab gear—not for our protection but to keep the integrity of the evidence, which in this case was the body of

Jonathan Buxton. She led us to the other room, and I paused. It still bothered me to see a human body with his chest spread open on an examination table. I was, however, adjusting to the smell of the place.

Dr. Coleman grabbed a clipboard where she'd attached her notes. "As you already know, his throat was cut with a very sharp knife. You also may have previously assessed that the drill wounds were made post-mortem." I nodded.

"What do you make of the letter V in his hand?" I asked.

"It matches the one on his forehead."

"Forehead?" Sam asked, finally inserting himself into the conversation. "Where?"

Dr. Coleman pushed Jonathan Buxton's bangs back, revealing another perfect V. "Right here."

"Made with the same knife?" Sam asked.

"Yes and no. It was made with the same knife as the other V, but the one used to cut his throat was different. It is about two inches wide and six inches in length, I would postulate—much like a hunting knife. The marks were made with a precision instrument like a scalpel or X-Acto knife." She showed us images of similar blades. "Like the drill holes, the letters were cut post-mortem."

"It's the strangest thing I've seen in a long time," Sam said.

"It's very similar to the markings made on the other victim," Dr. Coleman said.

"What other victim?" I asked. "Has someone else been marked with V's?"

"Same locations—the head and the right hand—but they were X's."

"X's?" Sam asked. "Can you show us?"

Dr. Coleman covered Jonathan's body and pulled a drawer from the wall of dead bodies. She lifted the dead man's hand and pushed back his bangs. "I told the other detectives about the markings, but they weren't interested."

"Which detectives?" Sam asked. "I haven't heard about this case."

Dr. Coleman looked at her notes. "Detectives Michaels and Schuster."

"Who?" I asked. She repeated the names and said she'd pointed out the markings, but neither man thought they were important to their case. I vaguely remembered hearing their names before in a joint meeting of the homicide detectives. "Aren't they homicide too?"

"Yes. They're on the weekend shift," Sam said.

"We need to let them know we may have the same killer." This could be a pattern."

"Let me handle it," Sam said. "We older detectives tend to be more territorial of our cases."

I looked at the body and noticed something was missing. "There are no holes in his hands or feet."

"Could be a different killer," Sam said flatly. "When did he die?"

"Sunday, August 31," Dr. Coleman said. "Ten days before your victim."

"So, he's the first victim," I said with my mind suddenly jumping to all kinds of scenarios. Maybe there was one before this. "At least so far."

"Don't get ahead of yourself, Abbey. Do the work and let it lead you to the right verdict."

"Come on, Sam. Letters carved into the victims' hands and foreheads. That's too strange to be random coincidences. And they were killed only ten days apart. That's not much of a cooling down period."

"Take a breath. Don't jump to conclusions. It takes more than two deaths to make a serial killer. Besides, Abbey, this is nothing to be excited about." Sam must have read my mind or at least my body language. He turned back to Dr. Coleman. "Any other similarities, Mandy?"

She smiled at the way he used her first name. "They have the same location of cuts to the throat and hands. Both are males in their mid to late forties."

"What about the drill marks? Anything similar?"

"No, Sam." He nodded, and Dr. Coleman pushed the drawer back into the wall. "I'll let you know if anything comes in like these."

We removed our lab protection and hung them on the wall. Sam walked halfway across the parking lot in silence. Then he stopped and said, "You ever hear of anything like this in the Army?"

"I've seen my share of mutilated and tortured bodies, but nothing like this. This is like a puzzle." I took out my phone and opened my internet search engine.

"What are you looking for, Abbey?"

"If it's a puzzle or a message, we need to decode it. I'm searching for words with V's and X's." I was shocked. "I never realized there were this many. We better sit down with those detectives today."

"We'll catch them at the end of today's shift. They'll be coming in for the weekend as we should be leaving." Sam scratched his head. "I feel like this should mean something to me."

"Me too, Sam. Me too." There was something eerily familiar about the markings on their hands and heads. Was it a case study in our training? "I need Deborah to file for the judge's order to check footprints of the Buxton employees in question."

"You don't even have enough to call suspicion, Abbey. No sense bothering a judge. Find something else to go on. You need a better reason than not liking their boss for a judge to sign off on footprints. Last thing you need right now is to be on the new DA's radar. Be patient. I'm going to access Detective Schuster's notes on that other case and see what they found."

Chapter Fifteen

Friday, September 12, 5:18 PM—Homicide

Ifocused on the footprints and thought of ways I could search their feet without a judge's order. I could go back to the manager and request voluntary footprints, but I needed to follow procedure, especially with the new DA. While we waited for the weekend crew to finish their briefing for the evening, I pulled up Dr. Teague's case. Could this be Skylar's doing? Could these two cases be the beginning of her cleansing?

"Abbey." Sam beckoned me forward. "We're meeting them in the conference room."

We entered the room and set our folder on the table. "Detective Rhodes, this is Detective Michaels."

I shook the man's hand. He squeezed hard, and I winced. If I'd known he was going to try to intimidate me right off the bat, I'd have prepared myself and deepened my grip. He was a buff, middle-aged, Black man with silver framed glasses and a serious look that told me they knew why we were here and had already taken a defensive stance. "I've heard of you," he said.

Trying to put on an air of confidence, I smiled and said, "All good, I hope."

"Not all." He left it at that. What a jerk. At least he could have elaborated. I don't mind critiques if I get explanations. He offered none.

"This is Detective Schuster," Sam said, moving the conversation on. Detective Shuster displayed strong Jewish features; he was close to Sam's age. Detective Shuster shook my hand. "I've seen you in several of our meetings. It's an honor," I said, trying to change the tone of our meeting.

"What's this about, Sam?" Detective Schuster asked. He folded his arms over his chest.

"Well, Reuben, I think we have a crossover case." I studied their reactions. While Detective Schuster would have made a great poker player, Detective Michaels would not. "We have a similar MO and strange markings that lead us to believe we have the same killer."

"Which case would that be?" Detective Schuster asked. Sam described the case. Before he could get more than a few sentences in, Detective Michaels cut him off.

"Impossible. We already have our killer in custody and are finalizing our case for the DA."

Detective Schuster put his hand up, signaling for his partner to calm down. "Let's hear them out first, Derek—see what they have to say." He motioned for Sam to continue.

"Dr. Coleman has identified similar markings on our victim and yours. Each one has a letter etched into his hand and forehead. Ours has a V and yours has an X."

"I told her that was irrelevant," Detective Michaels interjected. "We have the murderer dead to rights," he said, folding his arms and flexing his muscles which stretched the sleeves of his shirt. What a piece of work. "He made several threats, called the police on his neighbor three times, and shot down one of his drones two weeks before we found the neighbor dead."

Now I was wishing I'd looked over their file too. As it was, I found myself dependent on Sam's knowledge to counteract the confidence of Detective Michaels. I didn't like leaving the work to someone else. I really didn't like feeling ignorant either, especially in a room with three male detectives who all knew the details.

"How was his body displayed?" I asked.

"Displayed? He was found dead right next to his new drone," he said in a tone that inferred my ignorance was a nuisance.

"Was he laid out like an X?" I asked. I wasn't about to be silenced by an overbearing jerk, no matter how much larger he was than me. I'd worked six years on my confidence and feelings of inferiority with men. The Army was good for me. "You know—arms and legs stretched out."

"Yes." It was Detective Schuster who answered. "He was laid out like an X in front of his drone."

"Face up, or face down?"

"Down." It was Detective Schuster who responded again.

"And his throat was slit from ear to ear," Sam said, "just like ours." I watched Sam's body language change. He was confident and stalwart. He gave no sign of weakness or doubt. He suddenly looked several years younger. "We need to combine our efforts and find the real killer." The word *real* struck a nerve.

The moment Sam said it, the younger detective stood. "You trying to tell us how to do our job, Tidwell?" Detective Michaels leaned into the heavy conference table, shifting it our way. "You've got a lot of nerve." Detective Schuster motioned for him to ease up, but he wasn't having any of it. "Our case is solid: means, motive, and opportunity. David Smith killed his neighbor because he was sick and tired of the jerk flying his drone over his house to get videos of his wife. He'd warned Timothy Johnson multiple times and got no help from us. So Smith slit Johnson's throat and put his body beside the drone to send a message to us."

"What did he plead?" I asked Detective Michaels.

"Pardon?"

"David Smith. Did he admit to killing his neighbor?" I made eye contact with him and held it firm.

"Not exactly. He said he was glad he was dead." That logic would make every employee of Buxton Bolt and Screw guilty of murder.

"That's not exactly an admission of guilt," Sam said.

"He didn't deny it, either," Detective Michaels insisted.

I looked back and forth between the two detectives. Sam could not convince Detective Michaels he had the wrong man. On the other hand, Detective Schuster sat quietly in his chair, pensively taking it all in. "What about the markings?" I asked.

"What about them?"

"Why would he mark his neighbor's hand and head with an X?"

"The X was on his control hand, and the other one was right above his eye. I think it's obvious." That did seem to be a reasonable explanation.

"Surely, you have to admit that something ties these two cases together. Someone is making a statement, staging the victims this way."

"Listen, girl…"

Oh no he didn't. "Don't refer to me as *girl*, Detective," I snapped. "I am your equal…"

Schuster cut me off. "Detective Rhodes, our case is solved. I suggest you and Detective Tidwell work on yours."

"Reuben." Sam reached over the table and shook his hand. "I think you're making a mistake, but I won't say another word until I have proof." Sam turned and walked away. I wanted to scream at him. I wanted to shake some sense into Detectives Michaels and Schuster, but I followed Sam out of the conference room quietly. I could feel the heat in my face again, a regular tell-tale sign of my anger.

I needed a distraction or my head would explode. Thankfully, I would pick Dallas up in an hour for his mystery date. I didn't want to inadvertently vent my frustrations on Dallas or arrive in such a sour mood that I ruined the date. Dallas was old-fashioned and felt it was a man's responsibility to host the date. I had to show him it could go both ways. Besides, he deserved a treat.

Chapter Sixteen

Friday, September 12, 7:30 PM—Centennial Sportsplex

"**I** can't believe we're ice skating. I didn't bring thick enough socks."

I smiled and pulled a pair of men's large socks from my jacket pocket.

"You're not going to let me out of this are you?"

"Not a chance, Dallas. Be a good sport. It's my turn to pick the event and treat you." He scowled. "You can do this." I tilted my head and made big pouty lips.

"That's not fair." He smiled and took the socks from my hand. "When you said to dress comfortably and bring a jacket, I assumed we were going to be outside."

"You know what they say about assuming?" I asked. Then I wished I hadn't said it. Dallas wasn't the kind of man who'd know that saying. "Have you ever ice skated before?"

"No."

He wasn't very excited. Maybe I overdid this one.

"Roller skating?"

He shook his head.

"I'll teach you."

"In one night?" he asked.

I took Dallas by the arm and led him through the double doors of the Centennial Sportsplex. "Come on. You're athletic."

I pulled him to the counter and said, "Two for the public skate and two pairs of skates." I told the man my shoe size and waited for Dallas to do the same. Then I pulled out my credit card and paid. I could tell he was embarrassed about letting me pay, but it was good for him. It was also a little test to see if Dallas was the kind of man who could learn from a woman. We found the nearest bench and put on our skates. "Lace them tight, or your ankles will flop all over the place," I said as I pulled mine as tight as I could.

"When did you learn to skate? They have ice rinks in Guatemala?"

I shook my head. I wasn't sure if they did or not, but I didn't want to discuss my time in Guatemala. "I learned in Germany. My army buddies and I wandered across an ice rink near our base and taught ourselves to skate. I've loved it ever since."

Dallas finished tying his skates and tried to stand. Tried was the key word. His ankles buckled, and he fell to the rubber floor. His face was blood red. I was hoping it was from embarrassment rather than anger. He got to his hands and knees and worked back onto the blades of the skates. He wobbled, but I was there to steady him. "Honestly, Abbey, I can sit in the stands and watch you."

"That's not a date, and you're not getting off that easy," I warned. "Come on." After tightening his laces, I held him firmly by the arm and helped him walk to the opening of the rink. The temperature changed abruptly. He stepped through the gate and lumbered to the side. "Don't cling to the railing. It makes it harder to learn."

"What do I hold on to?"

"Me."

I held out my hand until he grabbed it. I eased him away from the side and out onto the ice. His height was his disadvantage, especially when he leaned forward. His center of gravity shifted forward.

"Stand up straight."

He tried to smile, but his eyes focused on his feet. He tried to walk on the skates like he would on concrete. Beginner's mistake.

"Dallas, relax. Glide smoothly; don't walk." I eased him back over to the wall. "Watch me." I skated off slowly, demonstrating the right way to push and glide. Then I picked up speed and took a couple laps around the rink. It felt good to have cold air on my face.

Someone patted my shoulder and dashed past me. He slid to an abrupt stop, spraying ice shavings in the air with his blades.

"Funny seeing you here."

"Lieutenant Daniels?" I skated to the side wall where he stopped. "What are you doing here?"

"Just getting a little exercise in anticipation of hockey season." He wore his Predators jacket and matching baseball cap.

"I forgot you were a hockey fan."

"Oh, yeah. And I just got the best gig ever," he said with a big smile. "I'm helping with security. The Preds' preseason starts next week."

"Do you get to watch the game at all?"

"Yes. I'll be in the rink area. The only thing better than watching hockey is getting paid to do it." He was giddy as a little kid.

"What does Sherry think about you working extra hours?"

"She gets to renovate our bathroom, and I get to watch hockey. It's a win-win." He waved at somebody who passed us.

I suddenly remembered the reason I was here and looked across the rink. Two young girls flanked Dallas on either side, helping him skate. "I gotta go." I raced to his side and said, "Sorry. I ran into a friend." The two young girls ignored me and continued to coach Dallas on his skating. "Who do we have here?" I asked.

"Oh, hey, Abbey," Dallas said, finally acknowledging my presence. "This is Ella," he said, tilting his head toward the young brunette holding his right arm, "and this is Lena." The one on his left was a cute little blonde. He didn't introduce me. He stared at his skates and moved awkwardly around the rink.

"And how do you know these young ladies?" I said with a hint of apprehension.

"He's our professor," the girls said on cue. "He's the best teacher in the world."

"I wish I could have him for every class," the blonde added.

I wanted to vomit as I heard their school-girl voices. "Oh, you're both from Belmont?" Freshmen I guessed. Eighteen, maybe nineteen. I moved closer. "I can take it from here, girls," intentionally overemphasizing the word *girls*. They didn't let go. "I appreciate your help, but we're on a date," I said stopping in their path.

"Oh, really? He was alone when we saw him," Lena said with a snotty tone.

"Yeah, he didn't say anything about a date. We just wanted to help," Ella added.

"Well, he's not alone now." I stood in their path with my arms closed.

Finally, Dallas said, "Thanks for your help, girls. I'll see you Monday." He shook his arms free and grabbed my hand. Reluctantly, they let go and skated off. Ella turned around and skated backwards, giving me a twisted smile.

"They're certainly friendly," I said. I steadied Dallas and helped him skate. "And cute, too."

"They're both in my first section of American Literature," Dallas said as if that justified their presence. "You left and talked to that man, and they showed up and wanted to help me."

Oh, so that's what it was about. "How convenient." He saw me talking with Lieutenant Daniels and thought he'd return the favor. I suppose we're both a little jealous. "That was Lieutenant Daniels," I said, offering and explanation. "He was my Lieutenant at East Precinct when I first started at Metro. He and his wife rented out a room to me for three years."

"He's married?"

"Of course, he's married. We're just friends."

"He skates well."

I knew he was making the comparison. "He's a former hockey player," I explained.

"Honestly, my students came to my aid. They said I looked helpless, and they showed mercy. That's it."

He smiled innocently. "I think I'm getting the hang of this."

"You are getting better." I turned backward and held both of his hands as we continued to skate. "I think your students like you."

"I'm just their professor. Nothing more."

"You're so naïve, Dallas."

He was innocent. Their intent was not. I turned around and put my arm around his waist. "It's one of your many great qualities." I leaned into him and rested my head on his arm. I guess he wasn't the kind of man who was afraid to learn from a woman after all. He relaxed. We laughed. We skated side by side.

"Thirty more minutes, and we can stop and get something to eat."

It turned out to be a great night.

Chapter Seventeen

Saturday, September 13, 10:10 AM—Harmony Apartments

I sat at my small table with copies of both forensic reports and compared the two cases. Both had obvious similarities such as the marks on the right hands and the foreheads. In contrast, one was a V and the other an X. Both killers chose white males in their mid to late forties for victims. Could it be a statement against white men. Cries of white supremacy and white man entitlement flooded social media. Maybe race was the motive. If this was Skylar, was she cleansing Nashville of white men? Was it somehow tied to Mark Ripley, the youth minister, and her father? No. She chose three women as her other victims. Maybe it wasn't Skylar after all.

The letters V and X led me to the word vixen. The first case with the drone fit if David Smith blamed his wife for her exhibitionism. Unfortunately, he was in custody during the time of the second murder. Maybe one of his neighbors felt sorry for him and killed his voyeuristic neighbor. What about Jonathan Buxton? Vixen didn't seem to fit his situation, which led me back to his father, V for Vince. The X must stand for something else like the symbol on his drone remote. The markings and their locations on the bodies were too similar for there not to be a connection. What was it?

Okay. Go back to the basics and review the facts. Women discovered both bodies. David Smith's wife heard a noise, looked out her bedroom window, and saw the body of her neighbor Timothy.

Ashley Buxton discovered her husband's body when she got home from her midnight to eight shift at the hospital. In each case, the murderers executed the men by slitting their throats. No signs of torture. The murderers displayed each body in the shape of an X. What is the significance of that X? Timothy Johnson's body lay beside his drone. Jonathan Buxton was attached by bolts and washers—an obvious reference to his business. Why would Jonathan's body be fixed to the floor? Was it about the bolts and washers, or was it to keep his wife, a nurse, from moving his body and trying to resuscitate him? Timothy lived alone. There was no reason to fix his position.

Were any footprints discovered at the Johnson crime scene? I flipped through my copies of the case notes. There was no mention of footprints. Of course, he was killed on his lawn and displayed right on the site of his death. There was no way of knowing if the killers were barefoot. What did the two men have in common? Nothing. Different sides of town. Different occupations. Timothy Johnson worked at home as a computer systems analyst. I found nothing to connect the victims except their age, gender, the method of death, the markings, and the staging of the bodies.

I opened my laptop and searched for anything dealing with letters carved in hands or foreheads. I wished I hadn't. Fourteen articles popped up—all about Charles Manson. Apparently, he carved an X in his own forehead shortly before appearing in court one day. His followers made similar markings on their own heads to show their loyalty to Manson. Could this be something similar? Did we have a Manson copycat? Manson cut his own mark. These were both done postmortem. I read details of the Manson case and determined the only thing it had in common with our cases was the letter on the forehead. I was thankful. I really didn't want to dig into the details of those murders.

I searched again. The only articles dealing with marks on hands and heads, other than the Manson case, discussed tattoos. I scanned the ME's reports again. Neither man had any tattoos.

Could that be significant? Was someone tattooing them? Were they being branded? If a brand, wouldn't it be of the same symbol, like cattle on a ranch? I was grasping at straws. This was fruitless work. I needed a break, so I walked down Broadway and listened to music, real music, country music, my favorite kind. If Nashville does one thing well, it's country music. A wagon of drunk women singing at the top of their lungs nearly ran me over. It was one of Nashville's many bachelorette events. I turned back to the many honkytonks and lost myself in the music. Within minutes I forgot all about the case.

Chapter Eighteen

Wednesday, September 17, 10:00 AM—Homicide Interrogation Room B

I'd reached the two young girls who quit Buxton and Son a few days prior to Jonathan Buxton's murder. They were roommates and agreed to come to the homicide offices for back-to-back interviews. I assured them this was simply routine and an attempt to gather any new evidence for our ongoing case.

Lisa Gatewood agreed to go first. She sat across from me and placed her hands on the cold metal table that separated us in the small room. I pointed out the cameras and explained that I needed her to voice all responses into the little black microphone in the center of the table. "Do you understand the instructions as I have explained them?"

She smiled, and her blue eyes twinkled in the fluorescent light. "Yes."

"Thank you. Would you state your name for the record?" I took notes as I went through the questions I wanted to ask.

"Lisa Gatewood."

"Lisa, did you work for Buxton and Son?"

"Yes."

"Why did you quit?" I'd already profiled the two girls and got the answer I expected them to give.

"It was boring."

I looked up, and she was staring right at me.

"It didn't pay well either."

"How long did you work for Buxton and Son?"

She thought for a moment. "Just short of three weeks, I think. Whenever I got the job at the restaurant."

"Did you give notice or just quit?"

She tilted her head to the side like she didn't understand my question. "What do you mean?"

"Did you tell them you were leaving or just not show up for work?"

"Oh, I called and told them we wouldn't be back next week."

I perked up. "You spoke for yourself and Meagan?"

"Yes. She was afraid to tell them. She hates to disappoint people."

I scribbled a few notes before asking, "What was she afraid of?"

"She doesn't like conflict," Lisa said matter-of-factly. "I can't even get her to pick a place to eat when we go out."

"Are you dating?"

She laughed. "No. We're not lesbians. We're just roommates."

"I see." I moved past the next couple of questions. "Did you have any interactions with Vince or Jonathan Buxton?"

"Jonathan is the son, right?" I nodded in affirmation. "He yelled at Meagan a couple of times for holding up the line. We were still learning, but he wanted the line to move faster."

"How did you feel about that?"

She gave me a school-girl look that said, *Duh.* When I didn't move away from the question, she said, "I thought he was a jerk."

"So, it bothered you?"

"I'm sorry, Detective, that's a stupid question. What am I supposed to say, *I loved being yelled at*?"

"Did he yell at you too?"

"No. I did my job."

"Did Meagan get angry?"

"You'll have to ask her." Lisa put her hands in her lap. "It didn't pay well, and we were treated like idiots. That's why we left. Now, we make twice as much money and leave work wanting to go back."

The interview was going nowhere. Obviously, they cut any

ties they had to Buxton and Son and moved on. This was not the kind of girl who would go to the trouble of killing her boss and staging a scene. If she got mad enough, she might *accidentally* hit him with her car.

"This is a strange request, but would you mind removing your shoes and showing me your right foot?"

She chuckled as she removed her ankle high boot, pulled off her sock, and plopped her foot on the table. "You're strange, lady."

Her foot was clean. No scar. I dismissed Lisa and began my interview with Meagan. Getting her to speak was like pulling healthy teeth. I changed strategies and asked a series of yes or no questions. She affirmed Lisa's account. She also had no problems showing me the bottom of her foot. Oh, well, at least I knew they weren't involved. I thanked them both for their cooperation and let them go. I typed my notes and put a copy on Sam's desk.

He thanked me and said, "I can't find any connection between Timothy Johnson and Jonathan Buxton."

"Me either, Sam." I flipped through the notes and thoughts I'd jotted in my notebook. "I know this is stupid, but the only connection I can find is their gender, race, and age."

"With all the hate on social media and in the news, it wouldn't surprise me if this was simply an attack on white men."

Sam and I worked into the night, searching for anything that we might have missed in the evidence. I kept searching for words with Vs and Xs that might fit our case, but I felt like I was forcing the issue instead of letting the facts lead me. The facts led me nowhere.

Chapter Nineteen

Saturday, September 20, 5:30 PM—Homicide

Sam and I spent more than a week going over the Buxton and Johnson cases with the rest of our homicide team. We found ourselves unwilling to leave work. We sat in our work cubby on a Saturday afternoon, still grasping at straws. The killers' MOs were so close that it seemed obvious to us both that we had the same killer. I still wondered what the letters meant. If we added their X to our V, there were too many possibilities of words to land confidently on one. Sam came up with the word vexed, which he said meant, *difficult and problematic…annoyed.* He joked that it applied to us. It certainly fit, but my mind kept returning to *Vixen.* I'm not sure what that said about me.

I shared my observations with a detective from the weekend homicide team. "The drone operator was obviously obsessed with his neighbor's wife. Even after several warnings, he continued to fly over her back yard streaming videos of the woman out by the pool, sunbathing or swimming. She didn't seem to mind the attention. Her husband, twenty years older, didn't have the same reaction to his voyeuristic neighbor. The killing made sense looking through that lens. The husband made a perfect suspect."

"I tend to agree," Sam said.

"So, you both agree with Michaels and Schuster now?"

Did we? The markings made no sense.

"Maybe Detective Michaels was right; the marks were to

indicate his control hand and his eyes," Sam added. He had a good point.

"If the murder wasn't out of jealousy or territorial defense, who would want the man dead?" I asked. He hardly left his home. What would the killers be telling us with the markings? An X? And why the hand and forehead? Did that mean something, or were they random choices that the murderer decided to continue?

"We're missing the obvious connection," Sam said as the other detective dismissed himself.

The footprints, three in number, nagged at me. Why barefoot? Everyone agreed that two of the prints were female and the other male. That scar on the big toe of one had a small angle at the base. Why leave such a unique, identifying piece of evidence?

If Vixen was the correct message, maybe one of the women at Buxton and Son was Jonathan's mistress. If so, maybe she became angry when Jonathan and his wife started their world tour and grew closer, leaving her out in the cold. But how did that connect to the Johnson case? My head was spinning out of control. Once again, we had too many questions and not enough hard evidence.

Detective Schuster called, announcing the discovery of another similar death. Sam put it on speaker. "Go ahead Reuben."

"Sam, if you're available, you might want to take a look at this." He explained the situation and gave us the address.

We rushed to Sam's car and went to the scene. When we arrived at the address, three patrols were already on site, taping off the area and taking photos of the crime scene. We got the basic information from the patrol officer as we entered the house. Detective Schuster greeted us at the door. Detective Michaels, on the other hand, walked out the back door as soon as he saw us on site.

The killers struck in the kitchen and drained the body of its blood. The trail was obvious. They dragged the body through the back door.

"Same three distinct footprints, Sam." I could see the same

scar in the big toe of the smallest. Again, they made no effort to hide their footprints. In fact, they displayed them for all to see.

"Who's our vic?" Sam asked Detective Schuster.

"His name is Zahir Khan, a thirty-two-year-old man of Indian heritage." Another male. This time he was not white, and he was ten years younger than the others.

"Is the body intact?" Sam asked, studying the swath of blood.

"Yes." Schuster pointed to the back door Detective Michaels just went through and said, "You need to see the back yard." He shook his head and apologized for sloughing us off before. "That's where you'll find the body. It's crazy."

CSI arrived before us. Like a machine, they took photos, gathered samples of the blood, and secured evidence to process later.

"Let's get at it, Abbey." I followed Sam through the house to the back door, making sure not to step in the blood and disrupt the prints. Sam's whistle caught my attention, and it only took a moment to realize why he was so impressed. I stood there with one hand still on the door. The garden was amazing. If I didn't know better, I'd have sworn we walked right through a portal and into an Indian temple.

Every corner of the back yard belonged to the elaborate garden. From the bottom of the back steps, a maze of circular concrete paths portioned off small ponds filled with water, flowers, shrubs, and lily pads. Three colorful statues formed a triangle on the paths, one directly in front of us, and one in each of the back corners of the lot. I'd seen pictures of these kinds of statues. In fact, there was something eerily familiar about this specific garden, as if I had seen it before. Impossible. I'd never visited India or been near a temple of this kind. And even though I patrolled East Nashville as a cop, I'd never been to this house before.

The body lay face down before the statue directly in front of us in the shape of an X. Blood stained his otherwise white linen jacket. Sam and I donned our gloves before touching anything.

Detective Michaels approached. "I don't like having to swallow my pride, but you got this right, Rhodes, and we didn't. Reuben and I think you two should take the lead."

Sam nodded and told him his suspect made sense for an isolated case. "We're just now connecting the dots." He said that it was up to the brass who led in this case. I knelt and examined the victim's right hand. There was another marking, the letter I. I pushed his thick black hair away from his forehead. "Here, too, Sam. Now we have X, V, and I. They're spelling something."

Sam knelt beside me and said, "I'll let Sarge know the situation. He can decide or pass it up the ranks."

"This makes three now. We need to get Sarge involved anyway. I'm afraid the killers are just getting started." We had to figure out the code soon, or others would die. The body of Zahir Khan pointed directly at the first statue. The godlike figure rested, with his legs crossed, on a large pink lotus flower. He had four heads and four arms, each holding some unique item. The statue was bright and colorful. "Strange figure," I said.

"Indian gods," Sam said. "Hindu, I think."

"I've seen pictures of things like this," I admitted. "Why do you think it has four heads and hands?"

"You'll have to look that up later. Right now, examine everything that might be significant to our case."

The statues were significant. He was positioned directly in front of one. If we learned anything to this point, the killers staged the bodies intentionally. I looked at the man and then the statue. I glanced at the two far corners. "The other two statues have four arms also."

"Take pictures. You can study them in more detail later," Sam advised. He seemed tense. Even his words were short and tight. Did Sam know something I didn't? "What do you notice, Abbey?"

"The killers want me to examine each body and the corresponding kill zone. Obviously, dragging his body here was important. Timothy Johnson was laid out beside his drone, the very object he used to stalk his neighbor's wife. Jonathan Buxton was set before the picture of him and his father at their company's front door. Now, Zahir Khan lay in his fabulous garden at the base of a four-headed god statue."

"What does it mean?" For some reason, Sam still expected me to know about these Hindu statues even though there were not based on Christianity. He knew my story, but Sam figured my little experience was better than none. Since he didn't *do* church, the interpretation fell to me.

"I don't have a clue, Sam. I admit it. I'm stumped." The X of the body was a common element, even though the other letters changed. Did X signify something significant?

"Maybe they're not letters at all, Abbey. Maybe their Roman numerals."

"Roman numerals?" I'd heard of them but couldn't tell you anything about them.

"If they are, instead of a X, V, and I, we have ten, five, and one."

"Okay. What does that mean?" It was his theory. I wanted him to explain the significance.

"I don't have a clue."

"Well, you can look out here. I'll study the crime scene inside," I said, walking back into the house. I entered each of the two small bedrooms before heading back to the kitchen. There were no pictures of Zahir with family. Most of the pictures were nature scenes. In his bedroom, I found a card reader/ID with a metal clip attached. Fulcrum Logistics, a shipping company based out of Nashville.

His house was immaculately clean. He'd filled his fridge and pantry with healthy foods. No sugar. No processed foods. Everything natural and organic. Zahir Khan lived a clean and healthy lifestyle—at least that's what the home presented. I wanted to retrace my steps and see what picture I could paint of the event. As I approached the front door, I noticed a smattering of white powder underneath it. I swung the door away from the wall and found an indention from the door handle, which had chipped the

paint and drywall. Someone swung the door open with a great deal of force.

"I noticed that too," Detective Michaels said, standing beside me. "Did the Buxton case have a similar MO?"

"Possibly," I said. "They had a doorstop that had dented the door, but I couldn't tell if it was new or old." I thought about the Buxton door. There was no forced breach. "For some reason, the victims are opening the door to the killers who feel the need to rush the victims from the threshold." I examined the lock and door frame.

"I agree," he said. "The handle and lock are intact."

I looked at the path more closely. I found another spot of powder beneath a small table on this side of the kitchen. "Look here." I drew his attention to the table. "Everything on the table is flush against the wall like someone put the items back on the table in a hurry." I pulled the table out from the wall. There was another indention, this one from the table. I got on my hands and knees and looked from the table's leg into the kitchen. I hadn't noticed them at first, but the chairs on the far side of the kitchen table were at least ten inches away, while the chairs on the near side were pushed flush. I quickly glanced from side to side of the kitchen and then up to the lamp. "The table's been moved too."

He stood behind me and examined the scene too. "Good eye, Detective Rhodes."

"Thanks." Did he just give me a compliment? "Zahir put up a good fight that led from the front door to the kitchen and the spot of pooled blood." Zahir was not surprised by them. He attempted to stop them and then ran away. The killers had to overtake and overpower him.

I stood near the blood. "He lost his battle right here."

Detective Michaels added, "Then, after they'd bled him out, they went to the trouble of moving his body to the four-headed statue."

Just as I thought. The stagings were critical. "Every man was set before his crime." At least, that was my working theory. I was trying to figure out Zahir's crime. Maybe it had to do with the statue. Was it stolen? The killers were sending a consistent message. Sam walked in just as I came to an astonishing conclusion. "The stagings are for us."

Chapter Twenty

Tuesday, September 23, 2:17 PM—Homicide

I tossed three photos on Sam's desk. "They're all Hindu gods, just as you suspected. These three form what is called the Trimurti—three Hindu gods that represent creation, preservation, and destruction." I pointed to a picture of the four-headed statue. "This one is Brahma. Each head is pointed in the four directions of a compass. Those four things in his hands represent sacred Hindu texts."

"Okay. You've done your homework, Abbey. What does it mean?"

I had many theories forming about that question. "The obvious is Zahir Khan was a deeply religious man—a Hindu. From what we gathered this morning from his boss and fellow employees, he was a quiet man and loved by all."

"We've heard that before," Sam said, rubbing his hands through his beard. "Go ahead."

"Unlike Jonathan Buxton, I believe Zahir was loved. Anyway, by having statues of all three gods, he sought balance." I sat in my chair and rolled up to Sam's side. "He bought into the whole circle of life thing," I said. I suddenly had the urge to break out into the *Lion King* theme song but refrained from it. Sam was still in a bad mood for some reason. Then it hit me. "How did the meeting with Sarge go?"

Sam turned. "He wants to meet with both of us."

Us? A vein in Sam's forehead bulged. I could see it throbbing with the beating of his heart. Sam Tidwell was a loyal detective. He knew how this would look on Shuster and Michaels. But Sam was also a just person, determined to make the right decisions with the case. He knew Michaels and Schuster were stuck. They gave the DA the wrong man even after meeting with us. Even if it hurt his relationship with his friend, Sam would be honest and straight with Sarge.

I didn't know if this was a time for encouragement or a forceful nudge. "I'll go by myself if you want me to."

"No. We're partners, and we do this together."

"Sam, if it hurts someone's feelings to get the right verdict, I'm okay with that."

"Sure, *you* are. You're not going to lose a friend over it." He turned around and looked at the three photos. "We're missing the obvious, Abbey. What connects all three victims?"

"I don't know, Sam, but I feel the same way. It's that old saying, 'You can't see the forest for the trees.'"

"So, you think we need to take a step back?" Sam grabbed the three folders and said, "Come with me."

He led me to the conference room and made a grid on the whiteboard. On the left side, he wrote the names of the three victims. "We're going to make sense of this before we meet with Sergeant McNally." Across the top, he put "Letter/Number," "Same," and "Different."

Sam wrote "Timothy Johnson, the letter X, and the number ten." He sifted through his folder and asked, "What elements of his case are the same as the others?"

While I was thinking, Sam wrote the other two names and their corresponding letters/numbers. "They're all men." He wrote that under "Same." I looked through my notes. "Each man had his throat slit from ear to ear." There were more similarities than differences. "Each one stretched like an X, face down before some significant object, and had marks on their hands and heads."

"Okay, Abbey. What makes each different?"

"Well, first of all, the letter etched in each body." We both looked at the letters momentarily before moving on. "Oh, Sam, another similarity is each man was found at his home."

"One inside, and the others in their back yards." Sam wrote the observations on the whiteboard. "What else is different?"

"Timothy Johnson and Jonathan Buxton were killed in the same location they were staged; Zahir Khan was killed in his kitchen and then moved." Then I remembered the door and table. "He's also the only one who showed signs of a struggle."

"Zahir is also the only one we can't find a motive for." Sam was right. I could see why the other two were killed. So far, we'd uncovered nothing as to the reason for Zahir's death. "What was it you said when I came in the kitchen yesterday?"

"That the staging was for us." I'd already forgotten that. "Who'd want us to see the victims where we found them? Maybe we're the thing that connects them, Sam."

He ran his fingers through his beard. "Abbey, we never did hear anything from Skylar after her warning back in April. Do you think this is the cleansing she promised?"

Of course, I did. I didn't want to say it aloud. Something about saying it made it true. "We do have two footprints we determined were made by females. Do you think one is Skylar?"

"Yes." He said it too quickly.

"How long have you been considering Skylar, Sam?" I studied his face.

He hemmed and hawed for a few minutes before admitting, "Since the Buxton case."

The very first crime scene? "Why didn't you say anything?"

"I didn't want to prejudice your opinion until I was sure." He reached inside a nine by twelve envelope in his stack of materials. "Take this tomorrow and ask the manager at Buxton if she recognizes the woman." He had a picture of Skylar. Sam was serious about this. Maybe that's why he'd been so pensive and sullen.

"Okay, Sam. On one condition." He nodded. "No more secrets and no more trying to protect each other from the truth."

He extended his hand and took mine. "Deal."

We completed the board, filling it with all the details we discovered to date. Then Sam called Sergeant McNally to the conference room. When he came in, I sat by the board, pointing to the facts as Sam bore the burden of defending our case to Sarge. It didn't take long to convince him all three cases had the same MO and probably the same murderers.

"We need to inform the FBI. This has all the markings of a serial killer." I objected, saying it was our case, and we could handle it. "Swallow your pride, Rhodes. We need all the help we can get. Besides, your team will still work the case. I'll speak to the Lieutenant and tell him to halt the other case with the DA." He scratched his chin. "Schuster and Michaels say you two should take the lead. Tidwell, you okay with that?" Sam nodded. "Okay." He left us with our whiteboard of facts.

"That stinks!" I cried. "You know the FBI will take over when they get here."

"No, they won't. The first step is to call them in and see if they're aware of any similar cases. If not, they'll consult with us unless we prove we can't handle the job."

I took a picture of the whiteboard for my own records. "We can do this, Sam."

His eyebrows furrowed. "You need to ask yourself, Abbey, which is more important, solving this case or being the one to solve it."

I honestly couldn't answer him. What did the Bible say? Pride comes before the fall?

Chapter Twenty-one

Wednesday, September 24, 9:10 PM—Ripley Home

Susan joined us in the kitchen. "Danny's asleep, and Hannah's listening to music. What's bothering you?"

"This case is eating at me. We're pretty sure Skylar is involved."

"What makes you think that, Abbey?" Dallas asked, rubbing my back. "You've heard nothing from her since April."

"This seems like a cleansing to us. Each person's body is set before a significant object. They're staged to give us some kind of message. We just can't figure it out."

"Tea?" Susan was of the belief that it wouldn't be right to have her company sit at the table with nothing in their hands. What would her mother say?

"Sure." I didn't want anything to drink, but if I refused, Susan would think she'd done something wrong. Dallas nodded. I think he understood as well.

"I still don't comprehend what makes you believe it's her," Dallas said. I didn't have a good answer. "I think that's what Skylar wants you to worry about. Ever since she left that note, you've been looking for something to connect to her. It's the classic trait of a terrorist. She's controlling your emotions without doing a thing."

He was right, but I still couldn't let it go. Skylar didn't issue empty threats, and she was a very patient girl. But then, how well did I really know her?

"Maybe if you give us some of the details, we can help give another perspective," Dallas said.

"Okay. I'll share what I can. One person was killed and left beside his drone."

"Why?" Susan asked, not letting me complete the thought.

"He used his drone to stalk his neighbor's wife, taking videos of her sunbathing and swimming." I expected another interruption, but they both remained unusually quiet. "The next person was killed and put in front of picture of him with his father. They worked together in the family business until the son pushed him out." Still no questions. "The last person was killed and set in front of a statue of Brahma…"

"The Hindu god of creation," Dallas said. He scratched his head.

"Yes." Of course he would know about the statues. "Each person had a letter etched into his right hand and his forehead."

"A letter?" Dallas asked. "What kind of letter?"

"The first one had an X, the second a V, and the last an I."

He smiled and said, "I don't think those are letters, Abbey."

"Sam thinks they may be Roman numbers," I said, giving him a smirk.

"I agree. Repeat what you said about each man." I thought he was making fun of me. "I'm serious."

I repeated the description of each staging and the letter/number etched into each man's hand and forehead.

Dallas snapped his fingers. "It can't be that simple." He leaned back in his chair and opened his Bible. He flipped through pages and said, "There it is. Just what I thought."

"What?" Susan and I asked simultaneously.

"They *are* Roman numerals, each one corresponding to one of the Ten Commandments."

"You've got to be kidding." Sam and I had worked many hours on this case. This never dawned on either of us. I'd be embarrassed if Dallas solved it in a matter of minutes. "What makes you so sure the numbers match the Ten Commandments?"

"You have paper and pen, Susan?" Dallas asked.

She ran to the study and came back with a variety of choices in different colors. He grabbed a pad and pen and talked as he wrote. "I, II, III, IV, V, VI, VII, VIII, IX, and X. That's one through ten in Roman numerals. Your victims are marked with ten, five, and one."

"So?"

He flopped his Bible on the table. "Let's see if they correspond like I think they do. Commandment number ten. 'You shall not covet your neighbor's house. You shall not covet your neighbor's wife.'"

"Covet means you like what another person has, right, and want something like it?" I asked, just to make sure.

"Not something *like* they have, but what they have...what is theirs. A person who covets makes plans to attain the object of desire from his neighbor."

I sat up in my chair. "Oh, my gosh. Our first victim was stalking his neighbor's wife and taking videos of her in her bathing suit," I said. How could Dallas figure it out so quickly? "What about the V?"

"V is five. Let me see. 'Honor your father and mother.'"

"The second victim kicked his own father out of the family business, a business the father built from scratch." I snatched a pad and pen and began writing all this down. "That's why he was pointed at the picture of their family business." I made another note. "And the last one, the I?"

"I is for one. 'You shall have no other gods before me.'"

That was Zahir to a tee. I stood up and kissed Dallas on the lips. "You're a genius. Why didn't we think of this?" Dallas stared at me.

"Sweety, don't kick yourself. If you didn't know they were Roman numerals, you could never have made the connection." Susan was nice to defend me, but Sam suggested they were Roman numerals, and it made no difference in our understanding. "That's why you have us. We're a team."

Dallas was so excited, he didn't respond to Susan's cheerleading. "If they're running Deuteronomy as their script, you need to hear this as well," Dallas said. He pointed to a highlighted section in his Bible. "In Deuteronomy five, thirty-three, it says, 'Walk in obedience to all that the LORD your God has commanded you, so that you may *live* and prosper and prolong your days in the land that you will possess.'"

Impressive. "How do you know all this?" I asked. If I didn't know better, I would have wondered if Dallas was the killer.

"I've been studying Deuteronomy since the new pastor shared his vision for the church. Listen, Abbey, there's more. In the next chapter, it says, 'Tie them as symbols on your *hands* and bind them on your *foreheads*. Write them on the doorframes of your houses.'"

"Doorframes?" Did we check their doorframes? "Dallas, this *is* a cleansing. You said they had to obey if they wanted to live. Right? So people who violated the commandments are being killed."

"Not exactly what it says, but that is the impression. Obey so that you may live and prosper." Silence settled over the room. It was so quiet I could hear Dallas's chair squeak as he leaned forward.

"So, Abbey, do you think this is Skylar?" Susan asked, rubbing the chill bumps from her arm.

"Yes, and she's out there executing judgement on people." This was too much for me to digest. I had chills running down my spine too. "Pastor Kelly was teaching on this very thing. It can't just be a coincidence."

"Not exactly," Dallas said. "He's teaching about sacrifices that cover or take away a person's sin. These people are being killed because of their sins." My hands began to shake. Suddenly, Susan took my right hand and Dallas my left. She uttered the most beautiful prayer I'd ever heard. All through it, I could hear Dallas whispering, "Yes, Lord. Yes." When they let go of my hands I didn't have a single quivering muscle in my body. I never believed in the power of prayer, but I did believe in Susan and Dallas. Besides, I'd take any help I could get.

Chapter Twenty-two

Thursday, September 25, 8:45 AM—Homicide

I paced the floor, excitement bubbling within me, my voice high and loud. Spence popped his head over the partition and said, "You're wound up today."

I ignored him. "Sam, Spence—look; Dallas figured it all out last night." I was so proud of him that I had to brag a little. "You were right, Sam, the letters are actually Roman numbers."

"Okay. Then what does that tell us?"

"They correspond to the Ten Commandments. I used my notes from last night's discussion and showed Sam a printout of the Commandments. "Chronologically, the first death was Timothy Johnson. He had an X cut into his hand and forehead." I read the verse where it instructed them to put the commandments on their hands, head, and doorposts. "We need to go back to each crime scene and see if there is a corresponding letter—number—on the front door frame."

"Okay," Sam said, still not following the lead. "So, what if there is?"

"Then we know for sure they are using the commandments as a cleansing. Remember the cleansing Skylar promised, Sam?"

"Don't jump to conclusions, Abbey. We have no evidence indicating anyone at this point. We're still looking for connections between the victims." Spence was always the stickler for procedure and process. If *by the book* had a name, it would be Spence.

"Sam was the one who suggested the link. Now, just follow

along, guys. Humor me." I read the part about it implying the penalty of death. "X is the Roman number ten. The tenth commandment is not to covet your neighbor's wife, which is what Timothy Johnson was doing."

"Enlighten me." Sam leaned back in his chair and crossed his arms like a skeptic challenging someone to prove he was wrong.

"He wanted his neighbor's wife, but the best he could do was take videos of her."

"And Jonathan Buxton? He coveted his father's business."

"Well, yeah, but his violation wasn't about coveting. His was the letter V, which is a five. The fifth commandment is to honor your father and mother. See where I'm going with this?"

"So far, so good. Keep going." Sam leaned in. Spence popped up again and listened to my explanation.

I took a deep breath. It felt good to have a grip on this case now. "Zahir Khan was etched with the letter I, which is the number one."

"No other gods, right?" Spence said.

"That's correct."

"This is actually making sense." It was rare for Spence to admit something like this unless it was his idea.

"Guys, it was right in front of our faces the whole time. We have to renew our search for Skylar."

"There were three prints in the blood. Remember? Two women and one man. We can't even be sure one of the women is Skylar."

"But Sam—"

"Don't *But Sam* me. Nothing connects Skylar except your desire to make her fit. We can't paint ourselves in a box. Let the evidence lead you, not your suspicions." Sam looked at the paper with all the commandments.

Spence chimed in. "If we follow the pattern, which one's next?"

"Let me see. Ten, five, and one. I assume that puts us back at nine next." It could just as easily be number two if the killer went from top to bottom and then back again.

"What's nine?" Sam asked.

"You shall not give false testimony against your neighbor."

"Man, Spence, you really know your commandments."

"You don't get through Catholic school without knowing them backward and forwards. I'm beginning to like this case." He answered his phone, "Detective Spencer. I'll be right there." He turned back to us. "Got a break in another case. Let me know if you need another eye on anything."

Sam nodded, and Spence grabbed his things. "Testimony. So, we're looking at a court," Sam said, getting us back on track.

"How do we know if someone's testimony was false or not? That's a huge net and a lot of fish. Are there any recent cases where neighbors had to testify against each other, Sam?"

Spence started to leave, but stopped to say, "You do know Jesus said your neighbor doesn't have to be the person who lives next to you. It can be anyone." That didn't help narrow our search. "Sorry. Got to go."

After Spence left, Sam said, "We can figure that out. What if you're wrong?"

"Then we try something else. It's the best lead we've had so far, Sam. Unless you have anything better, I'm going to dig into recent court cases with neighbors. Physical neighbors are so much easier to find." I was determined to catch them in the act. I know Sam warned me not to fixate on Skylar, but it fit her threat of a cleansing. She could be methodical like that.

"When is the next murder?" Sam asked. "Even if we can find the next victim, which is next to impossible, how would we know when the killers would strike?"

"Let's see what we have so far." I pulled my calendar off my desk. "When was Timothy's murder?"

Sam looked in the file. "August thirty-first."

"And Jonathan Buxton?" I asked.

"September tenth."

"Zahir was September twentieth, Sam. Every ten days there's

a killing. Today's the twenty-fifth. We have less than five days to figure it out and stop the next murder." It sounded like we just cracked the case wide open, and in a way, we did. But I knew we had an arrest warrant for Skylar since April, and nothing showed up. She'd managed to hide herself well. Why wait so long?

"If—and that's a big if—we just figured out the pattern," Sam cautioned my excitement, "we still need to find a neighbor guilty of giving a false testimony before twelve-o-one on the thirtieth."

I nodded and took a deep breath. How hard could that be? I was giddy with excitement. At least we had a direction and a plan. We didn't have to sit around and wait for the next body to be found.

We told Sarge our theory, and he took us straight to Lieutenant Stallings. "It's a sound theory, Rhodes. Good work. The FBI has a consultant on her way. Get her up to speed the moment she arrives. The clock is ticking, and we have a lot of work to do." We went back into the main room where the detectives sat in their cubicles, and Lt. Stallings called four other detectives to go into the conference room with us. There, he explained the theory and the problem.

"We need our top detectives on this. We need to be at the top of our game when the FBI shows up. According to our theory, we have another murder scheduled for this coming Tuesday." Our theory? I didn't mind him taking credit. It meant he was on board and taking responsibility for the gathering of other resources. "Tidwell and Rhodes say we're looking for any person who may have given a false testimony against his neighbor. Let's start with anyone caught in contempt of court and go from there." Good, this wasn't all on my head anymore. He asked for other volunteers to take a part in the task. "When Spencer gets back, pull him in."

Five detectives and an FBI agent all joined us on the case. Skylar didn't stand a chance. "So far, everything is in Nashville. I don't know if they will stick to their MO, but every victim has been male," I said.

Deborah came into the conference room and dropped a load

of papers on the table. "This is just from the initial search." We divided the cases of neighbor disputes. I was surprised how many there were. We returned to our desks, calling and searching databases. It was the proverbial needle in the haystack, but at least we now had a haystack. What other lead did we have?

"Sam."

"Yeah."

"They wanted us to know why they were killing these victims. The next one would have to be someone obvious, wouldn't it?"

"Would you have known about a stalker using a drone, or a son cheating his father out of business?"

"No. Not really."

"They're only obvious in retrospect, Kid. Hindsight's always twenty-twenty." He saw the emotional deflation in my body language and quickly added, "But we'll get them. Maybe not before they strike this Tuesday, but we will stop them. We always do. If we fail this time, it won't be the last time. Everyone makes mistakes. The key is to learn from them." Ever the mentor.

Sergeant McNally distributed photos of Skylar. Sam looked at me, and I shrugged my shoulders. "I didn't say anything about her." He didn't either. So, how did Sarge know about Skylar's possible connection to our case. Maybe he had the same impression we did, and this looked as close to a *cleansing* as we've had since April.

By Friday afternoon at four-thirty, we had trimmed it down to a list of five potential names. All involved neighborly disputes that appeared recently in the Nashville courts. Lieutenant Stallings called in patrol officers to watch each of the five individuals Sunday morning through the end of the day Tuesday. If they were the potential victims, we might just catch the murderers in the act—or before. It was the best we could do.

"Detectives, rest your minds. Let the patrol take it from here. If we miss them, I'll need you all fresh for the next opportunity."

How was I supposed to get my mind off Skylar and the case?

Dallas called. "Hey, Abbey, I know I said I had to work on my dissertation and wasn't available for the next couple of weeks, but I have a dinner meeting Monday night and really don't want to go alone. Would you come?"

"Sure. I'll take any opportunity I can to see you," I said, no longer trying to hide my affection for him. "What time?"

"I'll pick you up around six. You'll probably want to wear a dress or a nice pantsuit. I'll wear a tie."

"I guess I can drag something out of my closet. I'll try not to embarrass you."

He laughed and hung up.

Chapter Twenty-three

Monday, September 29, 6:30 PM—Cumberland Bend Baptist Church

I never dreamed Dallas would take me to Cumberland Bend Baptist Church for a dinner date. Was this Dallas's way of getting me back for ice skating? "Why are we at a church tonight?" I asked. I was exhausted from a trying week. Something about this church put me in a bad mood.

"It's a mission fundraiser," Dallas said. "I had to be here to follow up on previous research, and I wanted to be with you. It's the only solution I could find where I could do both."

I had to admit, that was sweet. "Why are you interested in a fundraiser here?" I asked. "Are they raising money for The Least of These Ministries?" Dallas was still co-chair of the ministry to Nashville's homeless population. He shook his head and said nothing. The church was huge from the outside, but when we walked into the main meeting hall filled with round tables, it felt like the inside was even bigger than the outside. "Tell me again why we're here."

"I'm following up on previous research I did for a paper on the relationship between American churches and foreign missions. A lot of churches give through a cooperative offering, but others, like Cumberland Bend, form a personal relationship with a missionary and channel all their mission money to support his ministry. That's why I'm here tonight. I want to hear the pastor and the missionary share how it works from each end. Don't worry so much about the program, just relax and enjoy the music. I hear the food will be fantastic."

"As long as there's good food, I can handle most any situation." I was glad the set up felt more like a political fundraiser than a church event. I'd done security for my share of those events.

"Here's our table." Dallas pointed to a table off to the far left, which was fine with me. It was near the restrooms. I looked down, and two placards were in his name.

"How did you know I'd come?"

"I didn't. I was going to ask you Wednesday if you'd accompany me to a boring dinner, but I got sidetracked with your case."

Sidetracked with my case? Ouch. After all of that, dinner was the very least I could do to help Dallas with his paper. "I'll take the chair with its back to the stage. You need to see the speakers for your research," I said. Honestly, I didn't care to watch preachers or missionaries talk. I grew up with that experience, and it still left a bad taste in my mouth. In fact, I could probably give Dallas a few stories about missionary fundraisers. Instead, I winked and said, "I'll just sit here and look pretty." I meant it in sarcasm.

"You do it well." He held out my chair and pushed me to the table.

What a gentleman. Where had he been all my life? I didn't deserve him. "I'm sure I'll enjoy the food and the music—and you." The host church showcased its various music programs, beginning with the adorable preschool and children's choirs.

After the children sang, we went back to talking with each other. I told him about our progress in the case since he decoded the secret messages. We chatted about each other's work. Realizing we were ignoring our tablemates, we turned our attention to them and exchanged pleasantries.

"Have you ever met a real missionary?" a little girl asked. Half of the adults nodded. She looked at me and asked, "What about you?"

I wanted to say something snide like, "There are no real missionaries," but she was just a little girl. I didn't want to pop her bubble at such a tender age. "Yes. My parents were missionaries."

Once it was out, I couldn't take it back. Why do I crumble with kids and spit out the truth?

"Really? Was it awesome?" I just smiled. A lie of omission.

"You never told me that," Dallas said, jumping at the new information. "When was this?"

"I was born here, but only because my father came to the states for an event like this. He had to raise funds for his ministry."

Just as Dallas was about to launch into a million questions, I was given a reprieve by the waitress. She set our salads at each place and two baskets of rolls. She took our drink orders, and I immediately stuffed my mouth with a fork full of salad. I know it wasn't very ladylike, but it was better than entertaining a discussion of my childhood. I continued to eat while Dallas perused a brochure from the missionary. He tucked one into his jacket pocket.

He leaned over to ask me something, but someone tapped the microphone and asked, "Is this thing on?" Everyone laughed, and he introduced himself as the senior pastor. The little girl and I whispered to each other while the pastor went on and on about his church's various ministries and its relationship with Central American missions.

I turned over the program and made a Tic-Tac-Toe grid. She went first.

"For the past five years, Cumberland Bend Baptist Church has partnered with Guatemala City Mission House."

I started to make my X, but I stopped abruptly. *Did he say Guatemala City Mission House? No. It can't be.*

"So, without further ado, I would like to welcome to stage, Pastor Joseph Abelard."

Please God, not him. It was the closest thing to a prayer I'd uttered in years. This couldn't get any worse. And then, it did.

"Thank you, Reverend Sayers. You are a kind and generous man. You always have been."

I turned my chair just in time to confirm the identity of the man leaving the stage. Sayers? It was the man who raped me and stole my childhood. He was a pastor now? Unbelievable!

The speaker washed away any doubt I may have had, saying, "Nick and I met over a decade ago. He was a youth minister who brought his group to our house to help us conduct Vacation Bible School in the remote villages of Guatemala." It *was* him.

I watched as the man stood in the wide hallway just off stage-right. He stopped to speak with a young red-head in a black dress. She was much shorter than he—probably much younger. I made that assumption based on what I thought of him. Nick Sayers was smiling way too much. I divided my attention between him and the man at the microphone—my father. I was in shock. How could he stand there and speak so piously about his ministry and about God's love? I looked at Nicholas Sayers and the girl in the hallway. How could he be so coy, laughing with that young girl? He *innocently* placed his hand on her lower back. This was the kind of hypocrisy that destroyed what little faith I had and cast me out into the streets of Guatemala to survive at the age of fourteen. And, like that girl, it all started with an innocent laugh.

I turned back to the stage. "Our mission is one of love. We do all we can to help the people of Guatemala experience the love of Jesus Christ." *Sure, you do.* "Our house is open to all Christian groups who wish to help us demonstrate God's love to the downcast." *Like your daughter?* "My wife and I live in such a way that when the sinner sees us, they see a reflection of God." *Hah! Liar.*

Wait. Did he say wife? Is Mom here too? I scanned the tables in front of the stage. What did she look like now? He had grey hair. Unless she dyed hers, she'd be gray now too. How old were they? They had to be in their mid to early sixties—or even older.

"Our daughter shared our ministry until she contracted an incurable infection. Now, my wife and I carry on alone with the help of native Guatemalans, which is why we desperately need your help." He had them all eating out of his hand.

"Isn't he fantastic?"

"What?"

"Isn't Pastor Abelard fantastic?" Dallas asked. He was spell-bound too.

As he continued to shower praise on my father, a sudden wave of fear overcame me. I caught myself running for the restroom, doing anything to get away. I tripped over a chair and stumbled into the wall divider. The chair bounced and disrupted the speech. I apologized profusely to everyone and raced to the hall. I couldn't take my eyes off my father. Now, he had locked onto mine. It was like we'd both seen a ghost. He stumbled in his speech, and I ran right into the Nicholas Sayers and the young redhead.

"Watch out!" he cried.

Too late. I knocked him down and fell on top. I quickly rolled off and looked for the girl who also crashed to the floor. She got up quickly and scampered off down the hall, hiking her dress up in her left hand. Nicholas Sayers bounced to his feet and stretched out his hand to help me up. I slapped it away. "How could you?"

"I'm sorry, Miss, but you ran into me." He boasted a grand smile as he kept his hand extended.

I got up on my own power. He didn't recognize me. "You stole my life!"

"Excuse me?" he put a hand on my shoulder and tried to calm me down.

I slapped it away. I was having none of his attempt to be charming. "You raped me. Now you stand here and act like you're perfect and sinless and doing everything God asks of you."

"I try." I scoffed aloud. "Do I know you?" he asked in a whisper. People from the side tables were looking at us. He grabbed me by the arm and attempted to pull me to the end of the hallway and away from the meeting hall.

I slapped his hand away for a third time. "You raped me back in Guatemala. I was only fourteen. How could you?"

He sniggered. "Are you that little Abelard girl? You were a

sweet girl, but very disappointing. Not even worth the effort."

"Sweet? I knew it. You told everyone I tried to seduce you!"

People sitting at the nearest tables were still looking our way. Dallas was standing and staring, but I didn't care at that moment. Nicholas jerked on my arm. "Will you hush?"

"No! I will no longer be quiet." He put his hand over my mouth and pulled me back down the hallway. I pushed free of his grip. I wasn't a defenseless little girl anymore, and I was much stronger than I looked. "I let you take everything from me, and I kept my mouth shut from embarrassment. You lied, and my parents bought the whole story."

A weird smile crossed his lips. Then, he hissed like a snake. "You were too easy, too trusting."

What? He was publicly admitting to the rape. "You got me drunk and…"

"Your word against mine. It was then, and it will be now. Who do you think they'll believe?"

"You'll pay for what you've done!" I slapped his face and turned away. I bumped into my father on my way back to the table to get my purse.

He turned to follow me. "Hannah, is that you?"

I spun on my heels. "Oh, hello, *father*. Nice speech." His mouth opened wide. "Hate to disappoint you, but I'm still alive." I turned and left him staring.

Dallas stepped in front of me to block my exit. "Abbey, how do you know Pastor Sayers?"

"Biblically. Is that what you want to hear?" It was all I could muster. If he'd heard any of my remarks, it made sense. If not… oh, well.

Dallas had a bewildered look as if he didn't know who I was. I'd seen that look before. Embarrassment. Shame. "Don't worry, Dallas. I understand. I'm used to being cast away." I rushed past him and the crowd of people gathering in the hallway before I burst into tears. I got out my phone and called for an Uber. Dallas called multiple times on my ride home, but I let his calls go straight to voice mail. I turned the phone off and stuffed it in my handbag.

Chapter Twenty-four

Tuesday, September 30, 4:38 AM—Harmony Apartments

Sleep evaded me. I couldn't stop the tape of my past; it ran over and over, taunting me and robbing me of what little peace I had left. I kept seeing the face of Nicholas Sayers saying, "You weren't even worth the effort." I pulled on my jacket, withdrew into the darkness of the hood, and headed out the door of my apartment. The elevator chimed, and I got in. I couldn't stop regurgitating the conversations with Nicholas Sayers, my father, and Dallas in my head. Nicholas and my father deserved my brusk responses. I should have said something long, long ago. Dallas, on the other hand, did not. I knew I was wrong lashing out at him, wrongly putting on him the years of being called worthless, years of fighting against my perceptions of men thinking I was weak. I stretched out in the lobby before going on a long run. I stepped outside, and the bitter cold wind slapped me in the face. I immediately pulled the strings on my hoodie, minimizing my face's exposure to the elements. Fortunately, the wind was at my back as I headed east on Demonbreun.

You adulteress! You Jezebel! Temptress of righteous men! Get out of my sight. You are dead to me. My father's words tore through my heart more bitterly than the wind at my back. *I never want to see you again. You will not turn my ministry into a tool of the devil.* And with those words, I was tossed eternally from my home at the age of fourteen. Never again did I step foot into a church or Christian building of any kind—until the murder of Mark Ripley.

The fourteen-year-old Hannah Abelard was lost in more ways than one as an abandoned American citizen in Guatemala City, Guatemala. My father must have told my story—my rapist's version—to everyone he knew and met. He'd cleansed his home of his sinful child, and he wore it like badge of honor. I wore it like a banner of shame. That man, proclaiming to be a minister of God, tricked me, gave me alcohol, and isolated me. He violated my innocence and took my virginity. I tried to come back home two times. I bypassed my father and appealed to my mother's heart. When that failed, I reached out to my older sister. She too shunned me like a leper. I was an outcast, as if talking with me would taint their precious souls.

Left to find shelter and food, I scrounged the city—digging in dumpsters, sleeping in drainage pipes. I did my best to hide from the other ragtag people, especially the older boys and men. They were drawn to me like flies to garbage, always wanting to look and to touch. Maybe my father was right. Maybe I was the cause of many men's temptations and weaknesses. My looks and my body were my curse—and my salvation.

I swore I would not bring Dallas down that road. He was better off without me.

A car horn blared, bringing me back to the present. I jumped back to the sidewalk. Somehow, without realizing it, I was crossing Wedgewood on Eighth. *How did I get here?* That thought catapulted me back to that night, hiding away in the storm, when Mr. Morales reached out and *rescued* me. I took his hand and his offer. He taught me the ways of business, got me back into school and soccer, and gave me stability that I desperately needed: food, shelter, clothing, and safety.

Yes, I was shocked and embarrassed when I caught him watching me bathe. I wanted to leave, but I knew what that would mean—scraping out survival on the streets. I was seventeen when I found the cameras and realized I had become the prophecy of my father—a temptress. But what could I do? Mr. Morales protected me from others. As long as I was a child under his protection, he kept his promise; no one laid a hand on me, not even him. For earthly protection I sold my soul—if I ever had one.

Not everything was dark and embarrassing though. Mr. Morales gave me a generous salary for doing research for his real estate business. He taught me to manage one of his stores too. I had no expenses, so I stuffed away my money, readying myself for the day I graduated and turned eighteen. Then, I could choose my own future, and I knew just the way to do it.

I studied the process of changing one's name. When I became an adult, I would file that very day for a name change. I already knew which judges to bribe, expediting the process. Mr. Morales taught me well. A name? Abbey Rhodes. That would really tick my father off—if he even knew I was alive.

"The Beatles are responsible for the downfall of modern society," my father said. He and the youth minister ruined the name and reputation of Hannah Leah Abelard. I would start anew as Abbey Rhodes.

I stumbled and nearly fell. Again, without consciously turning, I ran west on Battery Lane. The road was narrow, and cars were entering the roadway. The shoulder was negligible and the ground rough. The sun broke behind me. My runner's headlamp still bounced left and right as I ran. My legs and lungs burned, but I refused to give in to the pain. I turned north on Granny White and focused on my path as I was nearing Harmony Apartments.

I put the past temporarily behind me and wondered if I could ever swallow enough pride to beg Dallas for forgiveness. How would I even start the conversation? I knew he would forgive me long before I could forgive myself. Susan wasn't burning up my phone last night or this morning, which meant she didn't know about the incident. I assumed that meant one of two things: either Dallas was finished with my emotional outbursts, or he was graciously giving me time to explain, leaving the first move up to me. If the latter was correct, he was showing in his brainy way that he understood I didn't need to be rescued. He was acknowledging my strength and power to initiate reconciliation.

I truly hoped Dallas was interested in furthering our relationship. Yet I was torn. I wanted him back, but I didn't want to hurt him. The next move was up to me. How could I explain myself to him now? How much did he hear of my conversation with Nicholas? What would he do if he connected the dots and realized I was not born as Abbey Rhodes? Once again, I was paralyzed by fear.

When I got back to the apartment, I collapsed on my bed without even changing clothes.

Chapter Twenty-five

Tuesday, September 30, 9:27 AM—Harmony Apartments

The drum pounded in my head. I rolled onto my belly and stuffed the pillow around my head, but the noise wouldn't stop. It wasn't a dream. I glanced at the clock on my nightstand. Nine twenty-seven. I must have slept hard after that long run this morning.

The pounding continued, "Abbey, are you there?"

Susan.

"Give me a minute." I forced myself out of bed. My mouth was so dry, and my muscles ached. "Coming." I unlatched the door and let her in.

"I thought you did something stupid," Susan said, putting the back of her hand to my forehead. "I left a dozen messages, and you wouldn't answer the intercom either."

"Really? How did you get in?"

"Aaron recognized me," Susan said.

Aaron? "What did he have to say?" Then it hit me. "You called a dozen times? Who's hurt? Is it Hannah?"

"No one's hurt, Abbey. We're all fine." She took me by the arm and led me to the couch. "You look awful, girl."

"Thanks. I love you too." I was confused. Why was she here pounding on my door if there wasn't an emergency? "What's going on?"

"That's what I want to know."

"Did Dallas call you?"

He must have gotten her involved after all. Wonderful.

"We'll talk about that later. Right now, you have something more pressing." Susan continued to touch my forehead. "What's wrong with you?"

I didn't feel good physically, and now Susan was wearing me down. "Just spit it out, Susan. I messed up." There. I beat her to the punch. "I have an appointment with my counselor Thursday to discuss the PTSD and my heightened anxiety."

"You had to know Dallas would find out eventually, Abbey." She leaned in to smell of my breath and nearly gagged.

"Well, what did you expect? I slept hard and just woke up." Fixing a little pillow to my right, I added, "It's not like I'm the only one who's slept in late."

"Have you been drinking?"

"No. Absolutely not! I just have morning breath and a sour stomach."

"Honey, I've been trying to reach you all morning..."

"Why?" Was this about my temper tantrum last night or not? "I'm sorry, Susan, but I don't remember missing any calls."

"Where's your phone?" she asked in a challenging tone.

"Beside my bed." She squinched her eyes and headed down the short hallway. "What? Don't believe me?"

I followed Susan to my bedroom. She found the charger and pulled the cord. No phone. I pointed to my handbag. She opened it and grabbed the phone. "No wonder. Your phone is off. When did you turn it off?"

"Last night when I left Dallas."

"You left Dallas?"

"Long story, and I'm not in the mood to tell it."

Susan powered the phone on and used my face to unlock the screen. "Abbey, there. Twenty missed calls."

"Twenty calls?" I grabbed the phone and looked at the screen. The first five calls were from Dallas last night. Then a string of calls from Susan. The last three were from Sam. "Jeez. What's wrong with everybody?" Susan put her hands on her hips and looked on with disappointment. "Honest. I went for an early run and overdid it. That's why I slept late." I ran to pee.

Susan hollered down the hallway as I went to the bathroom. "Sam's been trying to reach you all morning. He says he came to your building and buzzed, but you didn't answer that either. He even called me to see if I knew where you were."

I pulled up my pants and stepped back into the hall. "Sam called you? Why?"

"He said there was another murder, and you were a no show."

Oh no! It was Tuesday, September thirtieth. "They must have struck again. Did they catch her?"

"I don't think so."

"That means we were wrong about the victim?"

She ran her fingers through my hair. "Oh, honey, you need a shower." She pointed to the bathroom. "You call Sam and go do your detective thing. Clean up first. When you're done with Sam, come to the house. We need to talk."

I nodded and called Sam. "So sorry, Sam. I went for a long run at four-thirty this morning and hit the sack hard. What's up? Where? So, we guessed wrong. Let me wash up and grab something to go. I'll meet you there. Text me the address."

"I'll see myself out, Abbey. See you after work."

I took a quick shower, brushed my teeth and gargled with mouthwash, then grabbed an oatmeal bar and a Diet Coke and headed to the newest crime scene.

Chapter Twenty-six

Tuesday, September 30, 11:06 AM—Home of Nicholas Sayers

I finally arrived on the scene. It was a huge house—no, it was a mansion. This person had the kind of neighbors who could afford to get even. "Detective Rhodes, this is Agent Carmichael from the FBI." Sam turned to her. "This is my partner, Detective Rhodes."

She was about five-seven with jet black hair and eyes to match. Her irises were so dark, I couldn't tell where the pupils ended. It gave her the look of one of those Anime characters. We shook hands. "I'm just here to observe—for now."

I nodded. Nice try. Not going to flinch at that. I turned to Sam. "Who's our vic, Sam?" I made sure to throw out his first name to say I wasn't going to play her intimidation game.

"His name is Nicholas Sayers."

"Who?" Surely I misunderstood him.

"Nicholas Sayers. He's the pastor of Cumberland Bend Baptist Church."

Nope. It was the same. That wasn't good, especially with the FBI scrutinizing my every move. "Where is he?" I had to confirm my worst fears. I also had to see if he was one of the commandment victims. I walked through the front door and examined the wall behind it. Nothing. There was a small table like the one in Zahir's home. I glanced underneath. Clean. No sign of forced entry. No sign of pushing through once the door was opened.

"Over here." Sam directed me to the body. It was him all

right. I examined his hand and forehead. Etched in both were the letters IX—the Roman number nine. We'd predicted the correct commandment, but we had no idea it would connect to someone like Pastor Sayers. Just like the other scenes, the murderers left three footprints in the blood pooled around his neck and head—a man and two women. As I was following the trail, I noticed a map pinned to the back of a dining room chair, which was set directly in front of the body. It was of Guatemala City, Guatemala. I nearly threw up. I was the victim of his false witness. Only a handful of people knew that story, and they were all in Guatemala. Well, not everybody. My mind suddenly recalled last night. Now, anyone who heard our argument on Monday night could be a person of interest.

"What's wrong, Abbey?"

"I think I'm going to be sick, Sam." I was sick. I hated this man, but I didn't want him dead. I just wanted him to pay for what he'd done, pay as in damage his reputation.

"Is there a problem, Detective," Agent Carmichael asked, leaning her head in between us.

I had to tell Sam about my encounter with Nicholas Sayers the other night. I knew it would make me a person of interest in his murder too. Despite Agent Carmichael standing beside me, I gave Sam the summary of my public breakdown. "I should have known better, but the last thing I said to him, in the hearing of witnesses, was, 'You'll pay for what you've done.'"

"I don't need to tell you how that looks, Detective Rhodes." She was right. I screwed up and at the worst possible time. She was explaining the standard procedure for an officer in my situation, saying something about being disciplined or put on leave, when a heard a familiar voice.

"Hannah?" I looked up the stairs. My mother stood there with one hand over her mouth and the other bracing herself against the wall. She looked so old. Her hair was a mix of white and gray; her face wrinkled from age and too much sun. "We thought you were dead."

"I'm Detective Tidwell. Who are you?" Sam asked.

"I was dead, Marilyn. You all made sure of it." She'd turned me away too. Of course, calling her by her first name was an added jab and obviously childish on my part, but it felt good.

"Okay. Everybody, take a breath and have a seat." Agent Carmichael was no longer just observing. She was taking charge.

Sam informed her this was still his case. Knowing this was getting complicated and looking bad on me, Sam wanted to limit the number of ears hearing the details. "Let's step into the next room and give our officers room to do their jobs." Sam gave them instructions concerning the crime scene and closed the office doors after he and Agent Carmichael entered the room. She stood with her feet spread a little farther than the width of her shoulders and crossed her arms. She was letting Sam know right now, he was under her scrutiny too. Sam focused on my mother. "Let's start at the beginning, if we can."

What was the knowledge of my changed name going to do to my job and my reputation? What about my place on the case? Did Agent Carmichael say something about having me put on leave? Could she do that? I could explain the change of name easily enough, but I didn't want to expose everything from my past. Sam knew enough already. The agent glared at me with her dark eyes. My life was falling apart. Someone knocked on the door. Sam had a brief discussion before opening it and letting my father in.

"Why are you here?" I asked. "Did you kill him?"

"Of course not!" my father shouted. "I was going to ask the same question of you."

"Joseph, please. Let's let the detective ask his questions." He sat with great reluctancy.

"I seem to be the only one in the dark here," Agent Carmichael said. She wasn't, but Sam wasn't going to throw me under the bus. "How do you three know each other?"

"This is our daughter Hannah," my mother said, pointing to me with watery eyes.

"Our only daughter died of an infection." My father folded his arms over his chest and looked away from me. "We have no other children."

"I'm confused," Agent Carmichael said. "Is she your daughter or not?"

Sam couldn't take it any longer. "Abbey, what's going on?"

"Abbey? Her name is Hannah," my mother corrected. "Hannah Leah Abelard."

"My name is Abbey Rhodes." My father's face turned blood-red. I'd waited a decade to say that to him—ten years to throw that name in his face. "I legally had it changed when I turned eighteen." I noticed out of the corner of my eye that Agent Carmichael was taking notes. I'm sure she'd want to know why I had to change my name.

"I don't know you!" my father shouted.

We all started talking at once. Sam's whistle pierced the air and stopped everything. "I'll ask the questions here." He looked directly at my father and said, "Don't speak unless I address you." My father started to protest, but Sam took two quick steps in his direction. There's one thing that shuts up a bully, someone who calls his bluff. Sam had a lot of anger and frustration to vent, and he seemed content to release it all on my father. He knew my side of the story and held more resentment than I did toward the man. "I only need to know how this connects to Pastor Sayers."

The FBI agent continued writing detailed notes.

Surprisingly, my father kept silent. I, however, reached a boiling point and everything spilled out all at once. I was thrust back into that little chapel at the age of fourteen. I spoke of my fears, and the youth minister who offered something to take the edge off the cold night. It tasted both bitter and sweet. He gave me more. "Next thing I knew, he was on top of me. His hands were everywhere. I tried to scream, but he shoved his hand over my mouth. Then, he was done. Refastening his belt he said, 'Well, that was disappointing.'" It was the same comment he made at the church last night.

I spoke of the shock, sitting there violated and not knowing what to do. "I ran to my parents for help, but when I got there, the story was backwards. He accused me of trying to seduce him—of throwing myself at *him*. My father immediately called me all kinds of names and kicked me out of the house."

"That's not true," my father said, finally looking directly at me.

"Yes, *Dad*. It is, and you know it. He lied to you, and you took his side. You never even gave me a chance to explain."

My mother started crying. I turned to her and said, "And you let him do it. You turned your back on me too."

"And where did you go? What kind of life did you live?" My father's judgmental side took over, and he tried to press me back into that little box. "You turned into the Jezebel I knew you to be."

Sam was on his feet again, but I assured him I was okay. It didn't matter if the FBI was there or not. Ten years of compressed garbage spilled out at once, and nothing I could do would put it back in the can. "I lived however I had to, Dad. I chose to survive, no matter what it took. What did you expect when you kicked me out?" There. I finally admitted it to myself and to them, and I was glad Sam heard it. "I was *fourteen*—and you threw me out like garbage. So, that's what I became—trash. You were right all along. Are you happy?" My mother was bawling. My father remained deathly silent. I turned to Sam. "I vented on Nicholas Sayers the other night because I wanted everyone to see him for what he really was, and yes, I wanted him to pay for what he did to me... for what he probably did to a lot of other young girls... but I didn't want him dead."

How many times had I heard that as an officer and detective?

"Abbey, you need to leave. We'll talk with the brass and see what they want us to do."

"You mean she works for you?" my father asked.

"No, sir. She's my partner. We work together." He put his finger in my father's chest. "Now, sit down, and I'll have an officer take your statements." He opened the door, avoiding Agent

Carmichael's stare, and gave instructions to the officers present. Then, Sam walked me back to my car. He put his arm around my shoulder and said, "We'll get through this, Kid. Head home, and I'll speak with the lieutenant about all this. Unfortunately, you and I both know what's hitting the fan."

I sheepishly nodded. I knew what that meant. I was off the case, and that was the best of the news. "I need to go see Susan first, if that's okay."

"Sure. In fact, I want you to stay with Susan until you hear from me." He started back toward the house. "I'll keep you in the loop, Abbey. I know how close you are to this case. Right now, go be with your friend. You'll hear from me soon enough."

Chapter Twenty-seven

Tuesday, September 30, 3:55 PM—Ripley home

I told Susan about the FBI agent, the church fundraiser, the encounter with my rapist, his death with the IX etched in his skin, my parents at the crime scene, and my precarious position with homicide now that I was also a person of interest.

She listened, prayed for me, and made sure I had something in my stomach—ever the hostess and friend. She separated the issues and led me through a discussion of each, one by one.

"I can't do anything about your work situation, but I can help you with the rest. Do you think Dallas heard you confronting Pastor Sayers?" I nodded. "All of it?" I shrugged my shoulders. "What did he do when you said that to him?"

"Nothing. He just stared at me as if I was an alien."

"But he called you several times after you left. What did he want?"

"I don't know. I didn't answer."

"Did he leave a message?"

"I didn't check. I took a quick shower and ran off to the crime scene; everything else fell apart."

Susan held out her hand. She wanted my phone. "Let's get this part over with. No sense dealing with the unknown if we don't have to." I gave it to her. She held the phone up to my face to unlock the screen and checked my messages. "You have three from Dallas." They were all from that night. "Are you ready?"

"No."

"I'm not going to make you listen to them, Abbey, but you need to." I nodded. Better to hear it with Susan than by myself. I expected the worst. "Okay. Message number one."

"Abbey, why won't you answer. We need to talk. I'm going to keep trying until you do."

"Well, at least he's still interested," Susan said.

"Did you hear the anger in his voice?"

"He's mad, but it may be because you're ghosting him. Let's check message two."

"Come on, Abbey. Answer the phone. I need to see if you're okay. I heard enough to know you're not. Please don't shut me out."

"That sounds even better, Abbey. He wants you to let him in. He wants to help." Susan pushed a lock of my hair behind my ear. She handed me a tissue. I feared we were going to need another box before this was all over. "Two down. One to go." I nodded.

"Abbey, I just talked with your father. I want to hear your side of the story." His voice was flat, calculated. "I also spoke with Pastor Sayers. I could tell he was lying. I told him after I spoke to you, I was going to have the state mission board look into the matter." There was a long pause where we could hear Dallas clearing his throat. "I told him he would have to deal with me if it was true." That was it. What did he mean by *my side of the story* and *if it was true*? Did he believe me or not?

"Well, I'm not sure what to make of that one, Abbey. At least he wants to hear your side of the story."

"*My* side, Susan? It means he's already heard theirs. It's like Nicholas Sayers said. Who's going to believe me over them? I can't go through this again. Why couldn't they all just stay in Guatemala and keep their version of that night with them?"

"Is that why you punished yourself by running until you had nothing left?"

Was that what I did? Was I punishing myself?

"Girl, you've got a lot of baggage to unpack. It's going to take a long time. Until then, give yourself some grace."

I wish my mind could lose baggage as easily as the airport did. Then I could just start over—again. That's what the new name and the new home were supposed to do. I made it through three years in the army without looking over my shoulder. Why did it suddenly hit me with the Ripley case? Why was everything coming to a boil now? Was it all about church? How much would Dallas need to hear? What would he think of me? Would it be like Aaron? *Face it, Abbey, you are damaged goods. Dallas deserves better.*

"Do you want to talk about it?" Susan asked, rubbing my weary shoulders.

"I thought I *was* talking. I guess that was all in my head." I leaned into her shoulder and let my only friend hold me for a while. She could speak her mind, but I always knew Susan loved me like a real sister. I could always count on her. She could even take it when I blew my top every now and then. "I don't know why I blocked him out, but I did. It seems like I'm always doing something wrong and pushing people away. I know I don't deserve a twentieth chance."

"He just wants the truth, Abbey. He needs to hear it." She ran her fingers through my hair. It felt good on my scalp. "How much of your story does Dallas know?"

"Nothing—other than what he heard last night."

Susan sat up and faced me. "Really? He doesn't know any of it? I just assumed…"

"I tried several times, but he always tells me, 'The past is the past. Leave it be.'"

"Wow." Susan scratched her head. "That's going to be an interesting discussion. You've said the worst. You might as well get it all out there now." She tried to smile encouragingly, but she was too much of an open book. "Look at me. I know everything, and I'm still here."

But I hadn't told Susan the worst yet, which is why my anxiety had been in orbit lately. I hadn't told a soul about my last night with Mr. Morales and why I joined the army. If I couldn't trust her with that, how would I ever tell Dallas? I sat up. "Do you think I unconsciously sabotage my relationships?"

"Is that counselor talk?"

"It's what Dr. Grissom wanted me to consider before our next appointment on Thursday."

"What do you think, Abbey?" Susan turned my face to hers and studied my eyes. "Do you?"

"If I do, it's not intentional." Was it a defense mechanism? A trick I taught myself so no one else could hurt me? If so, why did I let Aaron get past my defenses so quickly? I went six years without a date. It's not like the guys in the army or from East Precinct didn't try. I was able to be friends without any expectations. So, why Aaron and now Dallas? They were nothing alike, except good-looking. Was I that shallow? Unlike Aaron, Dallas was kind and patient. He'd never tried any physical advances. Was I not worthy of physical advances from Dallas? Is that what I wanted? Is that what I feared? My mind was all over the place. "Do you feel like I push you away, Susan?"

"You did when you thought I liked Dallas." We both laughed.

"I'm messed up, aren't I?" I wiped my eyes.

She pulled me in for a hug. "Aren't we all? That's what's so wonderful about Jesus and His grace. He loves us in spite of ourselves."

It sounded nice, but how could Jesus love me if I couldn't love myself. "I wish it was true."

"It is."

For Susan, faith was easy. She repeated that saying so often. What was it? *God said it. I believe it. I believe it 'cause He said it.* I looked away and stared at the blank wall. "I can't believe as easily as you do, Susan."

"It's true. You don't have to believe me. Believe Jesus."

"I think I trust you more." I could see her, read into her non-verbal cues. The only thing I knew about Jesus my father taught me. Half of that I didn't want to believe—to believe it meant believing my father. "It's too hard to believe in something I can't see, Susan."

"You don't have to believe in gravity to make it true." That actually made sense. I couldn't see gravity, but I could notice its effect on other things. Susan picked up a pillow and put it over my head. She let go. The pillow bounced off my head and onto the floor. "Give yourself some grace. Call him tonight. You're making it far worse by waiting."

How could it get any worse? My phone buzzed. "It's Dallas. How do you do that?"

She shrugged her shoulders.

I got up and walked to her den. "Hello."

"Are you okay? Why aren't you answering my calls?"

"Sorry. Sometimes it's easier to ignore problems than deal with them." That was an honest reply. Maybe I could do this.

"Seriously, I'm worried about you. I know you well enough to believe you have a different story. I need to hear it from you."

"It's not a very pretty story, Dallas."

"I'm sure it isn't. We can't change the past. But we do have to own it and embrace it if we're ever going to get past it."

"You told me to leave the past in the past."

"Well, now it's the present. Now, we must deal with it if we want to move forward." He paused to let that sink in. Was he saying he was on my side? "By the way, the cookies were delicious. How did you know Raspberry Cheesecake was my favorite kind?"

I rushed into the kitchen. "The cookies. I'm so glad you like them." I gave Susan a dirty look, and she gave a contorted facial apology. I glared at her. "Okay, Dallas. Ask whatever you want, and I'll give you the most honest answer I can."

"Did your parents kick you out of the house when you were fourteen?"

Okay. So, he's going to start with the easy questions first. "Yes. My father said I was dead to him."

"Why did they do that?"

So much for the easy questions. "Because my father thought I was dressing provocatively and trying to seduce one of the visiting youth ministers." I took a deep breath and swallowed back the vomit.

"Was that youth minister Pastor Sayers?"

How should I answer that? If I just said, "Yes," did that mean I was saying I tried to seduce him? Or would I just be confirming he was the one the story was built around? "I was fourteen years old when a new youth group came to our house to help us in our ministry. Their leader, Nick Sayers, asked me if I could show him one of the small chapels near our house. I didn't see anything wrong with it at the time. We walked two miles to the site. I remember, it was unusually cold that night, and I wasn't dressed for cold weather.

"He said he had something that would warm me up. I thought he was talking about coffee, but when I took a drink, it was cold with a harsh, yet sweet taste. He urged me to take another drink, and then another. He said it would help me relax. I felt woozy when he began to touch my breasts through my shirt. I backed away but stumbled. He helped me to a pew, and I sat down. Before I knew it, he was on top of me, and he had torn my shirt and my bra." I paused. I could feel the thumping of my heart. It was hard to get a breath. Dallas listened quietly. "He raped me."

"I'm so sorry, Abbey. I know this is hard, but I need to hear it all."

Susan leaned around the corner and mouthed, "Are you okay?" I nodded.

"How did everything get misinterpreted?"

Misinterpreted? "Are you asking how he convinced my parents that I came on to him and tried to seduce him?" My voice had an edge to it, and I didn't care to hide it. I felt like I was going through the judgment all over again. "He left me there in that chapel, half drunk, half naked. He went straight to my father and played the part of the pious leader concerned for his purity and reputation. He destroyed my life."

"Relax. I'm not accusing you of anything, Abbey."

"Easier said than done. You don't know what it's like to be thrown out like trash, treated like an animal, and to live with things you had to do to survive another day." I was hyperventilating. My heart was pounding. The room was spinning out of...

Chapter Twenty-eight

Wednesday, October 1, 6:05 AM—Ripley home

I woke to the smell of bacon.

"You gave us a scare."

I rubbed my eyes. "Where am I?"

"You're still at our house, Abbey." It was the voice of Hannah, Susan's fifteen-year-old daughter. "You scared us." She leaned over me and felt my forehead with the back of her hand. Like mother like daughter. "What's happening to you, Abbey?"

"I'm going through a bit of a bumpy period, Hannah. I'll get through it. I always do."

"I've never seen my mom so scared before."

"Yeah, I'm sorry about that." I gave her a quick hug and said, "Okay, now get out of here so I can get dressed." Someone changed my clothes last night and put me in a long T-shirt. I assumed it was Susan. Just as I pulled my pants up and fastened them, I heard a knock at the door. "Come in."

The door opened and Susan walked in, all dressed up. She had a pair of black high heel shoes in her hands. She sat on a small bench to put them on and asked, "How are you feeling this morning?"

"Okay. You look nice. What's the occasion?"

"I have a video conference at seven." She looked down at her outfit. "I know they can't see everything, but I need to look professional."

"You do."

"I'm concerned, Abbey."

"I know. That hasn't happened to me since I was a teenager. The stress of it all is really getting to me."

"You're welcome to stay here as long as you need to. Hannah can sleep with me."

"I appreciate it. Did Sam call last night?" I looked around for my phone.

"No. Was he supposed to?" Susan asked as she fastened one shoe.

"The last thing he said to me was to stay here until I heard from him." No missed calls.

"Breakfast is on the table. You can eat with us, or you can grab something later." Susan left and shut the door behind her.

Why didn't Sam call? Where were they with the case of Nicholas Sayers? What would Lieutenant Stallings do when he heard about my mistake. *Don't go there, Abbey.* I could feel the paranoia building. My phone rang, and I jumped. "Sam?"

"Where are you?" he asked.

"I'm still at Susan's. You told me to stay here."

"Good. We need to talk. Are you somewhere you can speak privately?" There was a sense of nervousness in his voice.

"Yes. I'm in Hannah's room, and the door is shut. What's going on, Sam? You're making me nervous."

"Does your boyfriend know about Pastor Sayers?" Did he want to know if Dallas knew he was dead, or did he mean the rape? "Was he with you the night you confronted the pastor?"

"Yes. I went to the fundraiser with Dallas. I'm sure he watched the whole altercation I had with Sayers."

"How did he react?" Sam was measuring his words. It was his investigative tactic. I'd seen him use it many times during interrogations.

"Get to the point, Sam. What are you really wanting to know?" I was growing even more paranoid.

"Would he have reacted in violence?"

"Whoa, Sam. Are you asking me if Dallas killed Sayers?" Where was this coming from?

"We have a witness that puts his car on the street in front of Pastor Sayers' house during the time of the murder. Agent Carmichael is already running with the lead. And Abbey, she's spoken with the captain."

Why would Dallas go to Sayers' house? Is Agent Carmichael running with him as a person of interest? I thought things couldn't get any worse. I was wrong. My hands shook. I began to hyperventilate.

"Could Dallas have done this?"

"There's no way, Sam."

"I know you don't want to go there, Abbey, but he had a motive, the opportunity, and certainly the means to do it." I wanted to scream, but I couldn't breathe. "He heard you accuse the man of rape. His car was on the scene. All he needed was a knife."

Dallas knew Nicholas Sayers. If he did come to his door, the man would have let him in. I replayed Dallas's phone messages in my mind. He said Nicholas would have to deal with him if my accusations were true. Did he mean that in a physical way? "Sam, I can't believe Dallas could do anything like that? Besides, it was part of the cleansing. Same MO."

"Think about it, Abbey. Who broke that code in less than a minute?"

Dallas! It was too easy. How could he make that sudden leap to the Ten Commandments? Ten. The bodies all staged in the letter X. It was telling us all the time, there would be ten killings, one for each of the Ten Commandments. "Oh, Sam." The size of the men's footprints in blood. They were the same as Dallas's.

"It's worse, Abbey. Lieutenant Stallings wants to know where you were during the time of the murder."

"Me? Am I being accused too?"

"Not yet. But with the department's desire for total transparency, he wants to make sure you are ruled out with a solid alibi."

Sam paused. I guess he was waiting for a response from me.

My mind was racing. Scenarios were pouring through my thoughts. First Dallas. Now Sam was wondering if I was involved too.

"Abbey, where were you between five and six that morning?"

"I was running."

"Can you verify that?"

"Are we really doing this, Sam?"

"Listen, Kid. I don't think you're anything but a victim here, but we need to prove that."

"What ever happened to innocent until proven guilty?"

"Unfortunately, we're held to a higher standard. Work with me. I've got to clear you before I lose this case to the Feds. Is there any way to prove you were running during the time of the murder? What route did you take? Maybe we can get camera images of you on the path."

I thought about my run that day. It was easy enough to show I ran through town, but the stretch as I passed Woodmont Boulevard to Battery Lane and up Granny White were all impossible to prove. I described my route that morning. "There might be cameras at the beginning and the end of my run, but the longest section in the middle is improbable."

"That's not going to be helpful. In theory, Dallas could have met you around Woodmont Boulevard, taken you to the home of Pastor Sayers, and dropped you back somewhere on Granny White after you both killed him."

It was true. Fate was against me. Of all days to take a long run. There was enough circumstantial evidence to cast suspicion on Dallas and me as the murderers.

"Skylar is playing us. She is good at it."

"I thought about that. Explain to me how she manipulated your run time and Dallas's visit to the Sayers' home."

I couldn't. Skylar didn't make me run. She didn't make Dallas go to Nicholas Sayers' home. Now, Sayers was dead too.

I thought of the redhead in the black dress. "Sam, could you do me a favor?"

"Depends. I'll do what I can." His voice was growing tighter each time he spoke. It made me wonder what he was thinking.

"Can you see if Cumberland Bend has cameras in the hallway outside of the fellowship hall."

"You want to see if it caught your conversation?"

"That too. There was a redhead in a black dress cozying up to Nicholas Sayers right before I literally bumped into him. Maybe she wasn't a future victim of his. Maybe it was the other way around. Maybe that's how they're gaining access to the homes of the men, Sam." It was all coming together. "If they have cameras, could you see if they have a good image of her face?"

"I'll go there today. They're having a special prayer service."

I suddenly thought of Mark Ripley. "I appreciate it. I'm heading back to my apartment. I'll stay there until I hear something from you." I started to hang up, but quickly added, "I assume I'm off the case."

"Definitely off the case, Abbey. I'm trying to keep you from losing your job—or worse." The air hung heavily over me as Sam uttered those last words. There was a long silence—too long. Finally, Sam tried to cheer me up. "Don't worry, Abbey, I'll clear you and get you back on the case as soon as possible." It was a sweet effort, but the words convinced neither of us that anything was going to be okay.

Chapter Twenty-nine

Thursday, October 2, 1:43 PM—Harmony Apartments

I busied myself by copying all of the pertinent details from the files and ME's reports. I knew Sam would have to take the original files back to Homicide. I might be grounded from the official case, but I could help from my apartment while I waited upon the action taken by the department. I knew I was innocent, and I believed the same of Dallas. I knew any evidence against us was purely circumstantial. I would have to speak with Dallas face to face. I would let him explain his own innocence before making my own plea.

It didn't take long for Sam to figure out why I needed the video from the church. This may be the first big break in the case, visual evidence of a person of interest. Having a face gave Sam the possibility of putting a name to it. With a name, he could find an address. The address would lead to an interview. Maybe Sam could pull magic out of the proverbial hat.

The intercom buzzed. "Yes."

"Abbey, it's Dallas. Can we talk?" I was expecting him to come sometime. I buzzed him in and waited for the elevator to chime for my floor. As soon as I confirmed it was Dallas who got off on my floor, I left the apartment door open and went back to my notes.

"You're mad at me?"

"It really doesn't matter what I think, Dallas."

"Of course it matters." He took the chair opposite mine. "Tell me what I did wrong."

I couldn't stop myself from laughing. It was a nervous habit. I was lost. "Where do I begin?" I didn't mean to say that aloud. It was a question I was asking myself. How far back should I go? "Why were you outside of the home of Nicholas Sayers the morning he was killed?"

His face lost all color. "He's dead?"

"As if you didn't know." I was taking on the demeanor of the investigator not the girlfriend.

"I didn't, Abbey. You have to believe me."

"Do I?" I stopped transcribing the notes and looked dead into his eyes. Today, they were not a source of warmth or comfort. Today they were windows into his fear and confusion. "Why were you there? We already have a witness that puts you outside of his home in your car during the time frame of his death."

"I…I…" Of all the time I'd known him, this was the first time I'd caught him at a total loss of words. I waited. No respite from me. If Dallas couldn't answer my questions, the detectives would have a field day with him. "I went to confront him about the…incident."

"The rape, Dallas. Call it what it was." I was cold. The old walls slammed back in place. The only faith I had left was in myself, and that was weak. "Because you were there, and I was out jogging at the same time, we are being considered as persons of interest."

"Persons of interest. What does that mean, Abbey? Does that mean we're both suspects?"

I explained how the incident at the fundraiser and our two veiled threats threw suspicion upon us both. "Couple that with your car being parked outside his house inside that window of time, you are the best lead Sam has right now."

"Why me?" Dallas asked. "I never got out of the car."

"Can you prove that?" I asked.

"No, but…"

"Dallas, I can't prove that you didn't pick me up in the middle of my nearly two-hour run that morning."

"Why would I do that?" He was innocently oblivious. Oh, his naivete was his blessing and his curse.

"So I could have time to kill Nicholas Sayers and get back to my apartment."

"Did you kill him?" He misunderstood my efforts to show why Sam and the other detectives would have reason to question us.

"Of course not, but neither of us can prove our innocence." His body melted into the chair. He was beginning to understand our predicament. "Why did you feel the need to go to his house?"

"You left on such a strange note, Abbey. You looked so hurt and lost."

"And you thought you would come to my rescue?" Dallas and I had this discussion many times before. "I'm not a damsel in distress, and you're not my white knight. I'm an army cop turned detective. I can handle myself." He didn't know what to say. I could see the confusion in his eyes. I was being hard on him because it was a stupid thing to do. "Dallas, both of us made threatening comments to Nicholas Sayers in the presence of witnesses. It was my fight. Not yours."

"I thought we were in this together, Abbey." He reached for my hand, but I pulled it away.

"Well, you thought wrong." It stung him, and that was my intention. Right now, Dallas needed to distance himself from me. If he had any chance of proving his innocence, it had to be apart from me. The words left a bitter taste in my mouth. I thought he would take the push and leave, but he didn't. He surprised me.

"You have my help, whether or not you want it. I'm going nowhere."

"Even if you're not wanted?" My heart ached. "Even if I tell you you're making my case harder to defend?"

"Yes." He leaned over the tiny table and took my face in his hands. This time, I welcomed the touch. "I'm staying because I can see the pain in your eyes. Your family may have kicked you out, Abbey, but you're not alone anymore. One of these days, you're going to have to admit that some people are on your side. I'm one of them."

I did my best to remain stoic. It wasn't easy. His eyes and his touch were melting my walls of isolation and defense. "Dallas…"

The intercom buzzed. Who could that be? "Hello."

"Abbey, it's Sam. Let me up. You've got to see this." Sam was surprised to see Dallas, which made for an awkward exchange of pleasantries between them. I was afraid it might look like we were corroborating our stories. That's what I would have assumed. Sam didn't seem to care. He pulled a laptop from under his arm and set it on the table. Sam opened the file and played the video.

A redheaded woman in a black dress stood in the hallway alone. The clock ran for a minute with no change. She was waiting for someone. "Can you get an angle that shows her face?"

"Just wait. You'll see her face in a couple of minutes. Tell me if she looks familiar." He let the video run. Nicholas Sayers entered the hallway, and the girl made a beeline for him. She touched his chest and face. He smiled and laughed. Suddenly, I plowed into both, sending the girl crashing to the ground and Nicholas stumbling. She turned, and Sam froze the image. "Recognize her?"

I searched my memory. "Yes!" I snapped my fingers. "The girl who visited Skylar at NCDC." I found the picture and held it up facing Sam. "Penny Thatcher. I thought she was dead."

"Me too. What was she doing at the fundraiser?"

I remembered her house and the blood. "Sam, they staged her death and disappearance."

"It sure looks that way."

I smiled. Now, everything made sense. "My guess is Penny Thatcher was marking her next victim. Pastor Sayers."

"Who's Penny Thatcher?" Dallas asked.

I met Sam's gaze, and we both smiled. "She's a religious fanatic obsessed with the Old Testament Temple."

"And sacrifices," Sam added.

"So, we're off the hook?" Dallas asked.

"Let me remind you, Mr. Gatlin, that you have some explaining to do, yourself." Sam was staring at him. "Why were you parked outside of his home during the window of his death?" Dallas explained his reason for going and his desire to confront the man. "As sweet as that is, Mr. Gatlin, that's the dumbest thing I've ever heard." Sam shook his head.

Dallas's gaze went to the floor, his shoulders slumped. Hearing me say it was one thing. Hearing it from Sam's lips hit him hard.

"Even with this video, you're still under suspicion. Even if you can produce alibis for the other three murders, you could be considered a copycat." I started to say something, but Sam shot me a glance that said, *Don't you dare.*

He sat in the chair between us. "Mr. Gatlin."

"Please, call me Dallas."

"Right now, I'm acting as a homicide detective, Mr. Gatlin, and you are still at the top of my list of probable killers." Sam shook his head again. "If you hadn't solved the mystery of the letters so quickly, I would have brushed this off for heroic passion. You came to the defense of your girlfriend and thought better of it, so you left."

"So, if I was stumped about the markings, I'd be off of your list?"

"Pretty much." Sam turned to me. "You're definitely off this case. Sarge said for you to take a week without pay and stay close to home while we continue the investigation. You're looking at the possibility of serious consequences, Abbey. Now, I'll take the video to the office and show everyone, including the brass. That should give us time to sort things out. I'll share what I can, but it's purely off the record. Understand?" I nodded. "That FBI agent is fully engaged now that you might be connected. She's digging into you, Abbey. Who knows what she'll find—or worse, what she'll do with it."

He turned away from me. "And you, Mr. Gatlin, go home and pack enough clothes for a week and a half. I want you both in one place where I can keep an eye on you." Before either of us could object, Sam said, "If the killers keep to their ritualistic schedule, they'll strike sometime on the morning of Friday the tenth. This fancy apartment building of yours has cameras everywhere. There's no way you can sneak out without being captured on video. Use that to your advantage."

"What if they pause the killings to make us look guilty?" I asked.

"You already look guilty."

"I can't stay here with Abbey. It wouldn't be right."

"Would you rather be suspected for sleeping around or taken in for murder?" I could tell Sam thought it was an easy choice.

Dallas, in classic Christian style, said, "Neither, if I can help it."

"You can't. I could put you in holding for the week if you'd rather." Sam reiterated his instructions and insisted Dallas be back here by dinner time. This was going to be awkward. It would be hard enough if we were on good terms. Dallas came over to see if we could mend things. Now, we'd be thrust together in one small apartment with a boatload of stress piled on top.

"What are people going to think?" Dallas asked.

"I don't care," Sam said. "You may not think Abbey's career or life is worth it, but I do. Order in for everything. Make sure you're seen by cameras. Step out in the hall ever so often just for good measure."

"Sam, I need to be out there solving this case, especially now that we know Penny Thatcher is involved. Get me back on the case. The sooner the better."

"Give me your gun and badge. They'll want it anyway."

I brought them back from my bedroom and slapped them in Sam's hands. "You know Sarge will be angry I didn't give them directly to him."

"Oops." Sam shrugged his shoulders. "Give me the file too." He could see my face. "Hey, Kid, don't think of this as a suspension or a lockdown. Consider it time off for a romantic vacation." He winked and left.

Oh, great. That's the last thing Dallas needed to hear. I could tell he felt guilty enough about being here with me in my apartment. What would he think about staying the night—for a week?

Chapter Thirty

Thursday, October 2, 5:01 PM—Harmony Apartments

Dallas returned at four-thirty with three bags of groceries, two suitcases, his laptop, and a backpack of books. He barely spoke to me. After the food was put away and his things stashed in the corner of my apartment, he said, "I'll take the couch."

"It makes a bed," I said. "I have sheets, blankets, and extra pillows in the hall closet."

"How are we going to work this, Abbey?" He stood with his hands on his hips. He couldn't keep his feet in one place. "People are going to talk."

"Let them."

"That's easy for you…" He stopped. Good for him. What did he mean by that anyway? I waited for an explanation. "Belmont has a policy, and I could lose my job."

"Dallas, it's not like I'm going to post pictures on social media saying my boyfriend is spending the week with me because we're both suspected of murder."

"Are we still…?"

"I suppose that's up to you. The only reason I was being cold with you was to protect you from further suspicion, But that ship has sailed." I was unusually calm considering the position we were in. "It's just eight days. Let's make the best of it."

"I told my boss I was going to take a couple weeks off to work on my dissertation. My graduate student can teach the class if other professors would check in on her occasionally."

"Her? I didn't know you had a female graduate student." He nodded and sat on the couch. "How old is she?"

"I don't know. Does that matter?" He grabbed the remote and turned on the television. "Honestly, Abbey. You sound jealous." Was I? *I don't know that I'd call it jealous. Insecure might be a better word.* "I'm only interested in one person, and that's you."

"Ah." I plopped next to him on the couch and put my arms around his neck. "Kiss me, handsome."

"Do you think that's a good idea?"

"I did until you said that." I removed my arms from his neck and scooted to the other end of the couch. "You act like I have an infectious disease. If it bothers you that much, I'll take my laptop and go to my room." I got no protest from Dallas as I grabbed my notes and laptop. "This is going to be a long week," I mumbled under my breath.

I worked on the case. It was the only thing that gave me peace. At least I felt useful. Out there with Dallas I felt rejected and cheap. It was like he feared that I would jump his bones and steal his innocence. Either that or give him some terrible disease. Maybe he did believe Nicholas Sayers' version. How could he love me and at the same time want me to be in another room? It didn't make sense.

Back to work. Since the killers started with the tenth commandment and went to the fifth next, I wondered if they would go to one of the adjacent commandments or drop all the way to number two. I wrote probable patterns. "10, 5, 1, 9, 4, 2, 8, 3, 7, 6," which would make remembering the Sabbath Day next. That didn't seem right. Then I wrote, "10, 5, 1, 9, 6, 2, 8, 7, 3, 4." What would be next in that pattern? "You shall not kill." No murder. That was ironic. I wrote a final pattern. "10, 5, 1, 9, 2, 8, 3, 7, 4, 6." That meant they were cleansing idolators next.

In both the first and last patterns, they would end with murderers. Then it dawned on me. That was their endgame. If we failed to stop them before they killed nine violators, they would end with suicide—the grand finale. So it had to be one of those patterns. Ending with the Sabbath Day was anti-climactic. I detailed my theory so when Sam contacted me, I could argue my case. Next on their hit list was about idols. It had to be. I reached for my Bible, but it was in the other room. I didn't want to go out there with Dallas. I googled the Ten Commandments in a modern translation, the ESV. Exodus chapter 20. Commandment two was super long. Why was it so much longer than the others? *Get to the point man.* I remembered that Dallas read from a different book. It started with a D. What was it? I went back to Google and found another reference for the commandments. Deuteronomy chapter 5. Good grief. Commandment two was just as long there. I checked Images. There we go. These were short and concise. Just the way I like them. "Do not make any idols."

What would be a modern-day idol? Those Indian gods certainly qualified. Was I supposed to see who made them? But then another image came to my mind—a recent and modern idol. Country legend Dolly Parton. There was a new statue of her in front of the Ryman Auditorium. I searched for an article about the unveiling. I found more than I bargained for. I narrowed them down to the ones I needed and printed them. I looked at one picture that showed two young women on their hands and knees, kissing Dolly's bronze feet. It looked like they were bowing down to worship her. This had to be it. The date caught my eye, June 30, the same as the drone article I finally found. I searched through my notes to see the date on the Buxton story, June 23, just a week prior. Could Nashville publications be their source for victims?

I searched the internet for Zahir Khan. Unbelievable. There was an article on his award-winning garden. I knew I'd seen it before. It highlighted the statues and the ponds. Dated June 16. This was the breakthrough I was looking for! So far, every one of the murders had corresponded to a Nashville journal or newspaper from June of this year. Curious. I searched for the names of Nicholas Sayers and Joseph Abelard. There was a brief announcement for the fundraiser event, but it was dated in late July. Wait a minute. How would Skylar know Nicholas Sayers lied about me? Did that mean she knew about my other name and my time in Guatemala? If so, how much did she know? Did she know about Mr. Morales? About the videos?

There was a knock at my door. "Abbey?"

"Come in."

Dallas opened the bedroom door, and a wave of savory smells rolled over me. "I hope you're hungry. I made dinner as a sort of peace offering for my rude behavior. Forgive me."

"Forgive you? For what?" I'd been so focused on the case I forgot about our earlier conversation.

"For being so paranoid, worrying about everyone's opinion of me instead of being more concerned about you and your feelings."

My stomach growled. "Let's talk about it over dinner." It smelled amazing. He led me back to the kitchen. I sniggered. Dallas used every pot and pan I had. "What is it?" Everything was already on the table. He found one of my candles and used it as a centerpiece. The light flickered in the breeze from the overhead vent.

"Tuscan butter salmon, glazed mixed vegetables, and dinner rolls."

"Wow! You never told me you could cook."

"Reserve that opinion until after we've eaten." He held out my chair and seated me at the table. Then he sat on the opposite side, extended his hand to me, and offered a prayer of thanks. "Heavenly Father, You know all things. We trust You are in charge and are providing a way to stop these killers and prove our innocence. Thank You for this unexpected time together. Bless our food and bless our relationship. Amen."

If God was in charge, why did anyone get killed? Why would an all-powerful, all-knowing God allow anything bad to happen? I appreciated Dallas's faith, but those words stirred ill feelings about a god who never bothered to protect and save me. I tried to brush aside the bitterness and focus on my time with Dallas. I took my first bite of the salmon and was blown away with the flavor. "This is better than restaurant food."

"Thanks."

"No, Dallas, I really mean it. I've never tasted anything this good." Maybe being sequestered in my apartment was going to be better than I thought. With Dallas cooking like this, other meals delivered right to my door, and the internet at my fingertips to search for clues, I could embrace the time away from others and make the best of it. The time with Dallas could be telling for both of us.

Friday, October 3, 2:15 PM—Harmony Apartments

I leaned into Dallas as we watched a movie we both finally agreed on. His arm settled around my shoulders as I nestled in against him. It was going to be a wonderful afternoon.

"We interrupt your regularly scheduled program for this breaking news. A source close to the investigation into the murder of Pastor Nicholas Sayers has revealed the ritualistic killing is the fourth in a series of murders committed by a group the Metro Nashville Police Department is referring to as The Commandments Killers."

I sat up straight. My muscles tensed. "What? Who's calling it that? Where did they get this?"

"According to a spokesman for the Metro Police, Pastor Nicholas Sayers suffered a fatal wound to his throat. Our sources tell us two possible suspects include a Nashville Homicide Detective and a Belmont professor, as each threatened Pastor Sayers the night before at a fundraising event held at Cumberland Bend Baptist Church. Our source shared this video evidence of the two encounters." The church security videos played where Dallas and I issued words of warning to Nicholas Sayers. Although the images of our faces were slightly distorted, anyone close to either of us would know. It infuriated and embarrassed me. The Chief would blow a gasket. I didn't realize Dallas had put his finger on Nicholas's chest when he said Nicholas would answer to him. The reporter promised more details would follow in tonight's news broadcast.

Two isolated snippets. They didn't include any of my

accusations or Nicholas Sayer's comments. Penny Thatcher was nowhere in sight.

I grabbed my phone and called Sam. The moment he answered, I went off. "Who leaked the story to the news, Sam? How did they get the church security video? Did you hear? They not only described us as possible suspects, but they showed video clips of our threats, nothing else."

"Take a breath, Abbey." But I was too wound up and too angry to stop. After a several minute rant, I stopped.

"Are you through? Can I speak now?" Sam snapped. He'd heard enough. I didn't mean to take it all out on him, but I did. "We just saw it ourselves and are looking into it already. Someone from the church must have sent an edited copy of the video to the news. We'll find out who. I promise."

"Sam, The Commandments Killers? How do they know about the connection between the killings and the Ten Commandments?"

"We caught that too. That detail had to come from someone inside." Captain Harris was shouting so loud he drowned out Sam's voice. I could hear everything he said.

"We either have a leak in this department, and if that's the case, I promise you; I'll find it and plug it up. Or, we have the killer showing her hand here, and that would mean she's trying to settle a score with Detective Rhodes." Captain Harris shouted a few obscenities and slapped his hand on a table or desk. "Get that reporter on the phone and find out who leaked the story. Tidwell, you contact the church and see who they sent the video to. Pressure from both sides until somebody breaks. I want to know how this happened, and I want to know now!"

He shouted at Sergeant McNally, telling him to talk to me personally and make sure I understood department protocol and my restrictions until this case was solved. Within moments, a second call came in. It was Sarge. I disconnected from Sam and took the call. Sarge questioned me about the video and the leak. "Tidwell told me Dallas Gatlin is with you."

"Yes, sir."

"Not a wise decision, but it's water under the bridge. Seeing as you two are already together, stay put in that apartment. I don't care if we have an earthquake, a tornado, or a flood. Don't you dare leave for anything. This killer's playing you like a fiddle, Detective. And Rhodes, leave the case to us. If I catch you sticking your nose in any part of it, I'll cut it off myself, and then you'll be fired, possibly behind bars. Understand?"

"Yes, sir."

"If this has anything to do with Skylar Watson, we'll find her. If you don't watch out, she'll bait you into another stupid move. You two watch your backs and keep your hands clean. That broadcast puts the department in a bad light, and you may pay heavily for it. We'll do our best to clear you both, but don't do anything else stupid."

I wanted to object, but he was right. We played right into Skylar's trap. "Sergeant McNally, I know which commandment is going to be next."

"I don't want to hear it, Rhodes. Stay out! We already have two teams working on it and they have solid theories themselves. Hear this: You can't get involved, Rhodes."

"Just hear me out, Sergeant, please. I've worked it out and know the sequence. The next victim will be Sondra Jennings who made the bronze statue of Dolly Parton."

"Are you deaf or just stupid?"

"Sergeant, the next death corresponds to commandment two, not to make idols."

His breathing was labored. He was angry. He hung up.

I was just about to complain to Dallas when someone knocked at my door. "Who is it?"

"Detective Rhodes, it's Agent Carmichael. I need to ask you a few questions."

Was she running the case now? "Just a minute." I gave Dallas a look an apologetic look and opened the door.

"What can I do for you, Agent?"

She looked past me. "Interesting."

"Agent Carmichael, this is my friend, Dallas Gatlin." He stood and extended his hand to her. She just looked at it.

"This is convenient," she said taking out her notebook and scratching something inside. "The two very people I needed to see, all in one place."

"I know it looks bad, but my…" I stopped. I had to watch what I said, or Sam's head would roll on this too. "My boyfriend came over without asking if it was okay." Dallas raised one eyebrow when I called him my boyfriend. I'm sure he wondered what I was doing, but he kept silent. "Discovering that he was here already, the department thought it best if we stayed in one place. You know—water under the bridge and all."

She quietly scanned the apartment and pointed to the couch. "You mind, Detective?"

"Make yourself at home, Agent." We were playing a game of cat and mouse, and I knew which role was mine. "I'm an open book."

She laughed. "We'll see what language it's in."

"Oh, that's clever," Dallas said, smiling and nodding his head. Ever the English nerd. Seeing my response, he pursed his lips and took a seat at the table.

"I was going to inquire as to the nature of your relationship, but you've already cut to the chase. I appreciate that." I nodded. How was she going to play this? She sat next to me on the couch. "I don't want to insult your intelligence, Detective Rhodes, but you have a lot to learn." Okay, the first jab. Say nothing. "We, in the law community, live under a microscope. We are expected not only to know the law, but we are supposed to be examples of how it is lived out in our society." She waited for a response, but I merely nodded in affirmation.

"You stood in a public place with hundreds of witnesses and threatened a man who turned up dead the next day." She crossed her legs. I watched as the black fabric stretched against her legs.

"Not only that, Detective, but you have a personal history with the victim that gives you a logical motive to want him dead." She paused to look at Dallas who was taking it all in from the table. "By your own admission, no less."

"I admitted to wanting him as embarrassed as I was. Never did I say I wanted him dead."

"Uh huh." She scribbled a note in her little book.

"Get to the point, Agent Carmichael. I know it's early in the afternoon, but at your pace, I'll be asleep before you finish." Counterjab.

"They said you lacked patience." Parry. I relaxed and said nothing in response. The left side of her mouth curled up in a smile. "You remind me a lot of myself as a rookie." *Rookie?* Another jab. She'd done her homework. She smiled a full smile.

Was it a true smile, or was she taunting me? *Wait it out, Abbey. Don't fall for it.*

"Personally, I don't think either of you killed anyone, especially Pastor Sayers. You don't strike me as being that stupid." Agent Carmichael stood and walked over the window overlooking downtown Nashville. "Nice view."

"I appreciate that," I said, using her earlier words. "I would have to be a total idiot to kill him, especially after I made a veiled threat at his church."

Dallas was fidgeting in his chair. He wanted to come to my defense, and it was killing him to stay out of the banter. He got up and got a drink of water. "Want something to drink?"

We both shook our heads.

"I'm sure in this day and age, someone will have a picture or video to support your morning jog."

I was hoping so, but I didn't even know if they had time to look. "Then why are you here?"

"Due diligence, Detective. You two are the most obvious people in the case. The city would cry foul if we failed to investigate the possibility. Besides, I must rule you out before I can move forward." She scratched a few more notes in her book. Her language was odd. It lacked a natural flow. She was being cautious.

"How can we help?" I asked, now willing to play her game.

"Give me the precise route of your run and the times you passed each neighborhood." I did what she asked to the best of my ability. She pulled up a satellite image of the route. "You must be in excellent shape, Detective." I bowed my head in appreciation of the complement. She took an abrupt turn and asked me to describe, in great detail, the rape she'd heard me accuse Pastor Sayers of. "And you claim your parents threw you out of the home after that?"

"Yes. You were there when I said it to them." She was getting under my skin.

"I want to hear it again." She looked at Dallas. "To be honest, I want to gauge his reaction as well."

I watched as Dallas looked back and forth between Agent Carmichael and me. She turned her back on us and looked out over the city. I repeated the details of the rape, and then I asked, "Well, did I pass?"

"I'm not a polygraph, but I'm pretty similar in the accuracy." She scratched a few more notes. She turned and leaned back against the window, now facing us again. After asking a barrage of other questions, Agent Carmichael changed directions again and asked about the case. "What would be your next move as a detective?"

"I'm off the case and ordered to let it go." Was she baiting me? Of course. She was waiting for me to slip—waiting to destroy me.

"And if you were free to speak of it?" As a gesture of openness, Agent Carmichael put the little notebook in her vest pocket and put her pen in the windowsill.

"I would speak freely, of course, but I'm not free to do so." *Well played.*

"I know you're not a part of the case anymore," she began with a slight tilt of her head, "but I think your team is shooting blanks." She walked back to the couch and sat beside me. She looked directly into my eyes. I still couldn't make out the line between

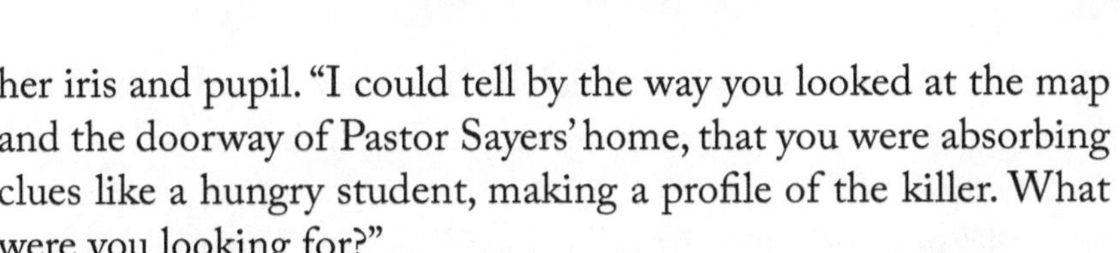

her iris and pupil. "I could tell by the way you looked at the map and the doorway of Pastor Sayers' home, that you were absorbing clues like a hungry student, making a profile of the killer. What were you looking for?"

Why not? "Okay. I can answer a direct question like that. I was looking for the presence of drywall dust behind the door and under the small table to indicate forced entry and a struggle."

"Why?"

"The crime scene didn't fit the pattern of Zahir's."

"Meaning?"

"Meaning that whoever came to the door was invited in and felt no need to burst through and subdue the pastor."

"Interesting."

"There you go with that word again," I said.

"Don't you find it interesting that the intruder subdued the pastor without a struggle?"

"Of course, I do. That's why I took note of it."

"Who might the pastor allow through his front door, not knowing she was a killer?"

"Interesting." It was a nice word. I know why she chose to use it. I never said the killer was a woman.

"What?"

"Agent Carmichael, you said, 'she.' Have you already determined the killer to be a female?" She shrugged her shoulders and poked out her lower lip. We bantered back and forth for a while before she turned to Dallas and said, "I understand you broke the code."

He looked at me, and I nodded. "It was a God thing."

"What does God have to do with it?" she asked. *Exactly.*

Dallas was ready to speak now. "Everything. They are using the Ten Commandments as a template after all." He said it in such a way that he made a dig of it being obvious to everyone but Agent Carmichael. I couldn't tell if he did it accidentally or intentionally.

"Okay. I'll bite. Why?"

"I'll leave the motives to you and Abbey. I'm just stating

the observable and obvious. Each victim has violated a particular commandment and is being singled out for punishment. The killer is playing God."

"I know this sounds off-subject," Agent Carmichael said, interrupting Dallas, "but I'm having a hard time imagining the two of you as a couple."

Ouch! "Okay, back to the case. If I were to speculate, I'd say they were going to kill a sculptor next, one whose works are being worshipped."

She pulled out her book and flipped back several pages. She returned to the window and retrieved her pen. "Your partner said, and I quote, 'They went to five after commandment ten. We believe they will either go after someone who broke commandment four, publicly denying the significance of the Sabbath Day, or someone who has committed murder recently, breaking commandment six.'"

"Those two theories make sense in a way, but they're flawed. The killer or killers have an endgame."

"Oh, really, and you've figured this out already?"

"Already? We have three dead people. I think we're behind the curve as it is."

"Okay, Detective Rhodes, spill it."

"Agent Carmichael, I have a viable theory and a specific person. All you have to do is watch Sondra Jennings and keep her safe on the tenth."

"That simple, is it?"

I explained my logic and what I believed to be their endgame of suicide. She addressed my history with Skylar Watson and wondered if I was making this case into some sort of personal vendetta against the young woman. I shrugged my shoulders. "Even if I am, that has no bearing on my prediction. If I'm wrong, you waste one night. If I'm right, you save a woman's life."

She scribbled something in her book. "It's a shame you made a careless mistake and, as such, have been removed from the case.

I would have enjoyed working with you, Detective." She thanked us for our time and let herself out.

The moment the door closed behind her, I let out a heavy sigh. "I said more than I should have. I've got to figure out how to let this go, or I'll be in an even deeper mess."

"That's probably for the best, Abbey." Dallas rubbed my back. He tried to cheer me up, but I wasn't having any of it.

I grabbed my laptop. "I'm sending the details of my theory to Sam. Maybe if he sees it, he'll reconsider."

"Abbey, you just said you were ordered to stay out of the case. The FBI agent heard your theory. Let her do something with it." He looked pleadingly at me. "Don't make things worse."

"Worse? How could they possibly get worse, Dallas? The whole city saw our threats and believes we may have something to do with the death of Nicholas Sayers. For all we know, they think *we're* The Commandment Killers."

"Abbey, 'God causes all things to work together for good to those who love…'"

"I don't want to hear it, Dallas. Is this good? Why is God letting these people die? How good is that?"

My phone rang. "What is it, Sam?"

"Oh, Abbey, I am so disappointed in you." It was a female's voice. "Why did it take you so long to figure out our simple code? Now, you're sitting back and letting others play our little game. That's not fair, and there are penalties for breaking my rules." It was Skylar! "I went to great lengths to design this for you. I thought you were a fighter like me, but you hide in the safety of your apartment while others do your work." Before I could respond, she added, "Don't try tracing the call. It's a burner, and I'll just throw it away when I'm done."

Dallas was listening over my shoulder. "How does she know all of that? Who's telling her what you're doing and what you're not?"

"I thought you would appreciate my generous gesture, but I haven't heard a single thank you."

"What gesture, Skylar? Killing people? How is that generous?"

"Pastor Sayers, duh!" Her voice changed from a sultry woman to a little teenage girl.

"Why did you choose him for commandment two?"

"Because he's a liar, Abbey. He turned your own family against you." I couldn't breathe. "The church needs integrity—more individuals with veracity."

"Ver—what?"

"Veracity. Look it up. Anyway, he deserved what we gave him."

"We? You and Penny Thatcher."

"So, you know about Penny. I suppose you know she killed Dr. Teague and Alex Carson for me."

I didn't know that until she said it, but I wasn't going to admit it. "How else could you have gotten the jump on them both? Besides, you never do your own dirty work."

"I don't like dirty hands. Now, back to Pastor Sayers. We killed him because he bore false witness and ruined your life." Reality crashed around me. How? "Yes, Abbey, I know all about poor little Hannah Leah Abelard and her time in Guatemala. Before you ask, I have those videos too." Dallas leaned back and gave a bewildered look.

"Work or home videos?" I tested her to see if she was bluffing or really knew about the shower videos. She gave a veiled response that answered the question without revealing details to anyone listening. I asked what she planned to do with them. She said they were simply for safe keeping. Only Susan and Sam knew about the shower videos, and I wanted to keep it that way. "Why are you doing this? What do you want from me?" I waited for her reply.

"I told you back in April. I'm the Yin to your Yang, the Moriarty to your Holmes. You hide in too many shadows, Abbey. I've gone to great lengths to pull the right team together. I'm here to make you great."

"Make me great? How?"

My question triggered something, and she screamed, "Stop lying around and solve the murders!"

Dallas said, "You're not supposed to get involved."

"I can't believe you're shacking up with your boyfriend. Maybe your father was right about you." That was dirty. I knew how she felt about men, especially fathers. "I was going to destroy the videos but maybe I should release them instead."

Dallas mouthed, "What videos, Abbey. What's she talking about?"

"Tell your boyfriend that's none of his business."

I started to respond, but a chill raced down my spine. Dallas didn't say it aloud. Oh, no. I looked up at the light. Why didn't I notice that before? I put my hand over the phone. "She's bugged us. She's been in my apartment."

"No, but I did have help. As you said, I don't do any of the dirty work myself, not even poor Dr. Teague. What's the fun in that?"

I'd covered the phone. She had another microphone. I grabbed a chair and reached for the ceiling light. It was out my reach. Dallas lifted me off the chair and got on it. He unscrewed the lamp cover and handed it down to me. The piece holding the glass in place was a hidden camera. I looked into it and said, "Goodbye, Skylar." I stomped on it and smashed the device. I covered the phone again. "She's been watching us, seeing everything we do and hearing everything we say."

"Of course I have." She heard that even though I crushed the bug. There were more. I hung up.

After calling Sergeant McNally about the phone call from Skylar and the bugs in my apartment, Dallas and I spent the rest of the afternoon searching everywhere for cameras. He found one in the kitchen, and I found one in my bedroom and another in the shower. When I found that one, I was suddenly and violently thrust back to Mr. Morales' house and the moment I discovered his cameras all over the bathroom.

Dallas found me in a fetal position on the shower floor. He

picked me up and carried me to my bedroom. I vaguely remember him laying me on the bed and pulling a blanket over me. I tried to pull out of the past, but I fell asleep.

Chapter Thirty-two

Saturday, October 4, 8:00 AM—Harmony Apartments

There was a knock at my apartment door. I scanned through the peephole. It was Jimmy from the lobby. I opened and thanked him for delivering the package.

"It came in at six this morning, but I thought I'd wait until a decent hour, Miss Rhodes." I started to shut the door as he turned, but he added, "It's a shame what they can say on the news these days. I know you didn't do it."

"Thanks, Jimmy." I handed him a tip and closed the door.

Dallas walked around the corner in my robe. I couldn't help but smile because of the length and the color. "You look cute."

He gave me a sarcastic smile and asked, "Who was that?"

"Jimmy from downstairs. He keeps an eye on the lobby, making sure none of the homeless try to come in." My apartment people may not let them in the building, but they treated them with dignity. That wasn't true in my neighborhood in Guatemala. Those first few weeks I was homeless, people kicked me, spit on me, soaked me with water, and called me all sorts of names. Dallas's voice pulled me out of the past.

"Security?"

"Of sorts," I said. "He brought up a package since he knows we're under house arrest."

"Oh, great! There goes my reputation. I've worked hard to build a name for myself…"

"I'm kidding, Dallas. I asked if he could bring it to me." Since the news played that video, Dallas's anxiety skyrocketed. To make matters worse, his university president called late last night to discuss the chatter at Belmont. "Calm down, Dallas. What was it you said about God making the best of the situation?"

"Fine. I know you may not believe that, but I do," he said. He stood there with his hands on his hips not realizing how ridiculous he looked.

"Then why am I the calm one?" If he only knew how I really felt.

He glanced at the box in my hands and said, "What is it? Are you sure it's not a bomb?"

"It's from Amazon, and I ordered it two nights ago."

"What is it?"

I looked at his legs and winked. "You want to see now, or would you rather get dressed first?" His face turned pink with embarrassment, and he ran to the bathroom to dress. I opened the box. Four night-vision trail cameras with video and still features. I grabbed the instructions from one of the camera boxes. It was something we used in the army to check up on people without alerting the brass or completing the necessary requisition paperwork.

"What are you doing with trail cams? Do you think someone is staking us out?" Dallas got a text on his phone and paused to reply.

I waited to answer until he looked up. "That's not why I got them, but it's not a bad idea. I asked Jimmy if anyone had been in my apartment the last couple of weeks. He checked the log and said I called the maintenance department May ninth and asked them to repair my ceiling light."

"May ninth? Are you sure it wasn't you?" Dallas asked.

"Yes. The scary thing is the call came from within the apartment, not from a cell phone."

"How do you know?"

"Whoever it was, she used my intercom to call it in. That's

why they didn't bother verifying the call." Skylar was smarter than I thought. "She's been spying on me for four and a half months."

"Aren't you afraid to sleep at night?" Dallas asked.

"I always bolt and chain the door when I come in. Anyone who's going to the trouble of breaking in while I'm here will be shot." I went back to the trail cams.

"What are those for?"

"Catching images of wild game in the dark."

"Don't patronize me, Abbey. What are you going to do with them?" He sat at the table with me. "I deserve the truth."

"I'm looking for a different kind of wild game." I wasn't going to lie to him, but I was hoping he would let it go. "What do you want for breakfast?" Maybe that would sidetrack him.

"I bought microwavable sausage, egg and cheese biscuits," he said, getting up and walking to the refrigerator. "Want one?"

"Sure. I'm going to flab out eating like this and not running every day."

"More to love," he said with his head in the freezer door.

I stopped looking at the cameras. *Let's test that theory.* "Do you mean you would love me if I was a plump couch potato?"

He turned and faced me. "Of course, but I know that will never happen."

I'd heard men say that to their girlfriends before, but they didn't really mean it. As soon as the girls gained weight, the men dumped them and went on to the next skinny girl. It was sad. "What makes you so sure?"

"Because you jog, work out in the gym, and take excellent care of yourself. Just as I'm worried about my reputation, you worry about your physical image."

My defenses fired up. "What does that mean?"

"It means you pride yourself on your looks and your shape, almost to a fault." He wrapped the biscuits in paper towels and turned on the microwave. Was he ignoring me? Dallas walked to the table and sat by me. "You're a complicated woman, Abbey. On one hand, you don't want me to love you for your looks, but on the other, you would be offended if I didn't." He put his hand up so I wouldn't interrupt him. "I love you for both, just in case you need to know. But I love your spirit and protective nature more."

Was that a compliment? My spirit? Did he mean soul or, like, spunky attitude? It didn't happen often, but I was speechless. "Thanks."

He immediately turned the tables on me. "What do you like about me?"

"The same." It was cheating, and I knew it.

"Unacceptable. Why did you come back the following Sunday? I know it wasn't for my preaching."

I thought for a moment. "Actually, that was a big part of it. You were—are—good looking, but you preached in a way that made sense and didn't condemn me. You were honest and unassuming." The microwave dinged. *Saved by the bell.*

We ate our breakfast sandwiches and drank some juice. He looked over at the box in the corner and remembered his question. "Really, Abbey, what are you going to do with the trail cams?"

"I'm hoping to catch an image of Skylar, Penny, and whoever else is killing people." I separated them in pairs and plugged their chargers into different outlets. I waited for the question. I could feel his eyes boring a hole in the back of my head. "I called in a favor and got the cell number and address for Sondra Jennings."

"You what!" Dallas clenched his teeth. "You have a direct order from your captain to stay out of the case. Abbey, you could lose your job."

"I've given a lot of thought and consideration to this, Dallas. I made a promise to protect members of this community. I know in my heart that Sondra Jennings is going to be the next victim of The Cleansing." He started to protest, but I continued and raised my voice a notch or two. "I've done everything I can to convince Sam and Sergeant McNally that they're wrong and Sondra is in danger. I even risked telling my plan to an agent who is watching everything I do. She probably ran right back to my superiors and told them."

"Can't you call your friend Lieutenant Daniels and let him do it?"

"I thought about that, but I would be putting him in the same position I am in, open to the same possible consequences."

"Why is that?"

"Her home is not in his precinct."

"What about calling that precinct's lieutenant?" Dallas was pushing me for another alternative, one that could accomplish both tasks: keeping us in the apartment as ordered and protecting the sculptor. Unfortunately, I'd run every scenario I could, and this was the only viable option.

"Any request I made to another officer would certainly set off a red flag and get back to Captain Harris. If I'm going to get in trouble, I might as well save her life first."

"What about calling her and having her go somewhere for a couple of days?"

"I already tried that. She's working on a bronze bust and is behind schedule. She said she can't afford to put it off for even a day." Dallas tried alternative after alternative, and I rebutted them all. I'd already had this argument in my head. "She agreed to have me stay in her home during that twenty-four-hour period and keep watch, but she wasn't moving." His eyes tightened and he glared at me. Dallas was sweet. He was trying to protect me *and* comply with orders. He was such a rule follower. I used to be, but my gut proved right too many times to sit by and ignore the truth.

"I don't like it, Abbey," he finally said with an air of defeat. "There has to be another way."

"Dallas, four people are dead already. They're going to kill the fifth one next Friday unless somebody stops them. No one else is willing. They don't believe my theory." I slumped in the chair. "They don't believe in me." I felt powerless and trapped. The only option I had left was to break my promise to Sam and Sarge. I had to protect her at any cost. I didn't like the thought of losing my life or my career, but I couldn't live with myself If I stood idly by and let her die. I'm sure Skylar had factored that in. She knew by now I was letting my instincts overcome my need to follow rules. Skylar knew me better than I knew myself.

"So, what's your plan?"

I explained the plan to cover all possible parking options with the trail cameras, hoping to get images of their vehicle and its license plate. Sondra already had Ring cameras installed at each door since her business was in her home and garage. Every death so far occurred before nine in the morning. If they kept to their MO, we should catch them that morning.

"Catch them? Are you going to try to arrest them all by yourself?" Dallas's demeanor changed. Now, he showed signs of anger and frustration.

"My first goal is to protect Sondra. If I can ID the people and get good solid images of them, I'll just scare them off. If they give me the opportunity, I will subdue and arrest them." I saw the flash in his eyes. "I'll call for back up immediately. But I need to be totally honest with you, Dallas. If they try to use force, I will respond accordingly."

"Meaning you are willing to shoot them?"

"Yes.'

"Thank God Sam took your gun."

"He took my Sig, but I have a Glock in my closet. Besides, if I have to shoot, I will wound them, just like I did Skylar. But if I need to take a life to save one, I will." I could see the fear in his body language. There was also a tinge of disgust.

"You know all life is precious, Abbey. God would not have us take the life of another."

"That's what I'm trying to stop."

"I meant you too."

A switch went off in my head, and I mistook his statement as a cry of hypocrisy. "What about all the times in the Bible where

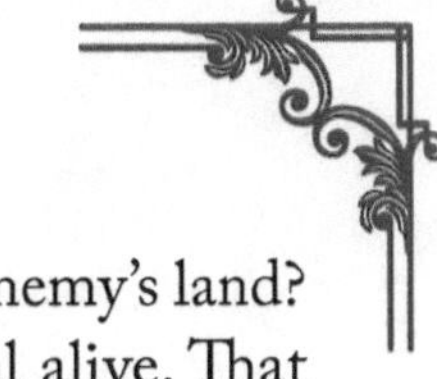

God commanded His children to kill everyone in an enemy's land? He told them not to leave a single person or animal alive. That included innocent children."

"God had a good reason to do that. He was protecting His chosen people."

"Well, I choose to protect Sondra Jennings against the enemy, and if means killing them to save her, so be it." I wasn't bloodthirsty. I wasn't even vengeful. It was a triggered response to church talk. Unfortunately, Dallas took the brunt of it. It seemed lately, I was doing that to him a lot. It used to be Susan, but she understood my PTSD. I wasn't sure how he would react. We sat in silence for at least ten minutes. It was awful.

"I'm sorry," I said. "You sounded so much like my father that I lashed out and couldn't stop myself."

"It's okay, Abbey. We all have our issues." He got up and went to the couch to study. "I truly worry about you, Abbey. I fear for your life, but I also fear for your soul."

Oh, no he didn't! I wanted to scream at him, to grab his Bible, and tear it to pieces. But I saw the genuine sadness in his eyes. It was the look of disappointment and fear my sister Miriam when she discovered I was pregnant from the rape. It was one of condemnation, and it didn't sit well. My biggest pet peeve was discovering that others felt I needed rescuing. I didn't. I suppose that's why I still had issues with God. When I needed Him, He wasn't there.

My doorbell buzzed. I looked through the peephole. It was the tech group from Metro, two hours late. They were here to get the bugs we found and scan for more. I let them and their equipment in and moved to the other room. I handed them all the devices we'd found so far and got out of the way for their more thorough search. Two and a half hours later they completed their scan and sweep of my apartment from one end to the other. Even though we'd found a handful, the team managed to locate five more devices. Skylar was seriously interested in my every move. In that case, she knew I bought trail cams. Would she warn the others? Maybe she was more concerned with my personal life. I secretly hoped she wasn't collecting anything embarrassing or compromising.

For some reason, I felt a deep need to talk with an unbiased person about my options. I couldn't speak with another cop. They would become a complicit accessory in my question and possible plan. Oddly enough, the person whose name kept popping up in my head was Susan's father, Charles. I had his number saved from the time Susan disappeared at the homeless sight. I went to my bedroom and closed the door.

"Hello."

"Dr. Pederman. This is Abbey. Do you have a minute to talk? I need some advice."

Chapter Thirty-three

Thursday, October 9, 11:55 PM—Harmony Apartments

I paced up and down the hallway of my apartment. Dallas slept soundly on the couch. My plans to stay with Sondra Jennings through the window of time the next victim was suspected to be killed all fell through. Dallas texted Sam my plans, which ticked me off to no end. I never realized how small my apartment was before that moment. I'd been climbing the walls like a caged animal.

Sam confiscated the trail cams and posted an officer on my floor supposedly to protect us. I knew better. He wanted to keep me in my cage. He did, however, agree to also post an officer across the street from Sondra's home. Sondra Jennings lived in the Creve Hall area of South Nashville. It was a heavily wooded area with very few options for parking. I tried to busy myself with details of the case, but getting any details was hard. Sam was already under great scrutiny from the department, and he risked everything to try and prove our innocence. I'd not heard back directly from Agent Carmichael since she left my apartment. Spence, the ultimate rule follower, hung up the moment I called.

I was stuck in my little apartment with only what the news stations would leak. So far, there were no reports of a strange vehicle near any of the crime scenes—except Dallas's. Thankfully, they verified he never left his car. I understand Agent Carmichael was also able to get an image of me during the time in question, which cleared me as well. I wanted to thank her personally, but I had no way to contact her. Still, I was on the outside looking in.

I stopped my pacing to study the image of Sondra, who was in her mid-forties and in great shape. She worked with her hands, lifting and molding heavy materials. Her skin was pale. I assessed that she spent most of her life indoors, working on her art. By my limited phone conversations with her, she seemed pleasant, a classic introvert.

I'd slept most of the afternoon and was well rested. Now, if I could just keep my mind from rehashing the last argument with Dallas, I would be okay. I was a mess.

I went back to my bedroom and sorted through my notes. I ran the details of all four murders in my head. Every victim, except Timothy Johnson who was discovered in the back yard with his drone, was killed inside the home. It suggested he was already outside when the killers came. His front door was still locked. All the others opened their front doors to greet the visitors. The murderers carried a sense of entitlement and purpose. Skylar's team entered through the main door. Skylar confirmed Penny Thatcher was involved, but Sarge said, "You have nothing to tie her to the crimes." Skylar's word was suspect with no evidence.

According to my theory, Skylar and Penny planned to kill Sondra Jennings for creating an idol of worship, commandment two. She designed and sculpted the new bronze statue of Dolly Parton in front of the Ryman Auditorium. I didn't believe Sondra Jennings meant the statue to be an idol of worship. She loved Dolly and appreciated all her accomplishments and altruistic gifts to society. But unless the posted officer stopped Skylar and company, my gut told me that Sondra would die this morning.

I glanced at the clock on my phone. Four-twenty AM. I assumed Sondra went to sleep several hours ago. I heard something in the other room. Dallas must've shifted on the couch. I thought being in close quarters with Dallas might bring us closer. Instead, it was driving a wedge between us. I wasn't sure our relationship would survive it.

I ran a mental scenario of my initial plans to be with Sondra. I stood with my back to the front door and imagined how they would enter and where they would go. Had they already scoped out her home? Did they know the garage served as her workshop? Certainly, they knew everything about her. Each crime scene indicated prior knowledge of the setting and how the body would be staged? The drone, the picture of Buxton and Son, the backyard temple, and the map of Guatemala. Nothing was random. Nothing left to chance.

"Coffee?"

I nearly jumped out of my skin. It was Dallas. "Yes, please."

"It's seven-twenty."

How did it get so late? Wasn't it four-twenty just five minutes ago?

"By the looks of things, you haven't slept a wink."

"No. I should be there." I looked away from him. "If my theory is correct, they will be there any minute." I followed Dallas into the kitchen.

"You still think she's in danger?" he asked as she put water in the coffee machine.

"Yes, I do. They think she created the statue of Dolly to be worshipped as an idol and needs to be purged from society. They'll come."

"I know you're mad at me for telling Sam."

"Yes. I don't need anyone protecting me. I can take care of myself."

He turned and folded his arms across his chest. "You think I did it to save you from the killers?"

"Of course, I do. You don't think I could handle the situation."

"Abbey, I did it to save you from yourself." I know my face expressed both my shock and anger. "You think you're the only one capable of solving the case and catching Skylar." I did. Was that wrong? "That's egotistical. You have a team of perfectly capable detectives working this case."

I stormed off, stomping all the way to my bedroom. *What nerve!*

"You're your own worst enemy!" he shouted at me. "If you leave this apartment and they strike again, you're going to continue to be a suspect."

"Is that more important that a person's life?" I slammed the bedroom door for emphasis. A doorbell chimed on my phone. It was her door cam link. I opened the app and watched. Sondra answered, "May I help you?"

"Yes, please. My van broke down, and my phone is dead. Could I please use yours to call a friend to come get me?" It was a petite, young female. Was she alone?

"Just a moment."

Sondra opened the door to let the girl in. "Oh, thank goodness. I really appreciate it." The girl made no effort to step in the house. I wished I could see Sondra's face. There was an awkward period of silence. "The phone?"

"Oh, sorry." Just as Sondra reached out with her phone, the door slammed wide open and five people rushed by the camera and into her house. Four of them were dressed in white robes. The young girl was dressed in jeans and a sweatshirt.

I minimized the app and called 9/11. I told the operator who I was, the address, and the situation. I said, "There's a patrol car on site." She contacted the dispatch who called the police. I could hear the struggle from the door cam, which was still activated. Sondra was fighting back. Someone yelled, "Get her."

"Stop!" I screamed into the phone. I could hear my voice on the app.

Sondra screamed, "No!"

I heard a young female voice shouting. Penny Thatcher took command of the operation. "My people, remove your shoes, for you're standing on holy ground. Sondra Jennings, I am Hadassah, and by my authority as priestess of the Most High God, you have been found guilty of creating idols..."

The camera timed out and cut off. I called Sam and frantically caught him up to speed.

"They got to her? How do you know this, Abbey?"

I explained I'd spoken with Sondra and had gotten the link to her door camera. "You said you had an officer across the street."

"We did. Abbey, you were ordered to stay clear of this case. Captain Harris is going to have your hide."

"Sam, that doesn't matter right now. Where's the officer on guard? He has to go help her now!"

Chapter Thirty-four

Captain Harris chewed me out. He used several expressions I hadn't heard since the army. He showed me my badge and firearm before he stuffed them in his desk drawer. "You are suspended until further notice. I know you think you did the right thing. You expect praise because you were right and could have saved her life, but you disobeyed a direct order. My order! I thought you would have been accustomed to following orders having served in the army, but I was wrong."

I started to object but bit my lip to keep it shut.

"Rhodes, it's high time you learned your place and where it falls in the chain of command. Get out of my office and don't come back until you hear from us! If I hear you've called Detective Tidwell, or anyone else related to this case, I'll have your head."

"Yes, sir." I slunk out of his office. I looked back just in time to notice Agent Carmichael entering it. I said goodbye to Sam and Spence before heading to my car. Now, I had to deal with Dallas. Sam had my email outlining the killer's pattern. Who knew if Skylar and Penny would keep to it now?

I sat in the parking lot and reviewed the door cam video. The video confirmed my suspicions. The young woman's voice belonged to Penny Thatcher, their leader and acting priestess. She entered last and wore an unusual breastplate over her robe. Unfortunately, Skylar was nowhere to be seen or heard.

Chapter Thirty-five

Friday, October 10, 1:12 PM—Harmony Apartments

I went through the door and slammed it behind me. Dallas sat at the table with two plates of food. "Sam said you'd be here a little while ago. I opted for sandwiches because I figured you might take the long way home."

"What else did Sam say?" How much did Dallas know?

"He said you could have saved her life." I nodded and sat at the table. "He also said you were suspended until further notice." I nodded again. I wanted to hear all that he was told before I offered anything new. "Abbey, I don't know what to say. I believe in rules and laws—I believe in order."

"I know I'm supposed to, but there are times when a life trumps all of that."

"I believe it's possible that both can coexist. I don't regret keeping you out of it—at least in person. I am, however, truly sorry she was killed."

I took a bite of the sandwich but couldn't taste anything. I washed it down with iced tea. "I appreciate what you were trying to do, Dallas. Honestly, I do." I paused. What was I trying to say? Was this the time to make decisions like this? "If we're going to be together, you're going to have to trust me."

"Trust you? I spent all morning wondering what I would do if you killed someone."

What did he mean by that? Would he give up on me? Would he leave?

"One of these days, it's going to come down to my life or someone else's. I'm prepared to make that choice."

He nodded. "For now, you're safe. I'll take that as a victory."

"Victory? A woman died unnecessarily last night. I could have and should have stopped that from happening." I took another sip of tea to wash the bread down. My mouth was so dry. "If I'd been suspended for taking action—for saving her life—I could have lived with that." I looked out the far window. "I don't know if I can live knowing I was so worried about losing my job that I let a woman be sacrificed in her own home." I looked across the table at him. "Dallas, I heard them threaten her. I can only imagine what she went through."

He reached for my hand. "We need to pray." I pulled it back

"No. You're going to have to pray by yourself. I don't know if I want to talk to a God who sits idly by and lets these kinds of things happen."

"Unfortunately, that's the price of free will." I wasn't sure what he meant by that, so I gave him a sarcastic smirk. I knew it was an attempt to explain God's lack of involvement and protection. "To me, it shows the depth of God's love, not the lack of it."

"Love? You call doing nothing love?" Now he was blowing smoke, just like every other preacher.

"Yes. Sometimes, letting go and doing nothing is harder than acting out your feelings." He covered my hand with his. This time I left it there. Was he talking about us or God?

"Elaborate."

"It was harder for you to stay here and rely on others."

"Of course, it was. She died because I did nothing! Don't you get that, Dallas?" I slipped my hand out and put it under my leg.

He looked deep into my eyes. "No, Abbey. You're wrong." I could feel the heat in my face. "She died because a group of evil people killed her. There's a huge difference." It hit me like a brick. "They acted, and that's their sin, not yours."

"Okay. Then why did God let them act that way? Why did

He give me the knowledge of the attack but not the ability to stop it?"

"Just as you made a choice to obey orders…"

"That choice was made for me, thanks to you." My look was hard. The walls were rising.

"You still chose to obey. I know you well enough to believe you could have found a way to get around the person on guard here." He was right, so why didn't I? "Something deep inside of you knew that disobeying a direct order would have jeopardized more than just one life."

"Don't ever say *just* one life. Every life matters." He nodded. "I told Sondra I would protect her. They won because I did nothing."

Dallas leaned into the table. "They haven't won, Abbey, and because you chose to obey an order, you're still in the game as you so aptly put it." I leaned back. I was still in it. The door cam footage proved it wasn't us. If I played my cards right, I might be reinstated and at least have an opportunity to help with the strategy. "Stop pouting and focus on the next victim. If not, Skylar will win."

I smiled. "Did you rehearse that, or was it off the cuff?"

He smiled back. "I may have run it through my head a few times this morning, just in case."

I took his hand in mine. "Thanks. I needed that."

"I know, without a doubt, someone is going to live because you stopped the killers." He took a deep breath, looked into my eyes, and said, "I know this has to be love because I'm so impressed and frustrated with you at the same time. I don't think I could love you any more than I do right now." He stood and leaned over the small table. Dallas kissed me. It was the best kiss I'd ever had.

I know I blushed because I wasn't expecting such a display of affection from him. We'd been stuck in this apartment since last Sunday, and this was the first time he even tried to kiss me. "I love you too, Dallas." I paused, wondering if I should say it or not. Oh, well. "I don't love myself very much right now."

"Why not?" He sat back down and put his hand over mine

again. "You're strong, fearless, protective—why, you're the knight in shining armor."

If he only knew the whole truth. "My armor is pretty rusted out. Nothing shiny about it."

"Abbey. You captured images of the real killers."

"Everyone but Skylar." I had Skylar's confession that she was orchestrating the whole thing, but it was my word against hers. She was much smarter than I was. She made that confession audibly, not in any written form. Skylar continued to leave no evidence of her involvement. Just as she had done with her father and youth minister, Skylar killed through Penny and her followers, always keeping her own hands clean. In her mind, that made her innocent. This was still just a game of cat and mouse to her.

Someone knocked on my door. "Are you expecting anyone?" Dallas asked.

"No." I started to get up, but Dallas motioned me to stay put. I didn't argue.

"Let me get it." He got up and looked through the peephole. "It's Mrs. Abelard—your mom."

"That's not funny," I said. He opened the door.

My mother looked at Dallas and gave visible signs of surprise. She didn't expect a man to answer. "Oh, I'm terribly sorry. I thought this was Hannah Abelard's apartment." She shook her head. "I think she goes by Abbey Rhodes now."

Dallas threw the door open wide. "This is the right apartment. Won't you come in?"

She stammered. "I didn't realize she was living with a man."

Of course, she just assumes my guilt. "I'm right here. You can say what you want and leave." I was in no mood for this, but I was curious to hear what she had to say. I could justify Dallas's presence, but I didn't feel the need, especially to her.

Unfortunately, he did. "I don't live here, ma'am. We've been sequestered because of the case and our supposed connection to the death of Pastor Sayers."

"We too have been asked to stay put." She looked around him and noticed the bedding on the couch.

"Then why are you here?" I sounded cold, but I didn't care.

"May I sit down so we can talk, Hannah?"

"Hannah Leah Abelard is dead."

"Abbey!" Dallas shot me a glance and said, "Mrs. Abelard, please sit on the couch." He picked up his folded sheets and blanket and put them in the corner of the room.

She sat on the couch, and I took a chair in front of her. "I'm tired."

She leaned forward and reached for my cheek. I avoided her touch by leaning back. "Will you ever forgive me?" she asked.

"I didn't know you felt the need." I wasn't going to make this easy. I could see in Dallas's eyes that he was praying for reconciliation. I was a long way from that. They didn't just hurt me or offend me. They tossed me out to sink or swim in the dark corners of Guatemala City. They left me to survive on my own at the age of fourteen. "Are you going to ask?"

"Of course, dear. Will you forgive us?"

"Us? He'll have to ask that himself." I leaned in and studied her dark brown eyes. "Why should I forgive you?"

"The Good Lord says if we confess our sins…"

"He is faithful and just and will forgive us our sins." She seemed shocked that I remembered that verse. "You'll have to take that part up with Him. I'm asking why *I* should forgive *you*?"

Her body slumped. "He said I shouldn't bother."

"So, my father sent you here. Are you preparing the way for the Lord?"

"How dare you!" She was up and on her feet. "I thought I might wave an olive branch and try to make peace between the two of you." She started for the door. "You're just like him you know. You're both stubborn as oxen."

I was nothing like the man. I didn't make it my life's work to convince everyone of their sin. "Well, I've survived without you for quite a while. I think I can make it in my new life." She reached for the door. "We haven't slept together if that's what you're thinking. He hasn't forced himself on me like your dear friend Nicholas did."

My mother turned and her face tightened. I could tell she wanted to say something ugly, but she didn't. She took a deep breath and let it out slowly. "If we knew he had raped you, we would have sent them home."

I took two steps toward her. I wanted to see her eyes. When I could tell she was uncomfortable from my proximity to her face, I said, "You did know. You all knew, and I'm sure Miriam told you about the abortion too." It was out before I knew it. Her jaw dropped at the news. I felt the images flooding my memory. I ran to my room and locked the door. I didn't want to look at Dallas's face. I couldn't face the shame anymore.

Chapter Thirty-six

Friday, October 10, 5:45 PM—Harmony Apartments

I woke up and glanced at my clock. I pushed myself out of bed, grabbed a change of clothes, and went to the bathroom. I looked in the mirror. Who was this hollow woman facing me? I got the shower water as hot as I could tolerate and stepped in. I just stood there for the longest time.

"Abbey, are you okay?"

"No."

"Do you need help?"

"Not the kind you can give me, Dallas. I'm going to soak my muscles for a bit and then wash up. I'll be out in a little while." My body missed our morning runs.

"Okay. Call if I can help."

I still felt like he was trying to rescue me. It was sweet, but I wasn't in the mood, so I said something spiteful to make him feel uncomfortable too. "Are you wanting to come in here?"

"No. I didn't mean it that way. I'm sorry. I'll leave you alone."

How did I get here? How did Skylar beat me at every turn? Without Dallas, I'd probably still be searching for the connection between the letters. Sondra Jennings died, but we have a good chance at stopping the next murder. When I got out, I vowed to tell him so. I suddenly felt really stupid. It reminded me of the time Sam and Skylar matched wits by quoting that old book. I had no clue what they were even talking about, but he was able to connect with Skyler, understand her on a different level. I was more of a chase an idea and rush into action kind of person. Because of my bull-headed pride, I nearly messed up and barely missed being tossed permanently out of the game.

I finished my shower, put on my clothes, and decided against makeup. Dallas was sitting at the table working on his laptop. "I'm surprised you're still here."

"Sam told me to stay put." Well, that didn't sound voluntary. He sounded distant. Maybe I embarrassed him.

"Why does Sam care?"

"He thinks you made us both targets by nearly interrupting their ordered sequence." I carefully eased onto the couch and laid my head on the arm. I could feel the tension headache coming on. "Not that I'm complaining," Dallas said with a smile.

I needed that smile. Maybe I still had a chance to rectify my mistakes. "Thanks, I guess."

He looked up from his laptop. "You know you have a habit of saying things most of us think but are too afraid to say."

"I'm really tired, Dallas. Speak plainly so this stupid girl can understand."

"Stupid? You must be kidding me." He got up and moved to the other end of the couch. He lifted my feet and sat down, placing my legs on his lap. "You're the only one who had it right. Two teams of detectives and an FBI consultant went in different directions. No one believed you, but you pressed on anyway."

"Why would anyone believe in me?" I was sinking deep into an emotional pit. It was a valid question. I barely graduated from high school, and I did just well enough on the MP exam to qualify. I was no genius, and Skylar was proving it at every turn.

"I believe in you." He rubbed my feet. It felt so good.

"The only clues they left us each time were footprints."

"I remember you saying something about that. What's the significance?"

"I thought they did it to taunt us. When Penny entered the home…"

"Penny?"

"Their leader. Anyway, when she entered the home, she told her followers to remove their shoes because they were on holy ground."

"Moses."

"What's Moses have to do with it?"

"When Moses encountered God in the burning bush, God commanded him to remove his sandals because he was standing on holy ground." Dallas paused for a moment. "Moses stood on holy ground because God's presence filled the place. Does she think she's God, or does she think she brings the presence of God with her?"

"I don't know about Penny, but Skylar probably thinks she's the god. Even this cleansing—she decided who deserves to die. She sent out her executioners to kill the guilty party. Skylar knows how I feel about God and church, and she's using the Ten Commandments to create serial killers."

"I'm not following you." Dallas rubbed my ankles. Wow. That felt incredible.

Focus! "She not only proved she was ahead of my every step, but she forced me to search the Bible if I want to beat her. Either way, I lose."

His eyes brightened, and a sly smile crossed his lips. "No, Abbey. You don't lose." He put his hand on my calf. "She's like Satan. He thought manipulating people into crucifying Jesus would gain him victory. God did the exact opposite. He planned the crucifixion and resurrection to defeat Satan, releasing the world from his control and power."

"There you go, getting all scholarly on me."

"It's basic really. God's word is your power." His face was shining. This was the kind of thing Dallas excelled at.

"You think by forcing me to read the Bible, Skylar is going to lose?" I had my doubts.

"I do. She already has in a sense. You knew they were going after Sondra Jennings."

"But I also lost. I'm suspended, and Sondra's dead." Dallas had both hands on my calves, massaging out the knots. It felt good. Too good. I was beginning to think about things I shouldn't. I couldn't focus on Skylar or the case. "I think you better stop, Dallas."

"Stop what?"

"Touching me."

"Oh, sorry. I didn't mean to hurt you. I just thought I could help ease the pain."

"You did. That's not why I need you to stop." I could feel the heat in my face—and other parts of my body—and it wasn't from anger.

His eyes widened and he immediately put his hands on the couch. "I didn't…" He lifted my legs so he could get up.

"Don't get up. Please. I want you here. I just think we better cool off—stop the massage." Where was I with Skylar? "Explain why you think the Bible is her Achilles heel?

Dallas put his hands under his legs. "Interesting metaphor." Whatever that meant. "She's using Penny Thatcher who, in turn, is using Deuteronomy as a script. How do you think Penny will respond to being caught on camera? She'll take it as a failure—not to herself, but to God. She's a believer."

"You think Penny Thatcher is a Christian?" I couldn't possibly make that leap. She was a cold-hearted killer.

"When I say she's a believer, I mean she truly believes she's doing the righteous thing. You'd be surprised what it says before and after the Ten Commandments in the book of Deuteronomy."

"Show me." For the next two hours, we sat side by side on the couch. I listened as Dallas explained the literal and figurative interpretations of the passages. He showed me how he believed it was meant to be. Then he told me how he thought Penny was seeing it. I was blown away. Which reminded me of something Dallas said earlier.

"Dallas, you called me a knight in shining armor." He nodded. "Well, I think you deserve all the credit. Without you breaking the

code for me, we would still be trying to figure out motive. You're saving the next person's life as much as I am."

He leaned into my shoulder. "We make a great team."

"Yes. We do." I ran my fingers through his hair. I was really lucky to have him in my life. He'd seen my worst, and he was still here. "Sorry about my mom. I saw your disappointment."

"I'm not going to lie. I was hoping you would forgive her and start afresh. I was more concerned for you than I was disappointed." He paused. I could tell he was thinking how to word the next thing he said. "I never knew what you suffered. You truly are a survivor."

"My past is dark, and I'm not proud of it. I did what I had to do to survive, and the moment I was old enough to join the army and leave Guatemala, I did."

"I've been thinking about what Sam said." It was like he didn't hear what I was trying to say about my life in Guatemala. "If you ruin Skylar's sacrifice and she decides to take it out on us, we'll help transition her from Moriarty to Voldemort."

"What's the difference?" I didn't understand all these book analogies. I didn't read for pleasure. My reading always had a purpose.

"I think she expected to outsmart you at every step. She hasn't. Now, she's out to destroy you, and anyone close to you is fair game."

That's what I feared. "I've been wondering what she'll do next. I think if Penny believes she's doing the right thing, she won't stop. I have to call Sam."

"You can't," Dallas said. "Don't push it. They'll come around soon enough."

"Okay." I smiled.

"Don't do it, Abbey."

"I tend to obey the letter of the command." That was following the law. Right? I called Susan. "Got a minute?"

"Give me a second to finish this email." A few seconds later, she said, "What's going on?"

I told Susan about the case, our sequestered situation, and the murder of Sondra Jennings. Susan asked a few personal questions about the situation with Dallas staying at my apartment, to which I gave yes and no responses. Dallas was staring right at me. I explained my situation at the department and the command I had to make no contact and to let the case go. I also explained Skylar's anger, disappointment, and threat to release the videos. Then, I told her Sam and Dallas's opinion of Skylar's response to her team being caught on video. "Susan, I need a huge favor."

"Anything, Abbey. You know you can count on me." There she was, the perky cheerleader, willing to do anything she could to help.

"I need you and the kids to go to your parents' house until this thing settles down. Skylar may come after you."

"Oh, Abbey. Do you really think so?" The peppy voice gave way to a somber whisper.

I'm sure Susan flashed back to the homeless camp and how close she came to death. In a way, I hoped she would be frightened enough to do what I asked. "Please take the kids and go to your mom and dad's house. Maybe all five of you should go to a hotel for a while."

"I don't know if my dad will leave his home, but if you think it's necessary, Hannah, Danny, and I will pack right now."

Chapter Thirty-seven

Friday, October 10, 9:01 PM—Harmony Apartments

I went into the kitchen to get some cold water from the fridge. Dallas was sitting at the table, watching a video. I glanced over and realized it was of a naked woman. "Dallas! Are you watching porn?" I couldn't believe it. Of all people, Dallas.

"You tell me, Abbey." He turned and held the laptop so I could see the screen. I dropped the glass, and it shattered on the tile floor. "What is this?"

"Turn that off!"

"When did you make this?" he asked. "You look young. Who's holding the camera?" He held the laptop to my face.

I snatched his computer and threw it across the room and into a far wall. "I didn't know he was filming my shower," I said, desperately trying to avoid another episode of PTSD.

"He who?" Dallas's voice was judgmental. It sounded like my father. "Who was in your bathroom filming you?"

I backed up and stepped on a sliver of glass. I immediately hobbled away and stepped on another piece with the same foot. I screamed and fell to the floor. Something pierced my side. I screamed from pain and embarrassment. A heavy thud landed against my door, then another. The front door broke and swung wide open. Sam entered with his gun drawn. "Police. Down on your knees. Now!"

Dallas dropped to his knees and said, "It's me, Sam. Don't shoot."

Sam noticed the blood all around me and pounced on Dallas. Within seconds he had Dallas face down on the carpet with his hands cuffed behind his back. Sam came to my side. My right foot was a bloody mess. "What did he do?" Sam asked.

I couldn't answer. My body shook from the pain from the piece of glass in my side. "She dropped a glass and stepped on it," Dallas said, doing his best to explain what happened.

"Why would she drop a glass? What did you do to her?" Sam was in his protective-dad mode.

"The video," I said, my voice quivering. "Skylar sent him the shower video."

Suddenly, Dallas made the wrong assumption and screamed at Sam. "You took video of Abbey in the shower!" He rolled over and managed to get to his feet. "You perverted—"

"Shut up! Everybody, shut up!"

"I called for help." It was Aaron, peeking around the corner of my broken door.

A few seconds later, the building's night security pushed through the entrance, pointing their guns at Sam. "Security. Hands in the air where we can see them. The police are on their way."

"Reaching for my badge," Sam said, slowly moving his hand to his jacket pocket. "Sam Tidwell, Nashville Homicide Detective."

After a lot of explaining, Sam, Dallas, apartment security, and the police had things worked out. I was on a stretcher heading to the hospital with a slit in my side and two cuts in my right foot.

"Why are your even here, Sam?" Dallas demanded.

"I was trying to keep Abbey up to date on this case, not that it's any of your business," Sam snapped back at him before turning back to me. "I'll be there after we finish here, Abbey."

Sam and Dallas exchanged hateful glances as the paramedics wheeled me out of the apartment and onto the elevator.

Chapter Thirty-eight

Saturday, October 11, 5:26 AM—St. Thomas Midtown

I woke when a nurse opened the door and spoke to someone else in the hallway. I was groggy and in great pain. I scanned the room. Sam slept in a reclining chair. I looked around for Dallas, but he wasn't there.

Sam jumped at the sound of voices. He noticed I was awake and came to my side. "How're you feeling, Kid?"

"Rough. Where's Dallas?"

Sam shrugged his shoulders and looked at the IV with a tube running to my arm. "I tried to explain everything to him, but he wasn't in the mood for me telling him anything. He still thinks I had something to do with the video."

"That's why Skylar sent it to him. She's going to take everyone away, one at a time."

"You're not getting rid of me, Kid, no matter how hard you try."

He paused as a nurse entered the room and emptied the urine container. She wrote the measurements on a chart and checked the IV. "I need to change the bandage on your side. If you will step in the hall, Detective, I'll let you know when I'm done." Sam left the room. "You're lucky Detective Rhodes. Your rib kept the glass from damaging your vital organs."

"I don't feel lucky."

I'd lost everything in a matter of days. First it was my job. I was pushing Susan away trying to keep her safe. Now, Dallas thought I was involved in pornography. Worse than that, he thought Sam filmed me. If Dallas wasn't willing to come to the hospital to check on me, he must be infuriated and disappointed. How could I blame him? He believed I willingly made the videos and kept them.

"This may hurt a little." She pulled the tape holding the gauze. I winced as the skin stuck to the adhesive. She freed the last corner and wadded the bandage upon itself. "The doctor did a nice job. You may not even have a visible scar when this heals." She put a new bandage on my side and did the same with my foot.

"How long will I be in here?" I asked—not that I had anywhere to go.

"That's up to the doctor. He'll be around about one after his last surgery. You can count on staying the night for sure."

She left, and Sam came back in. "You okay?"

"No." I started crying, and I didn't care if he saw me. "Why is God letting all of this come back on me? Didn't I suffer enough as a child?"

"I don't know, Abbey. I honestly don't know." He put his hand on my forehead. "You know more about that God thing than I do, but I'm here now. You're not alone."

"I'm done, Sam. Skylar won."

"You can't seem to catch a break." He put his hands in his pockets, looked down at the floor, and said something shocking. "I should have put a bullet in her brain when I had the chance."

Did he still feel guilty about that moment? "No, Sam. That isn't on you."

"On the plus side, you'll be happy to know the footprints of four cases match one woman we have in custody. She's a piece of work. They all are."

"You caught one of them? How?"

"Routine traffic stop if you can believe that. She had her robe in the back seat of her car. The officer spotted blood and brought her in."

"So she was a part?"

"Yes, and she has a mouth on her."

"You're kidding. I thought they were religious."

"Must have been an act. She's called us all kinds of names."

"What do we know...?" I forgot momentarily about the order. "I'm sorry, Sam. I shouldn't be asking. I don't want you to get in trouble."

He waved me off. "I don't know what you said to Agent Carmichael, but she's been singing your praises to the brass. She made it clear you have the best eye for this case and we need you. Captain Harris rescinded his order, especially now that we have video evidence of the cult." He realized what he had said. "Well, we have video, and we still have you."

"There was an officer outside her home. How did they get past him?"

"He got called away for a domestic." Sam shrugged his shoulders. He knew how it sounded.

"Was her body staged in front of another statue?" Sam nodded. "With the Roman numeral II?" He confirmed my suspicions. "What now?"

"What's next is that you heal," a man's voice said with command. "You've done enough." Dallas stood in the door with a vase of flowers. "I thought you might need cheering up."

I looked at Sam. "Sarge and I discussed it last night and think it would be best if you get someone to stay with you when they let you out." Sam put up his hand. "Before you object, you *have* to heal, Abbey. And you'll need help."

My body tensed as a wave of pain crashed over me. It felt like a knife had been thrust into my side. "Hit the button, Abbey. You need the pain medicine to rest and heal." Dallas was obviously upset Sam was discussing police business while I needed rest.

"Not until I catch up. What's today?"

"The eleventh." Sam answered. Dallas put the flowers on my food tray and folded his arms over his chest.

"Okay. We have nine days to figure out where Penny is going next."

"You don't need to do anything." Dallas's voice boomed throughout the tiny room. He was angry with both of us.

I tried to ignore him. I remembered something the woman said before the door cam disengaged. "By the way, who's Hadassah? I just remembered Penny's voice on Sondra's video feed calling herself the priestess Hadassah."

"I don't know," Sam admitted.

"Biblically speaking," Dallas said, "Hadassah was the Hebrew name for Esther."

I suddenly felt groggy. I looked over and Dallas held my morphine button in his hand. "That's not fair." I fought to stay lucid. "Who was Esther?"

"She risked her life to save her people from genocide. She was the queen…"

It was the last thing I remember hearing.

Chapter Thirty-nine

Saturday, October 11, 10:25 AM—St. Thomas Midtown

I heard a familiar voice and struggled to open my eyes. Susan and her father sat on either side of my bed. "Hey there, sleepyhead." Susan tried to put cheer in her voice for my benefit.

"What time is it?"

He looked at his watch. "Ten twenty-five."

"Where's Dallas?"

"He left right before we got here," Dr. Pederman said. "Sam said Dallas was exhausted and went home to get some rest."

"I'm thirsty." Susan held up a cup and guided the straw to my lips. "Thanks."

"Sweety, I'm really worried about you. Can you tell me what happened?"

I had to think. Why was I here? Oh, that. "Skylar sent the shower videos to Dallas. When he confronted me, I dropped my glass. I cut my foot on the broken glass and then fell."

"Bless your heart. So, he knows everything?" Susan asked.

"He knows enough."

I looked over at Dr. Pederman who pretended to look out the window. He was so sweet. He sat there quietly, ignorant of the conversation but never butting in. He was the kind of person who trusted you to tell him when you were ready.

I turned back to Susan and added, "Sam said they talked about everything."

"Did Sam say how Dallas took it?" Susan asked. Apparently, Sam didn't tell her. That couldn't be good for me.

"No, and I didn't ask."

"I'm going to go get some coffee and let you girls talk freely. Can I get you anything?"

"I'll take a sweet tea, Dad."

He leaned over the bed and kissed me on the forehead. "We're praying for you, Abbey."

As soon as the door closed behind him, I said, "He saw me naked, Susan. I was mortified."

"Did he say anything?"

"Plenty. He thought I was willingly involved in pornography." I remembered tossing his computer across the room. "I think I broke his laptop."

"How did Sam get involved?" Susan asked.

"Something about wanting to keep me up to date on the case. I don't know, but he heard my screams and kicked in the door. He thought Dallas hurt me. It was really confusing."

Susan gave me another drink of water. There was a knock at the door, and a nurse came in to check my vitals and fluids. Susan waited until she left to sit back down. I could tell she wanted to say something but wondered if it was appropriate. She had those telltale looks, chewing on her lower lip, eyes downcast, and twirling one lock of hair around her finger. "Spit it out."

"That obvious?" I forced a smile. I was still in a lot of pain. My foot throbbed, and my side hurt. "What do you think Skylar will do next?"

We talked about the next possible commandments. "I think Penny's calling herself Hadassah for some reason."

"You mean, as in Esther?"

"That's what Dallas mentioned, but I didn't get the explanation for who Esther is. I don't know for sure, but I think Skylar is getting upset and will go after someone close to me."

Susan didn't say anything. She was processing the information.

"For some reason, she doesn't want me dead."

"Well, that's good, isn't it?" That was Susan, always looking for the sunshine in the storm.

"Except she's determined to make my life miserable and to cut me off from everyone else."

There was another knock. "Is it safe to come in?"

"Yes, Dad."

Dr. Pederman entered the room with a coffee, a tea, and a pile of creamers. He also had a sack in one of his hands. "What's life without something sweet?" He handed the bag to Susan.

"Muffins! Can you eat one, Abbey?"

"I don't know. I guess I missed breakfast. Maybe half a muffin?"

We nibbled and talked. She told me about the kids and their concern for my health. Dr. Pederman searched inside his jacket pocket. "Danny made this for you."

He handed me a homemade get-well card. Danny drew a picture of his sister, Hannah, and me playing soccer in the back yard. I teared up. Something about Danny making a card for me was special. I'd never had anything like that. You'd have thought he gave me a diamond necklace. I held the card to my chest. "That is so sweet. Tell him it's perfect."

"You can tell him yourself when you get out of here." Susan began talking nonstop about the arrangements at her house while I healed. "I already decided to stay in our house. I work from home, and everything I need is in my office. Besides, my parents can watch the drive from their house." She seemed excited about the situation. "Maybe knowing you're at my house will keep us from harm too. You said she didn't want you dead."

I looked at Dr. Pederman. He scratched his buzzed head. It must have been freshly cut it was so short. I could tell he understood the situation. "Susan, the danger is to all of us, especially you and the kids."

"But they said there would be a police officer parked outside. That should scare them off."

"I wish that was true, Susan," I said. "I should go back to the apartment. That way I'm isolated just like she wants."

"Oh, just be the martyr then!" Susan began to cry and rushed out of the room.

"She'll be okay. She just wants to help. She's worried about you."

"I know she is, Dr. P, but she needs to worry more about the kids. That's her job. I signed up for this. They didn't." I tried to explain the dangers of my job. I talked about my time in the army. He could relate to that. He served two tours as a medic when Susan was a child. He understood the dangers. "This is far from over." I spoke fondly of my time as an MP and our motto of *Ever Vigilant*. I was accustomed to living that way. My apartment had security. It would be much more difficult for Skylar to reach me there. "Maybe she and the kids could stay with me."

"But didn't you tell Susan that Skylar got in and bugged your place?" He was a realist. We understood each other.

"Yes, but my security is on high alert right now. They are looking for anything suspicious, and anyone going to my place has to be buzzed in by me personally."

"That's good for you, Abbey, but Susan won't leave her house. We've tried and tried to get them to stay with us, and we're just across the street."

"She's stubborn." We both knew Susan wouldn't go for the idea. She was burdened with a purpose. Just as she risked her life to save the homeless missionary, she was willing to do the same for me. In Susan's mind, she had a best friend who was in danger, a friend who saved her life when she needed help. She would not be persuaded to abandon that sense of duty. There had to be a compromise. "Maybe the kids could stay with friends until this nightmare ends."

We went back and forth over different possibilities. The door opened. "Knock, knock."

"Lieutenant Daniels, come on in," Dr. Pederman said. "Let me step out and check on my daughter."

"Good to see you, Doc." They shook hands, and Dr. Pederman left. "Abbey, you look terrible."

"You always know how to make me feel loved."

"That's a given." He was serious. "Detective Tidwell caught me up to speed and said you might need someone to talk to who knows you well."

"Seems like too many people are worried about me. If you want to help, catch Skylar and Penny." I told him as much as I could remember about the cleansing, even the next two possible commandments. They would be extremely difficult to narrow down, but at least I found their sources of information. We could scour the Nashville journals and magazines from June and July, screening them against the remaining commandments.

"What can I do to help?"

"Bring my laptop. I want to go over Sondra's door cam video and see what I missed the first time."

A female voice chimed in. "That would be very helpful."

"Agent Carmichael," she said, introducing herself to Lieutenant Daniels. "And where might this laptop be?" she asked me. "I'd like to take a look myself."

"At my apartment. Lieutenant Daniels can take you to it."

"I'm not going to ask how you got the video," she said with a wink.

"I appreciate that. Maybe you could use facial recognition to identify the others."

"Well, let's go, Lieutenant. Time is of the essence." She started for the door.

"I'll join you outside in a minute, Agent. I need to finish checking on Abbey before I leave." Reluctantly, Agent Carmichael left the room.

"Do you need to talk first, Abbey? You're obsessing over this case, and it worries me."

"Look at me, L.T. This case is going to kill me if I don't solve it soon."

"It's going to kill you if you stay on it."

We had to stop the killings first. Then we could focus on Skylar. If I lay here and tried to outguess her, I'd be spinning my wheels. Take her down one brick at a time. Stop Penny and her cult, anger Skyler by doing so, and wait for her to make an emotional mistake. It was my best option. As soon as Lieutenant Daniels left, Susan and her dad came back in. No one was going to leave me alone. For once, I was glad.

Chapter Forty

Saturday, October 11, 7:12 PM—St. Thomas Midtown

The surgeon came by and said everything went well. If my vitals remained stable, I could go home tomorrow. They had to dig glass pieces out of my right foot. Thankfully, the shard that cut my side remained intact without leaving any fragments behind. Unfortunately, I would be confined to a wheelchair until my foot healed enough to bear weight. The doctor didn't want me to use crutches for fear the strain might tear the stitches in my side. I agreed to anything if it got me out of the hospital.

Lieutenant Daniels brought my laptop. "We copied facial images of Penny Thatcher and five of her followers. Agent Carmichal shared all the images with the Bureau to run them through their facial recognition software. "Since this was your case, we let Sam file the request." Lieutenant Daniels was always about protocol and following proper procedures.

"Thanks." I was glad things were moving forward on the case, but I was also sad to be on the outside of things.

"Okay, Abbey, everything is in motion. Tell me what's really going on." Lieutenant Daniels was always straight forward. He was also tenacious, yet patient. Once he latched on to something, he didn't let go. "I understand what happened officially with the department. I hear you'll be reinstated once you're physically able to return to work. What I want to know about is Dallas."

"He's great."

"Uh-huh."

He waited. Lieutenant Daniels leaned back in his chair and stared at me. The silence was so annoying.

"It's been an interesting week since Sam locked us in together."

He smiled and stared at me. I hated it when he did this. He knew exactly what made me tick.

"He's extremely patient with me and hasn't forced a physical relationship."

"I bet a guy like Dallas is waiting until marriage." He watched for a reaction to the word marriage. I didn't give him one. It was true. He discussed marriage and his commitment to stay a virgin when we first started dating. He said he wanted to be upfront with me. "How do you feel about that?"

"Good." It was what I'd hoped for but never believed a man could give me—time to date and learn to love without the expectations of sex. "He helps me relax and be myself. He wants me to have a renewed faith and get involved in the church, but he doesn't force it on me."

"Doesn't that trigger memories of your father? Seems weird that you would date a preacher." He had that look he got when he was examining the nonverbal signs of a suspect in interrogation. I could tell he was judging my answers for authenticity.

"He's not really a preacher. He's a professor of English and Religion." I took a breath when the pain flashed in my side. I waited until it subsided. "He fills in when pastors need him, but it's not his fulltime gig." Was I trying to convince Lt. Daniels or myself?

"But he does expect you to go to church with him, right?" Lt. Daniels and his wife Sherry heard all my rants about religious people and churches. Though Sherry was a faithful church-goer, Lt. Daniels was more of an Easter and Christmas Christian. When I lived with them, I refused to join them even on those two occasions. I know he thought it hypocritical of me to date a teacher of religion.

"I was already attending with Susan and the kids when I met him." That was true, but I came back because of him. At first, it was for his looks, but I was also intrigued by his views of Scripture and grace. These were new messages to me and flew in the face of the Bible my father taught. My father proclaimed a God of judgement; Dallas preached a God of grace.

"That's not what I asked, Detective. You know the difference between the fact you just gave and the inquiry I made."

"You make it sound so technical. I know why Sherry says you're not a romantic."

"So, it *is* romance." He acted like he just uncovered the deepest, darkest secret.

"Of course, it's a romance." I wasn't ashamed of that. "I've told you he's my boyfriend. Well, at least he was my boyfriend." Was he still? I felt that Dallas came to the hospital out of obligation, not love. The last image I had of him was of disappointment. Anger I could deal with. Apathy and disappointment were tough eggs to crack.

"Boyfriend who is currently living with you?" I know he said it with the inflection of a question, but it was really a statement to tease out our relationship.

"Not in the way you're implying, Lieutenant. In fact, not even to the extent that I was hoping." He raised his right eyebrow. "Yes. I was hoping it would be an extended date, but he's gone out of his way to eliminate those situations."

"Okay, you're going to have to explain that comment."

Before I could answer, someone knocked at my door.

"Come in."

I wasn't expecting my mother's face to appear around the door. "I know I'm not wanted here, but..." She paused and looked at Lieutenant Daniels. There was a quick recognition that he was not the same man she saw at my apartment. "And who is this?"

"Lieutenant Matthew Daniels," he said, standing and extending his hand. "Are you a friend of Abbey's?"

I didn't say anything. I wanted to see how she would answer.

"I hope to be."

He looked back at me to see if he should shield me from the strange woman.

"Lieutenant, this is my mother."

"Mrs. Abelard?" he asked.

She looked puzzled. "So, you know Hannah's real name."

I couldn't let that slide. "Abbey Rhodes is my *real* name. It's just not my birth name."

Her sullen facial expressions betrayed her disappointment. "I didn't come here to fight with you, Hannah."

"Then respect me enough to call me Abbey." I pushed the button to raise the head of my bed. Even though it hurt my side, I wanted to meet her eye to eye. I didn't like the feeling of being beneath her.

"You'll always be my little Hannah." I wanted to pounce all over that. Where was my big mother when I was struggling to survive? "I just came to see how you were doing?"

"How did you find me?" Someone was leaking information, and I was going to find out who. I only gave permission for Susan's family and members of Metro Nashville Police Department.

"You sent me the email and said you wanted to make peace. Then you gave me the hospital and room number. Don't you remember?"

"Maybe the painkillers dulled your senses, Abbey. Maybe you forgot," Lieutenant Daniels said.

"There aren't pain killers strong enough to make me do a thing like that. I would definitely remember." I opened my laptop and checked my outgoing mail. Nothing to her. I showed him. "Okay, Mom, sign into your email account and show me the letter."

"You don't believe me?" Even though she had always been passive-aggressive, she did not like being called a liar. She huffed as she came over to the tray.

"Oh, I believe you got the email, but I also know I didn't send it. But I think I know who did."

"Give me that," she said in a huff. She signed into her email account, pulled up the email, and showed me the letter where I pleaded with her to come see me since we got off to such a bad start.

I turned it to Lieutenant Daniels.

"That doesn't make sense. It says it came from your email address." He examined the email. "Someone must have used your laptop while you were asleep. Would Dallas have any reason to do that?"

Yes, but he would never go behind my back like that. "He hasn't been back. It has to be Skylar. She's a tech genius or something. She called me using Sam's number, but it wasn't his phone. She bugged my apartment and sent Dallas a vulgar video saying it was from me. And someone did something to edit the footage from the church. The church's staff swear they never sent the video to the news station."

"Why would Skylar want your mother to come here?"

I sat up. There was only one reason I could think of. *Surely, she wouldn't.* "Where's Dad?"

"Back at the hotel. He doesn't know I'm here."

"Which hotel, Mom? Be specific."

"The church put us in the Holiday Inn Express right by the airport."

I gave Lieutenant Daniels a desperate look. "I'm on it." He pulled his phone out and rushed into the hallway to make the call.

"You're being so opaque, Hannah." She put her hands on her hips. "Did you ask me here or not?"

"Not, but don't go anywhere. Wait until we get word from Dad."

"Your father's not ready to speak with you." She shook her head and sat down. "What happened to you?"

I was so focused on the current situation with my father that I didn't understand the depth of her question. "I broke a glass, slipped, and fell onto one of the sharp pieces."

"That's not what I'm asking. You used to be such a sweet and quiet little girl. How did you become…"

"A loud-mouthed jerk? Is that what you think I became?" She knew just how to push my buttons, and now that I was in such pain, I had no filters. Whatever I thought spilled right out of my mouth.

"No. You're twisting everything around." Her shoulders slumped. "That's not what I said at all." She looked into my eyes as if she was searching for that little girl back in Guatemala. "What did they do to you to make you so—on edge?"

"You mean triggered? And by *they* do you mean the police force, the army, or the men of Guatemala? Be specific, Mom. The answer varies."

"Why are you so hateful? I'm trying to make peace." She really didn't get it. I guess she thought we would pick back up like it was before the day Dad kicked me out and pronounced me dead to the family. "We didn't raise you that way."

"Raise me? You left that job to a stranger." Before I could launch into another tirade, Lieutenant Daniels burst through the door and said, "He's missing. His door was wide open, but he's nowhere to be found."

"Skylar has him."

She manipulated my mother to come across town to see me so she could get to my father, the source of my pain. "I need to call Sam. She's forcing us to fight on two fronts. A murderous cult has our full attention, and Skylar is jealous."

"What would this Skylar want with your father? Is she a friend of yours?"

"No, Mom. She's my enem—a ruthless, heartless killer. She wants my attention, and she's using your husband to get it."

"I don't understand," she said.

"You will."

Chapter Forty-one

Sunday, October 12, 7:30 AM—St. Thomas Midtown

I had a rough night with pain and had to have another dose of morphine before I could relax. I'm sure the stress didn't help the situation. When I woke, I noticed Sherry Daniels sitting beside me reading a book. "What time is it?"

She took out her phone and said, "Seven-thirty. I hear you were in a lot of pain last night."

I nodded. "Can I have some water?"

She grabbed my cup and gave me a sip. "Sam said he was going to stop by at ten to give you updates and talk about a strategy."

"Thanks." I leaned the back of the bed up a little. Once I felt a twinge of pain in my side, I stopped. "Any word on my father?"

"No. Abbey, please let them handle this. You don't need the undue stress. I understand you wanting to help find your father, but please let the other case go."

"You act like that's an easy thing to do. You wouldn't understand."

"You think I couldn't understand? I'm married to a cop, a lieutenant no less. He lives and breathes the job. It's what cost my Matthew his first marriage, and it almost cost us ours. You have to make a choice while you still can. Your health needs your priority right now." She searched my eyes. "Let us all help you so you can rest and get well."

Why couldn't I let the case go? Was it pride? Was it fear? Why couldn't I trust Sam or Lieutenant Daniels to solve the case and find my father? Metro was doing fine before I came. They could continue without me. "I'm sorry, Sherry. I didn't mean to take it out on you. Skylar's gotten to me, and I feel like I can't breathe as long as she's free."

"The stress is making you worse, Abbey. You need to rest and heal if you want to get back out there." She set her book on the tray. "You look weak. Are you hungry?"

"Very."

Sherry removed the lid from my breakfast tray. "You have sausage, eggs, and toast. What do you want first?"

"Is it still warm?"

She put her hand above the eggs. "I can feel some heat."

"Then I'll start with the eggs. I hate cold eggs."

Sherry maneuvered the tray as close as she could to my chest and handed me the fork. They weren't real eggs, but they didn't taste bad. I grabbed a little packet of salt and emptied it on the eggs. That was better. She sat there quietly watching me as I finished the meal.

"I hear your mother came by."

"You've been talking to your husband." I raised both eyebrows to signal a desire to know how that went.

"He acted like a father who's worried about his daughter." She smiled.

"Yes. He and Sam both treat me like a daughter. They're very protective."

She seized the opportunity. "Then they should protect you from Skylar and this case. If they love you like a daughter, why aren't they?"

"Because we're all cops at heart. We can't separate ourselves from work, no matter how hard we try." It was true. "That's why so many of us suffer from failed relationships." She understood that more than most. Lt. Daniels met Sherry after a brutal divorce over his lack of time and focus on home, his wife, and his boys. Sherry married Lt. Daniels understanding his duty and demands as a cop. Our significant others compete with the force for our attention. I wanted to explain that to Dallas, but I was afraid he might think I was pushing him away, if I hadn't already done so. "We try." What a feeble thing to say.

"I don't think you try hard enough. Cops, that is." I knew she meant it for Lieutenant Daniels more than me.

"You're probably right." I searched my mind for a biblical analogy she could understand. "I guess God could have saved us all without letting His Son die, but that's not the way He designed it." Oh, that was good.

"Touché." Despite her concern for me, she smiled. I think, deep inside, she was proud of my analogy. She'd tried for years to get me to attend Christmas church services with them. "I would ask why you think God did it that way, but it would take us so far off the given subject." She looked over the top of her book. "Do you not believe Sam and the other detectives can solve the case, or is it too personal for you to let go?"

Good question. I trusted Sam. Didn't I? He had Agent Carmichael's help. But Skylar made this personal, and I took it personally. She addressed the note to me. She brought me into this, and I had to take her out. That was it. She made it a game. She was disappointed that I brought others into it, but she used Penny and the others to carry out her plans.

To me, it was war. I could do the same thing Skylar was doing, orchestrating the action from afar, keeping her hands clean of blood and filth. She could move one chess piece, and I could move another. We'd continue the game until one of us could cry, "Checkmate."

"Abbey. Abbey?"

"Huh?"

"You didn't answer my question."

"I thought I was answering you. We were having a sparkling conversation in my mind. Sorry, I do that a lot." It was a bad habit, but it was better than saying every thought aloud.

"You were staring at the wall. I thought you were in a trance."

"What was the question?"

"Do you not believe Sam and the others can solve the case, or is it too personal for you to let go?"

"Of course, I trust him." I looked into Sherry's searchful eyes. "But this *is* personal. Skylar brought me into this, and she's not going to quit until *I* stop her."

"They can handle it."

"She took my dad so I would stay in the game."

"The game? This isn't a game, Abbey." Her voice was tight. I struck a nerve. I could see the muscles in her jaw tense and the veins in her neck bulge. I'd never seen Sherry this mad before. She closed her eyes and took a deep breath. "Anyway, Skylar knows you hate him. Why would she use him as leverage, unless…"

"No. I don't care about him." I didn't. I couldn't tell if I was going to cry or scream. "But I'm not going to let another person die because of me, even if it costs my own life." I tried to come up with another way of saying it, a way she could understand. "Didn't Jesus die for everyone, no matter how they felt about Him?"

She smiled. "I have to admit. That was smooth. Unfortunately, it proves the opposite of your point. Jesus loved the world, despite their responses to Him."

Bad analogy. "That's not what I was saying. Anyway, I have to stop Skylar. It's as simple as that." I pushed the button for the television and pretended to be interested in the first show I came across. Shery picked up her book and resumed reading. We were at a standstill.

Where was Dallas? What did his absence mean?

Chapter Forty-two

Sunday, October 12, 10:18 AM—St. Thomas Midtown

After an hour of silence, Sherry left, and Dallas came in. He too was quiet, despite my efforts to explain myself. I could cut the tension between us with a chainsaw, if I was lucky. We were in a stalemate. Time passed slowly, and neither of us wanted to be the first to break the silence.

Sam knocked and peeked inside the room. "Okay if we come in?" What a welcome distraction. Agent Carmichael eased around him.

"Sure. I'm going to get a soft drink from the machine downstairs," Dallas said. "She's all yours." He didn't try to hide his anger and disappointment from them. Sam's presence only seemed to make it worse. I wish I knew what happened between them while I was in surgery.

"I'm sorry, did we upset your boyfriend?" Agent Carmichael asked. I knew she would pick up on the conflict immediately.

"He's upset with me, actually." He knew I was making a choice to stay involved with the case.

"What's with him?" Sam asked. "I thought we worked everything out about that video." Sam sat in the chair next to my bed.

"I don't know, Sam." It was a lie. Dallas was upset about the dangers I walked through *and* the video Skylar sent him. "He wouldn't talk about the video. In fact, he didn't want to talk at all. I tried to explain the whole situation, but he didn't want to hear it. It's been like this since he came here." I pouted like a little girl, and I didn't care if Agent Carmichael saw it. "Besides, he's only here because Susan asked him. She is teaching the women's Sunday School class this morning. He agreed to give me a ride to her house later." I let out a heavy sigh. Just when I thought things were going well, my past crept in and ruined my life—again. "He can't understand why I'm still involved and getting stressed over the case and Skylar." I pushed the button to sit up.

"He's got a point, Kid. He worries about you and rightfully so." Sam sat in the chair by the window. "Look at you."

Agent Carmichael leaned against the wall at the end of my bed. She just listened, never asking what we were discussing. I assumed she could figure it out if she hadn't been told yet.

"I'm in here because Skylar sent him the videos. How did she even find them, Sam? I couldn't. Besides, I don't want him worrying about me. It's one thing to care for me and feel bad that I'm hurt, but I love my job. I don't know what I'd do if I couldn't be a detective." I took a sip of water. I wasn't thirsty, but I had to think about what I wanted to say next. I tried to convince myself that I had what it took to stop Skylar, but doubts were taking a foothold. I knew Dallas cared for me; at least he used to, but I needed him to care enough to let me be me. Was there a balance between caring for someone and letting them breathe? "He's got to loosen his grip, Sam. He's choking me."

"Love tends to do that." He paused for a moment. I could tell it triggered something deep within. He ran his fingers through his beard. "I wish my wife could press me about the job again." Sam looked away from me. "Kathy and Molly always fussed when I was a patrol officer. Every time I put on the uniform and went to work, they didn't think I'd come home." He looked out the window. "It's funny—funny strange that is—that they were hurt instead of me." He stood and fiddled with the blinds. "I made it my life's job to protect others, and I wasn't there to protect them."

I knew how he felt. "Sam?"

"It's okay, Abbey. It's taken me years of therapy to be able to say that. You need to hear it, especially now." He turned to face me. "I wish you could get your friend Susan to stay with you. Your apartment is much safer than her home. Since she won't, you need to stay with her, not because you need her, but because she may need you. Be there when she does. I don't want you to live with my mistake and wish you could change that one decision."

A sudden wave of guilt crashed upon my heart. "Susan's dad is more than capable of protecting them." Former military medic who kept guns in his house. He could handle any of Penny's followers. Skylar would never do her own work anyway. "She'd be better off without me." Another wave of guilt slammed against the shore of my thoughts. Susan sent her children away so she could take care of me and keep them safe too.

"You're going to be in a wheelchair. You need to be taken care of, whether you like it or not."

My muscles tensed. He hit it dead center. I didn't like being vulnerable and dependent on anyone else. I left those days in Guatemala. I worked my tail off in the army and at Metro to become independent and untouchable. Now with the Ripley family and Dallas, I had gotten soft. I worked hard with my counselor to keep my PTSD in check. Skylar was throwing my life off kilter, and the only way to stop that rollercoaster was to stop her—permanently.

"Don't think I'm oblivious to your kryptonite. You can pretend all you want, convince everyone else you're Supergirl, but I know you need people to lean on and to care for you." He moved closer to the bed. "What your parents did was horrible—unforgivable if you ask me. But one day you're going to have to deal with whatever happened at Mr. Morales' house, Abbey. If you don't, you'll rot from the inside out."

He was right, but I didn't want to hear it. I wasn't ready to deal with any more personal issues. We had a religious cult on the loose and a psychopathic puppeteer pulling everyone's strings. Now, my father—who I still hated—was taken as bait to bring me out in the open. "We have a case to solve, Sam. I don't have time to worry about where I put my head at night."

"I don't mean to butt in, but…"

"Then don't." It was cold, and I meant it to be. "This is a personal conversation."

"That's the problem, Detective Rhodes." I started to object, but Agent Carmichael said, "Hear me out." I nodded. "You have exceptional instincts. You pick up on connections and relationships of clues better than anyone I've ever worked with." I couldn't help but smile. "But you're also the most conceited detective I've ever met." My smile faded. My face felt hot. "You think you're the only one who can solve the case or catch the killers. Whoever this Skylar is has done a job on you, and you're willingly submitting to her plan."

"How dare you!"

"Somebody's got to tell you, Detective. You're so close to the tree, you can't even see the forest. Take a step back. Use this time to see the big picture." I started to say something, but she cut me off. "You have a wonderful partner with a lot of experience. Work with him, not against him. Take advantage of all the resources available to you. Swallow your pride for a moment and let us help."

"Wow. You've got nerve."

"The difference is, I don't care if you hate me. I'm here to help you all get the job done and save lives."

"Sam?"

"Okay, Kid. I can't say as I blame you for being upset, but she's right." I was stunned but silent. "Oh, I almost forgot." Sam searched his pockets. "You might want these." He held out four memory cards. "I took the liberty of setting these up around Sondra Jennings home after I left your apartment."

"You used the trail cams?"

"Yes, but I forgot I put them there. Anyway, I took the liberty of checking out the footage, and we got images of the van they use. We put out an all points on it and are waiting on a hit."

Sam and Agent Carmichael caught me up to speed on the search for the killers and the van. They also had the IT department of the FBI working on Skylar's ability to capture and mimic our communication.

"We have roughly seven days to figure out Penny Thatcher's next move. So far there have been no demands for your father."

The news perked me up. It was my turn to move the chess piece. "With all the cameras around Nashville, that van will turn up somewhere. Find it and you can follow them back to their home. If we can focus on Penny and stop her, Skylar will show herself. She hates to lose."

"Now that's a productive idea," Agent Carmichael said, pushing herself from the wall.

"And you were the one to beat her," Sam added. "I guarantee she's setting you up for a rematch of some sort." He ran his fingers through his mostly gray beard. "What ever happened to the Watson home?"

"I'm not sure." You'd have thought I would know with it being right across the creek from Living Water Church.

"I'll find out. If it's vacant and still in the family, I'm going to get a search warrant and make sure she's not holed up there." That hadn't even crossed my mind. Hiding in plain sight. Pain shot through my side, and I bent over the wound. I grimaced. "You better hit your pain button, Kid, and ease up."

"I can't, Sam. My mind is too foggy to think when I'm on it. I just need to relax my muscles, so they don't strain the stitches."

"Trust us," Agent Carmichael said. "You work the sequence and let us do the legwork."

"Abbey, when's the last time you took your medicine?" I didn't answer. "Abbey, I can check with the nurse if I have to."

"You're not allowed to know that. I have HIPPA rights." I was acting like a child. I hurt from the balls of my feet to the top of my head. "Two this morning."

"Push it, or I will."

I knew Sam would do it and then be mad at me for being so bullheaded. I hit the button.

"Work on what you can work on, Kid. You keep pushing yourself and you'll be no good to anybody." He got a text and read it. "Sarge needs me back at Homicide. We got a lead on the van." Before I could say it, Sam added, "We'll let you know." He and Agent Carmichael left, and Dallas came back in.

"He's worried about me too," I said, giving Dallas room to express his feelings.

"Actions speak louder than words." It was short and cold. "He came here to pull you into the case."

"No one pulls me into the case. I do that on my own." That wasn't what he wanted to hear, but it was the truth. "Sam made me take a dose of morphine. You'll be happy. I'll be quiet for a while."

He picked up on the sarcasm and said, "About time." Dallas pulled the chair up next to me and held my hand until I fell asleep.

I had strange dreams. Dallas and I were on a honeymoon cruise and people were disappearing all around us. Suddenly, everyone on the ship suspected me of killing passengers. They tied me up and threw me into the ocean. As I fell, I heard Skylar's laughter. I glanced back to the ship, and she had her arm around Dallas. "He's mine, now, and there's nothing you can do about it." I sank to the sound of her laughter.

When I opened my eyes, the room was dark and deserted. How long had I slept?

"Dallas?"

He didn't answer.

I heard a young woman's voice call my name.

"Susan, is that you?"

"Susan's not here anymore. You left her alone. Now, you have to live with that decision too."

"Who's there? Turn the light on."

"Don't you know my voice?"

The woman moved into a sliver of light from the hallway.

"Her family's dead, and it's your fault, Abbey."

"Skylar? What did you do?"

I reached for the nurse's call button.

"I moved the cord under your bed. You won't find it until I'm long gone. Now, come for me, or your dad will suffer the same fate as your precious friend."

"I will, and when I find, I'll kill you myself!"

"Dream on, Abbey. There's not a world that exists where you can outsmart me."

She flipped the light back on as she slipped out into the hallway.

"Nurse! Nurse!" No one came. I screamed louder, even though my side was killing me. "Why won't anyone come?"

"Abbey, wake up."

I opened my eyes. Dallas and Susan leaned over my bed. "Look at her, Dallas. Call for the nurse."

Dallas pressed the button. A nurse stepped in and asked, "May I help you?"

"Yes, she's burning up and breaking out in hives."

"Where is she?" I demanded. "Where's Skylar. She was here."

I was struggling to breathe. A team of nurses gathered around me. I couldn't focus. Everything went dark.

Chapter Forty-three

Monday, October 13, 10:10 AM—St. Thomas Midtown

"**S**he's awake." It was the sweet sound of Hannah Ripley. I felt her hand on my forehead. "She's cold and sticky. Is that good?"

"Yes. Hey, sweetie, can you hear us?" I nodded. My mouth was dry as a desert. I smacked my lips, and someone put a straw in my mouth. "Slow down, Abbey. Little sips. Hannah, don't let her drink so much. She'll get sick to her stomach again." *Again?* Hannah pushed the hair from my forehead.

"Did you catch her?"

"Catch who, Abbey?" Hannah asked.

"Skylar."

"No, but we tracked the van to their apartment and got a search warrant. We caught four, but Penny Thatcher got away. You were right. They're calling her Hadassah now."

"Let her rest, Sam Tidwell. You've pushed her enough." Only Susan would take that momma bear role for me.

"What happened?" I asked.

"It's okay, Abbey. I'm here." I reached my hand out and Susan took it. "You gave us quite a scare there. You had an allergic reaction to the antibiotic. You have to rest." She looked at Sam when she said it. I felt awful. The inside of my ears itched.

I told Susan about the dream, not thinking how awkward the honeymoon part sounded in front of everyone else. "When I woke, the room was dark, and you were all gone. I heard a voice.

It was Skylar." When I got to the end and repeated what Skylar said to me, everyone assured me that it was just a dream.

"It can't be. I remember waking up and seeing her there." I pointed to the place by the door.

"You must have had a dream within a dream," Hannah said.

"It was so real," I protested. "What day is it?"

"Monday."

"Why aren't you in school?"

"I had a dentist appointment this morning and asked Mom if I could come see you after."

"What can we get you?" Susan asked.

I looked around the room. I wanted to ask if Dallas had come back, but I wasn't ready for the answer. I moved to the one thing I could get my mind around—the case. "I want a Diet Dr. Pepper. Then, I want to know about the arrest." Susan's face tightened and her lips pursed. I knew that upset her. "It's the only thing that can clear my mind right now. Otherwise, I'll be obsessing over it and imagining all kinds of things."

"I don't think that's a good idea."

"Susan, I may be in the hospital, but I'm still a detective. You don't stop being a mother when you're hurt."

"That's different, and you know it." She got up. I thought she was going to leave, but she said, "All right, Sam. Get it over with. We both know she's not giving in on this." Susan moved to the window and looked out at the darkening sky. A storm was brewing. She handed Hannah her credit card and told her to go get me a drink.

Sam moved my tray to the bed and said, "I was pretty sure you'd want to see what happened, so I had Spence video everything. He's even spliced in bodycam footage for you. Abbey, you might want to sit up. You'll probably want to study it a few times."

I opened my laptop, signed in, and unzipped the file. I was stunned with the footage of the apartment. I watched them breach the door and felt my stomach muscles contract as if I was there.

The underlings were willing to sacrifice themselves to give Penny (Hadassah) a chance to escape. She pushed past Spence, knocking him, and the camera, down. That was the last piece of video of her.

Once everyone else was secure and in the hands of the officers, Spence painstakingly went over every inch of the apartment. Every wall in the den and first bedroom was covered with paper: copies of articles, pictures, timelines, and Bible verses. I watched the video all the way through three times. "This is incredible!"

Sam leaned in. "By the way, you had the sequence right, all the way down to their planned suicide. I'll be right here if you have any questions."

"Where is Agent Carmichael?"

"She and another agent are at the apartment studying the scene."

"Oh." I stopped the video several times and zoomed in on the materials. "All the articles are dated from the end of May to the beginning of July of this year. They spent all this time since April recruiting zealots and locating victims for each commandment." There were Nashville publications on each of our first five victims. There was a large X over each of their pictures. I noticed something and backed the video up. There was another name for commandment nine. They had a different victim for false testimony. It was someone who lied under oath and sent an innocent person to jail. The case was four years ago, and the perjury was discovered this past June. "Why did she switch to Nicholas Sayers? When did she find out about it? How did she discover my birth name and life in Guatemala?"

"Slow down. We're looking into all that. I had to tell the lieutenant and the IT people some of your story, so they knew what we were up against."

I nodded vacantly. I didn't really care at this point. I tried to keep my past from Dallas, and he saw it with his own two eyes. Now, he was distant: physically and emotionally. Penny had a huge section about me on one of the walls; she had both of my names and both of my lives. A chill ran down my back. Now, all the detectives and officers knew I had a life under another name. Thankfully, it just said, "shower videos," and didn't elaborate. There were pictures and descriptions of Sam, Dallas, Susan, Hannah, Danny, the Pedermans, and the Daniels family. Skylar had leverage. She not only knew about my past, but she also knew about the people I loved. "Sam, do you think Penny will continue the pattern and go after these people?"

"She's a fanatic, so, yes."

"But you said you got all of her followers. She can't do it alone."

"All that were in that apartment. That makes five so far. Who knows how many she has."

I started the video over and focused this time on all the Bible verses. "Hey Susan, can you look at these with me?"

"I wish Dallas were here. He's so much better at this than I am."

"I do too, Susan, but he's not. Just do what you can." I lowered the side rails of my bed, and she sat beside me. The first one was from Deuteronomy 5:1: Hear, O Israel, the statutes and the ordinances which I am speaking today in your hearing, that you may learn them and observe them carefully.

"That's the introduction to the Ten Commandments," she said. "They must feel as though God is directing them to ensure others learn and obey them."

I read the next one. "You shall walk in all the way which the LORD your God has commanded you, that you may live and that it may be well with you, and that you may prolong your days in the land which you will possess. Deuteronomy five, thirty-three. Look how they underlined those two phrases."

"Oh my," Susan said. "She thinks it's her duty to take the life of someone who breaks a command."

"Skylar knew all the way back to the death of her counselor that they were going to do this. She warned me that a cleansing was coming." It was chilling how thoroughly she planned this.

"Remember, Sam, Penny's visits with Skylar at NCDC? When she gave Skylar the religious materials?"

"Oh, yeah, I'm glad you brought that up. We matched surveillance video from the facility to the ring camera. I took great pleasure giving them to Sergeant McNally."

"Skylar is lightyears ahead of us."

Sam said, "She and Penny Thatcher probably planned the whole thing under our noses at the center."

Susan pointed to the screen of my laptop. "Look. There it is, Deuteronomy six, verses eight and nine. You shall bind them as a sign on your hand, and they shall be as frontals on your forehead. You shall write them on the doorposts of your house and on your gates." Susan got up and grabbed her Bible from the ledge of the window. "They're taking it literally." Hannah came in the room and set my drink on the tray. She sat beside Susan and listened in.

"Sam, did you ever find out if their doors were marked with the corresponding numbers?"

"Yes, they were, every single one. And get this, Abbey. The homes of the remaining victims are already marked."

"Are you kidding? They must have marked the homes, warning the owners to repent or die." Unfortunately, the messages were unnoticed or ignored—or, like us at first, just misunderstood. "Sam, I feel so stupid."

Sam said. "Well, we have their script now."

"If they stick to it. Skylar is the mastermind, and she's apparently been planning this since last spring. She definitely has backup plans…and backup plans to her backup plans."

Hannah moved over to the bed and pointed out the word, *fear*, was underlined in multiple verses. "Do they want the rest of us to live in fear, so we'll obey the commandments?"

"Probably," Sam said. "I could kick this over to the Feds as terrorism. Let them take charge and use their full force."

"But they'd take over the case, Sam." I didn't want to lose the

case. It was personal to me. "Isn't it enough that Agent Carmichael is involved and brought in another agent?"

"It's not a pissing contest, Abbey. It doesn't matter who gets the credit for stopping them." Sam was right, and I was embarrassed about making it that very thing, worrying about solving it myself. "She's a Fed, and she's involved, like it or not. Her partner's name is Agent Rogers by the way."

"Is that a bad thing?" Susan asked. "They could probably solve it quicker." That stung my pride. She was probably right, but I didn't know how Skylar would respond to their interference. "Don't forget, Abbey, she still has your father."

I had forgotten. "Has there been any word on him, Sam?"

"No word, no sign, and no contact demanding anything from us. The moment we hear anything on your father, I'll let you know. As far as the Feds are concerned, we're hanging on to the case for now. We've apprised them of everything to this point."

"Do you think she's already killed him?" I asked. Hannah rubbed the goosebumps on her arms. She was probably thinking the same thing as I was. Once they killed my father, who was going to be next? "Why else would she take him?"

Susan ran her fingers through my hair. I noticed she always did it to Hannah when she was trying to ease her daughter's anxiety. It was Susan's way of saying everything was going to be all right. It probably soothed Susan's nerves too. I knew she was praying that verse that God always makes a situation good. Thankfully, she didn't say it to me.

"She's punishing him for hurting me. There's still something in Skylar that wants to rescue me. It's so strange." On the one hand, she wanted to protect me. On the other hand, she did things that hurt or embarrassed me.

"It's as if she is telling you that she can hurt you but no one else can. My big brother did that to me," Sam said. I didn't know he had a brother. He never spoke of him. Of course, I never asked. I suppose it was because of my lack of family relationships. "He would make sure the block knew they couldn't touch me, but then he'd beat me up for the littlest things."

"Do you have any other brothers or sisters?" Susan asked. I was glad. I wanted to know too.

"I had one of each," he said. "They lived on opposite coasts. One in California, and the other in New York. Now, Maggie lives here."

"Sorry to interrupt, but what is Matthew twelve, verses thirty-six and thirty-seven?" I asked. There was no verse with it, just the reference.

Susan looked it up. "It says, 'But I tell you that every careless word that people speak, they shall give an accounting for it in the day of judgment. For by your words, you will be justified, and by your words you will be condemned.'"

"I guess they included actions as well as words," Hannah said. "I guess they forgot about judge not or you will be judged." She asked Sam, "What does that all mean for Abbey?"

"In my opinion, if this girl Penny believes she is called by God to punish those who have violated His primary commands, she won't stop. She'll think God will protect her until the task is complete." He turned to me. "In fact, capturing Penny's supporters will only serve to embolden her. Her sense of a special call will have been confirmed. Otherwise, God would have allowed us to capture her as well."

"Sam," Susan said, motioning to Hannah with her eyes.

Hannah needed to hear this too. "Susan, he's got a point. If that's all true, she will stick to the timeline and the sequence unless we stop her."

"Can't you just put all the others in protective custody until the timeline is finished?" Susan asked a good question. "Would that stop her?"

"It might," Sam said. "Captain Harris wants us to set a trap for her, kind of like you wanted for Sondra Jennings."

It was like he poured salt on an open wound. "We abandoned her and allowed Penny to make her sacrifice."

"He wants to put a patrol out front as a decoy."

"Out front? You know where she's going next?" I asked, somewhat bewildered.

"We think so."

"Who is it?" I asked.

"Relax, Abbey, and leave everything to us." They wouldn't give me the details, claiming that if I knew I might try to break out of the hospital. I argued, but it did no good.

Sam tried to reassure me by saying, "Spence and I will be inside the home."

"I don't know, Sam. Don't you think she'll suspect something like that after you raided her apartment?" Skylar was a genius. I didn't know how smart Penny was, but surely, she was still under Skylar's thumb and protection.

We bantered about the best strategy until the young man came in with my lunch tray. Susan and Hannah left. Sam pulled out a sack and ate his deli sandwich. His food looked far more appetizing than mine.

"I really think Susan and the kids should stay with you," Sam said.

"I've tried to get her to stay with me in the apartment. She insists on staying in her own home, so she and her parents can keep eyes on each other. The kids are both staying with school friends to keep their routines as regular as possible."

"I'm just saying. Your place is better." Sam paused and stroked his beard. I could tell he didn't feel right about something. "I have to get back to it. We've posted an officer outside your door. Call if you need anything. I nodded, and he left.

Around seven that night, the doctor finally came by and said if everything looked good in the morning, I could go home. He still insisted on a wheelchair until my side healed enough to bear weight without risk of reopening the wounds. Then he said I could transition to crutches.

I watched television for a little while but nothing good was on. I made some notes, mostly questions about the case, and then set them aside. I was so exhausted, I fell asleep without having to use any painkillers.

Chapter Forty-four

Tuesday, October 14, 3:25 PM—Ripley House

It took forever for the doctor to send the paperwork for my release. I also had to rent a wheelchair. Dallas called and said he had a meeting with his doctoral advisor and couldn't reschedule. He called Susan's dad to take his place.

Dr. Pederman waited with me. He was patient; I was not. Finally, we got to Susan's house, and he helped me inside. "I'll be across the street if you need anything."

"Thanks, Dr. P." He leaned in, gave me a reassuring but gentle hug, and whispered, "I appreciate this," like I was doing them a favor.

Susan put her hands together and smiled. "You'll be in Hannah's room until you can transition to crutches or a walker."

"I feel like a feeble invalid," I complained. I didn't want to put anyone out. I certainly didn't want to bring the fight to Susan's house.

"I know, Sweetie, you don't like anyone to wait on you, but you'll just have to swallow your pride for a week or two." There it was again, a jab at my pride. "Then you'll be back on your feet and isolated in your white tower in the sky."

"Wow. Laying it on a little thick, Mom." Hannah winked at me.

"You'll be no trouble at all," Susan insisted.

"Aunt Abbey!" Danny came running through the back door and gave me a hug. I didn't say anything, but he squeezed my side. I winced in pain.

Hannah noticed. "Danny! She just got out of the hospital. Don't send her right back."

"Sorry." He let go and pushed out his big lower lip.

"It's okay, little man. I feel the love." He stuck his tongue out at his sister and ran down the hall. I turned to Susan. "I thought they were staying with friends until this is over."

"They are, but I promised they could see you before Dad took them." She clapped her hands and said, "Okay, kids, Grampa is waiting for you. Your suitcases are already in his car." They pouted but obeyed. Susan and I watched as Hannah took Danny's hand and ran him across the street.

"Is there a place I can plug in my laptop? I want to look over the video and see if I can figure out where Penny might be."

"You just got here, Abbey. Get some rest, and then you can tackle the case."

"I know you mean well, Susan, and I appreciate everything you're doing. But in five days, unless we're absolutely right, Penny's going to kill someone."

"I thought Sam had the site and the person all figured out."

"Sam has her original script, but she knows that. I believe she'll continue the killings but find alternate victims." She rolled me into the den and set up a TV stand for my laptop. "Do you want anything to eat or drink?"

"Actually, I'd love a little of whatever you had for lunch if there are any leftovers."

"I was thinking snack, actually."

"I'm starving and could really use some good Susan Ripley food." Susan beamed and hustled to the kitchen. I could hear the microwave humming. I texted Sam:

```
Be careful on the stakeout tonight.
I sure hope the anonymous pans out, and
we'll have their new location.
```

We were all having to be ever vigilant now. I studied the video, going over every inch in sight.

Susan brought a hot plate of food and set it in on the tray, temporarily removing the laptop. She also put a large glass of sweet tea on the tray. Real southern sweet tea. "Eat first. Then you can play." She was going to spoil me. I dug my fork into the first of my chicken enchiladas. It reminded me of the meals I got at Mr. Morales's home. There were obvious triggers about my time with him, but he treated me to the best food. We also traveled to places I never dreamed I'd see. I got so lost in the memory that I didn't realize I'd eaten them both.

"Do you want me to make another, Abbey. I can bake more." She was happy as a lark, but I didn't need to take advantage of her hospitality.

"No. That was perfect. I can wait a couple hours until dinner," I said with a wink. I set the plate on the end table and grabbed my laptop. "I need to play now." She knew I loved what I did. Even though it dealt with life and death, being a detective was a thrill. It wasn't just a job. It was a part of my very being.

I glanced back through the video. On the wall, beneath the photo of Susan's family, someone had written her address. They had the street address and apartment number for me as well as Dallas. Under Sam's picture they had the address for Homicide and his house. The house address was underlined. I looked at next Monday's scheduled victim. Brenda Hollman, a sixty-two-year-old, white female who had been accused of auto theft. I zoomed in as best I could, but the type was so distorted, I couldn't read the details. It was from the website of one of the local news stations. I could barely make out the date. Searching online, I finally found the original post.

Brenda was caught with a brand-new Tesla. She stole it while someone else had set fire to a sign at the dealership. So, why was she free? I read further. The arresting officer failed to obtain a search warrant, so the evidence he found that day was inadmissible in a court of law. The news channel's investigative reporter dug into the case and convicted Brenda in the court of public opinion.

Still, she got away with the crime. Penny was out to correct that error and to bring what she believed to be the wrath of God upon Brenda Hollman.

They had her address, the commandment she broke (number eight—*Thou shalt not steal*), and the letters VIII to be etched into her hand and forehead. Penny's sentence would not be hindered by a failure to proceed legally. She was both judge and jury because she believed she acted by the authority of God.

I found it hard to believe they would continue with the previous schedule. They may have been fanatics and overconfident, but neither of them was stupid. That posed a different problem. What would they do instead?

I studied the wall and the individuals they selected. Who would be next if they chose not to kill Brenda? Would they skip her and move on? Would they flip the order? Would they pick new people? I had to think. They went to such great effort and detail to create the cleansing. Would they consider it defeat or a failure if they allowed us to force a change? Would they believe they could still outsmart us? Then I thought of my father. What was Skylar planning for him? In a way he was experiencing what he always called comeuppance—getting what you deserved. It was fitting that my father, who loved calling for punishment and considered himself God's spokesperson, was captive to Skylar who felt the same.

I had no clues to solve his kidnapping. On the other hand, I had a room full of clues about Penny and her beliefs. Somewhere in that apartment lay the answer to my questions. I dated the articles and sorted them in order. They didn't follow the chronological order for the first five victims. Why would they suddenly allow time to dictate the next victim? Before I realized it, Susan wheeled me to the kitchen table for supper. I looked at the kitchen clock—seven thirty. Even time was against me.

The Pedermans sat at the table which was full of food. "When did you get here?"

"About an hour ago," Dr. Pederman said. "We said hello, but you were oblivious to us."

"So sorry. I get lost in my job sometimes. Did Dallas call?"

"No, honey." Susan's mother used the same syrupy sweet names for me. "What did you mean when you said if you were Skylar what would you do next?"

"Just trying to get in her head."

Susan gave us both a glance indicating it was time to pray so we could eat while it was still hot. They bowed their heads and Susan's mother said a beautiful prayer of thanksgiving.

I looked at the food choices. Susan and Mrs. Pederman went all out. "Fried chicken, ham, baked potatoes, green beans, corn, salad, and hot rolls? Who else is coming for dinner?"

Her mom said, "We wanted you to feel at home after eating all that horrible hospital food."

Like mother, like daughter. "Thank you. This is way too much."

"Well, you don't get to eat it all, Abbey." Dr. Pederman took a piece of chicken and handed the plate to his wife. She grabbed a piece for herself and passed the dish to me.

The food was simple but amazing. The conversation was wonderful. It was funny. I used to thrive on time alone. Now, I enjoyed spending time with family. I felt at home. I felt my neck and back muscles relax. With that and a full stomach, I nearly fell asleep at the supper table. "Do you want to play a game or two of cards?"

"Thanks, Mrs. Pederman, but I can barely keep my eyes open. I think I'll get ready for bed. I didn't sleep well in the hospital and am looking forward to a comfortable bed." I couldn't figure out the puzzle of the case anyway. A good night's rest would refresh my mind, and I could get to it tomorrow. I had to trust Sam, Spence, and Agent Carmichael.

My foot and side were throbbing, and I had a hard time falling asleep. When I finally did, I had horrible nightmares about my father throwing me out onto the street. I relived those first few nights over and over again until the buzzing of my phone released me from the nightmare.

"Sam? What time is it?"

"Five in the morning."

"Did you catch them?"

"No."

"Is someone hurt?"

"Yes."

"Spit it out, Sam. You're killing me."

"We have your father. He's alive." Sam's voice contradicted such a victory. "Abbey, they stripped him and nailed him to my front door. He's in bad shape."

"But he's alive?" I put the phone on speaker and grabbed the clothes I took off last night which were still lying at the end of my bed. Sam described the condition of my father. They beat him and whipped him, leaving marks and cuts all over his body. "They gagged him and nailed him to a piece of wood, which they nailed to my door. He must have passed out from pain and shock."

"Is he conscious now?" I grabbed both arms of the wheelchair and maneuvered myself into the chair.

"No. Be thankful for that. He's barely recognizable."

"How did you find him?"

"Spence and I were on the stake out…" I took the phone off speaker and tucked it between my shoulder and ear. "…when dispatch called and said my paperman found him hanging from my front door." Sam cleared his throat. "They stapled a packet to his chest."

"Stapled? Like into his body?"

"Yes. It's a bunch of Bible verses and a note to you." I could tell he put his hand over the microphone and was talking to someone else. "Can I put the phone on video and walk you through the scene?"

"Of course." I heard the sound of an ambulance siren in the background as Sam was switching to video. "They're taking him now?"

"Yes."

"Where?"

"Vanderbilt. He's in bad shape."

"Okay, Sam, switch to video and walk me through it." My door opened and Susan slipped inside the room in her pajamas. I pointed to the phone.

"Who is it?"

"Sam. They found my father. He's alive—barely." I put the phone back on speaker so she could hear. Susan sat beside me as Sam walked me through the crime scene, which began with a blood from the street, up the sidewalk, to his front door. "Was his hand or forehead marked?"

"No. It was about the only place on his body they didn't touch. Abbey, why would they strip him, beat him, and nail his hands to a plank of wood?"

"To symbolize a crucifixion," Susan said. "What verses are on the note?"

Sam answered. "It says, 'Matthew twenty-three, thirteen.'"

"Is the verse written anywhere?" I asked.

"I don't think so."

Susan signaled something and ran out of the room. She came back with her Bible. She flipped through it and stopped. She pointed to the verse. "Sam, it says, 'Woe to you, teachers of the law and Pharisees, you hypocrites! You shut the door of the kingdom of heaven in people's faces. You yourselves do not enter, nor will you let those enter who are trying to.'"

"Wow. They punished him for hypocrisy. She wanted me to know she did this for me."

"That's pretty sick." Susan immediately covered her mouth. She mouthed an apology to me. I waved her off.

"Show me the rest, Sam."

The next verse was Matthew 18:6. Susan flipped a few pages back. "It says, 'If anyone causes one of these little ones—those who believe in Me—to stumble, it would be better for them to have a large millstone hung around their neck and to be drowned in the depths of the sea.'"

"So, why didn't they tie a large stone around his neck and drown him?" Sam asked. "They're so literal about everything else."

"Sam, move the camera back to the note. I want to see the next one." He did, and Susan found the verses. "If a man has committed a sin worthy of death and he is put to death, and you hang him on a tree, his corpse shall not hang all night on the tree, but you shall surely bury him on the same day (for he who is hanged is accursed of God). So that you do not defile your land which the LORD your God gives you as an inheritance. There's one more, Sam. I can't read it."

"It says James one, twenty-two."

Susan started to flip to it, but I shook my head. I knew this one. "'But prove yourselves doers of the word, and not merely hearers who delude themselves.' They used the words he preached over and over to judge him." I remembered what Dallas said about using the Bible to catch Skylar. But then I noticed, the note wasn't from her. It was from Hadassah, which was Penny's new name. She added a postscript that said, "No sacrifices this week. His punishment suffices for now." Wow. Somehow they knew so much about my father and what he preached. "Sam, does my mother know?"

"She's on her way to the hospital as we speak. What do you make of all this, Abbey?"

It was a lot. "Penny definitely believes she is the messenger of God and the exactor of His judgments." But those specific verses referred to his treatment of me as a child. Why was Penny defending me? Why did Skylar feel this strange attachment? No matter what we did, they were several steps ahead of us. We had to put our heads together and plan several steps out. "Sam, we've been playing defense. Can you come by around noon tomorrow, I mean later today? I think we need to pull in some of our resident Bible scholars and get their opinion of Penny's use of Scripture."

Scripture? I haven't called the Bible that since I was a young teenager. Something was happening to me—something stirring deep within.

Chapter Forty-five

Wednesday, October 15, 12:05 PM—Ripley House

Sam arrived at twelve-o-five for our lunch meeting. I introduced him to Pastor Kelly. He already knew Dr. and Mrs. Pederman and Susan. Dallas agreed to help us but seemed distant still. This was not the time to worry about my personal life. They placed several Bibles, a few Bible dictionaries, and a two-book commentary of the Bible on the kitchen table within everyone's reach. "First of all, thank you all for coming on such short notice. We're here to figure out a killer's message and see if we can't outwit her, biblically speaking. My Bible knowledge is limited, but you all know it backward and forward. We need your help."

"Are you two going to get in any kind of trouble, Abbey. Isn't this information confidential?" Pastor Kelly asked.

"If it makes you feel any better, I can deputize you," Sam said. His joke fell flat.

"Nice try, Detective Tidwell, but you're not a sheriff. I think he's concerned that you're stepping out of legal bounds here," Dr. Pederman said.

"Tell you what," Sam said. "While we're sitting around a table and talking, I'll call you Charles and you can call me Sam." They shook hands. "I'll keep it legal. If not, I'll turn in my badge."

"I'm still not sure why I'm here," Pastor Kelly said.

"The killers in our case are speaking through Bible verses," I said. "We can tell what they mean on the surface and apply them that way, but any symbolism or coded messages need to be discussed and applied to the case too. We need you to help us with that. Hopefully, we can figure out what they're planning next and stop them before they kill again."

"Okay, we're listening."

Everyone at the table knew Skylar Watson was involved, so there was no need to keep her name anonymous, but Penny was a different story. We agreed to refer to her as Hadassah instead. "Thanks, Dallas. It started with a message Skylar wrote for me and left on the body of her counselor. It said, *a cleansing is coming*. They took four months to recruit other followers who believed the same way Hadassah did. They also found ten victims by reading Nashville journals and papers published between the last week of May through the first week of July. Each person is accused of violating a specific commandment."

Sam chimed in. "They followed a specific pattern and calendar up until last night. A few days ago, we found their research and know who they planned to kill and when."

"Last night, they delivered a message to and through my father." I put copies of the verses on the table so they could pass them around and read each one. "It is our belief they plan to complete their cleansing because Hadassah is convinced she has a directive from God to do so. According to her note, they are suspending their schedule of a sacrifice every ten days for one week. No killing Monday because they tortured my father instead."

We spent half an hour discussing what we had just said and how we had come to those conclusions. Pastor Kelly asked for more background on the killers. He asked if we knew why the killer had changed her name to Hadassah. It didn't seem to fit with anything else in the case. We had to admit, we didn't know.

"The remaining commandments are eight, three, seven, four, and six." They opened their Bibles and found the commandments Sam mentioned. Here are the names of the potential victims matching each command. He set the names and commandments on the table. We were already amassing quite a pile of paper. "Is there anything in Hadassah's message that indicates a change in their plan other than the date?"

"I'm afraid to give my opinion," Mrs. Pederman said. "If I'm wrong, someone may die."

"That's the risk," I said, "but if we do nothing, they all will." She couldn't handle the pressure and excused herself from the room. "Anyone else need to bow out? Now's the time."

"We know we're asking a lot of you, but we're desperate," Sam said. "I don't know any of this Bible stuff."

"I'm no expert," Dallas said, "but I'll do anything I can to stop the killing. They're making a mockery of God's word." He grabbed the copy of Penny's message and studied the verses. Then, verse by verse, Dallas read what preceded and followed each one. "It seems to me, it's all about Abbey."

"What do you mean?" Susan asked.

"The original message was given to her. It was called a cleansing." He paused to make sure we were all listening. "What are they cleansing?"

"The earth—at least this little part of it," Pastor Kelly said.

"Specifically, Nashville," Charles Pederman added.

"Exactly." Dallas continued. "What are they cleansing Nashville of?"

"Criminals?" Susan asked.

"Sinners," Pastor Kelly said.

"Violators of God's Ten Commandments." Everyone looked at me. Dallas smiled. It was the first smile he'd given me since Skylar sent him the video file.

"Yes. And they didn't look for these people on their own," Sam said, following Dallas's logic. "They took the word of Nashville journalists. Each person was publicly accused of the crime before the killers sentenced them to death. That says a lot about the killers."

"So, my question is this," Dallas said. "If they're cleansing Nashville, why go after Pastor Sayers and Abbey's father, if their sins were committed in Guatemala?"

That never crossed my mind. I was so concerned about how they knew about it that I never wondered why. "Because they were in Nashville?" I wanted to know what Dallas was thinking too.

"Do you remember what Skylar texted you that night?"

"Which night?" I rolled back from the table.

"The night she killed her counselor. She said she was going to make you great."

"Well, I don't feel very great right now, Dallas. What's your point?" I pretended to look down at the pictures and notes.

"Skylar was going to make you great by being your counterpart." Dallas picked up the article about Timothy Johnson's drones. "It says here David Smith made several attempts to have Timothy arrested. He called the police, but they didn't fix the problem. The killers fixed what you all couldn't." He picked up another article. "Zahir Khan was praised for his colorful garden. It's not illegal to have a religious garden in your backyard. Even if there was a complaint, the police couldn't do anything about it." Dallas stopped and looked around the table. "But they could."

"You think they're trying to help Abbey clean up Nashville?" Sam asked. "Interesting theory, but it doesn't fit Jonathan Buxton or his father."

"Maybe—maybe not," Dallas said. "It's just a working theory."

"Not a bad one at that," I said, defending Dallas's effort to help us. "It certainly fits Nicholas Sayers and my father. Those were their attempts to right a wrong I suffered at fourteen, when I was powerless to do anything. Skylar and Hadassah used their power to exact retribution on my behalf."

"So, it does all center on you, Abbey." Susan's face was pale white. "What about the pictures they had of us? What does that mean?" Her hands were trembling. "Will she come after me and the kids?"

Dallas thought for a moment. "I'm not sure why they had pictures of Abbey's closest friends. Maybe as insurance."

Sam stood and ran his fingers through his beard. He paced

back and forth. "Skylar thinks this is a game between her and Abbey. She's already criticized Abbey for getting help." He looked out the back window and seemed to be watching something. "In fact, she would hate what we're doing right now."

"Except that I'm back in the game. The accident knocked me out, but I can use my mind even in a wheelchair. With the aid of technology, it's almost like I'm at the crime scene anyway." I was grasping at straws. Sam was right. By calling them all here and asking for their help, I just put a target on each person's back. "I'm sorry I pulled you into this." I spun the chair around so no one could see the trembling of my lips.

"God has a plan," Pastor Kelly said. "He's given each one of us a unique perspective and gift to help with this." He reached out, grabbed the arm of my wheelchair and turned me back to the table. "You may have the badge, Abbey, but order and responsibility belong to us all."

"Here, here," Dallas said.

"You were there when I needed you. I'm with you, Sweetie, through thick and thin." Susan was walking a precarious line between her support of me and protection of her children.

"If my daughter's putting her head on the chopping block, I'm not going to leave her alone."

"Thanks everyone, but Sam and I signed on for this. You didn't." I regretted my decision to include them in this puzzle.

"How about this?" Pastor Kelly asked. "What if we stick to the interpretation and you two handle the dangerous part?" Sam and I nodded.

They spent the best part of two hours giving possible interpretations and applications to the various Bible verses. What became painstakingly clear that night was Penny knew the Bible but was coming from a very literal point of view. Like many other false teachers, Penny was taking pieces of a whole—parts of a passage— and twisting it to make sense with her goal. She was everything I hated about religious people. Skylar's knowledge, however, was

limited like mine. Penny studied it and believed she was given a mandate to carry out a cleansing of some sort. No one found any indication of a change in Penny's plans or in the order she would carry them out. "They lay the victims out like sacrificial lambs," I said. "They even drain the bodies of their blood."

"These aren't sacrifices," Pastor Kelly said.

"That's what they call them."

"But Abbey, sacrifices were made to cover or pay for sins. The priests killed lambs and bulls to pay for the sins of the people so God would overlook them. They're using the Bible and these articles to excuse a mass execution."

"What's the difference?" Sam asked.

"Jesus gave Himself up as a sacrifice to save us. These women are killing others for the simple purpose of punishing them for their perceived sin."

"Oh." I didn't know if Sam got it or not, but it made perfect sense to me. Maybe Penny didn't know the Bible as well as she thought. So, these were executions, not sacrifices. "Why didn't she kill my father?" I asked as everyone was getting up from the table. "She did everything imaginable to him. Why not kill him? Didn't one of those verses say that the person hung on a tree was cursed and would die?"

"Not exactly. Paul was making a reference to a verse in Deuteronomy which gave God's people instructions on what to do with the body of a person hung on a tree. Paul was making an obvious reference to Christ," Pastor Kelly explained.

"Well, my father was no Christ," I snapped. "I'm sorry. I'm really tired and sore. I'm pushing myself too hard."

"Where's your medicine?" Susan asked. I told her and she ran to the back bathroom and grabbed two pills for me. "Don't force it, Abbey. You need to get well."

"I think that's a good cue for us to leave and let her rest," Dallas said. "Call you tomorrow?"

"I'd like that." He put his hand on my shoulder as he rose to leave. I felt warm all over. After they left, I rolled back to Hannah's room and took a nap until supper.

Chapter Forty-six

Thursday, October 16, 11:25 AM—Ripley House

"Why won't you go see him?" Susan asked. She was completely exasperated with me. "He's your own father."

"You of all people should know why I don't want to see him." I rolled down the hall, but she followed me. "He wasn't like your dad, Susan. He criticized me from day one, and when I needed him, he threw me out on the street." I rolled into the bedroom and tried to throw the door closed. She stopped it with her foot and came into the room.

"Abbey, they nearly killed him. Don't you care?" She plopped down on the bed with a huff. "Think of him as any other victim in one of your cases. Don't you at least check on them?"

"Sam checked on him this morning. He's still in critical care."

"What about your mother? Is she sitting there all by herself?"

"Probably." I grabbed the remote and turned the television on. Not that I cared about watching anything, but I wanted to drown out Susan's voice. Of course, it didn't work.

She stood between the television and me. "You're heartless, Abbey Rhodes."

"What do you want from me, Susan? They didn't care if I was alive or dead for the last ten years. They chose not to search for me, and they also refused to let me come crying back. I asked for forgiveness. My parents threw me to the wolves, and the wolves took me in. Mr. Morales, for all his faults, gave me food, clothing, and shelter." Susan tried to interrupt me, but I pounced on her.

241

"You grew up in this pretty little, safe world where you were the only child, loved and cherished by two parents. You were spoiled, Susan. The first tragedy you ever had to face was Mark's death, and even then, your parents sold their house and moved next door to help you. You have no idea what I went through. You have no idea the baggage I still deal with daily. So, don't call me heartless! I know I have a heart because it's broken." I paused to take a breath. "I'm doing the best I can." I rolled into the bathroom and slammed the door. She didn't follow. As I looked in the mirror and cried, I heard her shut the bedroom door. I'd gone too far. I was pushing the only one who loved me away. I felt the walls building, my heart going numb.

I had to get back to my apartment where I could do what I wanted to do without anyone's judgment. I had enough of that for a lifetime. I didn't need my best friend pouring it on too.

Someone knocked on the bedroom door. I ignored her. She knocked again. "Abbey, are you okay? It's Dallas." I heard the twisting of the doorknob. "I'm coming in."

I looked back in the mirror. I couldn't let him see me like this. "Give me a minute." I washed my face and reapplied my makeup.

"Are you all right? I could hear the screaming from the front porch."

"No, but I'll be okay in a minute." I finished fixing my appearance and opened the door. I rolled into the bedroom. "I thought you were going to call me. I didn't know you'd show up here."

"Is that a bad thing?" he asked. "I thought it would be a nice surprise, but now I'm not so sure." He sat on the side of the bed.

"It's a wonderful surprise." I reached for his hand, but he didn't reach back for me. "Your timing may not be the best, but I'll take whatever I can get." I needed him to hold me and make me feel wanted. He was still cold and distant.

"How are you feeling physically?"

"The side still hurts. My foot is getting better. I put a little weight on it this morning, and I think in a day or two, I can move up to crutches." It would give me greater freedom as well. Of course, my apartment building was completely accessible by wheelchair. I could go back this morning if I really wanted. I didn't want to leave Susan vulnerable. Somehow, I would have to swallow my pride and apologize for the things I said. I needed some time to get over the hurt first.

"I saw your parents this morning." Where was he going with this? "Your father is going to pull through physically. Emotionally, he has a lot of work and time ahead of him to get past this kind of trauma." He left it at that. Dallas was good at giving just enough to move me, but not so much as to put me on the defensive. There was no comment about my need to see them. His comment was informational only.

"You look good," I said. "I may not let you leave." He rolled me into the den. We sat and talked about all sorts of things. "Dallas, I've been thinking a lot lately, especially about why I can't give up on this case."

"Because you don't trust anyone else?"

That was partially true, but that wasn't my revelation. "I think it goes much deeper. I think I'm always afraid I'll never be enough. If I give up, I make it true."

"What do you mean?"

"I'll never be good enough for Susan, for you, for my job, and believe it or not, for God. Skylar knows my weaknesses and dangles her challenge in front of my face."

"That is deep, Abbey." He took my hand. "The beauty of it all is none of us will ever be good enough for God. If we could be, Jesus and His sacrifice are in vain. God loves us despite our short-comings." We chatted a little more about feelings of inadequacy. Eventually, we circled back around to the case. "You know, I bet Penny struggles with temptation."

"What is that supposed to mean?"

"It means that she's probably susceptible to temptation as well as you and I are." I must have given him a strange look because he quickly explained that it had nothing to do with physical temptations. "I bet she is tempted with pride and control."

Something went off in my brain, and a series of ideas streamed past my consciousness like a wall with seven televisions all on different channels. I silently watched as multiple scenarios revealed themselves. "Oh, Dallas, you're a genius. That's how we're going to capture her. We're going to bait her into a tirade, and she'll fall right into our hands."

"Thanks for the compliment. I'm trying to remember what I said that was so clever." Dallas stared at me, but I was still busy watching scenarios play out. He crossed his arms and waited.

"Remember when you said the Bible could be her undoing?" He thought for a moment and nodded. "If we can use the Bible to injure her pride and frustrate her sense of control, I think we can cause her to lash out."

"Wait. We want her to lash out?" Dallas began to debate the ethics and morals of using the Bible for personal gain. "I'm not sure I'm comfortable with this plan of yours."

"Think about it. Isn't that what Paul did when he got the Jewish leaders to argue with each other over the afterlife?" I remembered part of that story. Some believed in life after death and the others didn't.

"Not exactly. He created a debate amongst their ranks."

"So that he would get out of trouble, right?" I knew I was right. Dallas was just being stubborn. "If she is misinterpreting the Bible, isn't it kind of like your duty as a Bible teacher to correct her? You are a professor after all."

"I know what you're doing, Abbey, and it won't work." Dallas was trying to stare me down.

I put out my bottom lip and pretended to pout. "It will if you want it to."

"That's not fair," he said, looking away. "I'm not comfortable with the ethics of the request."

"I have a great idea, but I need your knowledge and ability

to sell it if I'm going to stop Penny from killing more people." I knew that wasn't fair either. This wasn't a time to play fair. I had to use everything at my disposal, which included Dallas's ability to debate and cite Bible verses at will.

"Let's say I agree. What's the plan?"

I laid out my new plan in as much detail as I could. I shared the name of my media contact from the Dean Swain case. If I could get Captain Harris to sign off on the idea, we'd be in business. After much back and forth, Dallas consented. He had one condition, and I had already planned for it. Now for the hard sell: Sam, Sarge, Lieutenant Stallings, and Captain Harris.

Chapter Forty-seven

Friday, October 17, 9:27 AM—Homicide offices

Sam rolled me into Captain Harris's office. Sergeant McNally got up and moved the chairs to make space for the wheelchair. Lieutenant Stallings smiled and said, "Some people will do anything to get out of work." It was nice to see him smile. I noticed Agent Carmichael wasn't present.

"If that were true, I'd be at home watching old movies right now." I knew he was kidding.

He handed me my badge and firearm. "Welcome back.

Captain Harris remained stoic.

"Captain, I appreciate you taking time to hear me out on this."

"Honestly, Rhodes, we're behind the ball on this case, even with the Fed's help. I'm willing to hear any plan that might gain some ground on them." He motioned for everyone to sit. "How long will you be in the chair?"

"I see my doctor Monday morning, and if the side has healed enough, I'll be on crutches when I leave. Thankfully the wounds on my foot weren't terribly deep."

"You're still officially on leave until cleared by a doctor," he said. "Let's not waste any more time. What's your plan?"

I looked at Sam, and he gave an encouraging nod. "We feel the best plan is to cause dissension between Skylar Watson and Penny Thatcher. We do this by publicly wounding their pride and making Penny feel like Skylar is using her for the endgame, which is to bring recognition to me as a detective."

"What makes you think Skylar Watson wants you to succeed?" Lieutenant Stallings asked. "It would seem like she's out to embarrass us."

All eyes studied me, gauging my plan and my confidence. "She told me so herself," I said. "In her own words, 'Let me be your Moriarty—your Lord Voldemort. You may be great now, but I can make you a legend.' She also criticized me for hiding out in my apartment instead of staying on the case."

"Sounds like a trap," Sergeant McNally said. We broke into debate over Skylar's message. Was Skylar setting me up to fail or succeed in view of all Nashville.

"Let's assume you're right. How would you turn them against one another?" Captain Harris pulled the conversation back on topic. "Explain your plan."

I took a deep breath. "This case is centered on the Ten Commandments. Penny is punishing people who violated them."

"We know this," Captain Harris said. "Get on with it."

He made me nervous. I began to doubt my plan. Captain Harris was a tough, no-nonsense man. As a black man in a predominantly white man's position, he'd worked hard to obtain the rank of Captain. He wasn't about to approve a plan that might embarrass the department or jeopardize his position. "Well, sir." Penny is using the Bible to communicate with us. She seems to have a thorough but superficial grasp of it." I used Dallas's words. Captain Harris tapped his fingers on his desk. He was growing more impatient. "Skylar only has a basic knowledge of it. My plan is to go on a television interview with Professor Dallas Gatlin and embarrass her with his interpretation, showing Nashville that Penny isn't as smart biblically as she is trying to portray."

"Pardon me for interrupting, Rhodes," Sergeant McNally said. "Won't that make her turn up the fire on the killings?"

"I believe it will make *us* the targets of her fury. Since Skylar has demanded that I not be hurt, she'll go after Dallas."

"You want to use your boyfriend as bait?" Lieutenant Stallings asked. "That's pretty bold."

"The department cannot use civilians as bait or in any other fashion that may bring harm to them." Captain Harris said it in such a way that he covered his legal bases but implied that Dallas was free to make his own decision.

"Tidwell," Sergeant McNally said. "You're unusually quiet. What do you think?"

"Abbey's given me the whole plan, and I think it might just work. If we play our cards correctly, we could wrap this case up by the end of the week."

I explained every detail of the plan, how we would use the Bible to contradict Penny's legalistic interpretations. Dallas would show Nashville how she was a hypocrite, not a spokesperson from God. Then, I would drive the wedge between Penny and Skylar. I knew the risk. If the plan worked, we would capture Penny Thatcher, but it came with a dire consequence I didn't discuss with my superiors. It would turn Skylar against me. Instead of making me great, she would try to destroy me. If I'd learned anything about psychopaths, it was that they didn't like being humiliated. They would not tolerate defeat. In essence, I was putting myself out as bait too.

After much discussion, they consented to my interview. If Dallas wished to join me, that was his decision. Spence and a new detective named Ginny Flinn volunteered to help us. They looked enough like Dallas and me to pull off our plan, a human shell game. First, we set a trap and hoped Penny would take the bait. I believed Dallas's theory was right and a bruised ego would set everything in motion. Now, I had to call on an old acquaintance for favor.

Chapter Forty-eight

Friday, October 17, 12:06 PM—Ripley House

Sam drove me to Susan's. "I sure hope you know what you're doing, Abbey."

"Me too. It's got to work, Sam." He pulled into the driveway and helped me get into the wheelchair. "I'll be glad when I can ditch this thing."

He wheeled me up to the front door. "I'm glad you have Susan to help you through it." I handed him the key. He unlocked the handle and deadbolt. We heard a woman's scream, and Sam threw open the door. He followed the sound of Susan's screams. I rolled over the threshold. Just as I was pushing myself toward the hallway, a man ran into me, flipping me out of the wheelchair. He tumbled to the floor and slid into the doorframe. I grabbed onto his pant leg and pulled with all my might.

He kicked at me and screamed at me to let him go. He kicked again, landing a solid blow to the side of my face. I grimaced and caught the other leg as he drew it back. I quickly wrapped both arms around his legs and held them firmly to my chest. He beat on my head and back, but I kept my face buried in his legs for protection.

A shot echoed through the hallway, and we both paused our struggle. "Sam!"

The moment I screamed, the man hit me in the back of my neck and shouted, "Let me go!"

Suddenly, the beating stopped, and the man's body slumped. "Abbey, are you okay?"

"Sam?" I opened my eyes. He was standing over me, holding his gun by the barrel. He'd hit the man with the handle, knocking him out cold. "I was afraid you'd been shot."

"No. I had to shoot him."

"Him? Him who? Is Susan all right?"

"She'll have a bruise around her neck, but she'll live. There was another guy with his hands around Susan's throat. He wouldn't let go, even after I hit him. Probably hopped up on something. Susan went limp, and he came after me."

"Is he…"

"Dead. Yes."

The man Sam knocked unconscious started to stir. Sam sat on him and pulled his arms behind his back. He got his cuffs and latched them on the man's wrists. "Friends of Penny's?"

"Where have these guys come from? I thought you got everyone when you raided the apartment?"

"There must have been more members of the cult than we expected." Sam called for an ambulance and the police. "Will this mess with your plan?"

"It might help it. If they were after Susan to send a message to me, our response will be perfect." I walked slowly using my heel on my bandaged foot to protect my wound. I found Susan crying in the corner of her bedroom. The covers were on the floor, and I feared the worst. I sat beside Susan and cradled her in my arms. "We got them both, Susan. It's okay now."

"No, Abbey. It's not okay. What if the kids had been here?" She sobbed so hard, her chest bounced with each fit. "Who *are* they?"

"We're going to find out," I assured her.

Susan's question gnawed at my mind. *Who were they?* Were they messengers from Skylar or Penny? This was not a random attack. They both knew where I was staying. Penny acted only in her version of righteousness. Susan would have to be guilty of violating a biblical law for her to order an attack. No, this was Skylar's work. She wanted to isolate me, to strip me of all help.

"An ambulance is on its way. I need to speak with Sam."

I made my way back to the foyer. "It's Skylar. I know it."

"What makes you so sure?"

I explained my reasoning, and then I added, "Either you or Dallas is next. We better make our move before she makes hers."

"You said it was Skylar's doing." Sam looked confused. He scratched the top of his head and leaned against the wall.

"I know. If we publicly blame Penny for it, and there is no biblical reason for Susan's attack, we can drive a huge wedge between them." I heard the sirens heading our way. "They've given us enough fuel for a bonfire."

The ambulance arrived first and took Susan. "The Medical Examiner's office is coming for him," a paramedic said as he rolled Susan out on a gurney. "We'll take her for scans to see if there is any internal damage."

I got back into the chair and helped Sam process the scene with the officers from East Precinct. Lieutenant Daniels arrived shortly after the ambulance left. "I heard the address on the scanner." He pushed my hair away from my face. "You have a cut under your eye. What happened?

"I'm fine."

"No, you're not, Abbey."

"I've had worse." I told him about my father. He asked about Susan, and Sam filled him in on the attack.

"What can I do to help?" He stared into my eyes. "Abbey, I know this is triggering all kinds of bad memories. Don't clam up and think you have to do this on your own."

"That's what Skylar wants," Sam said. "Don't let her win."

With Sam's permission, I explained our plan to bring Penny out of the woodwork and into our trap. He picked up immediately on the danger to me as well as Dallas.

"Is your boyfriend really okay with this? I thought he didn't like you being in danger."

"He doesn't. I guess he thinks he'll be there to protect me."

Despite the gravity of our current situation, Lieutenant Daniels laughed. "Even in a wheelchair, I'd put my money on you."

I rolled through the house looking for possible entryways for the attackers. Susan would not leave her house unlocked under any circumstances. Ever since she was pulled into the case in the homeless camp and was nearly killed, Susan worked desperately to somehow repay me for saving her life, though I never expected anything from her in return. Sam and Lieutenant Daniels worked with the officers to gather evidence from the scene.

As I passed Susan's room on the way back to the foyer, I noticed once again the bedding. She was changing the sheets. They surprised her from behind. She wasn't answering the front door. The door was still locked when we got there. They were either already in the house or they slipped in while she was making the bed. Where did they enter? I went door to door, window to window. Then I found it. The door to her garage was unlocked. I opened the door and discovered their entrance. Her car's back doors were open. How would they have gotten in without her noticing? She pulled into both schools through the parents' drop-off lanes. But the kids were staying with friends. Susan didn't take them to school.

I smelled the faint scent of brownies and remembered Danny's school was having a bake sale. Susan baked them last night and would have taken them into the school herself. Thinking she was making a quick drop-off, I bet she left her car unlocked. How bold of them to climb into her back seat under the scrutiny of school staff. They had to time it perfectly. They knew she would be going inside. But, that wasn't her normal routine, so how would they know?

"Sam. Lieutenant Daniels." They ran to me, not knowing if it was another emergency.

"What is it?" Sam asked. He was out of breath.

"I think this house is bugged. They knew Susan was going to break routine and go into Danny's school today. She never does that."

Agent Carmichael walked in just as Lieutenant Daniels called in a sweep of the house. We all stayed until they finished. They found three audio-visual devices like the ones found in my apartment. Thankfully, none were found where Dallas and I discussed the plan.

"If you don't mind," Agent Carmichael said, grabbing one of the devices, "I'm going to track these to the store and find out who bought these."

"Works for us," Sam said. She nodded and took off.

"How did they gain access?" Sam asked. "How long have they been here?"

It was one thing to use maintenance personnel in my apartment building to access my apartment and install listening devices. It was quite another situation to break into a person's home unnoticed and do it. Susan never mentioned any electricians, plumbers, HVAC companies, or appliance repairmen in her house. Of course, Dallas and I had been isolated to my apartment for a week, and then I was in the hospital. The hospital? Susan and Hannah visited me on two different days. I bet Skylar had it done then. How was she aware of our schedules? How was she able to convince people to plant bugs in my apartment and Susan's house? Where was she getting the money for all of this?

I suddenly wondered if Dallas's apartment had them too. If it did, we might be able to make use of them. We moved to the front porch, away from the bugs. "Can we scan Dallas's apartment without making a big deal of it? I just want to locate any, not remove them yet."

Sam made it happen. Unfortunately, they found nothing.

Chapter Forty-nine

Friday, October 17, 7:15 PM—Harmony Apartments

Dr. Pederman brought Susan home from the hospital. Her neck was already turning a dark blue and You could see the outlines of the man's fingers around the front of her neck in the bruising. Now, Dr. Pederman insisted on keeping Susan and the kids at his house.

I felt the weight of anxiety lift from my shoulders, when Captain Harris ordered two patrol officers to watch the house, and I moved back to my apartment with Dallas's help. We grabbed food on the way and decided to eat first and get his clothes after. With difficulty, I finally convinced him to come to my place to review the plan. It was the first time we'd been alone since that day. The tension was palpable.

In exchange for an exclusive interview, Sally Thomas of Nashville's NBC News agreed to let us talk on Tuesday morning's show. "Let me begin with the basics and make my comments about the relationship between Skylar and Penny. I'll create tension between them and hopefully cause a power battle. Then, I'll introduce you as our resident biblical scholar. You can make a public fool of Penny."

"Making her target me either for revenge or for my views on the Sabbath Day?" I made sure Dallas was up for this. He nodded, but the lack of color in his face showed he was overtaken with fear. "I can't believe you deal with this kind of tension every day."

"Well, it's not like this every day," I admitted. But the job did require dealing with murderers, who didn't value life and would likely kill us too if they got the chance. "I'm glad you're here."

"I couldn't possibly leave you alone right now, especially since you're in a wheelchair." I'm not sure what Dallas would do to protect me, but I was growing fond of the idea being valued. Tomorrow, I had the follow-up appointment for my side. Hopefully, I'd be free of the chair. "Monday is twentieth of the month. Do you think she will keep her word or continue with the schedule?"

It was a good question. "She promised no killings this week. Whether she falls into our trap, depends on your performance Tuesday." Could he truly humiliate her enough to make her break rank and seek personal revenge? Would his arguments be valid and sound? Could he perform on live television? Dallas had never been in this kind of spotlight. Lecturing to freshmen and sophomores in college was nothing compared to facing the tough questions of a news reporter on live television. "If you give sound arguments and add a hint of condescension and sarcasm, she may beat us to your house."

I knew that wasn't exactly true. Penny Thatcher proved she was a meticulous planner. She considered herself a prophetess and priestess of God. She would find affirmation in the Bible and use it to justify her actions. She still believed her cleansing would bring fear and repentance to all Nashville. If Dallas made her look like a fool, she might act sooner. However, I expected no kneejerk reaction. "Spence and Ginny are on board. He will double for you, and Ginny for me. She will make it look like I left your apartment with Spence, only Spence and I will be there the whole time."

"This is the part I don't follow. Is Spence leaving or staying?" Dallas's voice was thinner and softer.

"Once we are inside, Spence will swap clothes with you. It's supposed to be sunny Tuesday, which will help with the ruse. With sunglasses, no one will know it's you who is actually leaving with Ginny."

"How is she getting in the apartment?" he asked.

"We've already arranged for Ginny to be in the apartment across the hall. She and I will wear the same outfit. I'll give her my crutches."

"If you're on crutches by then."

"I'll give her my crutches." I vowed to have crutches—officially or unofficially. "That will help sell the story. When you open the door to leave, as Spence, she will join you and go to the car. It will look like Spence is leaving with me. Don't stop until you arrive at Homicide. Sam will take it from there."

"Did you come up with this plan, Abbey?"

"Yes. Why? Don't you like it?" I could tell he wasn't sure how to answer that question.

"It's quite devious."

I took that as a compliment even though he probably had a different intent. "We need to make them believe that you stayed in the apartment by yourself. You have to appear defiant and over-confident, which puts a target on your back. Penny must believe she can break in and overcome you."

"What if she doesn't buy it?" he asked. "What if she knows it's a set up and that I'm not alone?" He went to the sink and filled a glass with water. He gulped it down and filled it again. Classic dry mouth from anxiety.

"Then we go with plan B."

There wasn't a plan B yet. Hopefully, this plan worked, and we could subdue Penny. That would leave Skylar alone and vulnerable. We could turn the tables on them and go on the offensive. It was the first time we'd taken that initiative, and I finally felt we were gaining enough ground to pull ahead on this case.

"Relax, Dallas. You'll be great." He forced a smile. "I believe in you." It was true. My world was expanding. In the past two years I'd progressed from self-reliance—trusting no one else—to faith in Sam, Susan, and Dallas. Maybe, one day I could trust God again.

"Why should I stay the night here again?" he asked.

Dallas said it is such a way that I knew this was not a romantic getaway. He was here to help with the case, but that was all. I wanted to lie next to him, to smell his cologne and feel the beat of his heart.

"It's all a part of the ruse. We need them to believe you're caring for me until I'm out of this chair. If all goes well at the doctor Monday, I'll progress to crutches. You can stay through the interview Tuesday to make sure I'm okay with the transition."

"Skylar will believe I'm here to protect you."

Cute.

"No. Skylar knows me too well. She would never believe I resorted to you for protection."

"I think there's a putdown in there somewhere." He put his hands over his heart I'd stabbed him with a knife. If he only knew how true that image might be if we failed to pull this off.

"It wasn't intended to say anything about you. Skylar believes I'm much more than I really am. She's playing into my deepest fear, that I'm not enough."

If the interview Tuesday morning worked, Skylar would believe she succeeded, making me great in the eyes of the public. Then she would no longer need Penny. Skylar would emerge as the perfect antagonist to my story. Two strong women, equally matched in strength—yin and yang. She had superior intellect and skills with technology. I had a keen sense of analysis and physical skills with weapons and martial arts. By making me great, Skylar could devise a final showdown where she could show her superiority.

For now, I needed Skylar to turn on Penny. By giving Penny our full attention, attention that Skylar felt she herself deserved, we would drive a wedge between them. Penny would act first, and Skylar would let her fall. Penny was no longer of value to her. I feared what that meant for me. Even though Skylar was just eighteen, I couldn't match her wit. She'd proven she was miles ahead of me on this case. What could she do without restraints?

"Abbey, where's your head?" Dallas was waving his hands in front of my face. "You zoned out on me. Don't do that Tuesday."

"I won't. I was running scenarios in my head, making sure everything was in place." I sold the plan to my superiors, but I hoped beyond all hope Skylar and Penny were not ahead of me on this too. If I misjudged, Dallas would die. I couldn't handle that.

"Let's go over it one more time before I turn in for the night," he said. We reviewed it twice more. Finally, he felt he had a firm grasp on the gist of things and changed into his pajamas.

"Cute. *Lord of the Rings?*"

"Absolutely. The best fantasy trilogy ever. One day, I'm going to write something of that magnitude." We sat there another hour as Dallas described the stories he wished to write after they approved his dissertation and awarded his doctorate. It was nice to hear his dreams. I'd never asked about them before.

Did I have dreams beyond being a detective? What else was there for me? I went to my room and thought about my parents. Should I reach out to them or wait for them to apologize to me? I decided to check on them by phone tomorrow, and then I could focus on Tuesday's interview. After that, I'd go in person. They waited ten years. What was another day or so?

Chapter Fifty

Monday, October 20, 9:27 AM—Dr Nguyan's Office

Monday came, and Penny kept her word. No one died. Later that morning, Dallas drove me to my orthopedic doctor's office. I prayed for good news.

"You must have a little Wolverine blood in you," Dr. Nguyan said.

"Wolverine blood? That doesn't make any sense." What was he talking about?

"You know—Wolverine from Marvel's *X-Men*."

I stared at him. "Marvel? Like *The Avengers*?" I asked. It was the only reference to Marvel I knew. Maybe I should have let Dallas come in with me. He would know what the doctor was trying to say.

"Wolverine has the ability to heal quickly." He shook his head. I could tell he was disappointed that I didn't follow him. "Your foot is healing rather nicely. You can wear comfortable shoes—soft-soled shoes when you are at home. There's no need to fit you for a set of crutches. When you're out and about I'd like you to keep your foot in a protective boot for another two weeks. Then, if it continues like it has been, you can go back to wearing regular shoes." He noticed my smile. "Comfortable shoes, Abbey. No heels."

"Absolutely, Doctor Nguyan. Thank you so much."

"Really, you don't know Wolverine? Hugh Jackman?" I shrugged my shoulders, and he left.

His nurse came in shortly after with an orthopedic boot. He

put it on and let me try a few steps for confirmation. "Take it easy, Miss Rhodes. No racing."

"You got it." I was so anxious to untether myself from the wheelchair I would have promised anything. He held the door, and I walked through with a broad smile. Dallas stood as I came back to the waiting room. "What do you think?"

"You can make anything look good," Dallas said.

"Perfect answer."

He opened the door, and I hobbled down the hall to the elevator. The doors closed and I began fussing nonstop. "I still can't drive."

"You have plenty of friends that can drive you."

"I want to drive myself again." I talked on and on like a little girl after her first day at school. I listed all the things I wanted to do now that I was out of the wheelchair. I'd only been in it for a few days, but it felt like a lifetime. The clinic's double doors slid aside as I approached, and I made a beeline to the car.

I reached for the passenger door handle and asked, "What's on your mind?" He didn't answer. I must have really been hoofing it. I turned, but Dallas wasn't there. I quickly scanned the parking lot. No sign of him.

"Dallas?"

Nothing. I rushed back to the entrance, and the doors opened. He wasn't there either. I looked back to the parking lot to make sure I didn't miss him. I moved to the elevator as fast as I could in my new boot and pressed the button. The doors opened.

"Hi, I'm Dallas Gatlin." He stood in the elevator with his hand extended to shake mine.

I hit him in the stomach with my fist, and he doubled over in pain. I screamed, "Don't you ever do that to me again! I thought Skylar grabbed you." I hobbled away. My foot hurt from all the fast walking.

He pushed himself up from the side of the elevator and stepped off.

"You just took off and left me here. I thought I'd wait until you realized I was missing. It was a joke."

"Well, it wasn't funny." As I moved through the double doors once again, I said, "Maybe this interview is a bad idea."

He followed me all the way to the car trying to convince me he wasn't afraid of Penny or Skylar. He should be. I was more determined than ever to keep my eyes on him. This little innocent scare drove that message home.

Chapter Fifty-one

Monday, October 20, 6:30 PM—Pederman House

Dr. Pederman opened the door and greeted us. "Susan's been dying to see you."

I hobbled past him in my boot. I could feel the swelling of my foot. I hadn't followed my doctor's advice. "How is she?"

"In need of a good friend." He patted Dallas on the back. "Glad you both could come."

"Abbey!" Hannah Ripley ran around the corner of the hall and slid right past me in her socked feet. With a big smile, she hugged me tight. She nearly knocked me down.

"Easy there, girl." I hugged her back. It was good to have someone who understood me.

She pulled a card out of her back pocket and flashed it in my face. "I got it!"

"Too close. Pull it back a bit so I can see what you have." She did, and I felt horrible. She was supposed to get her learner's permit Tuesday, and I forgot to ask. "Have you driven yet?" She gave me that look.

Of course, Susan was sheltering her in the house. "Honey, I'll take you this weekend."

I could see the disappointment in her face. "Your mom was attacked yesterday. I know you're excited, but…"

"I know. Grampa already gave me the lecture." She looked into the next room to see if anyone was listening, before asking, "Do you really think they'll come back?"

"Come here." I went to the front window and pulled the curtain aside. "See that car?"

"Yes."

"Those are two good friends of mine. They promised they would take care of your family, and I trust them both." She sighed. "Listen, Hannah. We're going to catch them soon. Trust me." I was asking Hannah to do something I rarely did—trust someone enough to stop worrying. "I need to go see your mom right now. We'll talk later. Okay?"

I put on my happy face and hobbled into the next room. "Where's my stunt double?"

"Oh, sure, Abbey, I'm nearly killed, and you make it all about you."

"Susan Elizabeth Ripley!"

"She knows I'm kidding, Mom. Sheesh. Sometimes I think she would trade me for you if she could."

"Why trade when you can have both?" I asked. "Right, Mrs. Pederman?"

She gave me a gentle hug. "Look at you." We both looked rough. She wiped a tear from her eye. "What am I going to do with the two of you?"

Mrs. Pederman rushed to the kitchen when she heard a pot lid rattling from the steam.

I plopped beside Susan on the couch. I felt the pull of my stitches. "Seriously, Susan, how do you feel?"

"It looks worse than it feels—physically." She put her hand on mine. "Emotionally, I'm a basket case." She leaned into me.

"You keep interfering with our investigations. First the Dean Swain case and now the Commandment Killers."

"Commandment Killers? I thought you hated that name."

"I do, but I was on a roll." She laughed. Success. "Seriously, though, if you insist on being involved, I'm going to have to train you in self-defense."

"It wasn't my choice." Susan ran her fingers along the edges of the bruise on her neck. "I can't shake the feeling that I was dying. What would the kids do if I left them too?"

"You won't. We're close to catching Penny. We've already taken most of her crew."

"What about Skylar? You know, Abbey, one of these days she's going to turn on you."

"I'm ready for her." I tried to ooze confidence, but the words fell flat. "We're focusing on the immediate threat first." I explained pieces of our new strategy.

"You need to go see your father, Abbey." Susan leaned up and looked into my eyes. "You can't run forever."

"Who said I was running?" I wasn't running from him, but I wasn't about to go crawling back to him either. I tried that before, and it just made matters worse. He interpreted my groveling as an admission of sin. "He needs peace and quiet to heal right now. My presence would offer everything but."

"But he's your father."

We'd been through this discussion before, and it didn't go well. I took a deep breath and measured my word carefully. "Susan, you don't understand. Your dad has always been there for you."

"I know. I remember the lecture."

"I'm sorry. I keep taking my frustrations out on you and Dallas." She put her head on my shoulder. "My father not only disowned me, but he also pronounced me dead. Why would I go see him?"

"To reconcile with your parents." Even though battered and bruised from the attack, Susan's voice was full of optimism.

I tried to let my anger go—to move on—but it only worsened. "Susan, you're picturing some kind of Prodigal Son ending. It's not going to happen. There is no happily ever after with us."

"What about your mother? Surely, she could use your support right now." I didn't respond.

Thankfully, Mrs. Pederman hollered, "Supper's ready," from the kitchen. We washed our hands and moved to the table. Dallas and Hannah were helping her set the table.

Wait a minute. Someone was missing. "Where's Danny?" I should have noticed his absence earlier, but I was talking with Susan.

"I took him back to his friend's house," Dr. Pederman said.

"They're in the same class at school. I thought it would be better to keep him sidetracked and clear of here," Susan added. "I would have done the same with Hannah, but she put up a big fuss." Hannah gave her an ugly look. "I think she wanted to see her Aunt Abbey too."

Mrs. Pederman served an Italian dish with white sauce. It was fantastic. Creamy with small pieces of grilled chicken. We ate and steered the conversation clear of the case and recent events. Hannah finished her meal and moved to the den to do homework. Dallas and Dr. Pederman talked biblical history. I just listened and wondered if our plan would succeed. If it failed, how would that affect Susan and her family? Skylar sent men to hurt her; she would try again until she took Susan out of the picture. I knew Dallas wasn't far behind on her list. I made a personal vow to go after Skylar with everything I had once Penny was arrested. I wished I could go on television without the boot, but my foot hurt more than I was willing to admit. Maybe I could work on a sympathy angle. We thanked them for dinner and went to the car.

When we got to my apartment, Dallas noticed the swelling in my foot and said instead of leaving after the interview, he could stay an extra night at my apartment so I could keep it elevated. He fixed his bed on the couch. We stayed up another two hours watching an old movie before I made my way to my room and to bed.

One day, I thought, *I won't be going alone.*

For the first time, I didn't stop the dream. I let it go, and the scenarios of a future with Dallas and a family filled my mind. It was a nice dream, but I knew we had to survive Penny and Skylar first.

Chapter Fifty-two

Tuesday, October 21, 6:15 AM—Nashville's NBC Affiliate

We arrived early at the NBC studios in Nashville for preparation. Dallas protested the idea of wearing makeup, even though they explained he would look deathly pale without it. He finally agreed to a light brushing of powder to eliminate the glare on his cheeks and forehead. They pointed us to our respective chairs, attached our microphones, and showed where we should look when answering the questions. My nerves were shot. I hated being in the spotlight, but this was a necessity.

Sally Thomas flashed her Emmy-winning smile the moment the light signaled we were going live. "Good morning, Nashville. Today we have an exclusive interview with two specialists in The Commandment killings." I winced at that title internally, but kept my smile for the camera. "Let me introduce Homicide Detective Abbey Rhodes and Belmont religion professor Dallas Gatlin. So glad you could join me this morning."

"Thank you for having us," I said as politely as I could. Thankfully, my voice didn't squeak or stammer. "There are a lot of misconceptions and rumors flying about. We have important details we would like to give your listeners about the case." Dallas stared at Sally, unwilling to look at the camera. I wished I could read his mind.

"Well, then, let's get right to it," Sally said, pulling out a notebook of case details and questions. "When was the first death associated with the Commandment killings?"

My smile was less sincere at that point. She had no intention of letting us make our case and go home. Sally was going to milk this opportunity for all it was worth. "Sunday, August thirty-first. A man's body was discovered lying next to his drone. He—"

She cut me off. "I understand you originally believed the woman's husband was guilty, since he'd filed multiple complaints about the drone activity. What led you away from him as a suspect?"

How did she know those details? "In a case like this, you never expect it to be part of a series of killings. That only comes in hindsight after the second or even third murde. You always begin with the most logical suspects."

Sally looked into the lens of the camera. "Surely, when you have mysterious markings on the hands and foreheads like these do, you suspect more will follow."

Another detail we had not released. "You know what they say. Hindsight is twenty-twenty."

"At one point, even the two of you were considered persons of interest in the killings."

Dallas sat up in his seat. "My apologies for interrupting, but you led us to believe we were here today to talk about the current and future aspect of her case."

Sally's smile faded. "You are correct, Professor Gatlin. Of course, a teacher of English and Religion must appreciate the significance of this case's foundational details."

Dallas emboldened me. I leaned forward. "Oh, Sally, let's not waste your audience's time with information your competitors have already discussed at length. I thought you wanted fresh details." Having him by my side and jumping in to lend support was just what I needed. "I assumed you wanted to learn about the mind of our killer."

"We'll be right back after this word from our sponsors." The light went off, and she turned on us. "What do you think you're doing, humiliating me like that?" We listened as she reminded us of the great favor she was doing us. Then, I asked if we could focus on saving the lives of potential victims of our case. "This interview could bring a serial killer to her knees," I reminded her. I noticed the flash in her eyes, but she regained her composure just in time for the light to signal we were back on the air.

"We now segue to the mind of a killer. What makes the Commandment Killer tick? Tell us, Detective, what have you learned about our killer? Or should I say killers?"

"Most of the suspects are in custody. The leader of the group you refer to as The Commandment Killers is believed to be Penny Thatcher." I spent the next few minutes giving psychological details of Penny, doing what I could to paint a stark picture of a misguided fanatic. Then I made the shift to Skylar Watson, the mastermind behind the case. I created a sense of awe and respect for the puppet master who pulled Penny's strings. I offered my professional opinion that the two could not survive long as a team with Skylar's need to be in control of everything, even though her grasp of the Bible was childish at best.

"Penny is the means to force Skylar's endgame. Penny is a ritualistic and legalistic follower of the Law, God's Law." That struck me as funny, and I laughed (probably inappropriate considering our subject matter of murder). I quickly added, "I believe Penny's grasp of the Bible is superficial as well, but I'm no religion expert. Let's ask Professor Gatlin to fill in the details."

I glanced at Dallas and smiled. He was ready. There was a fire in his eyes.

"Professor Gatlin, do you agree with Detective Rhodes' assessment?"

"I do." He said it looking straight at me. I shuddered. Something about those words made me feel flush. Then Dallas looked at the camera as if he'd done this his entire life. "Penny Thatcher is a true believer. Now, when I say those words, I do not presume to know her personal relationship with Jesus Christ. However, Penny believes she is *the* spokesperson and hand of God." Dallas continued to distinguish between God's truth and Penny's version of the truth.

Apparently, Sally liked what she was hearing. "I hate to stop you for a commercial break, but they do make it possible for us to carry on." She turned to the camera, "We'll be right back after this." As soon as the light went off, she said, "This is good. As soon as we come back on, I want to hear details about this." She took a deep breath and smiled. "Maybe, if we're lucky, this Penny will be watching and call in."

I hadn't thought of the possibility of direct contact with Penny. Would we be able to do that on air? "If she does, what do we do?"

"We jump to a live debate. She can defend her interpretations, and you can defend yours."

Dallas raised an eyebrow. I had to trust him.

We came back on the air, and Dallas proceeded to make Penny look like a fool. "There are so many inconsistencies between her actions and the teachings in the Bible. Let's take her wish to be called Hadassah, which was the Hebrew name for Esther, the young Jewish girl who became Queen of Persia." Dallas opened his Bible and explained that Hadassah was taken into captivity and displayed before the King of Persia where he took her as his queen. Dallas described Esther's rise to a position of influence and the edict given against her people that would, in essence, wipe the Hebrew people from the face of the earth. "Esther risked her own life to save her people. Penny, on the other hand, sacrifices who she pleases. There is no greater good in her actions. She brings only punishment, not salvation."

He paused to take a drink of water provided by the news station. "The gist of Penny's murder spree is to punish those who have violated the Ten Commandments."

"Which is why we call her the Commandments Killer," Sally said, interjecting herself into his monologue.

"Exactly." He was good. Dallas stroked her ego before moving on. "But her claim as a purist and a prophetess who is killing to cleanse Nashville of violators of God's word is absurd. She and her companions killed their third victim on September twentieth."

"I don't follow," Sally admitted.

"September twentieth was a Saturday, the Jewish Sabbath day. Killing someone was an act of work, which in and of itself, violates the fourth commandment. It is also an act of murder violates the sixth commandment." He looked directly into the camera. "Penny Thatcher is a fraud. She may be a true believer, but God is not the object of her belief. She speaks for no one but herself and Skylar Watson. These points alone prove that. Sally," he spoke directly to the host, "Penny Thatcher is no better than Tobin, Ashbrook, or Berkowitz—killers who twisted the Bible to justify their own desires and actions. A true believer would align herself to God's will and His story of love. According to the Apostle Paul, God's love is patient and kind, and it certainly does not insist on its own way."

Sally asked several questions and made comments on our theories. She thanked us for our time and asked what we were doing to find Penny and to keep Nashville safe. I spun out the department's standard protocol about this being an active investigation and that we'd already given more details than we should. Dallas finished with comments about judging others and God's call to love your neighbor. He'd forgotten to prod Penny to go after him. I got his attention and mouthed, "Sunday as Sabbath."

"Sally, may I add one more thought?" She nodded and he made a quick argument about the Christian day of worship commonly being Sunday, not Saturday. Then he made a succinct case for Sunday being the new Sabbath Day. "If Penny Thatcher professes to be a Christian, she would adopt Sunday as her day of worship also. I don't think she really knows what she believes." Dallas left it with that.

We finished and thanked Sally as the sound technicians removed our microphones, then headed for the exit. As soon as the elevator door closed behind us, I jumped into his arms and put my legs around his hips. "I love you! That was so awesome."

"Thanks." He eased my feet back to the floor. "Let's hope Penny was watching and took the bait."

I was embarrassed by my unreciprocated show of affection.

Chapter Fifty-three

Tuesday, October 21, 1:22 PM—Vanderbilt Hospital

While Dallas and I were eating lunch in a very public and visible place, I received a call from my mother asking me to please visit my father in the hospital. I felt like a little girl hiding from a beating she knew was inevitable. I was a former Army MP, cop, and current homicide detective, and yet, my father still had a mysterious power over me. He still struck fear in my soul. I didn't want to go, but Dallas insisted. I agreed on the condition he would go with me. Why did my father's opinion still matter? What was I afraid of?

We exited the hospital elevator and looked for the Critical Care waiting room. I took a deep breath and squeezed Dallas's hand. My mother ran up to me and hugged me tight. I didn't know what to do. I didn't like physical contact unless I felt comfortable with the person. My body stiffened, and I put my hands to my side. She held me for an eternity. "Thank you so much for coming, Hannah."

Finally, she let go.

"It's Abbey." I searched her face for a response. Her brows furrowed and lips pursed. She was never going to like the fact that I gave up my birth name of Hannah Leah Abelard. It had religious significance. Abbey did not. Mission accomplished. "How is he?"

She looked past me at the door of the unit. "It's been touch and go, but he's stable."

"Good. Stable is progress from how they found him." I moved to a seat that had an end table on one side, and room for Dallas on the other. I nearly pulled him off his feet, guiding him to the chair so she couldn't sit by me. My mother took the seat on the opposite side of the end table.

"He's asked about you." She paused as if I was supposed to say something in response. "He wants to see you."

"I don't know if I can." I didn't want to see him, especially in his present condition. I didn't want to feel sorry for him. To be honest, I didn't want to feel anything for him. I just wanted to get back to the case, solve it, and have my parents return to Guatemala where they belonged. Then my life could return to normal. Right now, he was a major distraction. I know it was a cold and selfish way to think, but I'd closed that door years ago. I wasn't going backward under any condition. "I'm not ready."

"Please, Han…Abbey. It will only take a few minutes. Then you can go find the person who did this to him." Using my name helped to soften my defenses. I forced a smile.

"Want me to go with you?" Dallas asked.

I wasn't sure what my father would say. I didn't need Dallas to hear any of our conversation, or to see me weak and vulnerable.

"No. I can handle this."

I checked in with the nurse and entered the secured Critical Care Unit. I followed the circle of rooms until I came to his. It was walled off from the hallway with glass. I glanced through the slit between blinds and studied his face. He had bandages covering his scalp and several sutures on his face. He looked old and withered. How old was he now? He was twenty-four when Miriam was born. I'd heard that story enough to recite it in my sleep. She was ten years older than me. I was twenty-six. Put it all together, and that made him sixty-one. In his present condition, he looked eighty. How could an old man like that intimidate me still? It didn't make any sense, but he did.

I took a few deep breaths and let them out slowly. I kept telling myself, "He has no power. He has no power. He has no power." Why couldn't I believe it?

I knocked on the door and waited until I heard a faint, "Come in."

"You wanted to see me?" I stood to the side of the door, keeping five feet between us.

"Hannah, thank you for coming."

"Call me Abbey, please. I've gone by that name for eight years now."

"I'll try. Please sit down." He waved me over with a heavily bandaged hand.

"I can't stay long. We're deep into this case, and I need to get back to the office."

"I understand." We stared silently at one another, each waiting for the other to make the first move. I could play this game. A minute or two passed, and he fidgeted in his bed. He looked away and stared at a blank television screen. "I saw your interview." He watched us on the news this morning? "I was really proud of you."

It was the first time in my life he said those words to me. I'd heard him say them to Miriam incessantly. "Thanks."

"You and…I'm sorry, what is his name again?"

"Dallas. Dallas Gatlin."

"Yes. Dallas. Although I disagree with a few things he said, I can tell he is a biblical scholar who truly loves the Lord."

Another compliment. Where was he going with this? I took one step closer to his bedside. "He does. He's one of the most authentic Christians I know." Good. Compliment Dallas while taking a pot shot at my father. "My best friend Susan is the other."

"I can tell you feel a great sense of love for him." Did he hear me mention Susan too? "I'm glad you have someone like him in your life."

I cut him off before he said anything else. "If you're about to give your blessing, don't bother. I don't need one." I didn't want to feel indebted to my father in any way.

"Oh, I must have misinterpreted your looks. It seemed obvious that you cared for him."

"I do. I love Dallas very much. I don't need your blessing to affirm it." I felt the old protective walls slam into place. Besides, I wasn't sure Dallas felt the same way anymore. "Is this what you wanted to tell me?" I turned and put one hand on the door. "If it is, we're done here."

"No. Please don't go." *Please?* Was he begging me? What happened to that hard-hearted man who feared no one. "I wanted to talk to you about the girl."

"What girl?" I turned back to face him and studied his eyes. "Who are you talking about?"

"The young girl in charge, the one who told them exactly what to do."

"Dad, are you saying you remember your attackers? You told Agent Carmichael you couldn't remember anything." Was he trying to play me?

"I didn't. But, after watching your interview, something clicked. You said *Penny*."

"Did Penny Thatcher do this to you?"

"No. The young girl with the brown hair and sad eyes mentioned her name."

I moved to his bed and stood above him. "Sad eyes and brown hair? Was it Skylar?"

"Yes. That's the name the men called her. She said that Penny would be proud of her actions."

"Skylar Watson was there when they did this to you?" I described Skylar to him, and my father nodded. "What did she say?"

"She told them to make me suffer like Jesus did. She told them to wound me like the soldiers wounded Him." He looked away from me towards the only window in the room. "She told me that…" He paused and swallowed a few times. Whatever he had to say, I could tell he didn't want to say it. "She said you were an amazing woman despite my abuse." He looked at me. There were tears in his eyes. "She said you deserved a better father, and that I deserved to die."

Words eluded me. I couldn't look at him. As much as I had longed for him to suffer as I had suffered, I didn't want to look at this broken shell that used to be my father.

"Skylar Watson said that?"

"Yes." He shuffled in his bed, searching for a comfortable position. "She said a lot more."

"What did they do to you?" I forced myself to make eye contact.

He described everything in detail. They tortured him physically and mentally. Skylar took her time and broke him. When she'd finally crushed his spirit, they flogged him, put a crown of thorns on his head, cut him several times, stabbed him in his side, and nailed him to a plank of wood secured to Sam's front door. "It was horrible," he said. "But now I know firsthand what Jesus went through to save my soul."

This was the exact opposite of the father I knew and hated. "Do you think you could give physical descriptions of the men that did this?" He nodded. "I'll see if I can get a sketch artist here to make likenesses of them." It probably wasn't going to help. Like the ones who attacked Susan, these were probably hired guns Skylar used to carry out her wishes. It may even be the two men who attacked Susan. I had something better than descriptions of the thugs who did this. Now, we had an eyewitness who could testify to Skylar's direct involvement.

"I'm sorry, Hannah. I'm sorry for the way I treated you." He paused. I assumed he wanted me to say it was okay or that I forgave him. I remained silent. "I wanted you to be like your sister Miriam. I thought I could break you down and remold you in her image."

So, my suspicions were true. Why was he telling me this after all these years? "I'm not Miriam."

"I know. You had such a strong spirit. Now, I know what God had in store for you." He reached for my hand, but I just stared at him. "Please, forgive me for making you take the path of Joseph."

"Great analogy, Dad. You sold me into slavery. I guess that

means you were jealous of me." His eyes widened. "By the way, Miriam wasn't as perfect as you think; she made me get an abortion. Your little angel willfully killed a child, just to save your image."

It hit him like a sledgehammer. He gasped for air and grabbed his chest. The monitor showed the rise of his pulse and BP. "You were pregnant? What boy defiled you?"

"Oh, like you care! And it was no *boy*. Your precious friend Nicholas Sayers got me pregnant when he raped me."

"I refuse to believe that, Hannah. Why do you insist on spouting lies about a man of God? Do you have no respect for the dead?" I said nothing. I could feel the heat in my face. "Don't think I wasn't aware of your new lifestyle. You probably can't even name the father."

I leaned over him, my face inches from his. "How dare you. I never had sex with any other man in my life. Still to this day, that rape was the only time." My face was shaking. I wanted to choke the remaining life from him. I saw pure terror in his eyes.

"How was I supposed to know?"

I turned on my heels and mumbled under my breath. I had to leave, or I would do the unthinkable. I stood by the door and did my deep breathing exercises. Finally, able to face him again, I turned. "How were you supposed to know? I told you. I told you, and you were supposed to take my word for truth. My father was supposed to protect me. Instead, you took the word of a predator over your own daughter." It felt so good to utter those words that I didn't realize I was screaming until the nurse came in and scolded me for disturbing the unit. I waited until she shut the door to finish in a much softer voice. "I've never chosen to have sex outside of marriage. My virginity—my innocence—was stolen from me, and you befriended my rapist."

He stared at me. I thought he was processing my accusation and dealing with his guilt until he said, "And you took the life of an innocent child?"

He'd brushed aside the truth of his responsibility. "To this day I feel the guilt of that action." I could have refused Miriam. I could have run from her and had the child. Mr. Morales would have taken good care of it too. "I was fourteen and on my own. I was afraid and my big sister, the one who did everything right, took me to the clinic and signed for my abortion."

He was shaking his head. He couldn't accept the fact that his perfect angel did something like that. "Miriam would never…" He looked out the window. "She would never murder an innocent child."

"In a way, she killed two children that day," I said. My voice was cold and flat. I'd had these conversations in my head for over a decade. "She killed my baby to save your precious ministry."

"I don't want to hear it!" He pressed the nurse's button.

Before she could answer him, I added, "Somehow Skylar found out about all of this and made you pay. She knows about everything, Dad."

"May I help you?" the nurse's sweet voice asked. He didn't say anything. "Mr. Abelard?"

"Sorry. I hit the button on accident." As soon as the nurse hung up, his demeanor changed. He looked tired and old again. He was powerless now. I'd faced my demons. I told the truth, and there was nothing else he could do to me. I felt the weight of twelve years of guilt fall from my shoulders. If only I could let the rest go too. "I should have been there for you."

"Yes. You should have." I wasn't letting him off that easily. "I'm not going to live in the past anymore. I have a murderer to catch. I'll have a sketch artist stop by as soon as they can." I said goodbye and left him to deal with the pain. It was time he carried it for a while.

I found Dallas talking with my mother in the waiting room.

"Come on, Dallas. We need to go." We had a trap to set, and time was ticking away.

"How was he?" my mother asked.

"He's really tired. I'd let him rest for a while." With that, I left her sitting alone.

Chapter Fifty-four

Tuesday, October 21, 6:35 PM—Harmony Apartments

Dallas and I sat down to our Chinese supper. I started to take a bite but heard Dallas begin a prayer of thanksgiving. I closed my eyes and imagined what he might be feeling as he uttered those words. For me, it was still a senseless tradition. Did God really listen? Did He care that we were about to eat our food? What did it mean for God to bless our Chinese supper?

Dallas said, "Amen," and I opened my eyes.

"I know you still worry about what people think we're doing up here by ourselves," I said. I knew it wasn't going to be light conversation tonight, so I wanted to hear his feelings. What did Dallas think of this situation? What did he think, if anything, about a future with me?

He didn't say anything.

"I hope it doesn't tarnish your reputation, staying these nights with me."

Dallas put down his chopsticks and wiped his mouth with a napkin. "I'm not embarrassed being seen with you, if that's what you are asking. It's just different now."

Well, that was cold. Was he referring to the videos? "That's just what a girl wants to hear."

Dallas paused for a moment. "This is so much for me to process. I know you deal with this kind of thing all the time, but I'm just a simple professor. I live a vanilla kind of life. My biggest decision most days is whether to take a lunch to work."

"What does that have to do with being embarrassed of me?" His comment didn't seem to connect with mine. Was he processing the plan to catch Penny or a future with me?

"Before I met you, I got up, taught a few classes, graded papers, went home, and started the same thing over the next morning. Now, three people I know have been sent to the hospital, I just baited a murderer on public television, and I'm sleeping at your house for protection."

"You think you're here so I can protect you?"

"Come on, Abbey. I'm not stupid. Your apartment is secure. Besides, you have guns if anyone breaks in." He shifted his rice on his plate. "You don't think I can protect myself."

"That's not true." Well, it was partially true. I also wanted him here so I could be near him.

"Of course it is, Abbey. It stems from the same core trust issue you struggle with that keeps you from letting Sam and the others work the case."

"Core issue. What are you saying?"

"You think you're the only one who can fix problems."

"That's not true!"

"You find it hard to trust others. No wonder you have a hard time trusting God."

I didn't know what to say. I sat there with my mouth wide open, waiting for him to take it back. Dallas picked up the chopsticks and put some of his sweet and sour chicken in his mouth.

"I trust you and Susan."

"Do you? If you trusted me, you'd give me the whole truth. I wouldn't have to drag it out of you piece by piece."

"I thought we were talking about safety?"

I was totally confused.

"We were at first. I know this isn't about me being here for you. It's about you keeping an eye on me."

I put both hands on the table. I didn't know what to say. "Fine! What do you want to know?"

He looked up and slowly shook his head. "That's not the same, and you know it."

"You want to know everything, but you don't want me to tell you when I'm upset. I can't win."

"This isn't a game, Abbey. It's real life."

"I'm not good with relationships. I don't want anyone to get hurt, and I guess I—I do want to protect you and Susan." I put my head on the table and mumbled. "I don't even do that right."

"Trust us and let us help." He lifted my chin and looked into my eyes.

I suddenly realized how dangerous I was to those around me. The walls slammed into place.

"It was better when I pushed people away. At least then, I was the only one getting hurt." I didn't intend to say that aloud, but I couldn't take it back now. "Well, after this week, you'll be free of the drama and the danger. I promise, I'll catch Penny and put her away."

"You can't promise that, Abbey. And even when she's gone, there's still Skylar." He looked down at his food. "After Skylar there will be someone else. Evil is rampant in this world. Your job will never end."

Was he angry or afraid? Maybe both. He was right though. Skylar was out there, and we wounded her ego. Penny was still my primary concern. We went after her publicly, stripping away her very essence. She believed she was a prophet cleansing the world of sin. Dallas made her out to be a delusional fool. She was going to make him pay. I hoped she would try on my time and conditions. The only thing unknown was the date. Would she strike the moment Dallas went home, or would she stick to the schedule of every ten days?

I felt the cold. My walls were secure again.

"I promise that after we catch Penny, I will leave you out of the investigation. I'm sorry. I needed you and assumed you wouldn't mind." I paused so he could say something like, *It's okay* or *I don't mind at all.* He didn't. In fact, Dallas didn't say anything at all. He ate his food as if I wasn't even sitting at the same table. "It's just…" I took a deep breath. "Without you, we wouldn't have figured out the meaning of the markings."

He looked up and made eye contact with me. "I was just trying to help." He took a drink of his water. His hand was shaking. "It was like a game or a puzzle. I must admit, I was excited at first. But…"

"But the excitement has worn off."

"Oh, no. It's still exciting…dangerously so." He rubbed at the stubble on his chin. "I'm not wired for this."

I don't know why I expected everyone to feel the same way as I did. Susan was nearly killed because she is my friend. I put a bullseye on Dallas's back to catch an elusive killer. There must be something wrong with me to risk the people closest to me. Maybe Skylar was right. We were the same. We both used others for our own goals. "No, Dallas. You're not. You're too kind and loving. You have a big heart." This time, I looked down at my food. I'd lost my appetite. "What does that say about me?"

"You're the hero of the story, Abbey. You're the person who runs into a battle instead of taking cover. You risk everything to help and save others."

"I wished I could believe that was true."

"Don't push me away, Abbey."

"I don't want to."

Dallas stood and pulled me to my one good foot and planted the most passionate kiss on me. I melted in his arms. Then, he whisked me off my feet and carried me to the couch. He kissed me like he'd never kissed me before. He stopped and looked into my eyes. I sighed, rested against his shoulder, and fell fast asleep.

I woke a few hours later to discover Dallas had carried me to bed and put a blanket over me. I got out of bed, looked down the hall, and smiled. He was asleep on the couch.

Even knowing my past, Dallas treated me like a lady. Even at my worst, he loved me. I was never letting go. I was going to do whatever it took to keep him. If Skylar thought she could take him away, she had a fight on her hands.

Chapter Fifty-five

Wednesday, October 22, 5:22 PM—Apartment of Dallas Gatlin

Detective Spencer pulled up to the curb and stopped the car. "We swept the apartment a second time and found no devices. Captain's orders." Spence looked in the rearview mirror. "You two wait here while I check out the apartment."

Dallas and I sat in the back seat and waited for Spence to scan Dallas's apartment, the stairs, and the entryway. "It's going to be okay, Dallas."

"I'm not worried for myself," he said.

Five minutes later, Spence opened the lobby door and waved us on. I stepped out first and looked across the road making sure no one was waiting to ambush us. "Come on." I hobbled a few steps in my boot cast.

Dallas stepped out and shielded his eyes from the afternoon sun. He grabbed his overnight bag and followed me to the door. "Remember, there are multiple entrances to my apartment building, and none are guarded by security." It was a playful dig at my situation. "Some of us aren't rich."

We went up the steps to the second floor and entered apartment 207. A couple of minutes later, someone knocked on Dallas's door.

Spence checked through the peephole and opened the door. A young woman entered. Spence said, "This is Detective Ginny Flinn."

Dallas said, "She does look a little like you, Abbey." He looked back and forth between us. "Now what?"

"Now, you and Spence swap clothes." Ginny and I were already wearing the same outfit, so we waited for the men as they went into Dallas's bedroom and swapped clothes.

"I cut my hair to match your length. I think the rest matches up," Ginny said. She had a soft, sweet voice.

Once the men returned, we eyed each other. Spence's blue eyes sparkled, and I knew we needed to cover them. Dallas had rich brown eyes. "Spence, toss Dallas your sunglasses. We have to cover those beautiful brown eyes." Dallas put them on, and even from here I could believe he was Detective Spencer. "Okay, to make this work, just don't say anything. Dallas, you'll have to drive a few blocks. Then you can swap. Dallas, make sure you hop in the passenger seat instead of the back." I took my orthopedic boot off and let Ginny put it on. It might just work.

"Okay, everyone. Operation Shell Game is underway." Spence turned to Ginny. "Keep an eye out just in case."

Dallas winked before he left with Detective Flinn. "I saw that," I said in mock objection. "You look out the window, Spence. Act like you're going to miss me."

"I think I can manage." He punched me in the shoulder and glanced out of the window overlooking the courtyard. He sold it and then let the curtain fall back in place. "Do you think she'll strike tonight?"

"If she caught the interview, I'm betting she'll come tonight or tomorrow. We should be ready just in case."

We turned on the television, and they were still playing soundbites from Tuesday's interview. If Penny and Skylar were listening at all to the local channels, they knew we did our best to make them look like fools. Since my apartment had layered security and I'd initially been on the no touch list, our assumption was that Penny would take out her frustration on Dallas as the next best thing, especially after I had Dallas challenge her beliefs on the Sabbath. The point was to stir her up and put him on her alternate list for the fourth commandment, even if she didn't wait until the thirtieth.

"I've become a believer in your instincts, Abbey."

"With the news chatter, I can't see her waiting until the thirtieth. Their goal was to cause fear and repentance in Nashville. Dallas has Nashville laughing at them now."

Spence paced back and forth across the kitchen floor, wound up tighter than a string on a yo-yo. I was so used to Sam's laid-back nature, his ability to adjust on the fly, that Spence's anxiety began to bleed over onto my nerves. If this situation with our case did prolong until Sunday, we'd both go crazy.

"Settle down, Spence. I have the camera set up to notify me if anyone comes up the stairs. We're on the second floor, so I believe we can rule the windows out." He gave me a thumbs up to indicate he understood my message.

I took the opportunity to look around Dallas's apartment, especially the bedroom, while Spence got something to eat. He followed the plan and made several appearances by the main windows. If Penny was casing the apartment, she would have affirmation of Dallas's presence. I, on the other hand, avoided all the windows. We didn't need to spoil the ruse that Dallas was unprotected and vulnerable. To enhance the opportunity, Sam placed a patrol car outside of my apartment. A visible sign that Dallas was the easier mark.

Dallas kept his bedroom, like the rest of his apartment, clean and organized. He had an eye for color and décor, far better than I. He created a scene on his shelf in homage to the Lord of the Rings, using several small, colorful figurines. He was a grown man who embraced his inner child. I was a grown woman who desperately tried to forget my childhood. It was another example of what Susan called our dichotomy, adding in her cheerful tone, "Opposites attract." She was always the romantic optimist.

While Spence went to the kitchen, I peeled back Dallas's comforter and leaned over. I took a sniff of the pillow. It smelled like his cologne. A sense of calm fell over me. I longed for the day we could be together for good. Then, that little voice chided me for thinking of better times, for even considering a future with a man who was way out of my league. I heard Spence coming, so I put the comforter back in place.

"Do you want something to eat?" Spence asked from the hall.

"Maybe later." I had a few protein bars in my overnight bag Ginny held for me in the apartment across the hall from Dallas. She brought in a bag for Spence as well, but he was already ordering food for supper. He didn't like anything Dallas had on hand.

After Spence ordered his food, he moved his things into Dallas's bedroom. I moved into the other bedroom, which Dallas used for his office. He had a sleeper couch in there. For tonight, I decided to put some sheets on the couch. No sense making it into a bed if Penny did choose tonight for her revenge. If we were forced to wait longer, I could change it into the bed later. Her pattern was to strike in the early morning, just after daylight. Would she use the same ruse? Surely not, since we had that on video. She knew we'd expect it.

"I'm going to catch a few hours of sleep so I can be ready when she comes," I said softly.

"Okay. Now, am I supposed to fall asleep or pretend?" He took the hint and answered in a soft voice just in case someone was listening through the door or windows. Dallas's apartment had little sound insulation.

"You are Dallas. Follow the schedule. If they've been following him at any point, they may know his habits and sleep schedule." Everything Spence did was to make them believe he was Dallas, and therefore vulnerable to an attack. I was there to make sure they didn't carry it out.

"Okay."

Dallas said he spent a lot of time working on his paper. I decided to keep the office light on for a while.

There was a nervous tremor to Spence's voice. I assumed, since he was near my age, he had been on a stakeout before. From his behavior, I was now certain he hadn't. "Stop talking to yourself.

Someone may see your lips moving from the window and assume you're not alone." Spence looked down the hall to the office and put up his thumb. What a goofball.

I shut the door and changed into a sweatsuit. It was far more comfortable and still allowed me to jump into action at any moment. As I laid my head on the pillow, I thought of my father and the day my sister Miriam discovered I was pregnant.

Chapter Fifty-six

Twelve earlier—Streets of Guatemala City

At fourteen I did what I could to survive in Guatemala City. I moved closer to the city center because there were more opportunities to make money or to beg for food. I'd made it twelve weeks on my own after my family kicked me out for being raped by Nicholas Sayers. I was filthy, lonely, and bone tired from sleeping in places that weren't safe enough for me to do more than doze. But most of all, I was so hungry. I resorted to letting men touch me for money—only on top of my clothes, but it still made me sick to my stomach. After the ultimate violation by Sayers, I convinced myself it was understandable. It was that or starve.

That was the life my father condemned me to. Like Pilate with Jesus, he washed his hands of me. I was an embarrassment to the family. My entire family proclaimed I was dead; I ceased to exist. Word made back it to me that my father said he only had one daughter. When people asked about me, he said I was a local girl his family housed and tried to save. I was wild when they met me and wild when I ran away. They did what they could, but it was a big city. They said I didn't want to be found.

Of course, the truth was very different. When I came back, begging him to let me come home, he tossed me back to the curb, literally. I snuck back when I knew he was away trying to win souls for God. I begged my mother and my sister to let me in. They said they didn't know me. I asked them for a shower and clean clothes, but they refused. These things they granted to perfect strangers. I begged for clean food, but once again, they cast me away. I was left to beg in the streets. I found *employment* at a "dance establishment" owned by a man named Mr. Morales who scrupulously enforced the rules for his girls—outside of clothing was fair game, but he never allowed anyone to touch my flesh.

One day, I was in the market area buying fruit and bread with the money I made from *dancing*. I hoped I could eat most of my food before I being pushed to the ground and robbed. The lady sold me a mango and a papaya. I hid them under my shirt. Then I found someone willing to sell me day old bread for the money I had left. The bread was hard, and I found myself breaking it into two pieces so I could dig the softer part out with my fingers and eat it. I saw the two big boys who had stolen my meal three days ago—the last time I ate. Before they noticed me, I ran through three different tents. I was looking back over my left shoulder when I slammed into a car.

It knocked me to the ground, and I felt the fruit squish when I landed. The wind rushed out of my lungs, and I gasped for breath. The driver was beside me, telling me to calm down and relax. "You have to relax, or you won't be able to breathe." Finally, I did my best to stretch out and breathe. I felt the precious air fill my lungs.

"Are you okay?" She rolled me over to see if I sustained any physical damage from the collision. I couldn't believe my eyes. I could see her shock as well. "Hannah?"

"Miriam?"

"You look awful."

Of course, I looked awful. I was homeless. I tried to scamper away, but she held my arm tight. I stood and she gasped. "Are you pregnant?"

"What?" I had missed my last two periods, but I thought it was due to poor nutrition, bad water, and very little sleep. "No." What did she care anyway?

"Let me help you." Miriam pulled me close and held me to

her chest. I knew I was filthy. I knew I smelled awful, but she didn't seem to care about those things. "Come, get in the car."

I was filled with hope. I secretly praised God for this miracle. As I ran to the passenger door, I felt the guts of the smashed fruit sliding down the inside of my shirt. I'd been living like an animal for ten weeks. Now, in the presence of my sweet smelling and clean sister, I was filthy and ashamed. We drove out of the market area and away from the center of town. She handed me a box of tissues and said, "I have some wet wipes in the glove box. You might want to clean up your face before we get there."

I did as she directed and lowered the mirror concealed under the passenger visor. I didn't recognize the face looking back at me. I scrubbed and scrubbed until my face hurt. The wipes I used were black, and yet my face was still brown. I could see the red through the brown and realized I was rubbing off my skin. I looked like a native Guatemalan. I opened my mouth and gasped. My teeth were black. I used the wipes on them as well. I didn't care what they tasted like. I had to be clean when I was reunited with my parents.

"They'll take good care of you, Hannah. You won't have to worry any more about it."

"Thank you, Miriam. I don't think I could have made it another week." We drove for another twenty minutes. I still didn't recognize our surroundings. She pulled over in front of a dingy yellow building. "Where are we?"

"The doctor." Miriam looked in the side mirror and opened her door.

This wasn't our regular doctor's office.

"Miriam?"

"Don't worry, Hannah. I'll take care of everything." She ran around the front of the car and opened my door. I was confused. Was this doctor a new friend of my father? She took me by the arm and pulled me out of the car. Within seconds we were in the clinic. She pushed me into a seat and spoke to the receptionist in whispers. The woman waved her around the counter and introduced her to a man in tan scrubs. They both looked at me and continued to whisper. Miriam handed him some money, and he stuffed it into his pants pocket.

Miriam grabbed me out of my seat and pushed me past the desk. I stumbled into a smelly room with a dingy table and a weak light. "Where are we?" I asked.

"They're going to take care of you, Hannah. Please relax and this will be over before you know it. He'll fix everything."

"I'm not broken, Miriam. Why am I here?" I was irritated.

"We can't have you burdened with a child, especially living like you are."

"Burdened? Child? What kind of doctor is he?" As soon as I realized where she'd taken me, I tried to run out of the door. The doctor and two other men blocked my exit. They pulled me back into the room and forced me back onto the table. My arms hurt where they held me fast. "No!"

I tried to break free. The pain was unbearable.

Chapter Fifty-seven

Thursday, October 23, 6:20 AM—Apartment of Dallas Gatlin

I woke when my body hit the floor. I looked around and realized I was lying face-down on the rug in Dallas's office. My body was drenched with sweat, my hair matted to my face. *Get a grip, girl. You're safe now. Those days are over.*

I got up and hobbled to the kitchen for a glass of water, trying to keep my weight off my sore foot. After the third glass, I took a full one back to the office and sat on the couch. I looked at my phone. Six-twenty. I started the breathing exercises my counselor taught me, and I could feel my heartbeat slowing.

I heard a series of faint scratches on the front door, followed by a click. Someone picked the lock and eased the door open. They stopped suddenly when the door creaked. After a few minutes' pause, I could hear someone enter Dallas's apartment. I found my bag and eased the gun from it. I could hear Spence snoring, so I knew the creaking sound wasn't coming from him. Could it be Penny? A squeak from the wood floor. I was thankful that Dallas lived in an older apartment that kept the intruder from making much progress without having to pause after another betraying sound. I rolled out of view of the hallway connecting the kitchen to the two bedrooms—the master in which Spence slept and the office where I was. As quietly as I could, I pushed to my feet and readied my Sig for the intruder. I had to be careful to protect my bandaged foot from further injury. There wasn't time to put on shoes.

I had to catch Penny as close to the act as I could without

allowing her to hurt Spence. I peeked around the edge of the door-frame when I heard another squeak nearer to the master bedroom. A shadowy figure crouched beside the door. There wasn't enough light to determine if the person was in fact Penny Thatcher. I couldn't even be certain it was a woman. I held as motionless as possible. The intruder must have sensed my presence; the masked face was pointed toward the office. Spence continued to snore loudly, oblivious of the danger waiting outside of his room. I had the person for breaking and entering and could make an arrest on that violation alone, but we wanted to catch her over Spence with the intent to do harm.

Five minutes passed. I could feel the burn in my back and legs. My right foot was on fire. A muscle spasm was coming on, and I needed to move. Thankfully, the figure stood and opened the bedroom door. It stepped into the room and began to mumble something. Spence's snoring stopped. Did he wake? Did he just roll over in the bed? What would the intruder do?

I made up the distance to the doorway without a sound. I glanced inside and noticed the mask had been removed. It was a woman. It had to be Penny. She held something over her head and said, "You ruined everything."

"Police. Drop your weapon." I flipped on the light, temporarily blinding us all.

She glanced at me and then turned back to Spence with her knife. "I'd drop that if I were you." Spence held his Glock in his right hand. The barrel rested a few inches from her nose.

She lunged at him with the knife. Spence rolled away and out of her reach. It took less than a second for me to pounce. My body smashed hers into the bed. I had the arm with the knife. Spence removed it. We subdued her.

"Let me go. You're ruining everything."

"Penny Thatcher, you're under arrest for attempted murder. You have the right to…" I stopped in mid-Miranda rights. It wasn't Penny. "Who are you?"

"You pig! You heathen!" She spit in my face. "You both have stolen the spirit from our priestess, Hadassah of the Most High God."

I wiped the spit from my cheek with the sleeve of my sweat-suit. "Where's Penny?"

"There is no Penny. She is Hadassah."

"Right, and I'm St. Peter," Spence said. "You have the right to remain silent. Anything you say can and will be used against you in a court of law…"

"There is no law but God's. No court but His court."

She kept spouting off about our lack of authority, that God would be her judge. Spence wasn't fazed at all. He finished reading her Miranda rights as he cuffed her hands behind her back. Everything by the book.

"What was your plan here?" I asked. "Why didn't Hadassah come herself? Is she afraid?"

She screamed at the top of her lungs, telling me Hadassah was a priestess of the Most High God. She knew no fear. Then, she went on a tirade, accusing us of stealing her spirit again. Was she referring to the Holy Spirit? As I listened to her rant, I realized that Dallas's interpretations caused Penny to question herself and her legitimacy as a prophet of God. This woman, who still wouldn't give us her name, came here to kill Dallas for taking Penny's drive and focus. She still didn't realize Spence wasn't Dallas. That could work to our advantage.

I knew Penny would not come here now. The plan was solid, only we didn't account for an underling coming to carry out the revenge. Where was Penny hiding? How many more followers did she have? More questions without answers. After making a call to the local precinct to take this woman in, I called Sam and let him know what happened. He picked us up, handed me my orthopedic boot, and drove us to their precinct for questioning.

Chapter Fifty-eight

Thursday, October 30, 9:30 AM—Homicide

I sat in our cubical completely exhausted and deflated. A week passed since Helen March broke into Dallas's apartment. She insisted her name was Ruth. I got into an argument with her during the interrogation, saying, "Ruth was a nice and compassionate person, not a hateful witch." Sam rightfully removed me from the interview. Penny gave every one of her followers new names—Biblical names. I supposed it made them feel new and gave them some sort of validation to their calling.

Helen relocated to Nashville from Virginia after finding Hadassah on a dark web page called *The Chosen Few*. Spence located their page, which one could join by invitation only. Helen would not divulge the name of the person who recommended Penny's posts. Unfortunately, Spence could not penetrate their security, so he turned it over to the IT department. We were waiting on several things from them, including the answer to how Skylar found my humiliating videos. If we could break into Penny's site, it might help us find her before she killed again. In only five months, Penny had established her cult and recruited people from seven different states—that we knew of. She and Skylar devised a method of selecting victims, scoured local Nashville publications for individuals matching their needs, and studied the lives of the "sinners who violated God's holy Commandments." They found Bible verses which affirmed their evil plan and set in motion a *Cleansing* of Nashville.

Skylar wanted me to believe she was doing this for me, but I knew better. At the core of a psychopath is a narcissist who is superficially charming but lacks empathy. Everything Skylar did was for herself. She checked every box for a narcissist. She had a deep belief that she was unique and incredibly special. Skylar had a need for attention, praise, and power. Manipulation was her superpower. Somehow, she convinced her father that her mother was cheating on him and was out to destroy him. Skylar turned her father into a paranoid man, a man who eventually killed his wife, stuffed her into a deep freezer by breaking her legs, and filled it with water. He tortured her to ease his anxiety. Then, Skylar manipulated her father into beating her—so I would have sympathy and rescue her. I fell into her trap just like the others.

"Abbey, grab your stuff." Sam was shaking me. "We have another body."

"What did you say?" I was still lost in my thoughts.

"You need to come right now. She struck again." Sam grabbed his keys and said, "Move."

We didn't have to go very far. The tiny house was located on Lischey Avenue, on the other side of Ellington Parkway. The lower half of the one-story home consisted of moldy red bricks. The upper half was made of a dingy gray siding that showed signs of neglect. Three patrol cars were parked in the driveway, surrounding a brand-new Kawasaki Ninja ZX-10R. The fancy motorcycle didn't seem to fit anything else about this home. I paused at the porch to scan the doorframe for any letters. Someone had etched the Roman numerals VIII in the wood at the top. "Commandment number eight: Thou shalt not steal."

My heart sank. Our failure to catch Penny resulted in another person's death. It was another victory for Penny's Chosen Few cult. Instead of deterring Penny, Helen's capture only served to encourage her. This was victim number six. They were succeeding, and I was failing.

A young black female officer stood on the other side of the

yellow crime scene tape. I showed my credentials to the officer and said, "Detectives Tidwell and Rhodes."

"Agent Carmichael is already here," she said. "She's waiting inside."

We ducked under the crime scene tape and stepped into the house. Amazon boxes were everywhere, stacked four to six high depending on size. Most were still sealed. "That's a lot of boxes, Sam."

"Hope you don't mind, Detectives," Agent Carmichael said, stepping into the room to greet me. "I was two blocks away when I got word."

"No problem, Agent. My head wasn't in it today anyway. Still bummed about Penny eluding our trap."

"Let's get on with it, then," she said. "We have a lot to process. There are more boxes in the bedroom, office, and garage."

"Where's the body?" I asked. "I want to start with that."

"In the office. Let me know what you think after you make your observations. I'll be in here for a while."

"According to the doorpost, we're on the eighth commandment, do not to steal. Let me guess." Sam hated it when I guessed before studying the crime scene's facts. He claimed it closed my mind to the truth. I did it anyway. I was open to being wrong, but my gut was extremely reliable. I learned to trust it. "He stole someone's identity and bought all of these things in their name."

Sam crossed his arms. "I'll let the facts and evidence lead me to a conclusion. Take a hint from an old detective. Examine everything before you jump to any conclusions."

"I'm still impressed," Agent Carmichael said. "Let me know if you need me for anything. By the way, I called my partner and extended an invite. Sue me."

"The more the merrier," I said with heavy sarcasm.

The little, two-bedroom house was packed with all kinds of things from bicycles and scooters to cookware and electronics. I felt like I was walking through a hoarder's home, except for the fact everything was newly purchased and still sealed. I squeezed through the hallway and entered the office. As soon as I cleared a tall stack of boxes, I immediately recognized the same sacrificial staging of the body. It was a young black man with neatly trimmed hair, maybe an eighth of an inch long. He lay face down on the carpeted floor with a large circle of blood surrounding his head. His body, like the other victims' bodies, was stretched out in an X to signify the Ten Commandments and when the killings would be complete. We had to stop them before they struck again. Maybe it was better if the FBI took over. I was way out of my league.

I could see drops of blood on the desk but wanted to focus first on the body. With gloves on, I examined his neck. Just like the others, the killer made a clean slit just below the jaw line from ear to ear. Penny kept with her MO and etched the Roman numeral eight in his forehead and hand. I changed gloves, turning the other set inside out to contain the blood and stuffed them in my pocket.

This staging wasn't complicated. It confirmed what I already knew. He used his computer to purchase items on someone else's credit card. He was dressed in white boxers and an undershirt. No identification on him. There were no signs of a struggle, but there were spots of blood on the keyboard and chair. I grabbed the mouse and jiggled it. The screen lit up. If this were an indication of what he was doing when the killer found him, his last action was to fill a shopping cart with three expensive pieces of jewelry. The killer must have picked the lock on the front door, crept into this room, and put a knife to his throat while he shopped. The drops of blood on the keyboard and desk were not enough to indicate a slit throat, but they were typical of a superficial cut made as a threat. It's how the killer got him in position for the death blow.

I made a quick search of the desk. The victim had a postage meter and label printer set on the back right corner of the desk and a new HP laptop in its center. The top drawer was empty. The second contained bubble envelopes and labels. He had a little business going on here, where he received and shipped packages. I checked the package immediately to the left of his desk. The label read, "David Scott" and had the address of this house. Five boxes further to the left, I discovered another name. The package on the right displayed a third name with the same address. Everything fit the profile of an identify thief. How did Penny find him?

This was not the original person chosen for commandment eight. The image on Penny's apartment wall was a white woman who stole a Tesla and was released because of the arresting officer's mistake, searching without probable cause or a warrant. She was supposed to be the sacrifice for this commandment. This was a black East Nashville man. This confirmed that everything we gathered from Penny's apartment was now useless, at least as far as anticipating her next victim. Thankfully, she was sticking to her sequence of commandments and the schedule of killings, all dates ten days apart with the exception of the week with my father's release. Commandment three was next.

I suddenly had an overwhelming feeling of inadequacy. Everyone was looking for me to solve this case, and I had no clue how. We tried to lure Penny into jumping directly to the fourth Commandment, but she didn't take the bait. Helen, her passionate follower, only came after Dallas because he had weakened her leader's resolve. They were still believers. If anything, their belief was intensified. They felt called by God to cleanse Nashville. I was helpless to guess who might come next. Sadly, who didn't take the Lord's name in vain today? How could we possibly narrow our search to one specific person in ten days?

Sam's voice pulled me out of my private pity party. "I count two hundred and five boxes. All but four were shipped here. The four are labeled from here to various places." Sam flipped through his notes and caught me up to speed with the details gathered by the patrol officers and Agent Carmichael. "Roger Platt, twenty-three-year-old black male."

"Do we know if he owns this home? There were no records, bills, or invoices in his desk. I didn't search his laptop. Wanted to keep it on the site he was visiting at the time of his death."

"Good call, Abbey. Best to let IT look at it first." Sam surveyed the room full of boxes. "The earliest date I've found so far is from three weeks ago. Add a week for shipping, and…"

"Actually, with Amazon Prime, you can get a package delivered the same day," Agent Carmichael said.

"You're kidding me?" Sam said. "Well, that changes my timeframe."

"So far, I've found the packages in five different names. I wonder which person's identity was the first?" If we could line up the packages with the dates delivered, we could determine whether or not each name corresponded to a range of dates. If it does, we might get a better idea of how his little business started and how it progressed. "Sam, if he only started doing this three weeks ago, how on earth did they find him? Our efforts to drive a wedge between the two failed. Penny couldn't do this without Skylar. I knew she was good with technology, but this is next level."

"Safe assessment considering the surveillance, the research, and the hacking we've discovered so far," Agent Carmichael said.

"Sam, do you remember when we first looked into Skylar's bedroom in the house next to the church?"

"Vaguely. What's your point?" He put his notebook in his shirt pocket and faced me.

"The technology we found under her bed. The computer and gaming system. I assumed by her mother's journal that the parents purchased the items. What if Skylar was already a tech genius? She was able to send Mark Ripley an email from the church secretary's computer, easily bypassing her security code. And she advanced her knowledge at the detention facility. They said she excelled in her computer classes."

"Combine Skylar's mental prowess, paranoia, and sense of grandiosity and we have the birth of a tech-savvy psychopath we are trying hopelessly to find," Agent Carmichael added.

Skylar seemed to know exactly where we were and what we were doing. On the other hand, we actually knew little about her. "I still believe our best chance is to catch Penny. At least that should put an end to her religious killings."

"Let's get to work then, Abbey. We need to finish processing the scene and gathering as much evidence as we can." Sam knelt beside a tower of boxes and began to sort them by date. "Our killer may very well be Penny Thatcher, but we can't come at this from that conclusion, making everything we find prove her as our killer."

"That's good advice, Detective Tidwell."

"Agent Carmichael, it's about time you agreed with me on something," Sam said without turning to face her. "Up till now it's been Detective Rhodes this, and Detective Rhodes that."

"Jealous?" I asked.

"Yes." We all had a good laugh about it. We needed a little break in the tension.

Agent Carmichael's partner arrived to lend a hand. Together, we went over every inch of the little house. This time there was no evidence of a forced entry. Maybe he kept the door unlocked. He was killed at his desk. I took additional pictures and wrote descriptions of everything whether it seemed out of place or not. The bloody footprints led away from the body as usual but were not as identifiable on the carpet.

I finally discovered a rent contract and utility bills in the name of Roger Platt in a manilla envelope under a box in his bedroom. According to the documents, he'd lived in the house for nearly three years. Inside the envelope were warnings of eviction if he didn't start paying his rent on time and in the full amount. There were similar notices from the gas and electric companies.

The ME's office removed the body around one and said they would have our report ready tomorrow. "Sam won't be in the office tomorrow. It's Halloween."

"I'll be there," Sam corrected.

"But you always take the day off."

"Why is that?" Agent Carmichael asked.

"Ancient news," Sam said. "You guys hungry?"

Sam and I, along with the two agents, stopped for lunch around two and returned just thirty minutes later. We gathered all the information we could and left the crime scene just after four. We went back to Homicide and proceeded to sort through the evidence and clues from the house. Agent Carmichael called the Bureau to run additional searches. Sam left to meet with a couple of detectives from the night shift. I was utterly spent. I went home to microwave my supper and get some to sleep.

Chapter Fifty-nine

Thursday, October 30, 7:07 PM—Harmony Apartments

I sat at my table picking at a microwave meal I overcooked. By the time I finished, the chicken was hard, which was fine with me; I wasn't hungry anyway. I tossed the remains in the trashcan and moved to the couch. So many thoughts flooded my mind, the center of which was focused on Penny and Skylar. I kicked myself for not catching them immediately after the deaths of Dr. Teague and Alex Carson. If we'd done our jobs, six people would still be alive. Then Sam's voice played in my consciousness, saying, "The past is there to teach us, not subdue us." It was something his psychologist taught him, something she offered to free him from the *would have, could have, should have* feelings of guilt and shame. But It's one thing to know those truths and quite another to live by them.

What was I missing? What piece of evidence did I possess that could turn the tables on this case? If Skylar was using Penny to make me great in the eyes of Nashville, she was failing miserably. So far, the opposite had happened. Sam and I looked like fools, or in his words, *Keystone Cops*. He had to explain that one to me. I eventually googled the phrase and understood what it meant. We were clowns. It was getting to me.

The door buzzed. I hit the button, expecting it to be Susan or Dallas. "Hello."

"Hey, Kid, can I come up? I brought pizza and diet sodas."

"Come on, Sam. No beer?"

"No beer. I need a clear head, and I know you don't drink."

So much for sleep. I buzzed him in, and within minutes, Sam walked through my door with two boxes of pizza and a six-pack of my favorite diet drink.

"I'm getting déjà vu," I said, remembering the time during the Ripley case where Sam and I first broke the barriers between our years and experience. "Your FBI shadows not with you?"

"No, and I just got wind that the Chief may be turning the case over to the Feds. We need to get our heads together on this. I need some fresh ideas."

"Good. That's where I was tonight too." I went back to my bedroom and retrieved my personal notes on the case. "I was just thinking I was missing something obvious."

"Me too. Let's go back to the beginning. I think we rushed through something important."

We both went back to April, the day I received the text from Skylar. She used her psychologist's phone to text me. She wanted us to find the bodies right away. What clues did she leave us? She used the names of Moriarty and Voldemort for the personas she would use. That meant I was Sherlock Holmes and Harry Potter. I was familiar with Sherlock Holmes but read a few of his cases to do my due diligence. I also watched the Harry Potter movies with Dallas, who was able to explain what was happening. "What are their similarities, Sam?"

"Both were great detectives."

"Harry Potter was a wizard, not a detective," I argued.

"Did you really watch the movies?" I nodded. "In each one, he had to uncover the mystery that shed more truth of who he really was."

Something clicked. "What did you just say?"

"Harry solved mysteries, but the greatest mystery of all was Harry's truth—his true identity."

"Oh, my word, Sam! That's it." I left myself out of the picture, and I was supposed to be the key to this mystery. "She's peeling back the layers of who I am. Keep going, Sam. Don't stop there." I patted his arm. "What else do they have in common?"

"They both had a clever and powerful nemesis." Sam scratched his beard where it met his neck. "Let me see." He looked up at the ceiling. "I had a big list before you stopped me earlier."

"I'm so sorry, Sam. I'll shut up. Take your time."

He did. Too long. I was getting antsy. I stuffed a piece of cheese pizza in my mouth just to keep quiet.

"I don't know, now. For the most part Sherlock and Harry are worlds apart. Sherlock Holmes is a narcissist; Harry is humble. Holmes is expected to succeed; Harry is expected to fail. Holmes is older and established; Harry is young and a novice. Holmes meticulously works through a case, and Harry seems to always stumble upon the answer. In the end, I suppose they both win and are famous."

"Well, that is the goal Skylar stated for me." We really didn't have much more than we did when we started, except the realization that it had something to do with my truth. That was certainly the case with Nicholas Sayers, but not the others. Or was it? "We need to ask ourselves why they are using the Ten Commandments as an excuse to kill." Since Sam knew most of my story, I worked the theory out with him. "Let's see if the deaths correspond to *my truth* in any way without forcing the issue. I need your help."

We went through the case person by person, trying to connect the crimes to something in my past. Then Sam brought up the shower videos and said the men who watched those videos were coveting me.

Okay, maybe this wasn't a good idea after all. This triggered too many nightmares, and I worried that I would experience a flash of PTSD. But this was critical to solving the case, and I had to push through it. I had to test the theory. A flash of lightning startled me. I looked out the window and had failed to notice another storm brewing. Another flash. A rumble immediately followed. The storm was on top of us.

"Give it up, Sam. There's no semblance of a pattern tying to me." I took another bite. "I think Skylar's not only out to make me famous, but infamous as well. She leaked the video to Dallas. I think she knows everything about my hidden past and has been stuffing it in my face from the beginning."

I was so focused on the commandments and Penny that I separated Skylar from the murders. She was still the mastermind, but she still won't get her own hands dirty. Her game is to make someone else do the task for her.

Chapter Sixty

Friday, October 31 8:30 AM—Homicide

"**A**re you sure about this, Detective Rhodes?"

"I'm at least ninety percent positive, Lieutenant. It's the best lead we have."

"Detective Tidwell, do agree with her assessment?" He stared at Sam. Sam didn't answer right away. "I'll take that as a no."

"I trust her gut, sir. And to be honest, she was right about the sculptor. She took action even though you told her to stand down." That was a gutsy thing to say to his face. I understood Sam's hesitance to speak.

"I appreciate your honesty, Tidwell." He looked at me. "Okay, Rhodes. See if you can make it happen. Keep me informed." He cleared his throat. "If this doesn't work, we're turning this over to the Bureau. Dismissed."

With that, I left to work out the details.

As soon as the door closed to Lieutenant Stallings' office, I said, "I thought you were going to hang me out to dry there, Sam."

"I wouldn't do that. I had to muster the courage to put my career on the line and tell the truth." We headed back to our cubicle to put everything in motion to catch Penny and stop the killings.

I searched for the articles I'd read recently about the comedian coming to a Nashville comedy club this Sunday, the ninth. It was too perfect. Ten days from the last murder. She was infamous for her foul mouth and sacrilegious jokes. Rose O'Day proudly proclaimed her atheism and focused her routine on the hypocrisy of the modern church and Christianity. The local news criticized her for making inappropriate and unrepeatable comments about the Commandment Killers, calling them a symbol of religious intolerance. She hit all the buttons that would set Penny on fire. "I can't believe she's supposed to start her comedy tour here on the ninth. I don't think Penny could resist this one."

Sam ran his fingers through his beard. "I'm trying to find the connection to you. Anything?"

I smiled. "Her comment about the Commandment Killers dealt with Nicholas Sayers and my father. That's what caught my attention in the first place." My confidence was growing by the minute. We had the person and the date. Now, all I had to do was call Rose and persuade her to let us place someone in her hotel room on the eighth and ninth. Easier said than done.

I quickly discovered that Rose O'Day was not only an atheist, but she was a hardline antiestablishment advocate. Even if she believed my ruse, she had no intentions of subjecting her freedoms and rights to a dictatorial government official. How is it that someone who makes her living through comedy could be so hateful and rude? When I hung up, I searched online and found several videos of her comic routine. It would be generous to call her jokes funny. I wanted to call her back and say, "If you hate America that much, why don't you move?"

I was beginning to understand why a certain population of people were praising Penny and her cult of The Chosen Few. They were eliminating, for the most part, people who ruined the lives of others. These chosen victims were obnoxious, self-centered people. Many were calling Penny and her cult Religious Vigilantes. But the law is there for a reason. Otherwise, we are thrown into chaos.

"Sam, we'll have to get the hotel she's staying in to reserve us a room across the hall from hers." I told Sam which hotel she was staying in and asked if we would need a warrant for a stakeout.

"Let me run this up to Captain Harris. I think he knows the

manager there. It's not a high-class hotel with a grand lobby or ballroom, just a nice, decent place near the comedy bar."

I could imagine Rose making ugly comments about her accommodations and inconvenience. Having gone from Guatemala to the Army and then Metro Nashville Police Department, I had a great sense of confidence in and appreciation for America. It also made me very intolerant of people like Rose O'Day.

I pushed those thoughts aside and opened the ever-growing file on this case. "Do you have any more ideas about why they chose to use the Ten Commandments to kill these people?"

I heard Sam's chair creak as he leaned back to ponder my question. "When you look at Penny's file, it makes sense. And knowing Skylar doesn't do the killing herself, she needed someone she could manipulate and mold for her plan."

"I guess. Penny was already under the delusion she was chosen by God as a prophetess and priestess." I flipped through our file until I found her psychological assessment. "It says here that even as a little girl, she would kill small animals and burn them as sacrifices to God."

"She should have been in a mental hospital. She needs full-time care."

"Detective Tidwell, are you getting soft on Penny?"

"Oh, shut up, Rhodes. You know what I mean." Sam sat upright and shuffled through paperwork, making as much noise as he could. I took the hint.

I looked over the case from start to finish again. I had already memorized the victims' names and which commandments were used to justify each murder. "Sam, do you ever wonder why they chose this order? Why not start at ten and build to one, or vice versa?"

"Not really, Rhodes." When he was mad at me, he always used my last name. If he was really upset, he'd add the title of detective.

"There has to be a reason."

"Right now, I don't care why as much as I do that this plan

of yours will work. I don't know if you watch the news, but they're getting brash about our blunder of the investigation."

"I know, I know. The *Keystone Cops*." I could tell Sam wasn't in the mood to discuss anything, so I worked quietly. Why did Penny use this sequence? She started with a man who watched his neighbor sunbathe. "Sam, Penny didn't choose the sequence. Skylar did."

"What makes you so sure?" He didn't turn around, so I rolled my chair next to his.

"Penny had no clue who I was. She could not care less about my past. Skylar, on the other hand, made this all about me. She recruited Penny and set her loose—only Skylar dictated the order in which Penny had to work. She also issued a hands-off command on me."

That was another reason I knew this was about me and Skylar.

"And?" Sam said it in such a way that made me sound stupid for talking.

It was like a floodlight went off in my brain. "Sam, I understand her sequence. It began with a man who recorded video of his neighbor sunbathing, swimming, and walking around the pool. Mr. Morales taped me in the shower."

"Right. We figured out that one. Keep going." Sam turned around and faced me.

"From there, Penny's group killed Jonathan Buxton for the way he treated his father. They had a huge difference of opinion. In the eyes of many, I hated my father so much that I tried to sabotage his ministry." Sam moved closer. "Then we have Zahir Khan, a Hindu from India that made his own little garden sanctuary. His religion in a country that is still predominantly Christian."

"Okay, I think I'm following. Did you ever make negative comments about your father's ministry before he kicked you out? Did you complain to friends or adults?"

"All the time. Why?"

"Did men ever make inappropriate comments to you while you still lived at home?"

"Yes."

"Who did you tell?"

"No one. I wrote it all in my journal."

"Handwritten?" Sam was starting to scare me. He was only inches away now.

"No. I was afraid my father would find it, so I uploaded it to a private file." Where was he going with this?

"Did you do the same when you lived with Mr. Morales?"

"Yes."

My voice was a mere whisper. That's how Skylar knew. Somehow, she searched for me, backtracked my life, and discovered the computer journal.

"Sam. Skylar's a virtual stalker. She knows everything." The no other gods. "She must have found my other gods entry. It was done in sarcasm."

"What did it say?" Sam was writing notes now.

"I created a god, an all-powerful god who would rescue me from my father's abuse and captivity. It was written like a fantasy novel, where I was the virtual princess locked in the high tower. My father was the evil dragon. I was rescued, not by a knight in shining armor but a god who would punish him eternally." I stopped abruptly. "Sam, I'd pushed that out of my memory completely. She's used my allegory to make the sequence. It's not about my life in Guatemala. It was the prayer of my main character, the princess."

"Skylar thinks she's your god. You need to write the outline of that story and give me a copy."

The guilt weighed heavily upon me as I realized my story caused six people to die.

Chapter Sixty-one

Friday, November 7, 6:30 PM—Dallas Gatlin's Apartment

"**I**s it not good?" Dallas asked as I twirled the pasta around with my fork. "You've hardly touched your food."

"I'm sure it's wonderful." I set the fork down and looked at the wall opposite me. "I don't have an appetite tonight."

"You look a little peaked. Maybe you're coming down with something." He put his hand onto my cheek. "You're burning up, Abbey." He stood me up and guided me to the couch. "Lie down. I'm going to get a thermometer."

I grabbed a blanket from the back of the couch and covered up with it. "It's strange. This is only the second time I've seen your apartment."

He answered from the bathroom. "I don't think the first-time counts. You were here for a stakeout." Dallas came back into the den and said, "Open wide." He put the thermometer in my mouth and waited for the beep signaling it was finished measuring. "Huh. It's ninety-eight-point-six. You're perfect." He took the device out of my mouth.

"Aw, that's the sweetest thing you've ever said to me."

He knew I was teasing, but he smiled sheepishly anyway. I loved his innocence. We decided to start over as a couple and take our time getting to know each other. Dallas admitted he was still struggling with the video and the abortion, not to mention the dangers of me being a cop. I told him I understood. To be honest, I was still struggling with them too. He put his hand on my neck.

"I'm just tired. I keep running the scenarios through my mind, wondering how we could have caught her earlier."

"Don't beat yourself up, Abbey. Right now, you just need to be still and know He is God."

"That's from the Psalms, isn't it?" This case was bringing verses back to my mind that I'd forgotten long ago.

"Psalm forty-six, ten to be precise." He sat next to me and ran his fingers through my hair.

"How do you do that?"

"Do what?" He pulled his hand back, thinking I was referring to the touch.

"Recite specific books, chapters, and verses. I've been trying to remember verses from my childhood, but it's not going so well."

He leaned over and grabbed a black leather Bible from the end table nearest my head. He handed it to me. The leather was soft and worn. I could barely make out the words "Holy Bible" on the cover. I opened it and thought the thing would fall apart in my hands. He'd highlighted passages, made notes in the margins, and had numerous sticky notes attached to some of the pages.

"Was this your dad's Bible?"

"No. My mom gave it to me the year before she died." He turned to the page just past the cover. "I was fourteen."

"Did she buy it used?" It looked a century old.

"No. I've kind of worn it out." He smiled. "I've studied it cover to cover for twelve years, and I'm still learning new things every day." Dallas flipped to the back few pages which had an exhaustive list of Bible verses. "When I memorized a new verse, I would write the reference back here."

My mouth hung open. There had to be over a thousand verses written on those pages. He flipped back a page and pointed in the upper right corner. There it was, Psalm 46:10. I was amazed and impressed. All I could say was, "Wow."

"Memorizing is the easy part," he said. "Letting God write it on my heart is much harder." He put his hand over my heart, and it skipped a beat. "This is where they have to land, Abbey. It means absolutely nothing if it doesn't move your heart." I stared into his eyes. "That's Penny's problem. She wants to obey the literal words without ever knowing what it means or letting it move her heart first."

"That was my primary complaint against my father. Unfortunately, I used his shortcomings as my excuse to be ugly and hateful towards God and the church." That hateful heart drove me to write the allegory that Skylar was now using as a script to kill. I sat up and told Dallas all about the young Hannah Abelard and her allegory of hate. "Somehow, Skylar Watson found that computer journal. In fact, she's found everything about me. She probably knows more than I can remember." I knew the days of hiding were over. I would have to face everything from my past, even the one thing no one else knew.

"She's a dangerous woman, Abbey. You need to be careful." He looked down at the floor, and I knew at that moment he was reliving the experience of opening that video file of a teenage Hannah Abelard showering. I wanted to ask what he was thinking, but I couldn't muster the courage. He looked back up at me. "She has the power to destroy your life, and I'm afraid she's going to snap one day and do it."

"Now you know why I'm losing sleep. Even if—when—we catch Penny, I know it won't be over." I put his hand in mine. "I'm afraid she'll go after you or Susan again. I can handle a one-on-one fight with her, but I can't keep getting side-tracked worrying about the two of you. It makes me weak and vulnerable."

"You're wrong. Having us makes you stronger, just as having you makes us bolder."

My heart fluttered. "I know I said we were starting over, but I've changed my mind. I think it would be best if we cooled things off." He started to interrupt, but I continued before he could speak. "I need to focus everything I have on this case, and to be painfully honest, you're a huge distraction to me."

I could see the shock in his face, and it broke my heart to do this. I had to press on. It was the right thing to do.

"Abbey—"

"Please, Dallas, let me finish. This is really hard for me to do." That was the understatement of a lifetime. "I'm going to devote myself completely to this case until I have both Penny and Skylar in custody. I can't let you, Susan, or anything else get in my way."

Dallas stared at me. "You know it really frustrates me when you think it's your job to protect me."

"What?"

"It's hypocritical."

"Dallas."

"No. I listened to you. It's my turn to speak." I was shocked. He wasn't yelling, but there was such an intensity in his eyes. "You constantly say that you don't need to be rescued." I nodded. "Well, neither do we, Abbey. Susan and I are adults who are choosing to stand by your side, no matter what happens." He tenderly put his hand to the side of my face. "You can run away if you want, but you can't push me away. I won't budge. Penny Thatcher or Skylar Watson want to go after me? I say, Bring it on."

"Dallas, you don't…"

He pressed his lips against mine and kissed me.

Chapter Sixty-two

Saturday, November 8, 8:00 PM—Music City South Hotel

Sam and I sat at the little table eating our takeout food. I didn't have much of an appetite, especially for fried fish and chips, but I knew I had to eat something.

"What time do you think they will come?" Sam asked.

"If they keep to their regular schedule, they'll come shortly after sunrise. Dallas said that's how they measured their days in the Bible—sunrise to sunset." I looked at my phone. "Sunrise is at six-eighteen." I wondered if Penny would be alone, or if she would have an entourage of new followers.

As soon as we finished eating, Sam said, "Do you want to watch the hall camera first or hit the sack?"

I was exhausted still. "If it's all the same to you, I'll sleep first."

"You catch four hours, and I'll wake you. Then give me four. Assuming you're right on the time, we'll both be awake and ready when they come."

"Sounds like a plan."

I picked a bed and was asleep the moment I closed my eyes.

"Abbey, it's your turn to watch."

It seemed like I'd just fallen asleep. "It's been four hours?"

"Five. I let you sleep. There's been a lot of traffic down the hall, but no sign of Penny and company. Rose went into her room at eleven-twenty. She's been in there ever since."

I got up and looked at the clock. One-thirty. I settled onto the couch and watched the laptop screen. I was surprised with the number of people still awake between the hours of one and three. After that, things quieted down.

I found my mind wandering to my father and the way he looked in the hospital. Even his demeanor was different. Why, after all he did to me and to others, was I beginning to care what happened to him? I suddenly regretted leaving my mother in the waiting room alone. I'd fantasized for years about them feeling my pain. Now, the revenge wasn't as sweet as I expected it to be. I thought back to the song Miriam gave me, "If We're Honest." What did it say about us both being messes and broken?

I'd never thought about the incident from their perspective. Did they have regrets? Did my mother want to reach out to me? Was she afraid of my father and his reaction? And then, Dallas's words came to my mind, "Let the past stay in the past." *Easier said than done.* I think even Dallas was having difficulty leaving my past back in Guatemala. I kept rehashing every decision I'd made from that day, especially my conversation with Dallas about cooling things off. His response shocked me. Maybe we did have a future. But if that was going to happen, I'd have to take care of a few spiritual issues. Maybe Pastor Kelly would be willing to talk with me about finding forgiveness and moving on.

Something flashed past the camera at the far end of the hall. I glanced at the clock. Six-o-six. I'd been daydreaming for five hours. I woke Sam. We holstered our guns, Sam with his Glock and me with my Sig. We watched three people dressed in white robes slither down the hall and stop at Rose's door. Then, at the far end of the hall, Penny Thatcher stepped off the elevator in full priestess regalia, breastplate and all. We waited. Sam notified the awaiting patrol officers to make their way up to the fourth floor.

All we had to do was wait and watch. "Let them breach, and then we'll rush them," Sam said. "We want to contain them inside the room if possible. The officers will assist in blocking the exits."

We finally had them where we wanted them. I watched one of the robed figures pull out a hotel key card and access the room. Interesting. As soon as Penny entered behind the others, Sam and I bolted out our door and into Rose's, catching it before it closed.

"Police! Everyone down on the floor."

I'd been waiting for this moment. My heart pounded with excitement and fear. Two of the individuals rushed us. I heard Sam fire, and I watched the first man drop to the floor. The second continued, and I spun, landing a swift kick in her jaw with my orthopedic boot. She tumbled at Sam's feet. The others dropped to the floor with their hands held high.

"What's going on?" Rose ran into the entryway screaming at the top of her lungs. "What the…" With a swift spin from Penny and a slash of her knife, Rose fell to the ground, clutching her throat.

Penny Thatcher turned with her hands in the air. She looked at me and smiled. "Drop the knife," I shouted. I wanted to shoot her in the face, but I restrained myself.

"You have no authority over me," she said. "I answer only to God."

I kept my gun fixed on her while Sam knocked the bloody knife from her hand and secured her hands behind her back. The team of officers rushed into the room and subdued the others. One officer placed his hands over Rose's throat while another called for an ambulance. He looked our way and said, "It's superficial. She'll make it."

It was the first time I noticed the details of Penny's outfit. She was wearing a robe also, but hers was blue with all kinds of weird things on it. I finally got a clear look at her golden breastplate. It had twelve colorful stones distributed in four rows of three. Each one had something written in a strange language.

"What's with the crazy outfit?" Sam asked.

"This is the ephod and robe of the high priest," she said.

I noticed she was barefoot.

"Okay, I have to know for real. Why the bare feet?"

"I am always in the presence of the Most High God, and I walk on holy ground." I remembered her telling the others to remove their shoes at Sondra Jennings house.

It didn't make sense, but then, neither did she. I let it go. I took a deep breath and let it out. We did it. We beat them. Sam and I took Penny and said we would transport her in our car to the station. I wanted to press her about Skylar. As we pushed her onto the elevator, I could hear her whispering a prayer of apology to God for failing Him.

"What you did wasn't of God," I said, suddenly feeling bold in her presence. "He's a God of love and mercy." I surprised myself by saying it.

"He's also a God of justice," she said. "Yours is coming."

"The only justice you'll see is a life sentence, if you're lucky. You're finished, Penny," Sam said, coming to my aid.

"The name is Hadassah." She carried herself with pride and elegance, even though her hands were fastened behind her.

Sam stepped in front of her. "Tell us where Skylar is, and we might make a deal."

"You'll never catch Sky. She's seven moves ahead of you." Penny started to laugh.

"What's so funny?" I asked.

"Nothing, really. I was just thinking how perfect the number seven is." The door opened, and I gave her a little shove out of the elevator. She stumbled but managed to stay on her feet.

Chapter Sixty-three

Monday, November 10, 12:06 PM—Vanderbilt Hospital

Penny confessed to everything. She was proud of her *work* and gave us detailed descriptions of each murder. She even divulged the new list of individuals she was planning to sacrifice. I was right about her endgame. The final punishment would be upon her followers and finally herself for their hand in murder. She didn't, however, incriminate Skylar Watson in any part of the plan. Penny took full responsibility, even for what she called, "proselytizing the disciples." I had to look that one up. While we were happy to end the killings, I was seething that Skylar, once again, slipped through my fingers. I'd have to live with the fact that she was out there waiting for the perfect moment to set a new trap for me.

I suddenly thought of my parents. Guilt weighed upon me. My angry journal scripted the deaths of six people, nearly seven. It also caused my father to be tortured within inches of his life. I needed to see him.

The elevator door opened, and I made my way to the critical care waiting room to bury the hatchet with my mother and eventually my father. Lieutenant Daniels was right about one thing. Holding onto my anger was hurting me far more than it was them. This was a giant leap for me. Dealing with my father would come another day. I'd finally owned my truth and could begin the long journey back.

I passed the nurses' station and entered the waiting room. My mother wasn't there. I saw her jacket, so I figured she was either with my father or downstairs grabbing something to eat. After waiting thirty minutes, I asked the nurse if she knew where Mrs. Abelard went.

The young nurse thought for a moment. She asked one of the other nurses if she'd seen Mrs. Abelard. She nodded and said, "She went to the cafeteria with her daughter Abbey."

"That's not possible. I'm her daughter." There was a confused look on her face. "When did they leave?"

"About an hour ago, I think."

"No…no…no…no…"

She rushed to my side. "Is something wrong?"

I didn't take the time to respond. Not wanting to wait for the elevator, I rushed down the stairs, injured foot and all. I searched the cafeteria and the main halls. No sign of her. I pounded on the door to security and demanded to see the cameras from critical care, the cafeteria, and all exits. I flashed my badge and explained the situation. We watched the security video. A young woman in sunglasses, with a haircut exactly like mine, entered the waiting room and sat beside my mother. They talked and the young woman pointed to the door. All this within earshot of the nurses' station.

My mother sat still and stared at the woman. She nodded, and the stranger helped my mother to her feet. She bent over and slid a white envelope under my mother's jacket. They walked arm and arm toward the elevator, stopping to speak with the skinny nurse before continuing on. We picked them up on another camera as they entered the elevator going down. A third camera picked them up as they walked by the cafeteria. As they approached the main entrance to the hospital, the young woman pulled off her sunglasses and turned to the camera. She smiled. It was Skylar! They disappeared through the exit and the far side of the street.

I looked at the time stamp. Eleven-ten, an hour and forty-five minutes ago.

I called Sam as I rushed back to the waiting room. I threw

the jacket aside and snatched the envelope, tearing it open. Inside was a letter addressed to me.

Abbey, congratulations on your recent victory. I would have let you savor the moment, but you chose to make this contest personal. Fair warning. I've been grooming someone. He's coming for you, and he knows your Kryptonite. In the meantime, you might want to get a copy of Abbey Road. You'll need it.

Skylar

Abbey Road? Kryptonite? What was she talking about? And where did she take my mother?

Points to Ponder

1. Pastor Kelly encourages his church to accept a vision of loving God and loving others. How do the Ten Commandments fall into these two categories?
2. Penny Thatcher interprets the instructions in a way that makes her judge, jury, and executioner. How do we sometimes use the Bible for our own will?
3. Dallas originally told Abbey to leave the past in the past. Now, he is struggling with her past. What do you think will happen to their relationship?
4. Some people have given up on God and His church because of individuals like Nicholas Sayers and Joseph Abelard. How can we, as a church, help them past those hurts?
5. What are you holding on to from your past? Pray that God will help you give that shame and guilt over to Him and accept His forgiveness. Read 1 John 1:8-10.
6. Abbey is a complex character. In what ways is she both strong and fragile?
7. How does Susan serve as an encourager in Abbey's life?
8. Both Lieutenant Daniels and Sam act as father figures for Abbey. How do they contrast with Joseph Abelard?
9. If you had to choose, which character would you spend a day with? Why?
10. How did Skylar function as Abbey's Moriarty and Lord Voldemort?